the house of the
scorpion

NANCY FARMER

the house of the
scorpion

SIMON &
SCHUSTER
London • New York • Sydney

SIMON &
SCHUSTER

First published in Great Britain by Simon & Schuster UK Ltd, 2002
A Viacom company

This edition first published in Great Britain by
Simon & Schuster UK Ltd, 2003

Originally published in 2002 by Atheneum Books for Young Readers,
an imprint of Simon & Schuster Children's Division, New York.

Copyright © Nancy Farmer, 2002
Jacket illustration copyright © 2002 by Russell Gordon
Book design by O'lanso Gabbidon

1 3 5 7 9 10 8 6 4 2

Simon & Schuster UK Ltd
Africa House
64–78 Kingsway
London WC2B 6AH

www.simonsays.co.uk

A CIP catalogue record for this book is available from the British Library

ISBN 0689837704

This book is a work of fiction. Names, characters, places and incidents are
either a product of the author's imagination or are used fictitiously. Any
resemblance to actual people living or dead, events or locales is entirely
coincidental.

Printed and bound in Great Britain by
Cox & Wyman Ltd, Reading, Berkshire

To Harold for his unfailing love and support,
and to Daniel, our son. To my brother, Dr Elmon Lee Coe,
and my sister, Mary Marimon Stout.
Lastly, and no less importantly, to Richard Jackson,
il capo di tutti capi of children's book editors.

CONTENTS

CAST OF CHARACTERS

THE ALACRÁN FAMILY

Matt: Matteo Alacrán, the clone

El Patrón: The original Matteo Alacrán; a powerful drug lord

Felipe: El Patrón's son; died long ago

El Viejo: El Patrón's grandson and Mr Alacrán's father; a very old man

Mr Alacrán: El Patrón's great-grandson; husband of Felicia, father of Benito and Steven

Felicia: Mr Alacrán's wife; mother of Benito, Steven, and Tom

Benito: Oldest son of Mr Alacrán and Felicia

Steven: Second son of Mr Alacrán and Felicia

Tom: Son of Felicia and Mr MacGregor

Fani: Benito's wife

VISITORS AND ASSOCIATES OF THE ALACRÁNS

Senator Mendoza: A powerful politician in the United States; father of Emilia and María; also called Dada

Emilia: Oldest daughter of Senator Mendoza

María: Younger daughter of Senator Mendoza

Esperanza: Emilia's and María's mother; disappeared when María was five

Mr MacGregor: A drug lord

SLAVES AND SERVANTS

Celia: Chief cook and Matt's caregiver

Tam Lin: Bodyguard for both El Patrón and Matt

Daft Donald: Bodyguard for El Patrón

Rosa: Housekeeper; Matt's jailer

Willum: Chief doctor for the Alacrán household; Rosa's lover

Mr Ortega: Matt's music teacher

Teacher: An eejit

Hugh, Ralf, and Wee Wullie: Members of the Farm Patrol

PEOPLE IN AZTLÁN

Raúl: A Keeper

Carlos: A Keeper

Jorge: A Keeper

Chacho: A Lost Boy

Fidelito: A Lost Boy; eight years old

Ton-Ton: A Lost Boy; driver of the shrimp harvester

Flaco: Oldest of the Lost Boys

Luna: Lost Boy in charge of the infirmary

Guapo: Old man celebrating *El Día de los Muertos*

Consuela: Old woman celebrating *El Día de los Muertos*

Sister Inéz: A nurse at the Convent of Santa Clara

MISCELLANEOUS CHARACTERS

Furball: María's dog

El Látigo Negro: The Black Whip, an old TV character

Don Segundo Sombra: Sir Second Shadow, an old TV character

El Sacerdote Volante: The Flying Priest, an old TV character

Eejits: People with computer chips in their brains; also known as zombies

La Llorona: The Weeping Woman; mythical woman who searches in the night for her lost children

Chupacabras: The goat sucker; mythical creature that sucks the blood out of goats, chickens, and, occasionally, people

ALACRÁN FAMILY HISTORY

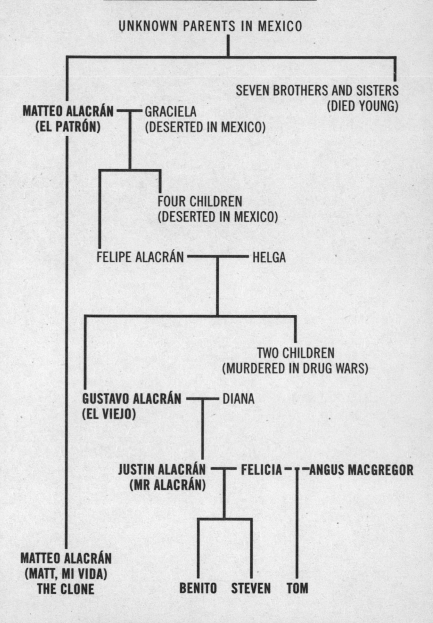

UNKNOWN PARENTS IN MEXICO

MATTEO ALACRÁN (EL PATRÓN) — GRACIELA (DESERTED IN MEXICO)

SEVEN BROTHERS AND SISTERS (DIED YOUNG)

FOUR CHILDREN (DESERTED IN MEXICO)

FELIPE ALACRÁN — HELGA

TWO CHILDREN (MURDERED IN DRUG WARS)

GUSTAVO ALACRÁN (EL VIEJO) — DIANA

JUSTIN ALACRÁN (MR ALACRÁN) — FELICIA — ANGUS MACGREGOR

MATTEO ALACRÁN (MATT, MI VIDA) THE CLONE

BENITO   STEVEN   TOM

BOLD TYPE = LIVING | LIGHT TYPE = DECEASED

the house of the
scorpion

YOUTH:
0 TO 6

1

IN THE BEGINNING

In the beginning there were thirty-six of them, thirty-six
droplets of life so tiny that Eduardo could see them only
under a microscope. He studied them anxiously in the
darkened room.

Water bubbled through tubes that snaked around the warm,
humid walls. Air was sucked into growth chambers. A dull, red
light shone on the faces of the workers as they watched their
own arrays of little glass dishes. Each one contained a drop
of life.

Eduardo moved his dishes, one after the other, under the lens
of the microscope. The cells were perfect – or so it seemed. Each
was furnished with all it needed to grow. So much knowledge
was hidden in that tiny world! Even Eduardo, who understood
the process very well, was awed. The cell already understood
what colour hair it was to have, how tall it would become, and
even whether it preferred spinach to broccoli. It might even

have a hazy desire for music or crossword puzzles. All that was hidden in the droplet.

Finally the round outlines quivered and lines appeared, dividing the cells in two. Eduardo sighed. It was going to be all right. He watched the samples grow, and then he carefully moved them to the incubator.

But it wasn't all right. Something about the food, the heat, the light was wrong, and the man didn't know what it was. Very quickly over half of them died. There were only fifteen now, and Eduardo felt a cold lump in his stomach. If he failed, he would be sent to the Farms, and then what would become of Anna and the children, and his father, who was so old?

"It's okay," said Lisa, so close by that Eduardo jumped. She was one of the senior technicians. She had worked for so many years in the dark, her face was chalk white and her blue veins were visible through her skin.

"How can it be okay?" Eduardo said.

"The cells were frozen over a hundred years ago. They can't be as healthy as samples taken yesterday."

"That long," the man marvelled.

"But some of them should grow," Lisa said sternly.

So Eduardo began to worry again. And for a month everything went well. The day came when he implanted the tiny embryos in the brood cows. The cows were lined up, patiently waiting. They were fed by tubes, and their bodies were exercised by giant metal arms that grasped their legs and flexed them as though the cows were walking through an endless field. Now and then an animal moved its jaws in an attempt to chew cud.

Did they dream of dandelions? Eduardo wondered. Did they feel a phantom wind blowing tall grass against their legs? Their brains were filled with quiet joy from implants in their skulls. Were they aware of the children growing in their wombs?

Perhaps the cows hated what had been done to them, because they certainly rejected the embryos. One after another the infants, at this point no larger than minnows, died.

Until there was only one.

Eduardo slept badly at night. He cried out in his sleep, and Anna asked what was the matter. He couldn't tell her. He couldn't say that if this last embryo died, he would be stripped of his job. He would be sent to the Farms. And she, Anna, and their children and his father would be cast out to walk the hot, dusty roads.

But that one embryo grew until it was clearly a being with arms and legs and a sweet, dreaming face. Eduardo watched it through scanners. "You hold my life in your hands," he told the infant. As though it could hear, the infant flexed its tiny body in the womb until it was turned toward the man. And Eduardo felt an unreasoning stir of affection.

When the day came, Eduardo received the newborn into his hands as though it were his own child. His eyes blurred as he laid it in a crib and reached for the needle that would blunt its intelligence.

"Don't fix that one," said Lisa, hastily catching his arm. "It's a Matteo Alacrán. They're always left intact."

Have I done you a favour? thought Eduardo as he watched the baby turn its head toward the bustling nurses in their starched, white uniforms. *Will you thank me for it later?*

2

THE LITTLE HOUSE
IN THE POPPY FIELDS

Matt stood in front of the door and spread his arms to keep Celia from leaving. The small, crowded living room was still blue with early morning light. The sun had not yet lifted above the hills marking the distant horizon.

"What's this?" the woman said. "You're a big boy now, almost six. You know I have to work." She picked him up to move him out of the way.

"Take me with you," begged Matt, grabbing her shirt and wadding it up in his hands.

"Stop that." Celia gently pried his fingers from the cloth. "You can't come, *mi vida*. You must stay hidden in the nest like a good little mouse. There're hawks out there that eat little mice."

"I'm *not* a mouse!" Matt yelled. He shrieked at the top of his voice in a way he knew was irritating. Even keeping Celia home long enough to deliver a tongue-lashing was worth it. He couldn't bear being left alone for another day.

Celia thrust him away. "¡*Callate!* Shut up! Do you want to make me deaf? You're just a little kid with cornmeal for brains!" Matt flopped sullenly into the big easy chair.

Celia immediately knelt down and put her arms around him. "Don't cry, *mi vida*. I love you more than anything in the world. I'll explain things to you when you're older." But she wouldn't. She had made the same promise before. Suddenly the fight went out of Matt. He was too small and weak to fight whatever drove Celia to abandon him each day.

"Will you bring me a present?" he said, wriggling away from her kiss.

"Of course! Always!" the woman cried.

So Matt allowed her to go, but he was angry at the same time. It was a funny kind of anger, for he felt like crying, too. The house was so lonely without Celia singing, banging pots, or talking about people he had never seen and never would see. Even when Celia was asleep – and she fell asleep easily after long hours cooking at the Big House – the rooms felt full of her warm presence.

When Matt was younger, it hadn't seemed to matter. He'd played with his toys and watched the television. He'd looked out the window where fields of white poppies stretched all the way to the shadowy hills. The whiteness hurt his eyes, and so he turned from them with relief to the cool darkness inside.

But lately Matt had begun to look at things more carefully. The poppy fields weren't completely deserted. Now and then he saw horses – he knew them from picture books – walking between the rows of white flowers. It was hard to tell who rode them in all that brightness, but it seemed the riders weren't adults, but children like him.

And with that discovery grew a desire to see them more closely.

Matt had watched children on television. He saw that they were seldom alone. They did things together, like building forts or kicking balls or fighting. Even fighting was interesting when it meant you had other people around. Matt never saw anyone except Celia and, once a month, the doctor. The doctor was a sour man and didn't like Matt at all.

Matt sighed. To do *anything,* he would have to go outdoors, which Celia said again and again was very dangerous. Besides, the doors and windows were locked.

Matt settled himself at a small wooden table to look at one of his books. *Pedro el Conejo,* said the cover. Matt could read – slightly – both English and Spanish. In fact, he and Celia mixed the two languages together, but it didn't matter. They understood each other.

Pedro el Conejo was a bad little rabbit who crawled into Señor MacGregor's garden to eat up his lettuces. Señor MacGregor wanted to put Pedro into a pie, but Pedro, after many adventures, got away. It was a satisfying story.

Matt got up and wandered into the kitchen. It contained a small refrigerator and a microwave. The microwave had a sign reading PELIGRO!!! DANGER!!! and squares of yellow notepaper saying NO! NO! NO! NO! To be extra sure, Celia had wrapped a belt around the microwave door and secured it with a padlock. She lived in terror that Matt would find a way to open it while she was at work and "cook his little gizzards," as she put it.

Matt didn't know what gizzards were and he didn't want to find out. He edged around the dangerous machine to get to the fridge. That was definitely his territory. Celia filled it with treats every night. She cooked for the Big House, so there was always plenty of food. Matt helped himself to sushi, tamales, pakoras, blintzes – whatever the people in the Big House were eating.

And there was always a large carton of milk and bottles of fruit juice.

He filled a bowl with food and went to Celia's room.

On one side was her large, saggy bed covered with crocheted pillows and stuffed animals. At the head was a huge crucifix and a picture of Our Lord Jesus with His heart pierced by five swords. Matt found the picture frightening. The crucifix was even worse, because it glowed in the dark. Matt kept his back to it, but he still liked Celia's room.

He sprawled over the pillows and pretended to feed the stuffed dog, the teddy bear, the rabbit (*conejo*, Matt corrected). For a while this was fun, but then a hollow feeling began to grow inside Matt. These weren't real animals. He could talk to them all he liked. They couldn't understand. In some way he couldn't put into words, they weren't even *there*.

Matt turned them all to the wall, to punish them for not being real, and went to his own room. It was much smaller, being half filled by his bed. The walls were covered with pictures Celia had torn out of magazines: movie stars, animals, babies — Matt wasn't thrilled by the babies, but Celia found them irresistible — flowers, news stories. There was one of acrobats standing on one another in a huge pyramid. SIXTY-FOUR! the caption said. A NEW RECORD AT THE LUNAR COLONY.

Matt had seen these particular words so often, he knew them by heart. Another picture showed a man holding a bullfrog between two slices of bread. RIBBIT ON RYE! the caption said. Matt didn't know what a ribbit was, but Celia laughed every time she looked at it.

He turned on the television and watched soap operas. People were always yelling at one another on soap operas. It didn't make much sense, and when it did, it wasn't interesting. *It's not real,*

Matt thought with sudden terror. *It's like the animals.* He could talk and talk and talk, but the people couldn't hear him.

Matt was swept with such an intense feeling of desolation, he thought he would die. He hugged himself to keep from screaming. He gasped with sobs. Tears rolled down his cheeks.

And then – and then – beyond the noise of the soap opera and his own sobs, Matt heard a voice calling. It was clear and strong – a child's voice. And it was real.

Matt ran to the window. Celia always warned him to be careful when he looked out, but he was so excited that he didn't care. At first he only saw the same, bleached blindness of the poppies. Then a shadow crossed the opening. Matt recoiled so quickly, he fell over and landed on the floor.

"What's this dump?" someone said from outside.

"One of the worker's shacks," said another, higher voice.

"I didn't think anyone was allowed to live in the opium fields."

"Maybe it's a storeroom. Let's try the door."

The door handle rattled. Matt squatted on the floor, his heart pounding. Someone put his face against the window, cupping his hands to see through the gloom. Matt froze. He had wanted company, but this was happening too quickly. He felt like Pedro el Conejo in Señor MacGregor's garden.

"Hey, there's a kid in here!"

"What? Let me see." A second face pressed against the window. She had black hair and olive skin like Celia. "Open the window, kid. What's your name?"

But Matt was so terrified, he couldn't squeeze out a single word.

"Maybe he's an idiot," the girl said matter-of-factly. "Hey, are you an idiot?"

Matt shook his head. The girl laughed.

"I know who lives here," the boy said suddenly. "I recognize that picture on the table."

Matt remembered the portrait Celia had given him on his last birthday.

"It's the fat old cook — what's her name?" the boy said. "Anyhow, she doesn't stay with the rest of the servants. This must be her hangout. I didn't know she had a kid."

"Or a husband," the girl remarked.

"Oh, yeah. That explains a lot. I wonder if Father knows. I'll have to ask him."

"You will not!" the girl cried. "You'll get her into trouble."

"Hey, this is my family's ranch, and my father told me to keep an eye on things. You're only visiting."

"It doesn't matter. *My* dada says servants have a right to privacy, and he's a United States senator, so his opinion is worth more."

"Your dada changes his opinions more often than his socks," the boy said.

What the girl replied to this, Matt couldn't hear. The children were moving away from the house, and he could make out only the indignant tone of her voice. He was shivering all over, as though he'd just met one of the monsters Celia told him haunted the world outside, the *chupacabras* maybe. The *chupacabras* sucked your blood and left you to dry like an old watermelon skin. Things were happening too fast.

But he had liked the girl.

The rest of that day Matt was swept by both fear and joy. He had been warned by Celia never, never to show himself at the window. If someone came, he was to hide himself. But the children had been such a wonderful surprise, he couldn't help running to see them. They were older than he. How much older

Matt couldn't tell. They were definitely not adults, though, and they didn't seem dangerous. Still, Celia would be furious if she found out. Matt decided not to tell her.

That night she brought him a colouring book the children had thrown away in the Big House. Only half of it had been used, so Matt spent a pleasant half hour before dinner using the stubby crayons Celia had brought on other occasions. The smell of fried cheese and onions drifted out of the kitchen, and Matt knew she was cooking Aztláno food. This was a special treat. Celia was usually so tired when she returned home, she only heated up leftovers.

He coloured in an entire meadow with green. His crayon was almost gone, and he had to hold it carefully to use it at all. The green made him feel happy. If only he could look out on such a meadow instead of the blinding white poppies. He was certain grass would be as soft as a bed and smell like rain.

"Very nice, *chico*," said Celia, looking over his shoulder.

The last fragment of crayon fell apart in Matt's fingers.

"*¡Qué lástima!* I'll see if I can find more in the Big House. Those kids're so rich, they wouldn't notice if I took the whole darn box." Celia sighed. "I'll only take a few, though. The mouse is safest when she doesn't leave footprints on the butter."

They had quesadillas and enchiladas for dinner. The food sat heavily in Matt's stomach.

"*Mamá*," he said without thinking, "tell me again about the kids in the Big House."

"Don't call me '*Mamá*,'" snapped Celia.

"Sorry," said Matt. The word had slipped out. Celia had told him long ago that she wasn't his real mother. The children on TV had *mamás*, though, and Matt had fallen into the habit of thinking of Celia that way.

"I love you more than anything in the world," the woman said quickly. "Never forget that. But you were only loaned to me, *mi vida*."

Matt had trouble understanding the word *loaned*. It seemed to mean something you gave away for a little while — which meant that whoever *loaned* him would want him back.

"Anyhow, the kids in the Big House are brats, you better believe it," Celia went on. "They're lazy as cats and just as ungrateful. They make big messes and order the maids to clean them up. And they never say thank you. Even if you work for hours making special cakes with sugar roses and violets and green leaves, they can't say thank you to save their miserable little souls. They stuff their selfish mouths and tell you it tastes like mud!"

Celia looked angry, as though the incident had happened recently.

"There's Steven and Benito," Matt reminded her.

"Benito's the oldest. He's a real devil! He's seventeen, and there isn't a girl in the Farms who's safe from him. But never mind that. It's adult stuff and very boring. Anyhow, Benito is like his father, which means he's a dog in human clothing. He's going to college this year, and we'll all be glad to see the last of him."

"And Steven?" Matt said patiently.

"He's not so bad. I sometimes think he might have a soul. He spends time with the Mendoza girls. They're okay, although what they're doing with our crowd would puzzle God Himself."

"What does Steven look like?" It sometimes took a long time to steer Celia to the things Matt wanted to know — in this case, the names of the children who'd appeared outside the window.

"He's thirteen. Big for his age. Sandy hair. Blue eyes."

That must have been the boy, thought Matt.

"Right now the Mendozas are visiting. Emilia's thirteen too, very pretty with black hair and brown eyes."

That must be the girl, Matt decided.

"She at least has good manners. Her sister, María, is about your age and plays with Tom. Well, some might call it play. Most of the time she winds up crying her eyes out."

"Why?" said Matt, who enjoyed hearing about Tom's misdeeds.

"Tom is Benito times ten! He can melt anyone's heart with those wide, innocent eyes. Everyone falls for it, but not me. He gave María a bottle of lemonade today. 'It's the last one,' he said. 'It's really cold and I saved it especially for you,' he said. Do you know what was in it?"

"No," said Matt, wriggling with anticipation.

"Pee! Can you believe it? He even put the cap back on. Oh, she was crying, poor little thing. She never learns."

Celia suddenly ran out of steam. She yawned broadly and fatigue settled over her right before Matt's eyes. She had been working from dawn to well after dark, and she had cooked a fresh meal at home as well. "I'm sorry, *chico.* When the well's empty, it's empty."

Matt rinsed the plates and stacked the dishwasher while Celia took a shower. She came out in her voluminous pink bathrobe and nodded sleepily at the tidied table. "You're a good kid," she said.

She picked him up and hugged him all the way to his bed. No matter how tired Celia was – and sometimes she almost fell over with exhaustion – she never neglected this ritual. She tucked Matt in and lit the holy candle in front of the statue of the Virgin of Guadalupe. She had brought it with her all the way from her village in Aztlán. The Virgin's robe was slightly chipped, which Celia disguised with a spray of artificial flowers. The Virgin's feet rested on dusty plaster roses and Her star-spangled robe was stained with wax, but Her face gazed out over the candle with the same gentleness it had in Celia's bedroom long ago.

"I'm in the next room, *mi vida,*" whispered the woman, kissing the top of Matt's head. "You get scared, you call me."

Soon the house shook with Celia's snores. To Matt, the sound was as normal as the thunder that sometimes echoed over the hills. It in no way kept him from sleep. "Steven and Emilia," he whispered, testing the words in his mouth. He didn't know what he would say to the strange children if they appeared again, but he was determined to try to talk to them. He practised several sentences: "My name is Matt. I live here. Do you want to colour pictures?"

No, he couldn't mention the colouring book or the crayons. They were stolen.

"Would you like some food?" But the food might be stolen too. "Do you want to play?" Good. Steven and Emilia could suggest something, and Matt would be off the hook.

"Do you want to play? Do you want to play?" he murmured as his eyes closed and the gentle face of the Virgin of Guadalupe floated in the candlelight.

3

PROPERTY OF THE ALACRÁN ESTATE

Celia left in the morning, and Matt spent the entire day waiting for the children. He had given up hope when, just before sunset, he heard voices approaching through the poppy fields.

He planted himself in front of the window and waited.

"There he is! See, María, I told you I wasn't lying," cried Emilia. Her hand rested on the shoulder of a much smaller girl. "He won't talk to us, but you're about his age. Maybe he won't be afraid of you." Emilia pushed the girl ahead of her and fell back to wait with Steven.

María wasn't at all shy about coming up to the window. "Hey, boy!" she yelled, rapping the glass with her fist. "What's your name? Do you want to play?"

With one blow, she stole Matt's carefully prepared speech. He stared at her, unable to think of another opening.

"Well, is it yes or no?" María turned toward the others. "Make him unlock the door."

"That's up to him," said Steven.

Matt wanted to say he didn't have the key, but he was unable to get the words out.

"At least he isn't hiding today," remarked Emilia.

"If you can't unlock the door, open the window," María said.

Matt tried, knowing it wouldn't work. Celia had nailed the window shut. He threw up his hands.

"He understands what we say," said Steven.

"Hey, boy! If you don't do something quick, we're going away," María shouted.

Matt thought desperately. He needed something to interest them. He held up his finger, as Celia did when she wanted him to wait. He nodded his head to show that he agreed with María's demand and was about to *do something*.

"What does that mean?" said Emilia.

"Beats me. Maybe he's a mute and can't talk," Steven guessed.

Matt raced to his bedroom. He ripped the picture of the man with the bullfrog sandwich from the wall. It made Celia laugh. Maybe it would make these children laugh. He ran back and pressed the newspaper against the window. The three children came close to study it.

"What's it say?" asked María.

"'Ribbit on Rye,'" read Steven. "Do you get it? It's a bullfrog going *ribbit, ribbit, ribbit,* and it's between two slices of rye bread. That's pretty funny."

Emilia giggled, but María looked uncertain. "People don't eat bullfrogs," she said. "I mean, not when they're *alive.*"

"It's a joke, dum-dum."

"I'm not a dum-dum! It's mean and nasty to eat bullfrogs! I don't think it's funny at all."

"Save me from eejits," said Steven, rolling his eyes.

"I'm not an eejit, either!"

"Oh, lighten up, María," Emilia said.

"You brought me out here to see a boy, and it was miles and *miles* across the fields, and I'm tired and the boy won't talk. I hate you!"

Matt stared at the scene with consternation. That wasn't the result he wanted at all. María was crying, Emilia looked angry, and Steven had turned his back on both of them. Matt rapped on the window. When María looked up, he waved the picture and then wadded it into a ball. He threw it with all his force across the room.

"See, he agrees with me," cried María through her tears.

"This is getting weirder by the minute," said Steven. "I knew we shouldn't have brought the eejit."

"I thought the boy would talk to a kid his own size," Emilia said. "Come on, María. We have to get back before dark."

"I'm not walking anywhere!" The little girl flopped down on the ground.

"Well, I won't carry you, fatso."

"Just leave her," said Steven. He started walking off, and after a moment Emilia followed him.

Matt was appalled. If the big kids went away, María would be all alone. It was going to be dark soon, and Celia wouldn't return for hours. María would be alone with nothing but the empty poppy fields and the . . .

The *chupacabras,* who came out after dark and sucked your juices and left you to dry like an old watermelon skin!

Suddenly Matt knew what he had to do. María had walked a few steps away from the window before sitting down again. She was shouting insults at the vanished Steven and Emilia. Matt grabbed the big iron cooking pot Celia used to make *menudo* and swung it before he could worry much about her reaction. She would be furious! But he was saving María's life. He smashed out the glass in the window. It fell in a tinkling, jangling mass to the ground. María jumped to her feet. Steven and Emilia rose up instantly from the poppy field, where they'd been hiding.

"Holy frijoles!" said Steven. All three stood openmouthed, staring at the empty hole where the window had been.

"My name is Matt. I live here. Do you want to play?" said Matt because he couldn't think of another thing to say.

"He *can* talk," said Emilia after the first shock had died away.

"Is that how you usually open a window, kid?" Steven said. "Stay back, María. There's glass all over." He stepped carefully to the opening and knocked out the remaining shards with a stick. Then he leaned inside to look around. Matt had to hold on to himself to keep from bolting to the other room. "This is creepy! The window's nailed shut. What are you, some kind of prisoner?"

"I live here," Matt said.

"You told us that already."

"Do you want to play?"

"Maybe he's like a parrot and only knows a few words," suggested Emilia.

"*I* want to play," said María. Matt looked at her with approval. The girl was struggling in Emilia's arms, obviously trying to get to him. Steven shook his head and moved away. He looked like he was really going to leave this time.

Matt came to a decision. It was frightening, but he'd never had an opportunity like this before and he might never have it again. He shoved a chair to the opening, scrambled up, and jumped.

"No!" shouted Steven, running forward to catch him. He was too late.

A terrible pain lanced through Matt's feet. He fell forward, and his hands and knees landed on the shards of glass.

"He wasn't wearing shoes! Oh, man! Oh, man! What're we going to do!" Steven pulled Matt up and swung him onto a clear patch of ground.

Matt stared with amazement at the blood dripping from his feet and hands. His knees sprouted rivulets of red.

"Pull out the glass!" cried Emilia in a high, scared voice. "María, stay away!"

"I want to see!" yelled the little girl. Matt heard a slap and María's shriek of outrage. His head was swimming. He wanted to throw up, but before he could, everything went black.

He woke to the sensation of being carried. He was sick to his stomach, but worse than that his body was trembling in a frightening way. He screamed as loud as he could.

"Great!" panted Steven, who supported Matt's shoulders. Emilia had his legs. Her shirt and trousers were soaked with blood, *his* blood. Matt screamed again.

"Be quiet!" Steven shouted. "We're running as fast as we can!"

The poppies, now blue in the long shadows of the hills, stretched away in all directions. Steven and Emilia were jogging along a dirt path. Matt's breath caught with sobs. He could hardly get air.

"Stop!" cried Emilia. "We have to let María catch up." The two children squatted down and let Matt's weight rest on the ground. Presently, Matt heard the patter of smaller feet.

"I want to rest too," demanded María. "It's miles and *miles.* I'm going to tell Dada you slapped me."

"Be my guest," said Emilia.

"Everyone be quiet," Steven ordered. "You've stopped bleeding, kid, so I guess you're not in too much danger. What's your name again?"

"Matt," María answered for him.

"We aren't far from the house, Matt, and you're in luck. The doctor's spending the night. Do you hurt a lot?"

"I don't know," said Matt.

"Yes, you do. You screamed," María said.

"I don't know what *a lot* is," Matt explained. "I haven't hurt like this before."

"Well, you've lost blood – but not too much," Steven added as Matt began to tremble again.

"It sure looks like a lot," said María.

"Shut up, eejit."

The older children rose, carrying Matt between them. María followed, complaining loudly about the distance and at being called an eejit.

A kind of heavy sleepiness fell over Matt as he was swayed along. The pain had died down, and Steven said he hadn't lost too much blood. He was too dazed to worry about what Celia would say when she saw the broken window.

They reached the edge of the poppy fields as the last streaks of sunlight slid behind the hills. The dirt path gave way to a wide lawn. It was a shimmering green, growing deeper with the blue light of evening. Matt had never seen so much green in his life.

It's a meadow, he thought, drowsily. *And it smells like rain.*

They started up a flight of wide, marble steps that shone softly in the darkening air. On either side were orange trees, and all at once lamps went on among the leaves. Lights outlined the white walls of a vast house above, with pillars and statues and doorways going who knew where. In the centre of an arch was the carved outline of a scorpion.

"Oh! Oh! Oh! Oh!" came a flurry of women's voices as they swept down the stairs to lift Matt from Steven's and Emilia's arms.

"Who is he?" asked the maids. They were wearing black dresses with white aprons and starched, white caps. One of them, a severe-looking female with deep creases down either side of her mouth, carried Matt as the others went ahead to open doors.

"I found him in a house in the poppy fields," replied Steven.

"That's Celia's place," a maid said. "She's too stuck-up to live with the rest of us."

"If she's hiding a child, I'm not surprised. Who's your father, kid?" said the woman who was carrying Matt. Her apron smelled like sunlight, the way Celia's did when it came straight from the clothesline. Matt stared at a pin fastened to the woman's collar, a silver scorpion with its tail curved up. Beneath the scorpion was a name tag that said ROSA. Matt didn't feel well enough to talk, and what did it matter who his father was, anyhow? He didn't know the answer, either.

"He doesn't talk much," said Emilia.

"Where's the doctor?" Steven said.

"We'll have to wait. He's treating your grandfather. At least we can clean the kid up," said Rosa.

The maids opened a door to reveal the most beautiful room Matt had ever seen. It had carved wooden beams on the ceiling and wallpaper decorated with hundreds of birds. To Matt's reeling eyes, they seemed to be moving. He saw a couch upholstered with flowers that shaded from lavender to rose like the feathers on a dove's wings. It was to this couch that Rosa was carrying him.

"I'm too dirty," Matt murmured. He had been yelled at before for climbing on Celia's bed with muddy feet.

"You can say that again," snapped Rosa. The other women opened a crisp, white sheet and laid it over the wonderful couch before Matt was laid down. He thought he could get into just as much trouble for getting blood on that sheet.

Rosa fetched a pair of tweezers and began pulling out fragments of glass from his hands and feet. "Ay!" she murmured as she dropped the bits into a cup. "You're brave not to cry."

But Matt didn't feel brave at all. He didn't feel anything. His body seemed far away, and he watched Rosa as though she were an image on a TV screen.

"He sure screamed earlier," observed María. She was dancing around, trying to see everything that happened.

"Don't act so superior. You yell your head off if you get an itty-bitty splinter in your finger," Emilia said.

"Do not!"

"Do so!"

"I hate you!"

"Ask me if I care," said Emilia. Both she and Steven watched in fascination as blood began to well out of Matt's cuts again. "I'm going to be a doctor when I grow up," announced Emilia. "This is very good experience for me."

The other maids had brought a bucket of water and towels, but they didn't attempt to clean Matt up until Rosa gave them permission.

"Be careful. The right foot is badly cut," said Rosa.

The air hummed in Matt's ears. He felt the warm water and suddenly the pain returned. It stabbed from his foot all the way to the top of his head. He opened his mouth to scream, but nothing came out. His throat had closed with shock.

"Oh, God! There must be glass left inside," cried Rosa. She grabbed Matt's shoulders and ordered him not to be afraid. She seemed almost angry.

The fogginess that had surrounded Matt had vanished. His feet, his hands, his knees throbbed with more pain than he had known existed.

"I told you he was crying earlier," said María.

"Be quiet!" said Emilia.

"Look! There's writing on his foot," the little girl cried. She tried to get close, but Emilia thrust her back.

"*I'm* the one who's going to be a doctor. Rats! I can't read it. There's too much blood." She snatched a washcloth and wiped Matt's foot.

The pain wasn't as bad this time, but he couldn't help moaning.

"You're hurting him, you bully!" shrieked María.

"Wait! I can just make it out . . . . 'Property of' – the writing is so tiny! – 'Property of the Alacrán Estate.'"

"'Property of the Alacrán Estate'? That's us. It doesn't make any sense," said Steven.

"What's going on?" came a voice Matt hadn't heard before. A large, fierce-looking man burst into the room. Steven immediately straightened up. Emilia and even María looked alarmed.

"We found a kid in the poppy fields, Father," said Steven. "He hurt himself, and I thought the doctor . . . the doctor – "

"You idiot! You need a vet for this little beast!" the man roared. "How dare you defile this house?"

"He was bleeding – " began Steven.

"Yes! All over the sheet! We'll have to burn it. Take the creature outside now."

Rosa hesitated, obviously bewildered.

The man leaned forward and whispered into her ear.

A look of horror crossed Rosa's face. She instantly scooped up Matt and ran. Steven dashed ahead to open the doors. His face had turned white. "How *dare* he talk to me like that," he hissed.

"He didn't mean it," said Emilia, who was dragging María along behind.

"Oh, yes he did. He hates me," Steven said.

Rosa hurried down the steps and dumped Matt roughly onto the lawn. Without a word, she turned and fled back to the house.

4

MARÍA

Matt gazed up. Hundreds of stars lay in a bright smear across a velvety, black sky. It was the Milky Way, which Celia said had spurted from the Virgin's breast when She first fed Baby Jesus. The grass pressed against Matt's back. It wasn't as soft as he'd imagined, but it smelled fresh, and the coolness of the air was good too. He felt hot and feverish.

The terrifying pain had subsided to a dull ache. Matt was glad to be outside again. The sky felt familiar and safe. The same stars hung over the little house in the poppy fields. Celia never took him outside by day, but sometimes at night she and he would sit in the doorway of the little house. She would tell him stories and point out a falling star. "That's a prayer being answered by God," she explained. "One of the angels is flying down to carry out God's orders."

Matt prayed now for Celia to come and rescue him. She'd be upset about the window, but he could live with that. No matter how loud she yelled, he knew that underneath she still loved him. He watched the sky, but no star fell.

"Look at him. He's just lying there like an animal," said Emilia from not far away. Matt jumped. He'd forgotten about the children.

"He *is* an animal," Steven said after a pause. They were sitting on the first step leading to the house. María was busy picking oranges from the trees and rolling them down the stairs.

"I don't understand," said Emilia.

"I've been stupid. I should have known what he − *it* − was the minute I saw it. No servant would be allowed to keep a child or live away from the others. Benito told me about the situation, only I thought *it* was living somewhere else. In a zoo, maybe. Wherever those things are kept."

"What are you talking about?"

"Matt's a clone," said Steven.

Emilia gasped. "He can't be! He doesn't − I've seen clones. They're horrible! They drool and mess their pants. They make animal noises."

"This one's different. Benito told me. Technicians are supposed to destroy the minds at birth − it's the law. But El Patrón wanted his to grow up like a real boy. He's so rich, he can break any law he wants."

"That's *disgusting*. Clones aren't people," cried Emilia.

"Of course they aren't."

Emilia hugged her knees. "It makes me feel goose bumpy. I actually touched it. I got its blood on me − María, stop rolling oranges at us!"

"Make me," jeered María.

"In about one second I'm going to roll *you* down the stairs." The little girl stuck out her tongue. She threw a fruit so hard, it shot off the bottom step and landed with a soft plop on the grass. "Want me to peel you one, Matt?" she called.

"Don't," said Emilia. The seriousness in her voice made the little girl pause. "Matt's a clone. You mustn't go near it."

"What's a clone?"

"A bad animal."

"How bad?" María said with interest.

Before Emilia could answer, the fierce man and the doctor appeared at the top of the stairs.

"You should have called me at once," the doctor said. "It's my job to make sure it stays healthy."

"I didn't find out until I walked past the living room. There was blood all over the place. I'm afraid I lost my head and ordered Rosa to throw it outside." The fierce man seemed less dangerous now, but Matt still tried to wriggle away. The movement sent a wave of agony through his foot.

"We'll have to take it somewhere else. I can't operate on the lawn."

"There's an empty room in the servants' quarters," said the fierce man. He shouted for Rosa, who pattered down the steps with a furious look on her face. She carted Matt to a different part of the house, a warren of dim hallways that smelled of mould. Steven, Emilia, and María were ordered away, to take showers and change their clothes.

Matt was deposited onto a hard, bare mattress. The room was long and narrow. At one end was the door and at the other a window covered with iron grillwork.

"I need more light," the doctor said, tersely. The fierce man brought a lamp. "Hold it down," the doctor ordered Rosa.

"Please, Master. It's a filthy clone," the woman objected.

"Get moving if you know what's good for you," the fierce

man growled. Rosa threw herself across Matt's body and grasped his ankles. Her weight made it almost impossible to breathe.

"Stop . . . stop . . . ," the boy wailed. The doctor probed in the deepest cut with a pair of tweezers as Matt struggled and begged and finally broke down entirely when the sliver of glass was extracted. Rosa held on to his ankles so tightly, her fingers burned like fire. When at last the wound was cleaned and stitched, Matt was set free. He rolled himself into a ball and looked fearfully at his tormentors to see if they planned anything else.

"I've given it a tetanus shot," said the doctor, putting away his instruments. "There may be permanent damage to the right foot."

"Can I send it back to the poppy fields?" inquired the fierce man.

"Too late. The children have seen it."

The men and Rosa went out. Matt wondered what would happen next. If he prayed very hard, Celia would surely come for him now. She would hug him and carry him off to bed. Then she would light the holy candle in front of the Virgin of Guadalupe.

Except that the Virgin was far away in the little house, and Celia might not even know where he was.

Rosa slammed open the door and laid newspapers all over the floor. "The doctor says you're housebroken, but I'm not taking chances," she said. "Do it in the bucket if you've got the brains." She placed a bucket next to the bed and picked up the lamp.

"Wait," Matt said.

Rosa paused. She looked distinctly unfriendly.

"Can you tell Celia where I am?"

The maid smiled maliciously. "Celia isn't allowed to see you. Doctor's orders." She went out and closed the door.

The room was dark except for a faint, yellow light filtering through the bars of the window. Matt craned his head up to see where it was coming from. He saw a bulb hanging on a wire from the ceiling. It was as small as the lights Celia used to decorate the Christmas tree, but it shone valiantly and softened what would otherwise have been complete darkness.

He could see nothing else except the bed and the bucket. The walls were bare, the ceiling high and shadowy. The narrowness of the room made Matt feel as though he were locked in a box.

He had never, never gone to bed alone. Always, even though it might be very late, he could count on Celia's return. When he woke in the night, her snores in the next room made him feel safe. Here there was nothing, not even the wind over the poppy fields or the murmur of doves in their nests on the roof.

The silence was terrifying.

Matt cried steadily. His grief went on and on. When it lessened, he remembered Celia and started crying again. He looked up with tear-blurred eyes at the little yellow light, and it seemed to waver like a flame. It came to him that it was like the holy candle in front of the Virgin. After all, the Virgin could go wherever She liked. She couldn't be locked up like a person. She could fly through the air or even knock down walls, like the superheroes Matt saw on TV — only She wouldn't do that, of course, because She was Jesus' mother. She could be standing outside right now, watching his window. Something let go inside of Matt. He sighed deeply and soon he was fast asleep.

He woke to the sound of someone opening the door. Matt

tried to sit up, but the pain made him lie down again. A flash-light shone in his eyes.

"Good. I was afraid this was the wrong room." A small shape ran over to the bed, unslung a backpack, and began taking out food.

"María?" said Matt.

"Rosa said they didn't give you dinner. She's so mean! I have a dog at home, and if he doesn't get fed, he howls. Do you like mango juice? It's my favourite."

Matt suddenly realised he was very thirsty. He drank the whole bottle without stopping. María had brought hunks of cheese and pepperoni. "I'm going to put them into your mouth one at a time – but you have to promise not to bite me."

Matt indignantly said he never bit people.

"Well, you never know. Emilia says clones are as vicious as werewolves. Did you see that story on TV about the boy who got hair all over him when the moon was full?"

"Yes!" Matt was delighted he and María had something in common. He had locked himself in the bathroom after that movie until Celia came home.

"*You* don't grow hair or anything, do you?" asked María.

"Never," Matt swore.

"Good," María said. She popped bits of food into Matt's mouth until he couldn't eat any more.

They talked about movies and then about stories Celia had told Matt of the dangers that lurked after dark. Matt found that if he lay perfectly still, his wounds didn't hurt too much. María bounced around and occasionally hurt him, but he was afraid to scold her. She might get angry and leave.

"Celia hangs charms over the doors to keep out monsters," Matt told María.

"Does that work?"

"Of course. They also keep out dead people who aren't ready to stay in their graves."

"There aren't any charms here," María said nervously.

That thought had occurred to Matt too, but he didn't want her to go away. "We don't need charms in the Big House," he explained. "There are too many people, and monsters hate crowds."

María's interest drove Matt to greater and greater heights. He talked feverishly, unable to stop, and he ground his teeth from sheer nervousness. He'd never had so much attention in his life. Celia tried to listen to him, but she was usually too tired. María hung on his words as though her life depended on them.

"Do you know about the *chupacabras?*" Matt said.

"What's . . . a *chupacabras?*" asked María. Her voice sounded a little high and breathless.

"You know. The goat sucker."

"It sounds nasty." María moved closer to him.

"It is! It's got spikes down its back and claws and orange teeth, *and it sucks blood.*"

"You're kidding!"

"Celia says it has a face of a man, only the eyes are black inside. Like empty holes," said Matt.

"Ugh!"

"It likes goats best, but it'll eat horses or cows – or a child if it's really hungry."

María was pressed right up against him now. She put her arms around him and he gritted his teeth to keep from wincing with pain. He noticed that her hands were icy.

"Last month Celia said it got a whole pen of chickens," Matt said.

"I heard about that. Steven said Illegals stole them."

"That's what they told everyone to keep them from running away out of sheer terror," said Matt, echoing the words Celia had used. "But they really found the chickens in the desert without a drop of blood inside. They were blowing around like dry watermelon skins."

Matt was afraid of Steven and Emilia, but María was different. She was his size and she didn't make him feel bad. What was it Rosa had called him? A "filthy clone." Matt had no idea what that was, but he recognised an insult when he heard it. Rosa hated him, and so did the fierce man and the doctor. Even the two older children had changed once they knew what he was. Matt wanted to ask María about clones, but he was afraid she might hate him too if he reminded her.

Meanwhile, he had discovered a wonderful power in repeating the stories Celia had told him. They had held him spellbound, and now they were impressing María so much that she was practically glued to him.

"The *chupacabras* isn't the only thing out there," Matt said grandly. "La Llorona walks in the night too."

María murmured something. Her face was pressed against his shirt, so it was hard to tell what she was saying.

"La Llorona drowned her children because she was angry at her boyfriend. And then she was sorry and drowned herself," Matt said. "She went to heaven, and Saint Peter shouted, 'You bad woman! You can't come in here without your kids.' She ran down to hell, but the Devil slammed the door in her face. Now she has to walk around all night, never sitting down, never sleeping. She cries, 'Ooooo . . . Ooooo. Where are my babies?' You can hear her when the wind blows. She comes to the window. 'Ooooo . . . Ooooo. Where are my babies?' She scratches the glass with her long fingernails – "

"Stop it!" shrieked María. "I told you to stop it! Don't you ever listen?"

Matt halted. What could possibly be wrong with this story? He was telling it exactly the way Celia had.

"There's no such thing as La Llorona! You made her up!"

"No, I didn't."

"Well, if she's real, I don't want to know!"

Matt reached out and touched María's face. "You're crying!"

"I am not, you eejit! I just hate nasty stories!"

Matt was horrified. He'd never meant to scare María that much. "I'm sorry."

"You should be," María muttered, sniffling.

"Nothing can get through the window bars," Matt said. "And there's tons of people in the house."

"There's *nobody* in the halls," María said. "If I go outside, the monsters'll get me."

"Maybe not."

"Oh, great! *Maybe* not! When Emilia finds out I'm not in bed, I'll be in really big trouble. She'll tell Dada, and he'll make me do the times tables for *hours,* and it's all your fault!"

Matt didn't know what to say.

"I'll have to stay here till morning," María concluded. "But I'll still get into really big trouble. At least the *chupacabras* won't eat me. Move over."

Matt tried to make room. The bed was very narrow, and it hurt to move even a few inches. His hands and feet throbbed as he clung to the far edge.

"You really are a hog," complained María. "Got any covers?"

"No," said Matt.

"Wait a minute." María jumped off the bed and gathered up the newspapers Rosa had spread out on the floor.

"We don't need covers," Matt objected as she began arranging them on the bed.

"They make me feel safer." María crawled under the papers. "This isn't too bad. I sleep with my dog all the time – are you sure you don't bite?"

"Of course not," said Matt.

"Well, that's all right," she said, snuggling closer to him. Matt's mind churned over the punishment María would endure because she had brought him food. He didn't know what the times tables were, but they were probably something awful.

So much had happened in such a short time, and Matt couldn't understand half of it. Why had he been thrown out on the lawn when everyone had been so eager to help him at first? Why had the fierce man called him a "little beast"? And why had Emilia told María he was a "bad animal"?

It had something to do with being a clone and also, perhaps, with the writing on his foot. Matt had once asked Celia about the words on his foot, and she said it was something they put on babies to keep them from getting lost. He'd assumed everyone was tattooed. From Steven's reaction, it seemed everyone wasn't.

María wriggled and sighed and flung her arms out in her sleep. The newspapers quickly fell to the floor. Matt had to scoot to the extreme edge of the bed to keep from being kicked. At one point she seemed to have a nightmare. She called, "Mama . . . Mama . . ." Matt tried to wake her, but she punched him.

In the first blue light of dawn Matt forced himself to get up. He gasped at the pain in his feet. It was worse than last night.

He dropped to his hands and knees and moved as noise-lessly as possible, pulling the bucket along with him. When he got to the end of the bed where he thought María couldn't see him, he tried to pee silently. María turned over. The noise made Matt jump. The bucket tipped over. He had to fetch newspapers to sop up the mess, and then he had to rest with his back against the wall because his hands and feet hurt so much.

"Bad girl!" shouted Rosa, flinging open the door. Behind her was a covey of maids, all craning their necks to see what was inside. "We turned the house upside down looking for you," Rosa yelled. "All the time you were hiding out with this filthy clone. Boy, are you in trouble! You're going to be sent home at once."

María sat up, blinking at the sudden light from the door-way. Rosa whisked her off the bed and wrinkled her nose at Matt cowering against the wall. "So you aren't housebroken, you little brute," she snarled, kicking aside the sodden news-papers. "I honestly don't know how Celia stood it all those years."

5

PRISON

That night, when Rosa brought him dinner, Matt asked her when María was coming back.

"Never!" snarled the maid. "She and her sister have been sent home, and I say good riddance! Just because their father's a senator, the Mendoza girls think they can turn their noses up at us. Pah! Senator Mendoza isn't too proud to have his paw out when El Patrón hands around money."

Every day the doctor visited. Matt shrank from him, but the man didn't seem to notice. He grasped Matt's foot in a business-like way, doused it with disinfectant, and checked the stitches. Once he gave Matt a shot of antibiotics because the wound looked puffy and the boy was running a fever. The doctor made no effort to start a conversation, and Matt was happy to leave things that way.

The man talked to Rosa, however. They seemed to enjoy each other's company. The doctor was tall and bony. His head was fringed with hair like the fluff on a duck's bottom, and he sprayed saliva when he talked. Rosa was also tall and very strong, as Matt had found out when he tried to get around her. Her face was set in a permanent scowl, although she occasionally smiled when the doctor told one of his bad jokes. Matt found Rosa's smile even more horrid than her scowl.

"El Patrón hasn't asked about the beast in years," remarked the doctor.

Matt understood that the beast was himself.

"Probably forgotten it exists," muttered Rosa. She was busy scrubbing out the corners of the room. She was on her hands and knees with a bucket of soapy water by her side.

"I wish I could count on it," the doctor said. "Sometimes El Patrón seems definitely senile. He won't talk for days and stares out the window. Other times he's as sharp as the old *bandido* he once was."

"He's still a bandit," said Rosa.

"Don't say that, not even to me. El Patrón's rage is something you don't want to see."

It seemed to Matt that both the maid and the doctor shivered slightly. He wondered why El Patrón was so frightening, since the man was said to be old and weak. Matt knew he was El Patrón's clone, but he was unclear about the meaning of the word. Perhaps El Patrón had loaned him to Celia and would someday want him back.

At the thought of Celia, Matt's eyes filled with tears. He swallowed them back. He would not show weakness in front of his tormentors. He knew instinctively they would seize on it to hurt him even more.

"You're wearing perfume, Rosa," the doctor said slyly.

"Ha! You think I'd put on anything to please you, Willum?"

The maid stood up and wiped her soapy hands on her apron.

"I think you're wearing it behind your ears."

"It's the disinfectant I used to clean out the bath," said Rosa. "To a doctor, it probably smells good."

"So it does, my thorny little Rosa." Willum tried to grab her, but she wriggled out of his arms.

"Stop it!" she cried, pushing him away roughly. In spite of her unfriendliness, the doctor seemed to like her. It made Matt uncomfortable. He felt the two were united against him.

When they left the room, Rosa always locked the door. Matt tried the knob each time to see whether she had forgotten, but she never did. He pulled on the window bars. They were as firmly attached as ever. He sat disconsolately on the floor.

If only he could see something interesting outside the window. A section of wall blocked off most of what lay beyond. Through a narrow gap he could see a green lawn and bright pink flowers, but only enough to make him want more. A thin ribbon of sky let in daylight and at night showed a few stars. Matt listened in vain for voices.

Scar tissue had formed a knot on the bottom of his foot. He inspected the writing frequently – PROPERTY OF THE ALACRÁN ESTATE – but the scar had sliced through the tiny lettering. It was more difficult to make out the words.

One day a frightening argument erupted between Rosa and the doctor. "El Patrón wants me by his side. I'll come back once a month," the man said.

"It's just an excuse to get away from me," said Rosa.

"I have to work, you stupid woman."

"Don't you call me stupid!" the woman snarled. "I know a lying coyote when I see one."

"I don't have a choice," Willum said stiffly.

"Then why not take me with you? I could be a house-keeper."

"El Patrón doesn't need one."

"Oh, sure! How convenient! Let me tell you, it's horrible working here," she stormed. "The other servants laugh at me. 'She takes care of the beast,' they say. 'She's no better than a beast herself.' They treat me like scum."

"You're exaggerating."

"No, I'm not!" she cried. "Please take me with you, Willum. Please! I love you. I'll do anything for you!"

The doctor pried her arms away. "You're hysterical. I'll leave you some pills and see you in a month."

As soon as the door closed, Rosa hurled the bucket against the wall and cursed the doctor by all his ancestors. Her face turned chalky with rage, except for two splotches of red on her cheeks. Matt had never seen anyone so furious, and he found it terrifying.

"You're responsible for this!" Rosa shrieked. She pulled Matt up by his hair.

"Ow! Ow!" yelled Matt.

"Bleating won't save you, you good-for-nothing animal. No one can hear you. This whole wing of the house is empty because *you* are in it! They don't even put pigs down here!" Rosa thrust her face close to his. Her cheekbones stood out beneath her taut skin. Her eyes were wide, and Matt could see white all around the edges. She looked like a demon in one of the comic books Celia got from church.

"I could kill you," Rosa said quietly. "I could bury your body under the floor – and I *might* do it." She let him slump to the floor again. He rubbed his head where she had pulled the hair. "Or I might not. You'll never know until it's too late. But one thing you'd better understand: I'm your master now, and if you make me angry – watch out!"

She slammed the door as she left. Matt sat paralysed for a few minutes. His heart pounded and his body was slimy with sweat. What did she mean? What else could she possibly do? After a while he stopped trembling and his breathing returned to normal. He tried the door, but not even rage had kept Rosa from locking it. He limped to the window and watched the bright strip of grass and flowers beyond the wall.

That night two gardeners, who refused to look at Matt, removed his bed. Rosa watched with a look of bitter satisfaction. She took away the waste bucket Matt had been forced to use since he arrived.

"You can go in the corner on the newspapers," said Rosa. "That's what dogs do."

Matt had to lie on the cement floor without any covers and, of course, without a pillow. He slept badly and his body ached like a tooth in the morning. When he had to use the newspapers in the corner, he felt dirty and ashamed. How long could this go on?

Rosa merely plunked down the breakfast tray and left. She didn't scold him. At first Matt was relieved, but after a while he began to feel bad. Even angry words were better than silence. At home he would have had the stuffed bear and dog and *Pedro el Conejo* for company. They didn't talk, but he could hug them. Where were they now? Had Celia thrown them out because she knew he wasn't coming back?

Matt ate and cried at the same time. The tears ran down into his mouth and onto the dry toast Rosa had brought. He had toast and oatmeal, scrambled eggs with chorizo sausage, a plastic mug of orange juice, a strip of cold bacon. At least she wasn't going to starve him.

In the evening Rosa brought him a flavourless stew with cement-coloured gravy. Matt was given no utensils and had to put his face in the bowl like a dog. With the stew came boiled squash, an apple, and a bottle of water. He ate because he was hungry. He hated the food because it reminded him of how wonderful Celia's cooking had been.

Days passed. Rosa never spoke to him. A shutter seemed to have come down over her face. She neither met Matt's eyes nor responded when he asked her questions. Her silence made him frantic. He talked feverishly when she arrived, but he might have been a stuffed bear for all the notice she took of him.

Meanwhile, the smell in the room became appalling. Rosa cleaned the corner every day, but the stench clung to the cement. Matt got used to it. Rosa didn't, and one day she exploded in another fit of rage.

"Isn't it enough that I have to wait on you?" she cried as he cowered next to the window. "I'd rather clean out a henhouse! At least they're useful! What good are you?"

Then an idea seemed to occur to her. She halted in mid-rant and looked at Matt in such a calculating way, he felt cold right down to his toes. What was she planning now?

Back came the sullen gardeners. They built a low barrier across the door. Matt watched with interest. The barrier was as high as his waist – not tall enough to keep him in, but high enough to slow him down if he tried to escape. Rosa stood in the hallway, watching and criticising. The gardeners said a few words Matt had never heard before, and Rosa turned dark with rage. But she didn't reply.

After the barrier was finished, Rosa lifted Matt outside and held him tightly. He looked around eagerly. The hallway was grey and empty, hardly more interesting than the room, but at least it was different.

Then something happened that made Matt's mouth fall open with surprise. The gardeners trundled down the hall with wheelbarrows piled high with sawdust. They dumped them, one after the other, into his room. Back and forth they went until the floor was full of sawdust heaped as high as the barrier in the doorway.

Rosa suddenly swung him up by his arms and tossed him inside. He landed with a *whump* and sat up coughing.

"That's what dirty beasts get to live in," she said, and slammed the door.

Matt was so startled that he didn't know what to think. The whole room was full of the grey-brown powder. It was soft. He could sleep on it like a bed. He waded through the sawdust trying to figure out why it had suddenly appeared in his world. At least it was something different.

Matt tunnelled. He heaped the shavings into hills. He threw it into the air to watch it patter down in a plume of dust. He amused himself this way for a long time, but gradually Matt ran out of things to do with sawdust.

Rosa brought him food at sundown. She spoke not a single word. He ate slowly, watching the tiny yellow light that belonged to the Virgin and listening for far-off noises from the rest of the house.

"What in God's green earth have you done?" cried the doctor when he saw Matt's new environment.

"It's deep litter," said Rosa.

"Are you crazy?"

"What do you care?"

"Of course I care, Rosa," the doctor said, trying to take her hand. She threw him off. "And I have to care about the health of this clone. Good God, do you know what would happen if he died?"

"You're only worried about what would happen to you. But don't lose sleep over it, Willum. I grew up on a poultry farm, and deep litter is by far the best way to keep chickens healthy. You let the hens run around in it, and their filth settles to the bottom. It saves their feet from getting infected."

Willum laughed out loud. "You're a very strange woman, Rosa, but I have to admit the beast's in good condition. You know, I remember it talking when it lived in Celia's house. Now it doesn't say a thing."

"It's a sullen, evil-tempered animal," she said.

The doctor sighed. "Clones go that way in the end. I did think this one was brighter than most."

Matt said nothing, hunched as he was in a corner as far from the pair as he could get. Long days of solitude in Celia's house had taught him how to be quiet, and any attention from Willum or Rosa could result in pain.

The days passed with agonising slowness, followed by nights of misery. Matt could see little from the barred window. The pink flowers withered. The strip of sky was blue by day and black at night. He dreamed of the little house, of Celia, of a meadow so intensely green, it made him cry when he woke up.

And gradually it came to him that Celia had forgotten him, that she was never going to rescue him from this prison. The idea was so painful, Matt thrust it from his mind. He refused to think about her, or when he did, he quickly thought of something else to drive her image from his mind. After a while he forgot what she looked like, except in dreams.

But Matt still fought against the dullness that threatened to overwhelm him. He hid caches of food under the sawdust, not to eat later, but to attract bugs. The window wasn't glassed, and so all sorts of small creatures could come in through the bars.

First he attracted wasps to a chunk of apple. Then he lured a glorious, buzzing fly to a piece of spoiled meat. It sat on the meat, just as though it had been invited to dinner, and rubbed its hairy paws as it gloated over the meal. Afterward Matt discovered a writhing mass of worms living in the meat, and he watched them grow and eventually turn into buzzing flies themselves. He found this extremely interesting.

Then, of course, there were the cockroaches. Small, brown ones struggled through the sawdust; and big, leathery bombers zoomed through the air and made Rosa scream.

"You're a monster!" she cried. "It wouldn't surprise me if you *ate* them!"

Oh, yes, there were all kinds of entertainment in bugs.

One magical day a dove pushed its way through the bars and rummaged through the sawdust. Matt sat perfectly still, entranced by the bird's beauty. When it flew away, it left a single pearl grey feather behind, which Matt hid from Rosa. He assumed that anything beautiful would be destroyed by her.

He sang to himself – inside where Rosa couldn't hear – one of Celia's lullabies: *Buenos días paloma blanca. Hoy te vengo a saludar. Good morning white dove. Today I come to greet thee.* Celia said it was a song to the Virgin. It occurred to Matt that this dove had come from the Virgin and that the feather meant She would watch over him here as She had done in the little house.

One day he heard footsteps outside. He looked up to see a strange, new face on the other side of the bars. It was a boy somewhat older than himself, with bristly red hair and freckles.

"You're ugly," said the boy. "You look like a pig in a sty."

Matt wanted to reply, but the habit of silence had grown too strong. He could only glare at the intruder. In the hazy background of his mind, he recalled a boy named Tom, who was bad.

"Do something," said Tom. "Root around. Scratch your piggy behind on the wall. I have to have something to tell María."

Matt flinched. He remembered a cheerful little girl with black hair, who worried about him and was punished for bringing him food. So she had returned. And she hadn't come to see him.

"That got you, didn't it? Wait'll I tell your girlfriend how cute you are now. You smell like a pile of dung."

Matt felt idly beneath the sawdust for something he'd been feeding to bugs. It was an entire orange. At first it had been green, but time had turned it blue and very soft. Worms filled the inside, diverting Matt with their wiggly bodies. He curled his fingers around the orange. It held its shape — barely.

"I forgot. You're too dumb to talk. You're a stupid clone who wets his pants and pukes all over his feet. Maybe if I spoke your language, you'd understand." Tom put his face against the bars and grunted. At the same instant Matt flung the orange. His accuracy was excellent because he had spent days aiming fruit at targets.

The rotten orange burst apart all over Tom's face. He jumped back, screaming, "It's moving, it's moving!" Pulp dripped off his chin. Wiggly worms dropped into his collar. "I'll get you for this!" he shrieked as he ran away.

Matt felt deeply peaceful. The room might look like a featureless desert to Rosa, but to him, it was a kingdom of hidden delights. Underneath the sawdust — and he knew exactly where – were caches of nutshells, seeds, bones, fruit, and gristle. The gristle was particularly valuable. You could stretch it, bend it, hold it up to the light, and even suck on it if it wasn't too old. The bones were his dolls. He could make them have adventures and talk to them.

Matt closed his eyes. He would like to lock up Rosa and the doctor. He would feed them wormy oranges and sour milk. They would beg him to let them go, but he wouldn't, not ever.

He fished up the dove feather and contemplated its silky colours. The feather usually made him feel safe, but now it made him uneasy. Celia said the Virgin loved all kind and gentle things. She wouldn't approve of throwing a rotten orange in Tom's face, even if he deserved it. If She looked inside Matt, She would see the bad thoughts about Rosa and the doctor and be sad.

Matt found he was sad too. *I wouldn't really hurt them,* he thought so the Virgin could see that and smile. Still, he couldn't help feeling the warm sensation of pleasure at having zinged Tom.

But as Celia had once told him, a smart person doesn't spit into the wind. If you throw a rotten orange into someone's face, you can bet the orange will sooner or later come flying back. In less than an hour Tom returned with a peashooter. Matt was clad only in a pair of shorts, so the peas landed on his bare skin. At first he tried to dodge them, but there was nowhere to run in the narrow little room. Matt settled in a corner with his head cradled in his arms to protect his face.

He instinctively understood that if he refused to react, Tom would lose interest. It still took a long time. The boy outside seemed to have an endless supply of peas, but eventually he called Matt a few bad names and went away.

Matt waited a long time to be sure. He could be very

patient. He thought of *Pedro el Conejo,* who explored Señor MacGregor's garden and lost all his clothes. Matt too had lost all his clothes, except for the shorts. Rosa said he would only ruin them.

Finally, he looked up and saw his kingdom was in disarray. Running around had destroyed the marks that told Matt what lay below. Sighing, he worked his way through the sawdust. He felt underneath to find his treasures. He combed the surface smooth with his fingers and renewed the lines and hollows that told him where everything was. It was very much like Celia moving the furniture out to vacuum the rugs and then moving it back again.

When he was finished, Matt sat in his corner and waited for Rosa to bring his dinner. But something shocking and unbelievable happened first.

"¡Mijo! ¡Mi hijo!" cried Celia from the window. "My child! My child! I didn't know you were here. Oh, God! They told me you were with El Patrón. I didn't know." She was holding María up to the window in the crook of her arm.

"He looks different," observed María.

"They starved him, the animals! And took his clothes! Come here, darling. I want to touch you." Celia jammed her big hand through the bars. "Let me see you, *mi vida.* I can't believe what's happened."

But Matt could only stare. He wanted to go. He had dreamed of nothing else, but now that the moment had actually come, he couldn't move. It was too good to be true. If he gave in and ran to Celia, something bad would happen. Celia would turn into Rosa, and María would turn into Tom. The disappointment would break him into pieces.

"Hey, eejit, I went to a lot of trouble to come here," María said.

"Are you too weak to stand?" Celia cried suddenly. "Oh, my God! Have they broken your legs? At least say something. They haven't torn out your tongue?" She began to wail like La Llorona. She stretched her hand through the bars. Her misery tore at Matt, and still he couldn't move or speak.

"You're squeezing me," complained María, so Celia put her down. The little girl managed to stand tall enough to peer through the window. "My dog, Furball, was like that when the dogcatcher got him. I cried and cried until Dada brought him back. Furball wouldn't eat or look at me for a whole day, but he got over it. I'm sure Matt will too."

"Out of the mouths of babies comes wisdom," said Celia.

"I'm not a baby!"

"Of course not, darling. You only reminded me that the most important thing is to get Matt free," Celia said, smoothing María's hair. "We can worry about the other stuff later. If I give you a letter, can you keep it a secret from everyone? Especially Tom?"

"Sure," said María.

"I hate to do it," Celia said, half to herself, "I hate like *crazy* to do it, but there's only one person who can save Matt. María, you must take the letter to your dada. He'll know where to send it."

"Okay," said María cheerfully. "Hey, Matt. Celia's going to put chillis in Tom's hot chocolate tonight, only you mustn't tell anyone."

"And *you* mustn't either," said Celia.

"Okay."

"Don't you worry," the woman called to Matt. "I've got more tricks up my sleeve than old man coyote has fleas. I'll get you out of there, my love!"

Matt was frankly relieved to see them go. They were an unwelcome intrusion in the orderly world he had created. He could forget them now and get back to the contemplation of his kingdom. The surface of the sawdust was combed smooth, the treasures hidden beneath marks that only he, the king, understood. A bee wandered in, found nothing, and left. A spider mended its web high up near the ceiling. Matt took out the dove feather and lost himself in its silky perfection.

MIDDLE AGE:
7 TO 11

6

El Patrón

"Get up! Get up!" shouted Rosa. Matt had been sleeping in a hollow formed by his body. As he slept, he sank down until the sawdust almost covered him. The sudden awakening made him gasp. The sawdust went up his nose, and he doubled over, coughing and retching.

"Get up! Oh, you're impossible! I've got to wash you, dress you, and who knows what else. You're nothing but trouble!" Rosa yanked him up by the hair and dragged him out of the room.

Matt was hurried down dingy hallways and past doorways that opened into rooms both cramped and gloomy. A maid scrubbed the floor with a big brush. She looked up with hopeless eyes as Rosa rushed him past.

Rosa pushed him into a steamy bathroom. A tub stained with rust was already full of water. The woman shucked Matt out of his shorts before he knew what was happening and dumped him inside.

It was the first bath he'd had since being locked up. Matt felt like a thirsty sponge soaking up water until he was so full that he could hardly move. The warmth soothed his skin, which had become itchy and sore. "Sit up! I haven't got all day," growled Rosa, setting to work with a brush almost as big as the one in the hallway.

She scoured him until he was pink, dried him with a big, fluffy towel, and tried to get a comb through his tangled hair. In a fury because it wouldn't come right, she grabbed a pair of scissors and cut it all off. "They want tidy, they'll *get* tidy," she muttered. She stuffed Matt into a long-sleeved shirt and trousers and gave him a pair of rubber sandals to wear.

Very soon he was being hurried across a courtyard to another part of the house. His legs ached with the effort of walking. Halfway across the courtyard his feet tangled in the unfamiliar sandals and he stumbled against Rosa.

She took the opportunity to lecture him. "The doctor will be there," she said. "And so will important members of the family. They'll want to make sure you're healthy. If they ask questions, don't answer. Above all, don't say anything about me." She brought her face down close to his. "You'll be all alone with me in that little room," she whispered. "I swear I'll kill you and bury you under the floor if you make trouble."

Matt had no trouble believing her. He forced his trembling legs to follow her to a part of the house as different from his old prison as the sun was from a candle. The walls were painted cream and rose and pale green. It was so bright and cheerful, it raised his spirits in spite of Rosa's dire threats. The floor gleamed with polish that made Matt feel like he was walking on water.

Windows looked out on gardens with fountains. They

splashed and glittered in the sun. A magnificent bird with a long green tail stepped delicately across a walk. Matt wanted to stop, but Rosa shoved him on, all the while cursing beneath her breath.

Finally, they came to a large room with a marvellous carpet woven with birds and vines. Matt wanted to kneel down and touch them. "Stand up," hissed Rosa. He saw windows framed by blue curtains that went from floor to ceiling. A small table set with a teapot, cups, and a silver plate of cookies sat next to a flowered armchair. Matt's mouth watered at the memory of cookies.

"Come closer, boy," said an old, old voice.

Rosa gasped. Her hand dropped from Matt's shoulder. "El Patrón," she whispered.

Matt saw that what he'd taken for an empty armchair actually contained a man. He was extremely thin, with shoulder-length white hair neatly combed beside a face so seamed and wrinkled, it hardly seemed real. He was wearing a dressing gown, and his knees were covered by a blanket. It was the blanket that had fooled Matt into thinking the old man was part of the chair.

"It's all right," said Celia from behind him. Matt whirled to see her in the doorway. His heart lurched with relief. Celia brushed past Rosa and took his hand. "He's had a bad time, *mi patrón*. For six months they've kept him like a wild animal."

"You lie!" snarled Rosa.

"I've seen it with my own eyes. María Mendoza told me."

"She's a baby! Who can believe a baby?"

"I can," said Celia quietly. "She hadn't been to the house for six months. When she arrived, she asked to see Matt, and Tom boasted that he'd shot him dead. She flew straight to me."

"*Shot* him? Is he hurt?" said the old man.

"He was already hurt." Celia described the injuries caused by the broken glass.

"Why didn't anyone tell me?" demanded El Patrón. His voice wasn't loud, but there was a quality to it that made Matt shiver even though he – for once – wasn't the one in trouble.

"It was the doctor's place to do it," Rosa cried.

"It was everyone's place to do it," said the old man in the same cold way. "Take off your shirt, boy."

Matt didn't dream of disobeying. He unbuttoned the shirt rapidly and dropped it to the floor.

"*¡Diós mio!* My God!"

"Those bruises must be from Tom's peashooter," said Celia, sounding ready to cry. "See how thin he is, *mi patrón?* And he's got some kind of rash. He wasn't like that in my house, sir."

"Call the doctor!"

Instantly – he must have been waiting outside the door – Willum entered and began examining Matt. He shook his head as though he were genuinely surprised by the boy's condition. "He's suffering from mild malnutrition," the doctor said. "He has sores in his mouth. His skin condition, I would say, comes from a combination of dirt and an allergic reaction to chicken litter."

"*Chicken litter?*" said the old man.

"I understand he was kept in a room full of sawdust to cut down on housekeeping."

"You knew about it, Willum," cried Rosa. "You didn't tell me it was wrong."

"I knew nothing about it until today," said the doctor.

"You're lying! Tell them, Willum! You thought it was funny. You said the beast – the boy – was in good condition!"

"She's suffering from delusions," the doctor told El Patrón. "It's a shame such an unstable individual was allowed to have a position of responsibility."

Rosa flew at the doctor and raked his face with her nails before he was able to grasp her wrists. She kicked and screamed, driving Willum back with the force of her rage. She actually bared her teeth like a wild animal, and Matt watched with interest to see whether she would manage to sink them into the man's neck. Everything seemed unreal to him – the sudden appearance of Celia, the old man, the furious battle between his two enemies. It was like watching TV.

But before Rosa could do any serious harm, a pair of burly men rushed through the door and dragged her away.

"Willum! Willum!" she wailed. Her voice grew fainter as she was carried off. Matt heard a door slam and then he heard nothing.

He became aware that Celia was hugging him. He felt her body tremble as she held him close. The doctor mopped his face with a handkerchief. He was bleeding from a dozen scratches. Only El Patrón appeared tranquil. He had settled back in the armchair, and his pale lips were drawn up in a smile. "Well. That's the most excitement I've had in months," he said.

"I apologize, *mi patrón*," said Willum shakily. "This must have been a terrible shock to you. I'll check your blood pressure at once."

"Oh, stop fussing," El Patrón said, waving him off. "My life is far too quiet these days. This . . . was most entertaining." He turned his attention to Matt. "So they kept you on litter like a barnyard fowl. Tell me, boy, did you learn to cackle?"

Matt smiled. He liked El Patrón instinctively. There was something so right about the way the old man looked. His eyes were a *good* colour. Matt didn't know why it was good, only that it was. El Patrón's face seemed oddly familiar, and his hands – thin and blue-veined – had a shape that appealed to Matt in some deep way.

"Come here, boy."

Without the slightest hesitation, Matt walked up to the chair and let the old man stroke his face with a paper-dry hand. "So young . . . ," El Patrón murmured.

"You can speak now, *mi vida*," said Celia, but Matt wasn't ready to go that far.

"*Mi vida*. I like that," the old man said with a chuckle. "I like it so much, in fact, it's what I'll call him. Can he talk?"

"I think he's in shock. In my house he chattered away like a tree full of birds. And he can read both English and Spanish. He's very intelligent, *mi patrón*."

"Of course. He's my clone. Tell me, Mi Vida, do you like cookies?"

Matt nodded.

"Then you shall have them. Celia, put his shirt back on and find him a chair. We have much to talk about."

The next hour passed like a dream. Both the doctor and Celia were sent away. The old man and the boy sat across from each other and dined not only on cookies, but on creamed chicken, mashed potatoes, and apple sauce as well. A maid brought them from the kitchen. El Patrón said these foods were his favourites, and Matt decided they were his favourites too.

El Patrón had said they had much to talk about, but in fact, only he did any talking. He rambled on about his youth in Aztlán. It was called Mexico when he was a boy, he said. He came from a place called Durango. "People from Durango are called *alacránes* – scorpions – because there are so many of them scurrying around. When I made my first million, I took that as my name: Matteo Alacrán. It's your name too."

Matt smiled, well pleased that he shared something with El Patrón.

As the old man talked, Matt pictured in his mind the dusty cornfields and purple mountains of Durango. He saw the stream that roared with water two months of the year and was dry as a bone the rest of the time. El Patrón swam with his brothers, but, alas, they died of various things before they had a chance to grow up. El Patrón's sisters were carried off by typhoid when they were so small, they couldn't look over the windowsill – no, not even if they stood on tiptoe.

Matt thought of María and worried. Those little girls weren't as old as she when they were carried off by the typhoid. He wondered if that monster resembled the *chupacabras*. Of all those children, only one lived: Matteo Alacrán. He was skinny as a coyote, with not even two pesos to rub together, but he was filled with a burning desire to survive.

At last the voice fell silent. Matt looked up to see that El Patrón had fallen asleep in his chair. Matt was exhausted too. He was so full of food, he had been half asleep for some time. The same men who had taken Rosa now entered, gently lifted El Patrón into a wheelchair, and rolled him away.

Matt worried about what would happen to him now. Would Rosa come back and throw him into the sawdust? Would she make good on her promise to bury him alive?

But it was Celia who triumphantly bore him away. She took him to her new apartment in the Big House. Her possessions had been moved from the old place, so Matt wasn't too disappointed about not returning home. The Virgin sat, as She always had, on a table by his bed. She had gained a new wreath of plastic roses about her robe and a white lace tablecloth beneath her from Celia, in gratitude for restoring Matt to safety.

All in all, he was pleased with the change, although he missed the doves cooing on the roof and the wind blowing through the poppies.

"Listen up, eejit," commanded María. "I'm supposed to make you talk." Matt shrugged. He had no interest in talking, and besides, María did enough for both of them. "I know you can do it. Celia says you're in shock, but I think you're just lazy."

Matt yawned and scratched his armpit.

"El Patrón is going away today."

Now María had Matt's interest. He was dismayed that the old man was leaving. He hadn't seen him since the day he was rescued. Celia said the excitement had been too much for someone who was 140 years old. El Patrón had to stay in bed until he felt well enough to travel to his other house in the Chiricahua Mountains.

"We have to say good-bye to him. Everyone's coming, and you'd better talk or you'll be in big trouble." María squeezed Matt's mouth as though she could force the words out. He snapped at her. The little girl scrambled away. "You said you didn't bite!" she screamed. She grabbed a pillow and hit him several times before collapsing on the bed.

"Bad clone!" said María, hugging the pillow to her chest.

Matt considered the idea. Being a clone was bad no matter what you did, so why bother being good at all? He reached over and patted her hand.

"Oh, why won't you talk?" stormed María. "It's been over a week. It took Furball only one day to forgive me after the dog-catcher got him."

Matt wasn't trying to upset her. He couldn't talk. When he tried to make the words, he was overcome with terror. To speak was to open a door into his carefully built fortress, and anything might rush inside.

"Matt was locked up a lot longer than your dog," said Celia as she entered the room. She knelt down and stroked Matt's face. "Furball was gone only two days. Matt was trapped for six months. It takes time to recover."

"Is that how it works?" the little girl asked. "The longer you're sick, the longer it takes to get better?"

Celia nodded. She kept stroking Matt's face, his hair, his arms. It was as though she were trying to bring feeling back into his body.

"Then I guess," María said, slowly, "it's going to take years for El Patrón to get well."

"Don't talk about that!" cried Celia so sharply that María hugged the pillow and stared goggle-eyed at the woman. "Don't say anything about El Patrón! Shoo! I don't have time to entertain you." Celia flapped her apron at the girl, who fled without another word.

Matt felt sorry for María. He purposely made his body go stiff to make it hard for Celia to dress him, but Celia didn't get angry. She hugged him and sang him her favourite lullaby: *"Buenos días paloma blanca. Hoy te vengo a saludar."* Matt shivered. It was the song to the Virgin, who loved all gentle things and who had watched over him in prison. Then he knew it was wrong to be mean to Celia and let himself go limp again.

"That's my good boy," murmured the woman. "You're a good boy and I love you."

Matt suffered a moment of panic when she tried to lead him outside. He felt safe in his old bed, with the stuffed animals and the tattered copy of *Pedro el Conejo*. He kept the blinds closed, even though the windows looked out onto a beautiful walled garden. He didn't want anything new in his life, no matter how beautiful.

"It's all right. I won't let anyone hurt you," said Celia, lifting him in her arms.

Matt had not seen the front of the Big House yet. He was enchanted by the marble-walled entranceway and statues of fat babies with stubby wings. In the centre was a dark pond covered with water lilies. Matt clutched Celia when he saw a large fish rise casually from the depths to look at him with a round, yellow eye.

They passed between fluted, white pillars to a porch with wide stairs leading down to a driveway. Everyone was lined up on the porch, servants to one side and family on the other. He saw Steven, Emilia, and María standing to attention. When María tried to sit down, Emilia yanked her up again. Matt saw Tom holding María's hand and felt an almost uncontrollable surge of anger. How dare he be friends with her! How dare *she* be friends with *him*. If Matt had another wormy orange, he'd hurl it again, no matter what.

El Patrón sat in a wheelchair with a blanket over his legs. The burly men Matt had seen before guarded him. Willum stood nearby, dressed in a grey suit too warm for the day. His face was shiny with sweat. Of Rosa, there was no sign.

"Come here, Mi Vida," said El Patrón. The old man's voice was clearly audible over the sounds of birds and fountains. It had a quality that commanded attention in spite of its weakness. Celia put Matt down.

Matt walked to the wheelchair eagerly. He liked everything about El Patrón – his voice, the shape of his face, and his eyes, which were the colour of the dark pond with the fish lurking in its depths.

"Show him to the family, Willum," the old man said.

The doctor's hand was damp. Matt felt a revulsion to him, but he allowed himself to be led around the porch. He was introduced to Mr Alacrán, the fierce man who had thrown Matt out that first night and who was Benito's, Steven's, and Tom's father. Benito, it was explained, was away at college and Matt would meet him another day. Mr Alacrán looked at Matt with undisguised loathing.

Felicia, Mr Alacrán's wife, was a frail woman with long, nervous fingers. She had been a great concert pianist, the doctor said, until illness forced her to retire. Felicia flashed Willum a quick smile that disappeared when she looked at Matt. With her was Mr Alacrán's father, an old man with white hair who seemed unsure of why he was on the porch.

Then Matt met – again – Steven, Emilia, María, and Tom. Tom gave Matt a scowl, which Matt returned. No one, except María, seemed pleased to meet him, but they all pretended to be friendly.

It's because they're afraid of El Patrón, Matt realised. He didn't know why, but it was very good that they were.

"Has *el gato* – the cat – still got your tongue?" inquired the old man when Matt was at last brought back to the wheelchair. Matt nodded. "Celia will have to work on that. Listen, all of you," El Patrón said in a slightly louder voice. "This is my clone. He's the most important person in my life. If you thought it was any of you sorry, misbegotten swine, think again." The old man chuckled softly.

"Matt is to be treated with respect, just as though I were here in his place. He is to be educated, well fed, and entertained.

He is not to be mistreated." El Patrón looked directly at Tom, who flushed red. "Anyone – *anyone* – who harms Matt will be dealt with severely. Do I make myself clear?"

"Yes, *mi patrón,*" murmured several voices.

"And to be absolutely sure, I'm leaving one of my body-guards behind. Which of you louts volunteers for the duty?"

The bodyguards shuffled their feet and looked down.

"Overcome with shyness, I see," El Patrón said. "I picked up this lot in Scotland, breaking heads outside a soccer field. Always choose your bodyguards from another country, Matt. They find it harder to make alliances and betray you. Well, Matt, you make the choice. Which of these shrinking violets do you want for a playmate?"

Appalled, Matt looked at the men. Anyone less playful could hardly be imagined. They were thick-necked and brutal, with flattened noses and scars wandering across their arms and faces. They both had curling, brown hair that grew low upon their foreheads, ruddy faces, and bright blue eyes.

"That one's Daft Donald – he likes to juggle bowling balls. Tam Lin is the one with the interesting ears."

Matt shifted his gaze from one to the other. Daft Donald was younger and less battered. He seemed a safer person to have around. Tam Lin's ears appeared chewed, they were so mis-shapen. But when Matt looked into Tam Lin's eyes, he was sur-prised to see a glint of friendliness.

Friendliness was so rare in Matt's life, he instantly pointed to the man.

"Good decision," whispered El Patrón. With the introduc-tions disposed of, energy seemed to desert him. He sank back in the wheelchair and closed his eyes. "Good-bye, Mi Vida . . . until next time," he murmured.

The Alacráns crowded around and assured El Patrón of their fond regards. He ignored them. Then Daft Donald lifted him, chair and all, and carried him down the stairs to a waiting limousine. Everyone followed, calling out their good wishes. When the car drove off, the family members hurried away. The servants parted around Matt as though he were a rock in a stream and vanished into the house.

He was ignored. Not mistreated, just ignored. Only María had to be dragged off, complaining loudly.

Celia waited patiently for the crowd to clear. And Tam Lin.

"Well, laddie, let's see what you're made of," said Tam Lin, scooping up Matt in one beefy arm and slinging him over his shoulder.

7

TEACHER

Matt avoided leaving the safe haven of Celia's apartment for as long as possible. But gradually, Celia and María lured him into the walled garden and, from there, to other parts of the Big House.

Matt didn't like these excursions. The servants drew away from him as though he were something unclean, and Steven and Emilia turned the other way if they saw him coming. And there was always the danger of running into Tom.

Tom insisted on playing with María. He made her cry, but she always forgave him. He followed her to Celia's apartment in spite of – or perhaps because of – Matt's hostility. He seemed to like being where he wasn't wanted.

"It's nice here," Tom said, picking up Matt's treasured teddy bear. "Catch, María." He swung the bear viciously by one of its ragged ears and smacked her in the face. The ear tore off. He tossed it to the floor.

"Ow!" she squealed. Matt scrambled for the ear, but Tom put his foot on it. Matt flew at him, and soon they were both down on the floor, kicking and punching. María ran to get Tam Lin.

The bodyguard watched impassively for a moment, then reached down and pulled the boys apart. "You were told to leave Matt alone, Master Tom," he said.

"He hit me first!" shouted Tom.

"He did," María said, "but Tom teased him."

"You're a liar!" yelled Tom.

"I am not!"

Matt said nothing. He wanted to throw Tom to the ground. He even wanted to kick Tam Lin. He tried to shout insults, but the words wouldn't come out. They stayed inside, getting bigger and bigger until he was sick to his stomach.

"You're right," Tom said suddenly. "I did tease Matt. I'm really sorry about it." Matt was amazed. Tom seemed to change right before his eyes. The angry red faded from Tom's cheeks. His eyes became clear and guileless. It was hard to believe it was the same boy who had been kicking and screaming only a minute ago.

Matt wished desperately that he could get over things that fast. Whenever he was hurt or angry or sad, the feelings stuck their claws into him until they were ready to let go. Sometimes it took hours.

Tam Lin studied Tom's earnest face for a moment and then loosened his grip on the boy's shirt. "Fair enough," he said. He turned Matt free too. Matt immediately took both Tom's and María's hands and dragged them to the door. He felt swollen with all the words he wanted to shout at them.

"You want us to go?" cried María. "After we made up and all?"

Matt nodded.

"Well, I think you're a pig! And I'm not going to be mean to Tom just because you don't like him. Besides, everyone thinks you're awful." María slammed the door behind her.

Matt sat on the floor with tears pouring down his face. He made snuffling noises like a pig and hated himself for doing it, but he couldn't stop. Celia would have comforted him if she'd been there. Tam Lin only shrugged and went back to his sports newspaper. Later, when Matt had recovered, he searched for the bear's ear, but it was gone.

Tom was a master of the near miss. He punched the air near Matt's head, practising – he said – karate exercises. He whispered insults too low for anyone else to hear. "You're a clone," he murmured. "Know what that is? A kind of *puke*. You were puked up by a cow."

Around important people, Tom was courteous. He asked how they were and listened politely to the answers. He brought drinks to his mother and opened doors for his grandfather. He was thoughtful and yet –

There was something a little off about everything Tom did. He brought his mother drinks, but the glass didn't always seem clean. He opened the door for his grandfather, but he let it swing shut on the old man's heel. It wasn't quite enough to make him fall and it *could* have been an accident. Everyone trusted Tom because he had such an open, innocent face, and yet – "He's an unnatural little weevil," growled Tam Lin. Matt was relieved to find that the bodyguard didn't like Tom either.

Tam Lin.

Matt spent the first weeks tiptoeing around him. The man was so large and dangerous looking. It was like having a tame grizzly bear in your house. Tam Lin planted himself in Celia's easy chair and watched silently as María and Celia tried to tempt Matt to read or do a puzzle or eat. Matt enjoyed these activities, but it pleased him to be coaxed. He could make María almost scream with frustration. Celia would only stroke his hair and sigh. The bodyguard seemed to be reading, but his eyes flicked up and back again as he took in the scene before him.

Matt thought he looked irritated, although it was hard to tell. Tam Lin's normal expression wasn't very pleasant.

The doctor visited often because of a cough Matt had developed. At first it didn't seem important, but one night he woke with his throat full of liquid. He couldn't get any air. He stumbled to Celia's room and doubled up on the floor. Celia screamed for Tam Lin.

Bursting through the door, the bodyguard upended Matt and gave him a whack on the back. Matt spat out a mass of thick slime. Tam Lin matter-of-factly ran his finger around the inside of Matt's mouth to clear it out. "Done that with lambs on me da's farm," he said, handing the boy back to Celia.

When Willum came later, Tam Lin watched everything the doctor did. The bodyguard said nothing, but his presence made Willum's hands slick with sweat. Matt didn't know why the doctor was so afraid of Tam Lin, but it pleased him deeply that it was so.

After that, all Matt had to do was cough and Celia or María would fall into a satisfying panic. Sometimes Matt really did have trouble breathing, but sometimes he only wanted to reassure himself that someone cared for him.

"I have to go to school, you eejit," said María. "The holidays are over." Matt stared out the window, punishing her for abandoning him. "I don't live here, you know. Sometime, maybe, they'll let you visit my house – you'd love it. I have a dog and a tortoise and a parakeet. The parakeet talks, but it doesn't mean anything."

Matt shifted his position to make his rejection more obvious. If María didn't notice she was being snubbed, the whole thing was pointless.

"I think you can talk if you want to," she went on. "Everyone says you're too stupid, but I don't believe it. Please, Matt," she wheedled. "Say you'll miss me. Or hug me. I'll understand that. Furball howls when I leave home."

Matt turned his back on her.

"You're so mean! I'd take you to school, but they don't allow clones. Anyhow, the other kids . . . " María's voice trailed off. Matt could guess. The other kids would run away like Steven and Emilia. "I'll be back on weekends. And you'll have a teacher here." She put out her hand tentatively. Matt shoved her away. "Oh, dear," she said with a catch in her voice. *She cried too easily,* Matt thought.

He felt a breeze as the door opened. How could she betray him by going away? She was probably visiting Tom now, asking *him* to go to school with her because she liked him better, the unnatural little weevil.

"You could've been nicer," remarked Tam Lin. Matt continued staring out the window. What business was it of Tam Lin to worry about María? He was Matt's bodyguard, not hers.

"Oh, you can understand me," the man said. "I've been watching you, with your sharp little eyes. You take in everything everyone says. You're like the old man. I don't know much about this clone business – I was twelve the last time I darkened a schoolroom door – but I know you're a copy of him. It's like the old vulture was being given a second chance."

Matt's eyes opened wide at Tam Lin's choice of words. No one *ever* criticised El Patrón.

"I'll tell you this: El Patrón has his good side and his bad side. Very dark indeed is his majesty when he wants to be. When he was young, he made a choice, like a tree does when it decides to grow one way or the other. He grew large and green until he shadowed over the whole forest, but most of his branches are twisted."

Tam Lin settled into Celia's chair; Matt could hear the springs groan with his weight.

"I'm probably talking over your head, laddie. What I mean to say is this: When you're small, you can choose which way to grow. If you're kind and decent, you grow into a kind and decent man. If you're like El Patrón . . . Just think about it." The bodyguard left the room. Matt heard him outside in the walled garden.

Tam Lin had energy to spare, and he didn't nearly use it up guarding Celia's apartment. He kept a rack of weights by the wall. Matt heard him grunt as he lifted them.

Matt didn't understand much of what Tam Lin had said. He'd never thought about growing up. Matt knew – theoretically – it was going to happen, but he couldn't imagine being bigger than he was now. The idea that if you were mean, you might stay mean forever had never occurred to him.

Celia said if you scowled all the time, your face would freeze that way. You'd never be able to smile, and if you looked into a mirror, it would fly into a thousand pieces. She also said if you swallowed watermelon seeds, they'd grow out your ears.

María was gone, along with Emilia. Soon Steven and Tom left for boarding school, and Matt found himself the only child in the Big House. If he was a child, that is. Tom said clones weren't the same as children. They weren't even close.

Matt looked at the mirror in Celia's bathroom. He couldn't see much difference between himself and Tom, but perhaps he was different inside. The doctor once told Rosa that clones went to pieces when they got older. What did that mean? Did they actually fall apart?

Matt hugged himself. His arms and legs might drop off his body. His head would roll around by itself, like in that monster movie he'd been watching before Celia ran in and turned off the TV. The idea filled him with terror.

"Time for school, laddie," called Tam Lin.

Still hugging himself, Matt emerged from the bathroom. A strange woman stood in the living room. She was smiling at him, but the smile didn't look right to Matt. It stopped at the edge of her mouth, as though there were a wall keeping it from getting any farther. "Hi! I'm your new teacher," said the woman. "You can call me Teacher, ha-ha. That makes it easy to remember." The laugh was weird too.

Matt edged into the room. Tam Lin blocked the door leading to the rest of the house.

"Learning is fun!" said Teacher. "I'll bet you're a smart boy. I'll bet you learn all your lessons fast and make your mummy proud of you."

Matt exchanged a startled look with Tam Lin.

"The lad's an orphan," Tam Lin said.

Teacher paused as though she didn't quite understand.

"He doesn't talk," the bodyguard explained. "That's why I have to answer for him. He can read a bit, though."

"Reading is fun!" Teacher said in a hearty voice.

She took out paper, pencils, crayons, and a colouring book

from a canvas bag. Matt spent the morning copying letters and colouring in pictures. Every time he finished a lesson, Teacher cried, "Very good!" and printed a smiley face on his paper. After a while Matt wanted to leave the table, and Teacher firmly sat him back down again.

"No, no, no," she cooed. "You won't get a gold star if you do that."

"He needs a break," growled Tam Lin. "So do I," he said under his breath as he ferried Matt to the kitchen for a glass of milk and cookies. He brought Teacher coffee and watched intently while she drank it. He seemed as puzzled by the woman as Matt was.

The rest of the day was spent counting things – beads, apples, and flowers. Matt was bored because he seemed to be doing the same thing over and over. He already knew how to count, even though he had to do it silently and write down the correct number instead of saying it.

Finally, in the late afternoon, Teacher said that Matt had been very good and he was going to make his mummy very proud.

Tam Lin presented a report of Matt's studies over dinner, when Celia returned. "You're my clever boy," she said fondly, giving Matt an extra slice of apple pie. She gave Tam Lin an entire pie for himself.

"Aye, the lad's that," the bodyguard agreed, his jaws full of food. "But there's something uncommonly strange about the teacher. She says the same thing over and over."

"That's how you teach little kids," said Celia.

"Perhaps," said Tam Lin. "I'm not what you'd call an expert on education."

The next day went exactly like the first. If Matt thought he'd been bored before, it was nothing compared to writing the same letters, colouring the same pictures, and counting the same wretched beads and flowers all over again. But he worked hard to make Celia proud of him. Days three, four, and five passed in exactly the same way.

Tam Lin went outside and juggled weights. He dug a vegetable bed for Celia in the walled garden. Matt wished he could escape that easily.

"Who can tell me how many apples I have here?" warbled Teacher on day six. "I'll bet it's my *good boy!*"

Matt suddenly snapped. "I'm not a good boy!" he screamed. "I'm a *bad clone!* And I hate counting and I hate you!" He grabbed Teacher's carefully arranged apples and hurled them every which way. He threw the crayons on the floor, and when she tried to pick them up, he shoved her as hard as he could. Then he sat on the floor and burst into tears.

"Someone isn't going to get a smiley face on his paper," Teacher said with a gasp, leaning against a wall. She started to whimper like a frightened animal.

Tam Lin thundered through the door and gathered Teacher up in a bear hug. "Don't cry," he said into her hair. "You've done very well. You've fixed something the rest of us hadn't a clue how to mend." Gradually, Teacher's breathing slowed and the whimpering stopped.

Matt was so startled, he stopped crying. He realised something momentous had just happened.

"I can talk," he murmured.

"You get two gold stars by your name today, lassie," Tam Lin said into Teacher's hair. "You poor, sad creature. I didn't know what I was looking at until now." He gently urged the woman out of the apartment, and Matt heard him talking to her all the way down the hall.

"My name is Matteo Alacrán," Matt said, testing his newly regained voice. "I'm a *good* boy." He felt dizzy with happiness. Celia was going to be so proud of him now! He would read and colour and count until he became the best student in the whole world, and then the children would like him and they wouldn't run away.

Tam Lin interrupted Matt's ecstatic thoughts. "I hope that wasn't a one-shot deal," he said. "I mean, you really can talk?"

"I can, I can, I can!" Matt sang.

"Wonderful. I was going bonkers with counting beads. The poor thing – it was all she knew how to do."

"She was an eejit," announced Matt, using María's worst insult.

"You don't even know what the word means," Tam Lin said. "Tell you what, laddie. We've got something to celebrate. Let's go on a picnic."

"A picnic?" echoed Matt, trying to remember the meaning of the word.

"I'll explain it to you on the way," said Tam Lin.

8

THE EEJIT IN THE DRY FIELD

Matt was wildly excited. Not only were they going on a picnic, but they would travel by horseback. Matt had seen horses from the windows of the little house. And of course he'd seen them on TV. Cowboys and big, tough *bandidos* rode them. His favourite hero was El Látigo Negro, the Black Whip. El Látigo Negro was on TV every Saturday. He wore a black mask and rescued poor people from evil capitalists. His favourite weapon was a long whip with which he could peel an apple while it was still on the tree.

Matt was more than a little disappointed when Tam Lin brought out a sleepy grey horse instead of the spirited steed El Látigo Negro rode. "Be reasonable, lad," said the bodyguard, tightening the girths on the saddle. "We're after reliability, not speed. El Patrón wouldn't take it at all well if you were dumped on your head."

Once Matt was perched on the saddle in front of Tam

Lin, he forgot all about his disappointment. He was riding! He was high in the air, swaying along with the smell of horse all around him. He felt the coarse hair of the mane and pressed his ankles against the warm coat of the animal.

After all those months without talking, Matt couldn't wait to catch up. He chattered about everything he saw — the blue sky, the birds, the flies buzzing around the horse's ears.

Tam Lin didn't stop him. He grunted occasionally to show he was listening and directed the horse along a dirt path. They plodded through the poppy fields and gradually moved away from the Big House toward the grey-brown hills that lay on the horizon.

The first fields they encountered were covered with a mist of new leaves. These were the seedlings. Matt had watched the growing cycle from the window of the little house, and he knew what to expect. The older plants were larger and rounder — like small cabbages — and the leaves were tinged with blue. As they rode, the plants became larger until they were as high as the belly of the horse. Buds opened into crinkled petals in a glory of white under the hot sun. A faint perfume hung in the air.

They came to fields where the petals had fallen. These lay in drifts all over the ground while the seedpods they left behind stuck up like green thumbs. The pods had swelled until they were the size of hen's eggs and ready for harvest.

Matt saw the first Farm labourers. He'd observed them before, but Celia had warned him to hide from strangers, so he hadn't watched them closely. Now he saw that both men and women wore tan uniforms and wide, straw hats. They walked slowly, bending down with tiny knives to slash the pods. "Why are they doing that?" Matt asked.

"To release the opium," replied Tam Lin. "The sap oozes out and hardens overnight. In the morning the workers scrape it off. They can collect from the same plant four or five times."

On and on the horse plodded. The fields shimmered with heat, and a sweet odour with something rotten at its core filled the air. The workers bent and slashed, bent and slashed in a hypnotic rhythm. They didn't speak. They didn't even wipe the sweat off their faces.

"Don't they get tired?" Matt asked.

"Oh, aye. They do," said Tam Lin.

At last the horse came to a deserted field. The plants were beginning to dry. A hot breeze rattled the leaves. "Look! There's a man lying on the ground," cried Matt.

Tam Lin halted the horse and got down. "Stay," he ordered the animal. Matt clung tightly to the mane. He didn't feel at all safe so far off the ground. Tam Lin strode over to the man, bent down, and felt his neck. He shook his head and returned.

"Can't we – can't we help him?" faltered Matt.

"It's too late for that poor soul," grunted the bodyguard.

"What about the doctor?"

"I told you it's too late! You want to get your ears cleaned!" Tam Lin hoisted himself back into the saddle and ordered the horse to go on. Matt looked back, tears stinging his eyes. The man was quickly hidden by the poppy plants.

Why was it too late? Matt wondered. The man must be terribly hot, lying as he was in the full sun. Why couldn't they stop and give him water? Matt knew they had water. He could hear it sloshing in Tam Lin's backpack.

"We could go back – " Matt began again.

"Damn it!" roared the bodyguard. He halted the horse and sat for a moment, breathing hard. Matt looked at the ground and wondered whether he had the nerve to jump off if Tam Lin really lost his temper.

"I forget. Kids your age don't know anything," said Tam Lin at last. "The man is dead. Heat or lack of water killed him. The cleanup crews at the end of the day will find him."

The horse moved on. Matt had even more questions now, but he was too unsure of Tam Lin's temper to ask them. Why hadn't the man gone home when he got sick? Why hadn't the other workers helped him? *Why was he being left out there like a piece of rubbish?*

All the while, they were riding along a range of hills that bordered the fields. Now they turned off into a dry streambed that led into the hills. Tam Lin got down and led the horse under a cliff, where it would have shade. Nearby was a trough and a pump, which he worked vigorously to bring up the water. The horse was sweating. Its eyes watched the trough, but it didn't move.

"Drink," said Tam Lin. The horse trotted forward and dipped its muzzle. It blew noisy bubbles as it drank ravenously. "We'll walk the rest of the way."

"Can't we take the horse?" said Matt, looking doubtfully at the streambed snaking into the hills.

"It wouldn't obey. It's programmed to stay on the Farm."

"I don't understand."

"It's a Safe Horse, which means it has an implant in its head. It won't bolt or jump. It won't even drink unless you tell it to."

Matt digested that idea for a moment. "Not even if it's very thirsty?" he said at last.

"It was thirsty just now," said Tam Lin. "If I hadn't told it to drink, it would have stood in front of the trough until it died. Stay," he told the horse.

Shouldering a backpack, he started up the dry stream. Matt

scrambled after him. At first the way wasn't difficult, but soon it was blocked by boulders they had to climb. Matt wasn't used to exercise, and he quickly found himself out of breath. He didn't stop, though, because he was afraid Tam Lin would leave him behind. Finally, the bodyguard heard him gasping and turned back. He hunted through the backpack. "Here. Drink some water. Have a bite of beef jerky too. The salt'll do you good."

Matt devoured the beef jerky. It tasted wonderful.

"Not much farther, laddie. You're doing very well for a hot-house plant."

They came to a giant boulder that seemed to block the trail until Matt saw a round hole in the middle. It was worn smooth like the hole in a doughnut. Tam Lin climbed through and reached back to help Matt.

The scene on the other side was completely unexpected. Creosote bushes and paloverde trees framed a small, narrow valley, and in the centre of this was a pool of water. At the far end Matt saw an enormous grapevine sprawled over a man-made trellis. In the water itself, Matt saw shoals of little brown fish that darted away from his shadow.

"This is what you call an oasis," said Tam Lin, throwing down his pack and taking out food for the picnic. "Not bad, eh?"

"Not bad!" agreed Matt, accepting a sandwich.

"I found this place years ago when I first started working for El Patrón. The Alacráns don't know about it. If they did, they'd run a pipe in here and take out all the water. I hope I can count on you to keep the secret."

Matt nodded, his mouth full of sandwich.

"Don't tell María either. She can't help blabbing."

"Okay," said Matt, proud that Tam Lin considered him responsible enough to keep a secret.

"I brought you here for two reasons," said the bodyguard. "One, because it's nice. And two, because I want to tell you a few things without being spied on."

Matt looked up, surprised.

"You never know who's listening to you in that house. You're too young to understand much, and I wouldn't say anything if you were a real boy." Tam Lin tossed bread crumbs into the pool. The little fish rose to the surface to feed. "But you're a clone," he went on. "You haven't got anyone to explain things to you. You're alone in a way real humans can't understand. Even orphans can look at pictures and say, 'That's me ma and that's me da.'"

"Am I a machine?" Matt blurted out.

"Machine? Oh, no."

"Then how was I made?"

Tam Lin laughed. "If you were a real boy, I'd tell you to ask your big brother that tricky little question. Well, lad, the best way to describe it is this: A long, long time ago some doctors took a piece of skin from El Patrón. They froze it so it would keep. Then, about eight years ago, they took a bit of that skin and grew it into a whole new El Patrón. Only they had to start at the beginning with a baby. That was you."

"That was me?" asked Matt.

"It was."

"So I'm just a *piece of skin?*"

"Now I've gone and upset you," said Tam Lin. "The skin was what you might call a photograph. All the information was there to grow a real copy – skin, hair, bones, and brain – of a real man. You're exactly like El Patrón when he was seven years old."

Matt looked down at his toes. That's all he was: a photograph.

"They put that piece of skin into a special kind of cow. You grew inside, and when the time came, you were born. Only, of course, you didn't have a father or a mother."

"Tom said I was puked up by a cow," said Matt.

"Tom is a filthy little pustule," said Tam Lin. "And so is the rest of that family. If you quote me, I'll deny it." He brought out a bag of trail mix and passed it to Matt. "To continue: Being a clone, you're different and a lot of people are afraid of you."

"They hate me," Matt said simply.

"Aye. Some do." Tam Lin stood up and stretched his big muscles. He paced back and forth on the sand where they were having their picnic. He hated to sit still for long. "But some love you. I'm speaking of María and, of course, Celia."

"And El Patrón."

"Ah, well. El Patrón's a special case. To be honest, the number of people who love you is small and the number who hate you is large. They can't get around the fact that you're a clone. It makes it hard to send you to school."

"I know." Matt thought bitterly of María. If she really loved him, she'd take him with her and not care about how the other kids felt.

"El Patrón insists that you be educated and live, as nearly as possible, a normal life. The problem is, no private teacher wants to teach a clone. And so the Alacráns got an eejit."

Matt was startled. He'd heard the word so often – mostly from María – he'd thought it was only a swear word, like *dumdum* or *cootie face*.

"An eejit is a person or animal with an implant in its head," said Tam Lin.

"Like the horse?" said Matt as a terrible thought occurred to him.

"Correct. Eejits can do only simple things. They pick fruit

or sweep floors or, as you've seen, harvest opium."

"The Farm workers are eejits!" cried Matt.

"That's why they work without resting until the foreman orders them to stop and why they don't drink water unless someone tells them to."

Matt's thoughts were whirling. If the horse could stand there and *die* in front of a trough of water, then the man —

"The man," he said aloud.

"You're bright as a button, lad," said Tam Lin. "The man we saw on the ground probably lagged behind the other workers and didn't hear the foreman tell them to stop. He might have worked all night, getting thirstier and thirstier — "

"Stop!" shrilled Matt. He covered his ears. This was horrible! He didn't want to know any more.

Tam Lin was at his side at once. "That's enough lessons for one day. We're on a picnic and we haven't had any fun yet. Come on. I'll show you a beehive and a coyote den. Everything lives around water in the desert."

They spent the rest of the day exploring the burrows, the crevices, the hidden lairs of the secret valley. Tam Lin might not have gone to school for too long, but he knew a great deal about nature. He taught Matt to sit still and wait for things to come to him. He told him how to tell the mood of a beehive by its hum. He pointed out droppings and tracks and bone fragments.

Finally, as shadows began to fill up the oasis, Tam Lin helped Matt climb through the hole in the rock and return to the horse. It was waiting exactly where they'd left it. Tam Lin ordered it to take another drink before they set off.

The fields were empty, and the long shadows of hills flowed across the land. Where they ended, the late-afternoon sun made the poppies glow with a golden light. They passed the dry field where the man's body had lain, but it was gone.

"Teacher was an eejit," said Matt, breaking the silence.

"She was one of the brighter ones," said Tam Lin. "Even so, she could do only one lesson over and over."

"Will she come back?"

"No." The bodyguard sighed. "They'll put her to work mending curtains or peeling potatoes. Let's talk about something more cheerful."

"Could *you* teach me?" asked Matt.

Tam Lin let out a bellow of genuine laughter. "I could if you wanted to learn how to break desks with karate chops. I reckon you'll do your schooling off the TV. I'll be around to hang you out the window by your ankles if you don't study."

9

THE SECRET PASSAGE

On the surface Matt's life settled into a pleasant rhythm. He studied via distance learning over the TV, Tam Lin sent off the homework, it came back with excellent grades, and Celia praised Matt lavishly. María praised him too when she visited. It didn't hurt either that Tom had lousy grades and managed to stay in boarding school only because Mr Alacrán sent the headmaster a large donation.

But underneath Matt felt a hollowness. He understood he was only a photograph of a human, and that meant he wasn't really important. Photographs could lie forgotten in drawers for years. They could be thrown away.

At least once a week Matt dreamed of the dead man in the field. The man's eyes were open and staring up at the sun. He was terribly, horribly thirsty. Matt could see how dusty his mouth was, but there was no water anywhere, only the dry, rattling poppies. It got so bad that Matt demanded a jug of water by his bed. If only he could take that jug into his dreams. If only he could *dream* it there and pour water into the man's dusty lips, but he couldn't. And when he woke up, he drank glass after glass to get rid of the dry, dead feel of the poppy fields. Then, of course, he had to go to the toilet.

On such occasions Matt would tiptoe past Celia's bedroom. He could hear her snores and, across the hall, Tam Lin's thunderous reply. This should have made him feel safe. But Matt never knew, just before he opened the bathroom door, whether the dead man might be lying on the other side, staring up at the big light in the middle of the ceiling.

María started bringing Furball on her visits. He was a shrill, rat-sized dog that forgot his house training when he got excited. Tam Lin often threatened to suck him – and the mess he deposited – up the vacuum cleaner. "He'd fit," he growled over María's horrified protests. "Trust me, he'd fit."

What Matt hated about the creature was everyone's assumption that he and Furball were the same. It didn't matter that Matt had excellent grades and good manners. They were both animals and thus unimportant.

During Easter vacation Tom said good manners were no harder to learn than rolling over or playing dead. Matt threw himself at him, and María ran shrieking for Tam Lin. Tom was sent to his room without dinner. Matt wasn't punished at all.

Which was okay with Matt, except that Furball wasn't punished for his crimes either. He couldn't understand the difference between right and wrong. He was a dumb beast and so, apparently, was Matt.

When María wasn't visiting, Matt amused himself by exploring the house. He pretended he was El Látigo Negro scouting out an enemy fortress. He had a black cape and a long, thin leather belt for a whip. He skulked behind curtains and furniture, and he hid if he saw one of the Alacráns in the distance.

Felicia – Benito's, Steven's, and Tom's mother – played the piano in the afternoons. Her crashing chords echoed from the music room. She attacked the piano with a fervour completely different from her usual, sluggish self, and Matt liked to hide behind the potted plants to listen.

Her fingers flew from one end of the keyboard to the other. Her eyes were closed and her mouth was pulled back in a grimace that wasn't pain, but something close to it. The music was wonderful, though.

After a while Felicia would run out of energy. Trembling and pale, she would hunch over the keys, and this was the signal for a servant to bring her a brown liquid in a beautiful, cut-glass bottle. The servant would mix a drink – Matt loved the clink of ice – and place it in Felicia's hand.

She would drink until the trembling stopped. Then she would wilt over the piano like one of Celia's spinaches when Tam Lin forgot to water the garden. Maids had to carry her away to her apartment.

One day Felicia didn't come at her usual time, and Matt hovered behind the potted plants as he worked up his courage to approach the piano. If she caught him, he knew he'd be banished from the room forever. His fingers tingled with the desire to play. It looked so easy. He could even hear the music in his head.

Matt crept out of his hiding place. He reached out to touch the keys – and heard Felicia's listless voice in the hallway. She was telling a servant to bring her a drink. Matt panicked. He darted into a closet behind the piano and shut the door an instant before Felicia came into the room. She immediately started playing. Matt sneezed from all the dust in the closet, but Felicia was making too much noise to hear him. Matt felt around until he found a light switch.

It was a disappointing place. Sheet music was stacked against the walls. A heap of folding chairs filled up one corner. And it was so covered with dust and spiderwebs that Matt sneezed again. He rolled up a sheet of music and began sweeping off the inner wall, more for something to do than from any real curiosity.

On the inner wall, under a knot of webs that would have made Dracula happy, Matt found another light switch. He flipped it on.

He recoiled against a heap of music when part of the wall slid open and threw up a cloud of dust that made him choke. He reached for the asthma inhaler Celia insisted he carry at all times. When the dust had settled, Matt saw a narrow, dark hallway.

He peered around the corner. An empty passage stretched both to the left and to the right. By now Felicia had stopped playing the piano. Matt held very still, listening for the clink of ice in glass. After a while he heard the maids carry Felicia away.

Matt flipped the switch once more and saw, to his great relief, that the wall closed up again. He slipped out of the closet, leaving dusty footprints across the carpet, and was scolded by Celia when she saw the state of his clothes and hair.

This was even better than an episode of El Látigo Negro, Matt thought, hugging the secret to himself. This was a place that belonged to him alone. Not even Tam Lin could find him if he wanted to hide.

Slowly and carefully over the next few weeks, Matt explored his new domain. It seemed to snake between the inner and outer walls of the house. He found peepholes in the wall but saw only empty rooms with chairs and tables beyond. Once he saw a servant dusting furniture.

A few of the peepholes looked into dark closets like the one in the music room. Matt didn't understand until one day, while feeling his way along the passage, his hand struck against another switch.

He flicked it on.

A panel slid open just like the one in the music room. Matt's heart beat wildly. He could walk right into the closet! It was full of musty clothes and old shoes, but if he pushed them aside, he could get to the door on the other side. He heard voices. The doctor and Mr Alacrán were pleading with a third person whose replies were muffled. The doctor spoke harshly, bringing bad memories back to Matt. "Do it!" Willum snarled. "You know you have to do it!"

"Please, Father," said Mr Alacrán, gentler than Matt had ever heard him be.

"No, no, no," moaned Mr Alacrán's father.

"You'll die without chemotherapy," his son begged.

"God wants me to come."

"But I want you here," Mr Alacrán pleaded.

"This is a place of shadows and evil!" The old man was clearly becoming irrational.

"At least get a new liver," Willum said in his harsh voice.

"Leave me alone," wailed the old man.

Matt retreated to the passageway and closed the opening. He didn't understand what the men were arguing about, but he knew what would happen if someone caught him listening. He'd be locked up. He might even be given back to Rosa.

Matt made his way to the music room, and for a long time

he didn't venture into the secret passage. He did, however, keep listening to Felicia's music. It was something that had gotten inside him, and no matter how dangerous it was, he couldn't go long without hearing it.

One afternoon Matt was alarmed to see the doctor arrive with Felicia's drink instead of a servant. "Oh, Willum," she moaned as he mixed in the ice. "He doesn't talk to me anymore. He looks right through me as though I weren't there."

"It's all right," soothed the doctor. "*I'm* here. I'll take care of you." He opened his black bag and took out a syringe. Matt held his breath. The doctor had given him a shot when he was sick and he'd hated it! Matt watched, fascinated, as Felicia's arm was swabbed and the needle jammed in. Why didn't she cry out? Couldn't she feel it?

Willum sat next to her and draped his arm around her shoulders. He murmured things Matt couldn't hear. It must have pleased Felicia, because she smiled and rested her head against the doctor's chest. After a while he guided her from the music room.

At once Matt was out of his hiding place. He sniffed the glass and sampled the contents. Ugh! It tasted like rotten fruit. He spat it out at once. He listened carefully for footsteps outside in the hall and sat down at the piano. He carefully pressed a key.

The note rang softly in the music room. Matt was entranced. He tried other keys. They were all beautiful. He was so enchanted, he almost didn't hear the servant coming down the hall, but fortunately, he woke up soon enough to scuttle behind the potted plants.

After that day Matt studied the comings and goings of the servants, to work out when it was safe to visit the music room. Felicia never used it in the morning. In fact, she didn't get up until the afternoon and was active for only an hour or so then.

Matt discovered he could re-create the songs Celia sang to him, using one finger. Felicia used all ten, but he hadn't figured out how to do that yet. Even so, the ability to create music filled him with a joy too large to contain. He forgot where he was. He forgot he was a clone. The music made up for everything – the silent contempt of the servants, Steven's and Emilia's snubs, Tom's hatred.

"So this is where you get to," said Tam Lin. Matt swung around, almost tumbling off the bench. "Don't stop. You've got a real talent there. Funny, I never thought of El Patrón as being musical."

Matt's heart was beating wildly. Was he going to be barred from the room?

"If you're musical, *he* must be," said the bodyguard. "But I guess he never had time to study. Where he lived, they chopped up pianos for firewood."

"Can you play?" asked Matt.

"You must be joking. Look at these."

Matt saw stubby fingers sprouting from large, awkward hands. Some of the fingers were crooked, as though they'd been broken and healed again. "You could use one finger," he suggested.

Tam Lin laughed. "Music has to be in the head first, laddie. The good Lord passed me by when He was handing out talent. You've got it, though, and it'd be a shame not to use it. I'll talk to El Patrón about finding you a teacher."

This proved difficult. No human wanted to teach a clone and no eejit was smart enough. Finally, Tam Lin found a man who had gone deaf and was desperate for work. It seemed odd to Matt that someone who couldn't hear could teach music, but so it was. Mr Ortega felt it through his hands. He placed them on the piano as Matt practiced and caught every mistake.

It wasn't long before Matt added musical ability to his growing list of accomplishments. He could read ten years beyond his level, do maths that left Tam Lin bewildered – and irritated – and speak both English and Spanish fluently. In addition, his art grew better by the day. He threw himself into studying everything that came before him. Matt could name the planets, the brightest stars, and all the constellations. He memorised the names of countries, their capitals and chief exports.

He was in a rage to learn. He would excel, and then everyone would love him and forget he was a clone.

10

A Cat with Nine Lives

Y ou're like a wild animal," complained María as she stood in the doorway of Matt's room. "You hide in here like a bear in a cave."

Matt looked indifferently at the curtained windows. He liked the safe, comfortable darkness. "I *am* an animal," he replied. Once those words would have pained him, but he accepted his status now.

"I think you just like to wallow," said María, striding in to open the curtains and windows. Outside lay Celia's garden filled with stands of corn, tomatoes, beans, peas. "Anyhow, it's El Patrón's birthday, and that means you'd better take that snarl off your face."

Matt sighed. He could unnerve almost everyone by growling at them, but not María. She only laughed. Of course, he never dreamed of growling at El Patrón on those rare occasions when the old man visited. To do so would have been unthinkable. Each time, El Patrón looked more frail and his mind seemed less in order.

It broke Matt's heart to look at him. He loved El Patrón. He owed everything to him.

Matt could hardly remember those terrible days three years before, when he was kept in a pen with cockroaches for friends and old chicken bones for toys. But he knew he'd still be there – or buried under the floor by Rosa – if the old man hadn't rescued him.

"El Patrón's 143 today," said Matt.

María shivered. "I can't imagine being that old!"

"Celia said if they put that many candles on the cake, it would melt the paint off the walls."

"He was kind of strange last time he was here," said María.

That's one way to put it, thought Matt. El Patrón had become so forgetful, he repeated the same sentence over and over again. "Am I dead yet?" he asked. "Am I dead yet?" And he held his hand before his face, studying each finger as though to reassure himself that he was still there.

"Are you ready?" cried Celia, rushing into the room. She made Matt turn and adjusted the collar of his shirt. "Remember, you're sitting next to El Patrón tonight. Pay attention and answer all his questions."

"What if he's . . . weird?" said Matt. He remembered answering the question "Am I dead yet?" over and over the last time the old man visited.

Celia stopped fussing with the shirt and knelt before him. "Listen to me, darling. If anything bad happens tonight, I want you to come straight to me. Come to the pantry behind the kitchen."

"What do you mean, bad?"

"I can't say." Celia looked furtively around the room. "Just promise me you'll remember."

Matt thought it was hard to promise something like that – nobody planned to forget – but he nodded.

"Oh, *mi hijo,* I do love you!" Celia flung her arms around him and burst into tears. Matt was both startled and dismayed. What could have upset her so much? He saw María out of the corner of his eye. She was making a face that indicated how totally soppy she found this display. That was María's favourite word recently: *soppy.* She'd picked it up from Tam Lin.

"I promise," Matt said.

Celia sat back abruptly and wiped her eyes with her apron. "I'm a fool. What good would it do if you understood? It would only make things worse." She seemed to be talking to herself, and Matt watched her anxiously. Then she stood up and smoothed the wrinkles in her apron. "Run along, *chicos,* and have fun at the party. I'll be in the kitchen serving up the best dinner you ever saw. You look wonderful, both of you, like you stepped out of a movie." The old, confident Celia was back, and Matt was relieved.

"I have to get Furball from my room," said María after they left.

"Oh, no! You can't take him to dinner."

"I can if I want. I'll hide him on my lap."

Matt sighed. There was no point arguing with her. María took Furball everywhere. Tam Lin complained that it wasn't a dog, but a hairy tumour growing out of her arm. He offered to take her to a doctor and have it removed.

Tom was in María's room, and Furball was nowhere to be seen.

"You didn't let him out?" cried María as she looked under the bed.

"I never even saw him," said Tom, glaring at Matt. Matt glared back. Tom's bristly red hair was slicked down, and his fingernails were neat, white crescents. Tom was always perfectly groomed for these occasions, and it earned him many admiring comments from the women who came to El Patrón's birthday parties.

"He's lost!" wailed María. "He gets so scared when he's lost. Oh, please help me find him!"

Reluctantly, Tom and Matt left off their glaring contest and began looking under pillows, behind curtains, in dresser drawers. María whimpered softly as the hunt dragged on without any results.

"He's probably running around the house having a great time," said Matt.

"He hates being outside," said María, weeping. Matt could believe that. The dog was such a loser that he ran from sparrows, but he probably *was* outside hiding in any of a thousand places. They'd never find him before dinner. Then something odd struck him.

Tom.

Tom was searching, but he didn't seem to be really *looking*. It was hard to describe. Tom was going through the motions, but all the while his eyes were watching María. Matt stopped what he was doing and listened.

"I hear something!" he cried. He dashed into the bathroom, lifted the toilet lid, and there was Furball, so waterlogged and exhausted, he'd been able to utter only the faintest whine. Matt pulled the dog out and dropped him hastily on the floor. He grabbed a towel and wrapped up Furball. The dog was so tired, he didn't even try to bite. He lay perfectly limp as María snatched him up.

"How did he get in there? Who put the top down? Oh, darling, sweet, sweet Furball" – she cuddled the revolting creature next to her face – "you're okay now. You're my *good* dog. You're my honeybunch."

"He's always drinking out of the toilet," Tom said. "He must have fallen in and pulled the lid down on top of him. I'll call a maid to give him a bath."

He went out but not before Matt saw a flash of real anger on his face. Tom had wanted something and hadn't got it. Matt was sure Tom had dumped Furball in the toilet, although he'd never shown dislike for the dog before. That was like Tom, though. He could be courteous and helpful on the surface, but you never knew what was going on underneath.

Matt felt cold. Furball would have drowned if he hadn't found him. How could anybody be that cruel? And why would anyone want to hurt María, who was so tenderhearted, she rescued black widow spiders? Matt knew no one would believe him if he accused Tom. He was only a clone and his opinion didn't matter.

Or it didn't matter most of the time, Matt thought as a delightful plan occurred to him.

Most of the time the servants ignored Matt and the Alacráns looked past him as though he were a bug on a window. Mr Ortega, the music teacher, rarely said anything to him except, "No! No! No!" when Matt struck a wrong note. Mr Ortega didn't say "No! No! No!" very often now. Matt was an excellent piano player and thought it wouldn't have hurt the man to say "Good!" now and then. But he never did. When Matt played well, an expression of joy crossed Mr Ortega's face that was as good as a compliment, though. And when Matt played really,

really well, he was too enraptured to care what the music teacher thought.

Everything changed during the annual birthday party. It was really El Patrón's party, but it had developed into a celebration for Matt as well. At least Celia, Tam Lin, María, and El Patrón celebrated for him. Everyone else just gritted their teeth and got through the day.

It was the one time when Matt could ask for anything he wanted. He could force the Alacráns to pay attention to him. He could make Steven and Tom – yes, Tom! – be polite to him in front of their friends. No one dared to make El Patrón angry, and therefore no one dared to ignore Matt.

Tables were set for the party in one of the vast gardens surrounding the Big House. The lawn was flawlessly smooth, with the grass all of the same height. It was cared for by eejits who trimmed the ground with scissors just before the event. It would be trampled into oblivion by tomorrow, but now it glowed like a green jewel in the soft afternoon light.

The tables were covered with spotless, white cloths. The dishes were trimmed with gold, the silver cutlery was freshly polished, and a crystal goblet sat by each plate.

In a corner, under a bougainvillea arbour, sat an enormous stack of presents. Everyone brought gifts to El Patrón, although there was nothing he didn't already own and not much he could enjoy at the age of 143. There were even a few presents for Matt – small, loving tributes from Celia and María, something useful from Tam Lin, and a large, expensive gift from El Patrón.

The guests wandered around, choosing delicacies brought to them on trays by the maids. Waiters offered drinks of every description and brought water pipes for those who wished to smoke. There were senators and famous actors, generals and world-renowned doctors, a few ex-presidents, and half a dozen dictators from places Matt had heard about on TV. There was even a faded-looking princess. And of course there were the other Farmers. The Farmers were the real aristocrats here. They ruled the drug empire that formed the border between the United States and Aztlán.

The Farmers stood in a knot around a man Matt hadn't seen before. He had bristly red hair, a soft, doughy face, and deep circles under his eyes. He looked unwell, but in spite of that, he was in a good mood. He harangued the others in a braying voice and punctuated his statements by poking them in the chest with a finger. By that alone Matt knew he must be a Farmer. No one else would dare to be so rude.

"That's Mr MacGregor," said María. She had come up behind Matt with a fluff-dried Furball draped over her arm.

"Who?" For an instant Matt was back in the little house in the poppy fields. He was six years old, and he was reading a tattered book about Pedro el Conejo, who got trapped in Señor MacGregor's garden. Señor MacGregor had wanted to put Pedro into a pie.

"He has a Farm near San Diego," said María. "Personally, I think he's creepy."

Matt studied the man more closely. He didn't look like Señor MacGregor in the book, but there was definitely something unpleasant about him.

"They're signalling everyone to go into the salon," said María. She hitched Furball into a more comfortable position. "You'd better not howl," she told the dog, "no matter how awful the company is."

"Thanks a lot," said Matt.

The salon stood at the top of marble steps leading up from the garden. The party guests drifted toward it, dutifully obeying the summons to greet El Patrón. Matt braced himself for a shock. Each time he saw El Patrón, the old man had deteriorated more.

The guests arranged themselves in a semicircle. All around the edge of the salon were giant vases of flowers and the marble statues so dear to El Patrón's heart. The conversation died down. The sounds of birds and fountains became clearer. A peacock shrieked from a nearby garden. Matt waited tensely for the hum of El Patrón's motorised wheelchair.

Then, amazingly, the curtains at the far end of the salon parted and El Patrón walked in. He moved slowly, to be sure, but he was actually *walking*. Matt was delighted. Behind the old man came Daft Donald and Tam Lin, both pushing wheelchairs.

A gasp echoed around the salon. Someone – the princess, Matt thought – cried, "Hip hip hooray!" Then everyone cheered and Matt cheered too, filled with relief and joy.

Someone behind Matt muttered, "The old vampire. So he managed to crawl out of the coffin again." Matt turned quickly to see who it was, but he couldn't tell which of the party-goers was guilty.

When El Patrón reached the middle of the salon, he signalled for Tam Lin to bring up his wheelchair. He sank down, and Tam Lin stuffed pillows around him. Much to Matt's surprise, Mr MacGregor came forward and sat in the other wheelchair.

So they are friends, Matt thought. Why hadn't he seen Mr MacGregor before?

"Welcome," said El Patrón. His voice wasn't loud, but it commanded instant attention. "Welcome to my 143rd birthday party. All of you are my friends and allies – or family members." The old man laughed softly. "I imagine *they* hoped to see me in my grave by now, but no such luck. I've had the benefit of a marvellous new treatment from the finest doctors in the world, and now my good friend MacGregor is going to be treated by these same people."

Mr MacGregor grinned and held up El Patrón's arm as a referee would hold up a victorious boxer's arm. What *was* there about the man that was so repulsive? Matt felt his stomach knot, and yet he had no reason to dislike him.

"Come forth, you miracle workers," said El Patrón. Two men and two women separated themselves from the crowd. They approached the wheelchairs and bowed. "I'm sure you'd be satisfied with only my heartfelt thanks" – El Patrón chuckled as the doctors tried to hide their disappointment – "but you'll be even more satisfied with these one-million-dollar cheques." The doctors immediately cheered up, although one of the women had the grace to blush. Everyone applauded, and the doctors thanked El Patrón.

Tam Lin caught Matt's eye and nodded to him. Matt stepped forward.

"Mi Vida," said El Patrón with real warmth. He beckoned with his gnarled hand. "Come closer and let me look at you. Was I ever that handsome? I must have been." The old man sighed and fell silent. Tam Lin indicated that Matt was to stand next to the wheelchairs.

"I was a poor boy from a poor village," El Patrón began, addressing the assembled presidents, dictators, generals, and other famous people. "One year during Cinco de Mayo, the ranchero who owned our land had a parade. I and my five brothers went to watch. Mamá brought my little sisters. She carried one, and the other held on to her skirt and followed behind."

Matt saw the dusty cornfields and purple mountains of Durango. He saw the streams that roared with water two months of the year and were dry as a bone the rest of the time. He had heard the story from El Patrón so often, he knew it by heart.

"During the parade the mayor rode on a fine white horse and threw money into the crowd. How we scrambled for the coins! How we rolled in the dirt like pigs! But we needed the money. We were so poor, we didn't have two pesos to rub together. Afterwards the ranchero gave a great feast. We could eat all we wanted, and it was a wonderful opportunity for people who had stomachs so shrunken that chilli beans had to wait in line to get inside.

"My little sisters caught typhoid at that feast. They died in the same hour. They were so small, they couldn't look over the windowsill – no, not even if they stood on tiptoe."

The salon was deathly still. In the distance Matt heard a dove calling from the garden. *No hope,* it said. *No hope. No hope.*

"During the following years each of my five brothers died; two drowned, one had a burst appendix, and we had no money for the doctor. The last two brothers were beaten to death by the police. There were eight of us," said El Patrón, "and only I lived to grow up."

Matt thought the audience looked bored, although they tried to conceal it. They had heard the same speech for years.

"I outlived them all as I outlived all my enemies. Of course, I can always make more enemies." El Patrón looked around the audience, and several people tried to smile. They met El Patrón's steely eyes and immediately sobered up. "You could say I'm a cat with nine lives. As long as there's mice to catch, I intend to keep hunting. And thanks to the doctors, I can still enjoy it. You can start clapping now." He glared at the audience, and they began – first hesitantly and then loudly – to applaud. "They're just like robots," El Patrón muttered under his breath. More loudly he said, "I'm going to take a brief rest, and then we shall all have dinner."

11

THE GIVING AND TAKING OF GIFTS

Matt wandered around the garden, admiring the ice sculptures and a fountain of wine with orange slices bobbing in a red pool. He dipped his finger in to taste. It wasn't as good as it looked.

He checked the place cards on the tables and saw that he was, as usual, seated next to El Patrón. Mr MacGregor was on El Patrón's other side. The other favoured guests were Mr Alacrán and Felicia, Benito, back from college – or rather, *expelled* from college – and Steven and Tom. Mr Alacrán's father rounded out the guests at the head table. Everyone called him El Viejo these days because he seemed even older than El Patrón.

Humming to himself, Matt removed Tom's card and put it at the baby table. A nanny sat at each end to keep order, and high chairs were lined up on either side. Matt located María's card and placed it next to his.

Next Matt explored the edge of the garden, where the

bodyguards formed a sullen, dark perimeter. Each of the presidents, dictators, and generals had brought his own protectors, and of course the Alacráns had hired a small army for the party. Matt counted more than two hundred men.

Who were they guarding against? he wondered. Who was likely to come charging across the poppy fields? But Matt was used to bodyguards at all family affairs, and it seemed natural for them to be there.

The sun was setting, and the garden was full of a cool, green light. The Ajo Mountains still glowed purple-brown in the distance, and the poppy fields were tipped with a gold that faded even as Matt watched. Lamps went on in the trees.

"You pig!" cried María, who had Furball ensconced in a bag slung over her shoulder. "Just once you could be nice to Tom. I've moved his card right back."

"I'm punishing him for trying to drown Furball," said Matt.

"What on earth are you talking about?"

"Furball couldn't have fallen into the toilet and pulled the top down. It isn't possible. Tom did it."

"He couldn't be that evil," said María.

"Since when? Anyhow, it's my party, and I get to say who sits where." Matt was beginning to lose patience with María. He was trying to be nice to her, and she was taking it all wrong.

"They eat *mush* at the baby table."

"Good," Matt said. He fetched Tom's card and replaced it. María reached for it again, and he grabbed her wrist quite hard.

"Ow! That hurts! I'm going to stay here."

"No, you aren't," said Matt.

"I'll do whatever I like!"

Matt ran back to his table with María trying to push past him and grab her place card. El Patrón had arrived, along with

MacGregor and the others.

"What's this? What's this?" said El Patrón. Matt and María skidded to a halt.

"I want her to sit next to me," said Matt.

The old man laughed: a dry, dusty sound. "Is she your little girlfriend, your *novia?*"

"That's disgusting," said Mr Alacrán.

"Is it?" El Patrón chuckled. "Matt's no different than I was at that age."

"Matt's a clone!"

"He's *my* clone. Sit here, girl. Make room for her, Tam Lin." Tam Lin found a place setting for María. He frowned at Matt.

"Where's Tom?" Felicia said. Everyone turned to look at her. Felicia was so quiet and so seldom seen, most people seemed to forget she existed.

"Where is Tom?" El Patrón turned to Matt.

"I put him at the baby table," said Matt.

"You pig!" shouted María.

El Patrón laughed. "That's the stuff, Mi Vida. Get rid of your enemies when you can. I don't like Tom either, and dinner will be better without him."

Felicia balled up her napkin in her fist, but she didn't say anything.

"I don't want to stay here! I want to be with Tom!" cried María.

"Well, you can't," Matt said flatly. Why did she always have to stick up for him? She didn't even stop to think. There was no way Furball could have pulled the lid down on top of himself. But she didn't believe Matt because he was only a "disgusting clone." A dull rage at the unfairness of it swept over him.

"Do as you're told, girl." El Patrón suddenly lost interest in the drama and turned to Mr MacGregor on his other side.

María, choking back tears, was pushed up to the table by Tam Lin. "I'll see he gets the same food as the rest of us," he whispered.

"No, you won't," said Matt.

Tam Lin raised his eyebrows. "Is that a direct order, Master Matt?"

"Yes." Matt tried to ignore María's soft whimpers as she strove not to draw attention to herself. If she couldn't bring herself to punish Tom, he would do it for her. Food was brought and served. María selected bits to feed Furball and continued to stare down at her lap.

"Foetal brain implants – I must try that sometime," said MacGregor. "It's done wonders for you."

"Don't put it off too long," El Patrón advised. "You have to give the doctors at least five months' lead time. Eight is better."

"I won't be able to use – ?"

"Oh, no. He's *much* too old."

Felicia was staring down at her plate with almost as much dejection as María. She wasn't even pretending to eat. She drank from a tall glass that was regularly filled by a servant. She looked pleadingly at MacGregor, although Matt couldn't guess what she could want from him. In any case, he ignored her – and so did her husband and everyone else for that matter.

El Viejo, Mr Alacrán's father, spilled his food and made a mess on the tablecloth. No one paid attention to him, either.

"See, there's an example of someone who didn't get his implants when he should have," said El Patrón, pointing at El Viejo.

"Father decided against it," said Mr Alacrán.

"He's a fool, then. Look at him, Matt. Would you believe

that's my grandson?"

Matt hadn't worked out the exact relationship between El Viejo and El Patrón before. It hadn't seemed important. El Patrón looked ancient, no doubt about it, but his mind was sharp. At least now it was. After those whatever-they-were implants. El Viejo could hardly string a sentence together, and some of the time he sat in his room and *screamed*. Celia said that happened to some old people and that Matt mustn't worry about it.

"I could believe he's your grandfather," said Matt.

El Patrón laughed, spraying food particles over his plate. "That's what comes of not taking care of yourself."

"Father decided implants were immoral," said Mr Alacrán, "and I honoured his decision." A sudden intake of breath around the table told Matt that Mr Alacrán had said something dangerous. "He's deeply religious. He thinks God put him on earth for a certain number of years and that he mustn't ask for more."

El Patrón stared at Mr Alacrán for a long moment. "I'll overlook your rudeness," he said at last. "It's my birthday and I'm in a good mood. But someday you'll be old too. Your body will start to fall apart and your brain will deteriorate. See if you're so high-minded then." He went back to eating, and everyone relaxed.

"May I check up on Tom?" Felicia said in her uncertain way.

"Stay out of this," growled Mr Alacrán.

"I — I only wanted to see if he had food."

"For God's sake! He's capable of standing on his own hind legs and finding something to eat!"

Those were Matt's sentiments too, but he was surprised at the anger Mr Alacrán showed toward Felicia. How could anyone get mad at her? She was so helpless. Felicia hung her head and withdrew into silence.

After dinner Tam Lin rolled El Patrón to the bougainvillea arbour for the gift giving. Mr MacGregor excused himself because he had to rest up for an operation. Matt was glad to see him go.

El Patrón set great importance on gifts. "You can tell how much someone loves you by the size of the present," he often told Matt. He preferred to receive gifts, rather than give them. "The flow of wealth should be from outside" – El Patrón opened his arms wide, as though he were about to hug someone – "in." El Patrón gave himself a big bear hug instead. Matt thought this was very funny.

Daft Donald and Tam Lin brought the boxes to El Patrón. Matt read the cards and tore off the wrappers. A secretary recorded who had given what and the value of the gift. Watches, jewellery, paintings, statues, and moon rocks piled up on the lawn. Matt thought the moon rocks looked like something you could find anywhere in the Ajo Mountains, but they came with a certificate and were very expensive.

The faded princess gave El Patrón a statue of a naked baby with wings – one of the few gifts he seemed to like. Matt gave him a wallet that had looked good in the catalogue and now seemed shabby next to the other presents. "You'd need a wallet as big as the Grand Canyon to hold El Patrón's paper money," Celia had said, "and you'd have to drain the Gulf of California for the small change."

The Farmers, one and all, gave weapons: guns that responded to one's voice, lasers that could burn an intruder to a crisp from the other side of a wall, flying minibombs that clamped themselves on to an enemy's skin. The latter were programmed to recognise specific people. Tam Lin took the weapons away the minute Matt unwrapped them.

"Open your presents, Mi Vida," El Patrón said after a long while. His eyes were half closed, and he looked almost bloated with all the gifts he'd received. A mountain of new possessions surrounded his wheelchair.

Matt eagerly tore open a small box from Celia. It was a hand-knitted sweater. Where she'd found the time to knit, Matt didn't know. Tam Lin gave him a book identifying edible plants in the desert. El Patrón gave him a battery-driven car big enough to sit in. It had flashing lights and a siren. Matt was too old for such things, but he knew the car had been very expensive and therefore that El Patrón loved him very much.

María snatched away the present she'd brought him. "I don't want to give you anything!" she cried.

"Give that back," Matt said, angry that she'd made a scene in front of everyone.

"You don't deserve it!" María started to run away, but she was halted by her father, Senator Mendoza.

"Hand him the box," said Senator Mendoza.

"He was mean to Tom!"

"Do it."

María wavered for a moment and then flung the box as far away as she could.

"Pick it up and bring it to me," Matt said. He was in a cold rage.

"Let her go," said Tam Lin in a low voice, but Matt wasn't in any mood to listen. María had insulted him in front of everyone, and he intended to make her pay.

"That's the stuff," El Patrón said gleefully. "Make your women toe the line."

"Get it *now*," said Matt in the same cold, deadly voice he'd heard El Patrón use on terrified servants.

"Please, María," Senator Mendoza coaxed gently.

Sobbing, she retrieved the present and thrust it at Matt. "I hope you choke on it!"

Matt was trembling and afraid he'd lose control and start crying too. Suddenly he remembered what El Patrón had said earlier: *Is she your little girlfriend?* Why shouldn't María be his girlfriend? Why should he be different from everyone because he was a clone? When he looked into the mirror, he saw no difference between himself and the others. It was unfair that he was treated like Furball when he had good grades and could name the planets, the brightest stars, and all the constellations. "One more thing," Matt said. "I demand a birthday kiss."

Gasps ricocheted around the crowd. Senator Mendoza turned ashen, and he put his hands protectively on María's shoulders. "Don't do this," murmured Tam Lin. El Patrón beamed with delight.

"It's my party too," said Matt, "and I can have anything I want. Isn't that so, *mi patrón?*"

"It's so, my little fighting cock. Give him the kiss, girl."

"He's a clone!" Senator Mendoza cried.

"He's *my* clone." Suddenly El Patrón wasn't the jovial birthday host anymore. He seemed dark and dangerous, like a creature you might stumble on in the middle of the night. Matt remembered Tam Lin's words about his master: *He grew large and green until he shadowed over the whole forest, but most of his branches are twisted.* Matt was sorry he'd started this whole affair, but it was too late now.

"Do it, María," said Senator Mendoza. "I won't let it happen again. I promise."

The senator didn't know that María had kissed Matt on several occasions, just as she kissed Furball and anything else that pleased her. Matt knew this was different, though. He was humiliating her. If it had been Tom asking for the kiss, no one would have cared. People would have thought it cute for a boy to flirt with his *novia*.

Matt wasn't a boy. He was a beast.

María came up to him, no longer angry or rebellious. She reminded him of Felicia bent sadly over her plate. For an instant he wanted to say, *Stop. It was a joke. I didn't mean it.* But it was too late. El Patrón was watching them with obvious glee, and Matt realised it might be dangerous to draw back now. Who knew how the old man might punish María if he had his fun spoiled now?

María leaned forward, and Matt felt the cold brush of her lips on his skin. Then she ran to her father and collapsed in tears. He gathered her up and shouldered his way through the crowd. The paralysis that had seized everyone broke. Everyone started talking at once – not about what had just happened, but about anything else. But Matt felt their eyes on him – accusing, disgusted, repelled.

El Patrón had wearied of the excitement. He signalled Tam Lin and Daft Donald to take him away and was already being carried up the steps before Matt noticed.

The party went on with renewed spirit now that El Patrón was gone, but no one talked to Matt. No one seemed to notice he was even there. After a while he gathered up his smaller presents, leaving the battery-driven car for the servants to attend to.

Matt made his way to Celia's apartment and laid out Celia's sweater and Tam Lin's book. Then he opened María's gift. It was a box of toffee she'd made with her own hands. He knew because she'd told him about it ahead of time. She was no good at keeping secrets.

Matt knew María hoarded things – worn-out shirts, broken toys, and gift-wrapping paper – and she got hysterical if anything went missing. Celia said it was because she'd lost her mother when she was only five.

One day María's mother had walked out of the house and never returned. No one knew where she'd gone, or if they did, they weren't talking about it. When María was small, she imagined her mother had got lost in the desert. She woke up at night crying that she could hear her mother's voice, but of course she couldn't. Ever since then, Celia said, María had hung on to things. It was why she rarely let Furball out of her sight and why the dog was such a wimp.

María had cut squares from her treasured gift-wrapping paper and used them to wrap Matt's toffee. He felt terrible looking at them. Why hadn't he listened when Tam Lin told him to let her go? He closed the box and put it away.

Celia had drawn the curtains in his room. As always, she had lit the candle in front of the Virgin. The Virgin looked shabby with Her chipped robe and cheap plastic flowers, but Matt wouldn't have wanted Her to look any other way. He crawled under the covers. Feeling around, he found the lump that was his stuffed bear. He would have died rather than admit to María that he still slept with it.

12

THE THING ON THE BED

Matt woke up feeling gritty and hot. The candle in front of the Virgin had burned out, leaving a waxy smell that the curtains held in. He opened the window, wincing at the sudden invasion of sunlight. It was late morning. Celia had already gone to work.

Rubbing his eyes, Matt saw María's present on a shelf, and the birthday party came back with hideous clearness. He knew he had to make things up to her, but he also knew she needed time to cool down. If he approached her now, she'd only slam the door in his face.

Matt dressed in cool clothes and found leftover pizza for breakfast. The apartment was empty, the walled garden deserted except for birds. He went out and watered the vegetables.

The day after a birthday party was always a letdown. The power Matt enjoyed as El Patrón's clone vanished. The servants went back to ignoring him. The Alacráns treated him like something Furball had coughed up on the carpet.

The hours dragged on. Matt practised on his guitar, a skill he was developing without Mr Ortega's help. The music master was unable to keep his hands on the instrument and thus was unable to detect mistakes. After a while Matt switched to reading Tam Lin's present. The bodyguard was fond of nature books, although he read them at a painfully slow rate. Matt already had books on wildlife, camping, map reading, and survival that Tam Lin fully expected him to study. Tam Lin drilled him when they went on expeditions in the Ajo Mountains.

All Matt's activities were supposed to be risk free. Thus, he was allowed to ride only Safe Horses, and he could swim only if two lifeguards were present. He could climb ropes only if there was a mountain of mattresses underneath. Any bruise or cut was treated with extreme alarm.

But once a week Tam Lin took Matt on educational field trips. The trips were disguised as visits to the Alacráns' nuclear power plant or the opium processing plant – a stinking, clanking horror even an eejit would find unbearable. Halfway there Tam Lin would turn the horses toward the hills.

Matt lived for these expeditions. El Patrón would have had a heart attack if he'd known how many cliffs Matt climbed and how many rattlesnakes he teased out of the rocks. But they made Matt feel strong and free.

"May I come in?" said a faint, uncertain voice. Matt jumped. He'd been daydreaming. He heard the person enter the living room. "It's . . . Felicia," said Felicia hesitantly, as though she weren't quite sure of her identity.

This is completely weird, Matt thought. Felicia had never shown the slightest interest in him. "What do you want?" he asked.

"I . . . thought I might . . . visit." Felicia's eyes looked heavy, like she might fall asleep at any moment. A vague odour of cinnamon hung around her.

"Why?" Matt knew he was being rude, but when had the Alacráns been anything else to him? Besides, there was something creepy about the way Felicia swayed back and forth.

"May I . . . sit?"

Matt pulled a chair over to her, since it didn't look like she'd make it by herself. He tried to help her, but she pushed him away.

Of course. He was a clone. He wasn't supposed to touch humans. Felicia half fell into the chair, and they stared at each other for a moment. "You're a guh-guh-good musician," Felicia stammered, as though it hurt her to admit it.

"How do you know?" Matt couldn't remember ever playing when she was around.

"Everyone . . . says so. It's such a surprise. El Patrón doesn't have a – have a . . . musical bone in his body."

"He enjoys listening," Matt said. He didn't like to hear El Patrón criticised.

"I know. He used to listen to me."

Matt felt uneasy. He'd probably taken away what little attention Felicia got from other people.

"I was a great concert pianist once," she said.

"I've heard you play."

"You have?" Felicia's eyes widened. "Oh. The music room. I was much better . . . before I had my – my . . . "

"Nervous breakdown," said Matt. Her hesitant speech was getting on his nerves.

"But that isn't why . . . I came. I want to – to . . . "

Matt waited impatiently.

"Help you," finished Felicia. There was another long pause

as Matt wondered what kind of help she thought he needed. "You upset María. She cried all night."

Matt felt uncomfortable. What did Felicia have to do with this?

"She wants to . . . see you."

"Okay," said Matt.

"But she . . . Don't you see? Her father won't let her come here. It's up to you."

"What should I do?"

"Go to her," cried Felicia with more energy than Matt had expected. "Go *now*." The outburst seemed to exhaust her. Her head drooped and she closed her eyes. "You wouldn't have something . . . to drink?" she whispered.

"Celia doesn't keep alcohol," said Matt. "Should I call one of the maids?" he said.

"Never mind." Felicia sighed, rousing herself enough to stand. "María's waiting at the hospital. It's . . . important." With that, Felicia made her way to the door and drifted into the hallway like a cinnamon-scented ghost.

The hospital wasn't a place Matt went willingly. Set apart from the rest of the buildings, it was surrounded by a wasteland of sand and low, flat bullhead vines. The vines protected their turf with the meanest, nastiest thorns ever and could even stab through shoes.

Matt picked his way carefully through the wasteland. Heat radiated off the ground, making the grey, windowless building shimmer. The hospital was like a prison with a strange, alarming smell inside that permeated everything. Matt was dragged there twice a year to undergo painful and humiliating tests.

He sat on the front steps and inspected his sandals for bullheads. María was probably in the waiting room. It wasn't too bad there, with chairs and magazines and a cold-drink machine. Sweat ran down Matt's face and stuck his shirt to his chest. He opened the door.

"I don't see why I should talk to you at all," said María. She was sitting in one of the chairs with a magazine open on her lap. Her eyes looked puffy.

"It was your idea." Matt bit his tongue. He wanted to make up with her, not pick a fight. "I mean, it was a good idea."

"You're the one who invited me," said María. "Why couldn't you find somewhere nice? This place is creepy."

Matt's alarm system went on at once. "I didn't invite you. Wait!" he cried as María started to get up. "I do want to see you. I guess – I guess – I was a pig at the birthday party."

"You *guess?*" María said scornfully.

"Okay, I was. But you didn't have to take back the present."

"Of course I did. A present's no good if it's given in anger."

Matt stopped his first reply before it could get out. "It's the nicest gift I ever got."

"Oh, sure! Nicer than that tiny sports car El Patrón gave you!"

Matt sat down next to her. She moved away as far as she could. "I really like how you wrapped the toffee."

"It took me a long time to decide which papers to use." María's voice trembled. "You'll only ball them up and throw them away."

"No, I won't," promised Matt. "I'll spread them out carefully and keep them for always."

María said nothing. She stared down at her hands. Matt edged closer. The truth was, he liked it when she kissed him, even if she kissed Furball sixty times as often. He'd never kissed her back, but he might try it now, to make up.

"Good. You're both here."

Matt recoiled. Tom stood in the doorway. "How did you find us?" Matt snarled.

"Of course he knew where we were. You told him to bring me here," María said.

"No kidding," said Matt. The pieces were falling into place now. Tom had pretended to carry a message to María, and Felicia had done the same with Matt. They had to be working together. Matt had never thought of Felicia as dangerous, but he didn't really know her.

"I thought you might like to see something," Tom said. His face was open and friendly, and his blue eyes shone with innocence. Matt wanted to roll him in the bullheads.

"Here?" said María doubtfully.

"It's like Halloween, only better. It's the ugliest, grossest thing you ever saw, and I bet both of you wet your pants," Tom said.

"I've done things that would make your eyes drop out," María sneered. "Tam Lin showed me how to pick up scorpions, and he let a tarantula walk up my arm."

Matt was surprised at María's daring. Tam Lin had shown him the same things, and Matt had almost done what Tom described.

"This is worse," Tom said. "Remember that Halloween when you thought the *chupacabras* was outside and Matt put chicken guts in your bed?"

"I did not! It was you!" cried Matt.

"You put your hand right in it," said Tom, ignoring Matt, "and screamed your head off."

"That was so *evil*," María said.

"*I* didn't do it!" protested Matt.

"Well, this is worse," gloated Tom. "I don't know if you have the – pardon the expression – guts for it."

"She doesn't," said Matt.

"Don't tell me what to do!" María got a mulish look in her eyes and Matt's heart sank. He knew Tom was up to something foul, but he hadn't figured out what it was yet.

"Come on. He's only trying to start trouble." Matt tried to grab María's hand, but she yanked her arm away.

"Listen." Tom opened the door leading from the waiting room to the rest of the hospital. Matt's stomach hit rock bottom. He had bad memories of some of those rooms.

Tom's face glowed with joy. It was then, Matt had discovered, he was most dangerous. As Tam Lin said, if you didn't know Tom well, you'd think he was an angel bringing you the keys to the pearly gates.

In the distance they heard a mewling sound. It went on for a moment, stopped, and began again.

"Is that a cat?" said María.

If it is, it isn't yowling for milk, Matt thought. There was a level of terror and despair in that sound that made the hair stand up on his neck. This time he did grab María's hand.

"They're doing experiments on cats!" María cried suddenly. "Oh, please! You've got to help me rescue them!"

"We'd better ask permission first," said Matt. He was deeply unwilling to go beyond that door.

"No one's *going* to give us permission," María stormed. "Don't you see? Adults don't see anything wrong with those experiments. We have to take the cats away – Dada will help me – and the doctors won't even know where they've gone."

"They'll only get more." Matt felt cold as he listened to the sound going on and on.

"That's the dodge people always use! Don't help anyone. They'll only find more Illegals to enslave or poor people to starve or – or cats to torture." María was working herself into a state. Matt despaired of getting her to listen to reason.

"Look, we should ask your dada first – " he began.

"I won't listen to that cat suffer one more instant! Are you with me or not? If not, I'm going by myself!"

"I'll go with you," said Tom.

That decided Matt. There was no way he was letting Tom take María by herself to see whatever horror he had stashed away.

María strode down the hall, but she slowed the closer they got to the cries. Matt still held her hand. It was cold and sweaty, or maybe his hand was. The sound wasn't exactly like a cat. It wasn't like anything Matt had heard before, but there was no mistaking the anguish in it. Sometimes it rose almost to a shriek and then faded, as though whatever was making the noise was exhausted.

They arrived at the door. It was closed, and cravenly, Matt hoped it was locked.

It wasn't.

Tom threw it open. Matt could hardly register what lay on the bed before them. It rolled its eyes and thrashed helplessly in the straps that restrained it. Its mouth opened in a horrible O when it saw the children, and it screamed louder than Matt thought possible. It screamed until it ran out of air, then it wheezed until it didn't have the strength to do that anymore, and then it lay there panting and gasping.

"It's a boy," whispered María.

It was. Only at first Matt thought it was some kind of beast, so alien and terrible was its face. It had doughy, unhealthy skin and red hair that stuck up in bristles. It seemed never to have been in the sun, and its hands were twisted like claws above the straps that held it down. It was dressed in green hospital pyjamas, but these had been befouled by its terror. Worst of all was the terrible energy that rolled through the trapped body. The creature never stopped moving. It was as though invisible snakes were rippling beneath the skin and forcing its arms and legs to move in a ceaseless bid for freedom.

"It's not a boy," Tom said scornfully. "It's a clone."

Matt felt as though he'd been punched in the stomach. He'd never seen another clone. He'd only felt the weight of hatred humans had for such things. He hadn't understood it because, after all, clones were like dogs and cats, and humans loved them. If he'd thought about it at all, he had assumed he was a pet, only a very intelligent one.

Matt became aware that María no longer held his hand. She'd shrunk against Tom, and he had his arm around her. The creature – clone – had regained its energy and was screaming again. Something about the children terrified it, or perhaps it was terrified all the time. Its tongue protruded from its mouth and drooled saliva down its chin.

"Whose – ?" whispered María.

"MacGregor's. He's a real wreck – his liver's all eaten up with alcohol," said Tom in a casual, chatty way. "Mum says he looks like something the Grim Reaper forgot to pick up."

Mum, thought Matt. *Felicia.*

"Are they going to – ?" said María.

"Tonight," Tom said.

"I can't bear to look at him!" wailed María. "I don't want to think about it!" Tom pulled her away, and Matt knew he was enjoying every minute of this.

"Shall I leave you two alone together?" Tom inquired from the doorway.

Matt had trouble tearing his eyes away from the thing on the bed. There was no *way* he could be the same sort of being as that creature. It wasn't possible! The creature opened its mouth to make another horrible scream, and Matt suddenly knew who it looked like.

It resembled MacGregor, of course, because it was his clone, but MacGregor was an adult with differences that made it hard to see the connection. It was a lot closer to – close enough to show a kinship with – "It looks like you," Matt said to Tom.

"You wish! You *wish!*" yelled Tom, dropping his cheerful grin.

"Look, María. It has the same red hair and ears."

But she refused to look up. "Take me out of here," she moaned with her face buried in Tom's shirt.

"I'm not like that thing!" shouted Matt. "Use your eyes!"

He tried to pull her from Tom, and she shrieked, "Don't touch me! I don't want to think about it!"

Matt was beside himself with frustration. "You wanted to come down here to rescue a cat. Well, look at *this!* It needs rescuing!"

"No, no, no," whimpered María. She was in a state of utter panic. "Take me away!" she wailed.

Tom hurried her down the hall. He glanced back with a look of savage triumph, and Matt had to clench his teeth very hard to keep from running after them and pounding Tom to within an inch of his life. It wouldn't do María any good. It wouldn't do Matt any good either, except to convince her he really was a beast.

Their footsteps died away. Matt stood for a moment in the hallway, listening to the mewling of the thing on the bed. Then he closed the door and followed them.

13

THE LOTUS POND

Matt had to talk to someone. He had to do something to keep from howling like a dog at the horror of it all. He wasn't a clone! He couldn't be! Somehow, somewhere a mistake had been made. Words he'd overheard from the doctor came back to him: *Clones go to pieces when they get older.* Was that going to happen to him? Was he going to end up strapped to a bed, screaming until he ran out of air?

Tam Lin was with El Patrón, and not even Matt was allowed into that heavily guarded part of the house without permission. He ran to the kitchen instead. Celia took one look at his face and hung up her apron. "Finish the soup for me, would you?" she told a junior cook. She took Matt's hand and said, "Let's take the afternoon off, *chico.* The Alacráns can eat their shoes for dinner for all I care."

Alone of all the servants, Celia could and did insult the Alacráns whenever she felt like it. Not to their faces, of course, but she was less servile in their presence than the others. She, like Matt, was protected by El Patrón.

Celia said nothing more until they were inside her apartment with the door closed. "Okay. Something bad happened," she said. "Is María still mad?"

Matt didn't know where to begin.

"If you say you're sorry, she'll forgive you," Celia said. "She's a good kid."

"I did apologise," Matt managed to say.

"And she wouldn't accept it. Well, that happens sometimes. Sometimes we have to grovel to show we really mean it."

"That isn't it."

Celia pulled him onto her lap, something she rarely did now that he was older, and held him tightly. Matt's reserve snapped. He sobbed uncontrollably, clinging to her, terrified she would push him away.

"Hey, María won't hold a grudge. You have to make her a list of who she's mad at, 'cause she doesn't remember more than half an hour." Celia rocked Matt back and forth, all the while murmuring comforting words he could hardly take in. All he sensed was the music of her voice, the warmth of her arms, the fact that she was *there*.

Finally, he calmed enough to tell her everything that had happened in the hospital.

For a moment Celia sat perfectly still. She didn't even breathe. "That . . . little . . . *creep*," she said at last.

Matt looked up anxiously. Her face had turned pale and her eyes stared into the far distance. "Tom is MacGregor's son, you know," said Celia. "I shouldn't tell you these things at your age, but nobody gets a decent childhood in the Alacrán household. They're all scorpions. Boy, did El Patrón have it right when he picked the name."

"How can Tom be MacGregor's son? Felicia's married to Mr Alacrán."

Celia laughed bitterly. "Marriage doesn't mean much to this crowd. Felicia ran off with MacGregor, oh, years ago. I guess she got bored hanging around here. Only it didn't work out. El Patrón had her brought back – he doesn't like people taking his possessions – and MacGregor let him do it. Felicia was beginning to bore him.

"Mr Alacrán was very, very angry because he didn't *want* her back, but El Patrón didn't care. Mr Alacrán doesn't talk to her anymore. He won't even look at her. She's a prisoner in this house, and the servants supply her with all the booze she can handle. Which is a lot, let me tell you."

"What about Tom?" Matt urged.

"Tom showed up about six months after she returned."

Matt felt slightly better after learning this information. It pleased him that Felicia was in disgrace, but he still had questions. He steeled himself to ask the most important one. "What's wrong with MacGregor's clone?"

Celia looked around nervously. "I'm not supposed to talk to you about this. You weren't supposed to know about him."

"But I do know," Matt said.

"Yes. Yes. That's Tom's doing. You don't understand, *mi vida*. All of us have been warned not to talk about clones. We don't always know who might be listening." Again Celia looked around, and Matt remembered what Tam Lin had told him about hidden cameras in the house.

"If you tell me, it'll be Tom's fault," Matt said.

"That's true. I really don't see how I can avoid explaining after what you've seen."

"So what's wrong with MacGregor's clone?"

"His . . . brain has been destroyed."

Matt sat up straight when he heard that.

"When clones are born, they're injected with a kind of drug. It turns them into idiots," said Celia. She wiped her eyes with her apron.

"Why?"

"It's the law. Don't ask me why. I can't tell you."

"But I wasn't injected," Matt said.

"El Patrón didn't want it to happen to you. He's powerful enough to break the law."

Matt was filled with gratitude for the old man who had spared him such a terrible fate. Matt could read and write, climb hills, play music, and do anything a real human might do – all because El Patrón loved him. "Are there any others like me?" he asked.

"No. You're the only one," Celia said.

The only one! He was unique. He was special. Matt's heart swelled with pride. If he wasn't human, he might become something even better. Better than Tom, who was an embarrassment to the family. Then a horrible thought occurred to him. "They won't – the doctors won't – inject me later?"

Celia hugged him again. "No, darling. You're safe from that. You're safe for as long as you live." She was crying, although Matt couldn't understand why. Perhaps she was afraid because she had said something in front of the hidden cameras.

Matt felt limp with relief. He was exhausted by all that had happened and he yawned broadly.

"Take a nap, *mi vida,*" said Celia. "I'll bring you something nice from the kitchen later." She led him to his bedroom, turned on the air conditioner, and closed the curtains.

Matt stretched out under the sheet and let a delicious sense of ease sweep over him. So much had happened: the disastrous party, the sinister hospital, MacGregor's clone. Matt felt hurt that María had run from him after seeing the thing on the bed. He would seek her out later and show her that he was completely different.

As Matt drifted to sleep, he pondered why MacGregor would want a clone when he had a son. It was probably because Tom had been taken away from him by El Patrón. And because Tom was an unnatural little weevil no father would like to have around.

But then, Matt thought hazily, *why replace him with a horribly damaged clone?*

María refused to talk to Matt. She hid in her father's apartment or managed to be with a group of people every time he saw her. But Matt had faith in María's intelligence. If he could get her alone and explain how he was different from all other clones, she would understand.

MacGregor was back from his operation. He still looked – as Felicia put it – like something the Grim Reaper forgot to collect, but he was getting better all the time. He and El Patrón sat in adjoining wheelchairs and cackled over old memories – rivals they had destroyed and governments they had overthrown.

"Got me a new liver," MacGregor said, patting his stomach, "and went in for a set of kidneys while I was at it." He gazed at Matt with those bright blue eyes that were so much like Tom's. Matt thought he was disgusting. He couldn't wait for the man to go home.

María would be leaving for boarding school soon. Matt realised he had to act now. As he watched her across the garden, playing chase at a slow pace because she had Furball in her side bag, the solution came to him. María didn't have the dog with her all the time. Now and then Senator Mendoza banished him to the bathroom in their apartment. What if Matt stole the animal and sent her a ransom note?

There was a pump house by the lotus pond. It was concealed by a giant wisteria vine and reasonably cool inside. Matt could hide Furball there. But how could he keep the dog from yapping? Even a spider swinging down on its web sent the animal into hysterics.

He won't bark if he's asleep, Matt thought.

Matt had spent a lot of time in the secret passage behind the music room. He liked to pretend he was a superhero creeping up on his enemies. He'd replaced El Látigo Negro as his hero with Don Segundo Sombra – Sir Second Shadow – an international spy. The Black Whip was for kids, but the Don did adult things like drive race cars and parachute out of jet planes. An even better hero was El Sacerdote Volante, the Flying Priest. The Flying Priest bombarded demons with holy water that ate holes in their scaly hides.

One of the closets reachable from the secret passage belonged to Felicia. It was full, top to bottom, with liquor. More interesting – and useful now – was a shelf of small bottles with eyedroppers. They contained laudanum. Matt knew all about laudanum, having studied the opium business as part of his regular homework. Laudanum was opium dissolved in alcohol, and it was very strong. Three drops in a glass of fruit juice would knock you out for eight hours. Felicia had enough stored in her closet to knock out an entire city. It explained why she was so dopey all the time.

Matt waited until he saw her dozing on a lawn chair, and then he hurried through the secret passage and stole one of the small bottles.

The lotus pond was one of a dozen pools of water in the vast gardens of the house. It was deserted in summer because it had little shade. Ibises, with wings clipped to keep them from flying away, stalked through papyrus grass and hunted frogs under the lily pads. It was El Patrón's idea of an ancient Egyptian garden. The walls enclosing the place were painted with stiff figures of ancient gods.

Matt pushed aside the wisteria and went into the pump house. It was dark and damp. He made a bed for Furball out of empty sacks and filled a bowl with water.

He stepped outside and froze. Tom was on his hands and knees at the other end of the garden. His back was turned, and he was absorbed in watching something on the lawn. Matt eased carefully out of the wisteria. He moved quietly through the papyrus to sneak back into the house.

An ibis rose from the grass. It flapped its mutilated wings and blundered across the pond.

Tom jumped up. "You! What are you doing here?"

"Watching you," Matt said coolly.

"Well, it's none of your business! Get back to your part of the house!"

"All parts of the house are mine," said Matt. He looked past Tom and saw a frog on the lawn. Its hind legs had been nailed to the ground, and it flopped frantically, trying to escape. "You're disgusting!" Matt said. He went over and freed the frog's feet. The creature threw itself into the water.

"I was only doing a science project," said Tom.

"Oh, sure. Even María wouldn't believe that."

Tom's face flushed with rage, and Matt braced himself for a fight; but just as suddenly the anger drained away, as though it had never been there. Matt shivered. It bothered him when Tom made a lightning shift like that. It was like watching a crocodile submerge in a nature movie. You knew the crocodile was planning an attack, but you didn't know when.

"You can learn a lot from studying a place like this," Tom said in a casual voice. "The ibises live on frogs, the frogs eat bugs, and the bugs eat one another. It teaches you about the meaning of life." Tom had on his professional Cute Kid smile. It didn't fool Matt for one second.

"Let me guess. You're on the side of the ibises," Matt said.

"Of course. Who wants to be at the bottom of the food chain?" Tom said. "That's the difference between humans and animals, see. The humans are at the top, and the animals – well, they're just walking T-bone steaks and drumsticks." He strolled off – an easy, good-natured stroll to show he wasn't concerned that Matt had disturbed his evil game. Matt watched him disappear into the house.

What rotten luck, Matt thought. He didn't want Tom poking around while he was talking to María. If only he could slip *Tom* the laudanum. For a moment Matt savoured the idea, but he knew that would be going too far.

María had the dog glued to her all morning and all through lunch the next day. Finally, Senator Mendoza said, "For God's sake, María. It stinks."

"Did you roll in something icky," she said fondly, holding the creature up to her nose. "*Did* you, sweet-ums?"

"Get it out of here," her father snapped.

Matt was observing this from behind a wall hanging. He slithered along the curtains and followed María. If he could talk to her now, he wouldn't have to kidnap the stupid dog. She thrust Furball into her apartment and closed the door.

Agonised yips broke out from the other side.

"María – " began Matt.

"Oh, hi. Listen, I've got to run. Dada will get mad if I don't come back right away."

"I just want to talk."

"Not now!" cried María, dodging past him. She ran down the hall, her sandals slapping against the floor.

Matt felt like crying. Why was she making things so difficult? Would it kill her to listen?

He hurried to Celia's apartment to get a bowl of raw hamburger he'd noticed in the refrigerator. When he returned, he looked around carefully for servants coming down the hall. The minute he opened María's door, Furball yelped and scurried under a sofa. *Great.*

Matt picked up the side bag María used to cart the animal around. He opened it temptingly and placed a chunk of hamburger inside. The dog whined and drooled as he watched. María fed him a special diet recommended by a vet, but it didn't include raw meat. She didn't like the idea of raw meat.

"You want that. You know you do," said Matt.

Furball licked his chops.

Matt held up a glob of the stuff and blew the smell toward the animal.

Furball trembled all over and swallowed several times. Finally, he couldn't stand it anymore and darted out. In an instant Matt had him trapped inside the bag. Furball snarled and tried to claw his way out. Matt poked a crumb of hamburger into the bag and got a bite that drew blood. Furball howled piteously.

"Here! Eat yourself silly," Matt cried, shoving fistfuls of meat inside. Matt heard slurping, gulping, and frantic licking. Then – miraculously – the animal stretched out in the bag and fell asleep. Matt peeked inside to be sure. This was even better than he'd hoped.

He slung the bag over his shoulder, expecting outraged yips when the dog felt himself being moved. There was nothing. Furball was used to being hauled around. He slept in the bag all the time and probably felt safe wrapped up in his dark little cave. Matt could understand that. He was fond of dark hide-aways himself.

He left a note under María's pillow: *Meet me by the lotus pond at midnight and I'll tell you where your dog is.* He signed it *Matt.* Then, *P.S. Don't tell anyone or you'll never see him again!!!* Matt supposed the last line was mean, but he was fighting against impossible odds.

He slipped out of the apartment, leaving the door ajar so it would seem the dog had worked it open. The halls were empty and the lotus garden deserted, except for ibises meditating on the existence of frogs. Everything was working out perfectly. Furball stirred slightly when Matt laid the bag down in the pump house, but he didn't bark.

Matt decided to leave him in the bag. He could come out when he felt like it and find water and the rest of the hamburger. Matt put the laudanum on a shelf. He was frankly relieved he didn't have to use it. As much as he disliked Furball, it seemed wrong to feed him the same stuff that turned Felicia into a zombie.

María discovered Furball missing right after lunch. She enlisted everyone – except Matt – to hunt for him. Matt could hear voices calling, but anyone familiar with the beast knew he wouldn't answer. He would cower in whatever hiding place he'd found until dragged out, snapping and snarling.

Celia was asleep when Matt left. Most of the hall lights had been turned off, and black areas yawned between them. Not long ago Matt would have been afraid to go out so late. He no longer believed in the *chupacabras* or vampires, but the dark, dead stillness of night brought them back. What if María was too frightened to leave her apartment? Matt hadn't thought of that. If she didn't come, the whole plan would be ruined.

His footsteps echoed on the floor. He stopped many times to be sure no one was following him. He checked his watch. It was fifteen minutes to midnight, when the dead – according to Celia – threw off their coffin lids like so many blankets. *Stop that,* Matt told himself.

The lotus garden was lit only by starlight, and the air was warm and smelled of stagnant water. Not a frond of the palm trees stirred. Not a mosquito whined. Somewhere in the papyrus the ibises were sleeping, or perhaps they were awake and listening to him. What would they do when they realised he was there?

Don't be a coward, Matt told himself. *They're only birds. They're long-legged chickens.*

A frog grunted, making Matt almost drop the flashlight he carried. He shone it on the pond. He heard a splash and a rustle of feathers.

Matt walked as silently as he could toward the pump house. It would be truly awful to hear Furball whine right now. Maybe María wouldn't come. After all, if he was this jumpy, she must be terrified. But she'd come for her dog. Matt didn't underestimate her courage when she thought something was important.

He reached the wisteria. Would it be better to wait here or to check on Furball? He didn't much like going into the dark little house. Anyhow, if he went inside, María wouldn't know where to find him. He heard a noise – floodlights lit up every corner of the garden. It was El Patrón's security system! Matt was blinded. He backed into the wisteria and was grabbed by powerful hands. "Let me go!" Matt shouted. "I'm not an enemy! I'm El Patrón's clone!"

Daft Donald and Tam Lin frog-marched him to the middle of the lawn. "It's me! It's me!" Matt cried. But Tam Lin remained silent and grim.

Senator Mendoza came out of the Big House. He stood in front of Matt, flexing his hands as though he had to keep them under control. For a long, long moment he said nothing. Then: "You are worse than an *animal*." He spoke with such concentrated venom that Matt flinched back against the hands restraining him.

"Oh, I won't hurt you. I'm not that kind of man. Besides, your fate lies with El Patrón." Another long pause. Just when Matt began to think the man wasn't going to say anything else, Senator Mendoza hissed, "You can count on one thing: You will never . . . *ever* . . . see my daughter again."

"But – why?" said Matt, startled out of his fear.

"You know why."

Matt didn't. This was all a horrible nightmare, and he couldn't wake up. "I only wanted to talk to her. I meant to give Furball back. I didn't mean to upset her and I'm sorry now. Please let me see her. To say I'm sorry."

"How can you possibly apologise for killing her dog?"

For an instant Matt wasn't sure he'd heard right. Then the full enormity of the situation sank in on him. "But I didn't! I wouldn't! I couldn't do such a thing to María! I *love* her!" The minute Matt said it, he knew he'd made a terrible mistake. Senator Mendoza looked as though he wanted to strangle Matt right there and throw his body into the lotus pond. Nothing could have been more infuriating than a reminder of how close Matt and María had become – so close that Matt had demanded a kiss from her in front of everyone at El Patrón's birthday party.

It was unthinkable. It was as though a chimpanzee had demanded to wear human clothes and to eat at the same table as people. Worse. Because Matt wasn't even a normal, forest-living beast. He was the thing on the bed.

"I'm sorry. I'm sorry." Matt's mind had frozen. All he could think of was to keep apologising until Senator Mendoza heard him and forgave him.

"You're lucky you're under El Patrón's protection." Senator Mendoza turned and strode into the house.

"Move along," said Tam Lin as he and Daft Donald propelled Matt from the garden.

"I didn't do it!" cried Matt.

"They found your fingerprints on the laudanum bottle," said Tam Lin. Matt had never heard him like this before – so cold, so bitter, and so disgusted.

"I *did* take the laudanum, but I didn't use it." They were moving rapidly through the halls with Matt's feet only brushing the floor. They arrived at Celia's apartment. Tam Lin paused before opening the door.

"I always say," Tam Lin said, breathing as hard as if he'd run a long way, "I always say the truth is best even when we find it unpleasant. Any rat in a sewer can lie. It's how rats are. It's what makes them rats. But a human doesn't run and hide in dark places, because he's something more. Lying is the most personal act of cowardice there is."

"I'm not lying." Matt couldn't help crying, even though he knew it was a babyish thing to do.

"I can believe you made a mistake," Tam Lin went on. "The bottle said *three* drops – that's the dose for a full-grown man. But Furball was a dog. A dose like that would kill him. Did kill him."

"Someone else gave it to him!" Matt cried.

"I'd feel sorry for you if I hadn't seen María first. And I'd feel more kindly if you stepped up and took the blame you deserve."

"I'm not lying!"

"Ah, well. Perhaps I'm expecting too much of you. You're confined to quarters until María leaves. And now is as good a time as any to tell you El Patrón is leaving at the same time. And taking me with him."

Matt was so stupefied, he couldn't speak. He stared at Tam Lin.

"It had to happen sometime, lad," Tam Lin said more kindly. "You're able to look after yourself now. If anything goes wrong, Celia can send a message." He opened the door, and Matt was swept up by Celia, who obviously had been waiting on the other side.

He couldn't talk to her. As had happened when he was deeply upset before, the power of speech left him. He was six years old again, master of a kingdom of gristle and bone and rotting fruit hidden beneath the sawdust in a little room.

14

CELIA'S STORY

Matt was inside his room when María left. He heard the hovercraft whine as it prepared to lift off. He heard the whoosh of air and felt an eerie stir on his skin as the antigravity vessel passed overhead. He had never travelled in one. El Patrón discouraged such things, preferring to keep his Farm close to the memory of his youth.

As a boy, El Patrón had observed the grand estate of the wealthy rancher who owned his village. He remembered a statue of a winged baby and a fountain tiled in blue and green. He remembered the peacocks that haunted the garden. In every respect – he told Matt – he tried to duplicate that memory, only of course being vastly more wealthy, he could have dozens of statues, fountains, and gardens.

The Alacrán *estancia* was laid out over a large area. No part of the house was taller than one story. The walls were a brilliant white, the roofs of fine red tile. Modern conveniences were kept to a minimum, except in special areas like the hospital. Thus, Celia cooked over a wood-burning stove when El Patrón was visiting because he liked the smell of burning mesquite. At other times she was allowed to use microwaves.

The gardens were cooled with fine sprays of water, and the rooms, for the most part, depended on shaded verandas to tame the hot desert air. But during the annual birthday party modern conveniences came out. The famous celebrities would have been miserable without their air-conditioning and entertainment centres.

Not that El Patrón cared whether they were miserable. He merely wanted to impress people.

Matt listened for the purr of El Patrón's limousine. The old man preferred to travel by road. If it had been possible, he would have gone by horse, but his bones were far too brittle to attempt such a thing. He would sit in the back with Tam Lin for company. Daft Donald would drive. They would whisk along the long, shimmering highway to El Patrón's other house in the Chiricahua Mountains.

Matt stared up at the ceiling. He was too depressed to eat or watch TV. All he could do was play out the events of the past few days in his mind. He went over them again and again. If only he hadn't put Tom at the baby table. If only he hadn't made María kiss him in front of the others. If only he hadn't gone to the hospital.

The regrets piled thickly on one another until Matt's thoughts were running around in his head like a hamster on a wheel.

Everyone thought he'd poisoned Furball. His fingerprints were on the bottle, and he'd left a note, a signed note! – how dumb can you get? – in María's room. Matt had to admit the evidence against him was pretty good.

Tom must have seen him come out of the pump house and decided to finish the job he'd started when he dumped Furball into the toilet. But how did Tom use the laudanum without leaving *his* fingerprints on the bottle?

Round and round went Matt's thoughts. *Squeak* went the wheel in his mind. He heard the limousine start up, the distant slam of a door, the fading roar of the engine.

So El Patrón was gone now. And Tam Lin. Matt grieved for him. *Any rat in a sewer can lie,* Tam Lin had said. *It's how rats are. . . . But a human doesn't run and hide in dark places, because he's something more.* Matt thought he could make María understand if he ever got to see her. She'd forgive him because he was a dumb animal and didn't know any better. But Tam Lin had called Matt a human and expected much more from him. Humans, Matt realised, were a lot harder to forgive.

For the first time he saw a huge difference between the way the bodyguard treated him and how everyone else did. Tam Lin talked about courage and loyalty. He let Matt do dangerous things on their expeditions and go off by himself to explore. *He treated Matt as an equal.*

Tam Lin often talked to him about his childhood in Scotland as though Matt were another adult. It wasn't like El Patrón's memories, which tended to fall into a rut. Matt had those stories memorised right down to the last word. Tam Lin's stories were about the difficult decisions you made to become a man. *I was a proper fool,* the bodyguard had said. *Turned my back on my family, ran with a rough crowd, and did the thing that brought me here.* What that thing was Tam Lin never revealed.

At the memory of those picnics, tears came to Matt's eyes and rolled down his cheeks. He made no sound. He had learned that safety lay in silence. But he couldn't stop the tears.

Yet in the midst of his sorrow, Matt found a glimmer of hope. Someone, out of all the people who thought he was no better than a dog, believed he could be something more.

And I will be, Matt promised as he stared up at the blurry ceiling.

Not everything was depressing. Tom was banished from the house. María, when she was hunting for her dog, had innocently asked her father to look in the hospital. Senator Mendoza wanted to know how she knew about the place. The whole story came out about MacGregor's clone and Tom's part in luring María to see it. El Patrón banished Tom to a year-round boarding school with no holidays.

"Why doesn't Mr MacGregor take him, if Tom's his son?" Matt asked.

"You don't understand," Celia said as she cut cheesecake with fresh raspberries for dessert. Ordinarily, Matt would have demanded two slices. Now he didn't think he could choke down one. "Once El Patrón decides something belongs to him, he never lets it go."

"Never?" said Matt.

"Never."

"What about the presents he gets for his birthday?" Matt thought of all the gold watches, jewels, statues, and moon rocks people had given El Patrón for over one hundred years.

"He keeps it all."

"Where?"

Celia dished up the cheesecake and licked her fingers. "There's a secret storeroom under the ground. El Patrón wants to be buried in it — may the Virgin keep that day away forever." Celia crossed herself.

"Like" – Matt had to think – "Like an Egyptian pharaoh."

"Exactly. Eat your cheesecake, *mi vida.* You need to keep your strength up."

Matt ate mechanically as he imagined the storeroom. He'd seen pictures of King Tutankhamun's tomb. El Patrón would lie in a golden box with all the watches, jewels, statues, and moon rocks around him. Then, because Matt didn't want to think of El Patrón dying, he said, "What does that have to do with Tom?"

Celia settled back in her easy chair. She was much more relaxed now that everyone had left. "El Patrón thinks a person belongs to him the same way a house or car or statue does," she said. "He wouldn't let that person go any more than he'd throw away money. It's why he wouldn't allow Felicia to escape. It's why he keeps everyone under his control so he can call them back in an instant. He'll never let MacGregor have Tom, even though he can't stand the boy."

"Do you and Tam Lin belong to El Patrón?" Matt asked.

Celia flinched. "¡*Caramba!* The questions you ask!"

Matt waited.

"Maybe you wouldn't get into so much trouble if people explained things to you," she said with a sigh.

"I didn't poison Furball."

"You didn't *mean* to, darling. I know your heart is good."

Matt badly wanted to argue his case, but he knew Celia wouldn't believe him. His fingerprints were on the laudanum bottle.

"I grew up in Aztlán," she began, "in the same village where El Patrón was born. It was poor then and it's worse now. Nothing grew there except weeds, and they were so bitter that they made the donkeys throw up. Even roaches hitchhiked to the next town. That's how bad it was.

"As a girl, I went to work in a *maquiladora* – a factory – on the border. All day I sat on an assembly line and put tiny squares into tiny holes with a pair of tweezers. I thought I'd go blind! We lived in a big grey building with windows so small, you couldn't put your head outside. That was to keep the girls from running away. At night we climbed to the roof and looked north across the border."

"Our border?" asked Matt.

"Yes. The Farms lie between Aztlán and the United States. You couldn't see much because the Farms are dark at night. But *beyond,* where the United States lay, was a great glow in the sky. We knew that under that glow was the most wonderful place. Everyone had his own house and garden. Everyone wore beautiful clothes and ate only the best food. And no one worked more than four hours a day. The rest of the time people flew around in hovercrafts and went to parties."

"Is that true?" asked Matt, who knew almost nothing about the countries bordering the Farms.

"I don't know." Celia sighed. "I guess it's too good to be true."

Matt helped Celia clear the dishes, and together they washed and dried. It reminded him of those days, long ago, when they lived in the little house in the poppy fields.

Matt waited patiently for Celia to pick up the story again. He knew if he pushed her too hard, she'd stop talking about her past.

"I lived in that grey building forever, getting older and older. No parties, no boyfriends, no nothing," she said at last after the dishes were put away. "I hadn't heard from my family in years. Maybe they were all dead. I didn't know. The only change in my life happened after I learned to cook. I was taught by an old *curandera,* a healing woman who took care of the girls. She taught me all kinds of things.

"I was the best student she ever had, and soon I got off the assembly line and started cooking for the whole building. I had more freedom; I went to the markets to buy herbs and food. And one day I met a coyote."

"An animal?" Matt was confused.

"No, darling. A man who takes people over the border. You pay him and he helps you go to the United States. Only first you have to cross the Farms." Celia shivered. "What an idiot I was! Those people don't help you go anywhere. They lead you straight to the Farm Patrol.

"I packed everything I owned, including the Virgin I had brought from my village. About twenty of us crossed into the Ajo Mountains, and that's where the coyote abandoned us. We panicked like a bunch of scared rabbits. We tried to climb down a cliff, and a woman fell into a gorge and died. We abandoned most of our belongings so we could move faster, but it didn't do us any good. The Farm Patrol was waiting at the foot of the mountains.

"I was taken to a room, and my backpack was dumped out. 'Be careful!' I cried. 'Don't hurt the Virgin!' That's how She got the chip on Her robe – when the Patrol dumped Her on the floor.

"They laughed, and one of them was going to crush Her with his foot when someone shouted 'Stop!' from the doorway. Everyone snapped to attention then, you better believe it. It was El Patrón in his wheelchair. He was stronger in those days, and he liked to check up on things personally.

" 'Your accent is familiar. Where are you from?' he asked. I told him the name of my village, and he was very surprised.

'That's my hometown,' he said. 'Don't tell me the old rat's nest is still there.'

"'It is,' I said, 'only the rats have moved on to a better slum.'

"He laughed and asked if I had any skills. From that moment on, I belonged to El Patrón. I'll always belong to him. He'll never let me go."

Matt felt cold. It was good that Celia had crossed over the border. Otherwise, she wouldn't have been around to care for him. But there was something so bleak about her last words: *He'll never let me go.* "I love you, Celia," Matt said impulsively, putting his arms around her.

"And I love you," she said softly, hugging him back.

It felt so safe then. Matt wished he could hide in her apartment forever and forget about the Alacráns, the scornful servants, and MacGregor's clone.

"What happened to the other people who crossed the border?" he asked.

"Them?" Celia's voice was flat and expressionless. "They were all turned into eejits." And she refused to say any more about it.

OLD AGE:
12 TO 14

15

A Starved Bird

The days passed with unvarying sameness. Now Matt could no longer look forward to María's visits. Both she and Emilia had been sent to a convent to turn them into proper young ladies. "María's the one they're trying to tame," Celia said. "Emilia's about as wild as a bowl of oatmeal." Matt asked Celia to send María a letter, but she refused. "The nuns would only hand it over to Senator Mendoza," she said.

Matt tried to imagine what she was doing, but he knew nothing about convents. Did she miss him? Had she forgiven him? Was she visiting Tom instead?

With María and Emilia gone, Benito and Steven went elsewhere for their vacations. Mr Alacrán was away on frequent business trips, and Felicia and El Viejo stayed in their rooms. The halls and gardens were deserted. The servants still went about their duties, but their voices were muted. The house was like a stage with all the actors missing.

One day Matt ordered a Safe Horse from the stables and waited tensely to see whether the request would be denied. It wasn't. An eejit brought out the animal. Matt, uncomfortable, cast his eyes down. Few eejits worked in the house, and he preferred not to think about them. He reached for the reins and glanced up.

It was Rosa.

Matt felt that old thrill of terror, as though he were still a small boy and she his jailer, but this woman posed no threat at all. The hard, bitter lines of her face seemed unconnected with anything going on inside. Rosa gazed straight ahead with her hand outstretched. It was unclear whether she even saw him.

"Rosa?" Matt said.

She looked at him. "Do you wish another horse, Master?" The voice was the same, but the old anger was gone.

"No. This one is fine," Matt said.

Rosa turned and shuffled back into the stables. Her movements were jerky compared to what he remembered.

Matt rode away from the house. The horse walked steadily. It would move in a straight line until Matt told it to go right or left, and it wouldn't pass the boundary implanted in its brain. *Like Rosa,* Matt thought. For the first time he realised what a terrible thing it was to be an eejit. He hadn't known any of the others before their operation. They were simply there to do boring jobs. But Rosa had been a real, though cruel and violent, person. Now she was merely a shadow with the life sucked out of her.

On an impulse he turned the animal west rather than east and skirted the poppy fields to where he thought Celia's little house lay. He shaded his eyes to make out its shape. This part of the Farm was at an early stage in the growing cycle. The plants were hardly more than a grey-green shadow, and a gentle mist wafted up from sprinklers in the ground. The air was sharp with the smell of wet dust.

A few eejits bent over the earth, tweezing up weeds and squashing bugs. This was their country, the country of the eejits. Matt wondered what would happen if they suddenly woke up. Would they turn on him like the villagers in that movie about Frankenstein? But they wouldn't wake up. They couldn't. They'd go on weeding until the foreman told them to stop.

Matt couldn't find the little house. It must have been torn down when he and Celia moved. Sighing, he turned east toward the oasis in the mountains.

When he got to the water trough, Matt alighted and filled it from the pump as Tam Lin had always done. "Drink," he told the horse. Obediently, it slurped until Matt decided it had had enough. "Stop," he said. He led it into the shade and told it to wait.

He felt a whisper of fear as he walked into the mountains. This time he was alone. This time no one would come to his aid if he fell off a rock or was bitten by a rattlesnake. He got to the hole in the rock and climbed through. The pool was low since it was the end of the dry season and the thunderstorms of August and September were yet to come. The branches of a creosote bush trembled on the other side as some animal slunk into hiding. Wind whistled through the bare rocks with a lonely, keening sound.

Matt sat down and took out a sandwich. He didn't know what he was doing here.

At the upper end of the little valley was the grapevine sprawled over its man-made arbour. Someone had lived here long ago, and the vine had grown so heavy, part of the arbour had collapsed. Matt walked carefully into its shade, keeping his eyes peeled for snakes that also liked the cool dark.

He saw a large metal chest on the ground. On one side was a roll of blankets and a cache of water bottles. Matt halted. His heart started to gallop. He glanced around to see where the intruder was hiding.

There was nothing except the keening wind and the rasping call of a cactus wren somewhere in the rocks.

Matt retreated into the cover of a creosote bush. The oily leaves broke against his skin and released a pungent smell. Who had dared to invade his special place? Was it an Illegal trying to the reach the United States? Or had one of the eejits woken up?

As Matt considered the possibilities, he realised that no Illegal could have hauled a metal chest through the dry hills and canyons Celia had described. And no eejit ever woke up.

Heart thumping, Matt ventured from his hiding place and examined the chest. It was secured by two metal clasps. Carefully, he undid the clasps and lifted the lid.

On top of neatly packed parcels was a note. *Deer Matt,* it began. Matt sat back in the dirt and breathed deeply to contain his shock. This stuff was for *him*. When he'd calmed down, he took up the note again.

Deer Matt, it said. *Im a lousy writer so this wont be long. El Patron says I have to go with him. I cant do anything about it. I put supplise in this chest plus books. Yu never know when yu mite need things. Yor frend Tam Lin.*

It was written in a large, childish scrawl. It surprised Matt to see how poor the man's writing was, when his speech was so intelligent. Tam Lin had said he'd never been educated, and here was the proof of it.

Matt eagerly unpacked the chest. He found beef jerky, rice,

beans, dried onions, coffee, and chocolate. He found a bottle of water purification pills, a first-aid kit, a pocketknife, matches, and lighter fluid. *Pots in blanckets* said another note halfway down. Matt immediately unwrapped the blankets and found a nest of cooking utensils and a metal mug.

At the bottom of the chest were books. One had foldout maps and another was titled *A History of Opium*. Two more were manuals on camping and survival. A note at the very bottom read, *Keep chest clossed. Koyotes eat food. Books tu.*

Matt sat back and admired the treasures. Tam Lin hadn't deserted him after all. He read and reread the last words of the note and it was like drinking many cups of fresh, cool water: *Yor frend Tam Lin*. Then Matt packed everything up, stowed the chest in the shadows, and made his way back home.

The house was in turmoil when he got there. Hovercrafts landed, servants ran to and fro. Matt found Celia waiting anxiously inside the apartment. "Where have you been, *mi vida?*" she cried. "I was about to send out a search party. I've laid your suit on the bed."

"What happened? Why is everyone running around?" he asked.

"No one told you?" She distractedly pulled off his shirt and thrust a towel at him. "Take a quick shower before you get dressed. El Viejo is dead." Celia hastily crossed herself and left.

Matt stared at the towel as he collected his thoughts. The old man's death wasn't a surprise — he hadn't emerged from his room in months, and he'd clearly been very sick. Matt tried to feel sorry, but he hardly knew the man.

Matt showered and dressed as rapidly as possible. "I didn't tell you to wash your hair," wailed Celia when she saw him. She combed it down frantically. She was wearing a fine black dress with jetbeads sewn on the front, and Matt thought she looked strange without her apron.

"El Patrón insisted on us being present," Celia said as they hurried through the halls.

They came out to the salon. The statues had been replaced by pots of flowers. Black crepe hung in swags around the walls, and hundreds of holy candles glittered in a rack at one end of the room. The smoke and pall of incense made Matt break into a coughing fit. Everyone — and there were at least fifty people in the salon — turned to frown at him. Celia handed him the inhaler she always carried.

Presently Matt's wheezing subsided and he was able to look around the room. In the centre was an elegantly carved coffin with brass handles. Inside, looking more like a starved bird than anything else, was El Viejo. He was dressed in a black suit, and his sharp nose stuck up like a beak against the ivory silk lining.

Celia wept softly, dabbing her eyes with a handkerchief, and Matt felt bad about that. He hated to see her cry. The mourners kept their distance from the coffin. They clustered against the walls and made low conversation. Matt saw Benito, Steven, and Emilia. Steven and Emilia were holding hands.

The crowd thickened. MacGregor entered, looking thirty years younger than the last time Matt had seen him. Now he really did look like Tom, and Matt felt an unreasoning surge of dislike. The hot, close smell of burning candles made his head swim. He wished he could go outside. On the far side of the house was a huge swimming pool that was hardly used by any-one except Felicia, when she was sober. Matt thought about the swimming pool now, with its cool blue depths. He imagined himself skimming along the bottom.

"Don't say anything," whispered Celia in his ear. If she hadn't waked him, he would have missed María's entrance on the far side of the salon. She was taller and thinner, and she looked very adult in her slim, black dress. Her hair fell in a shiny veil over her shoulders. She wore diamond earrings and a small, black hat trimmed with more diamonds. Matt thought she was the most beautiful thing he'd ever seen.

She was holding hands with Tom.

Matt felt Celia grip his arm. He stared at María, willing her to look at him, willing her to drop Tom's hand or (even better) push Tom away. María melted into the crowd without once glancing Matt's way.

El Patrón was rolled into the salon by Tam Lin. Mr Alacrán was with them, and for the first time Matt saw signs of real grief on someone's face. Mr Alacrán went up to El Viejo's casket and kissed the old man on the forehead. El Patrón looked annoyed and signalled Tam Lin to wheel him along the crowd so he could be greeted by people.

Matt waited tensely. He wanted desperately to thank Tam Lin, but now was obviously a bad time. Somehow Matt knew the contents of the metal chest were forbidden. He didn't want to get Tam Lin into trouble. But everything stopped when a door opened and the officiating priest entered. He was followed by boys swinging balls of fuming incense and a children's choir.

Their sweet voices stilled the conversation in the salon. They were dressed in white robes like a troop of angels. Their hair was neatly combed and their faces scrubbed and shining. They were all about seven years old and they were all eejits.

Matt could tell by the empty look in their eyes. They sang beautifully – no one was more able to appreciate good music than Matt – but they didn't understand what they were singing.

The children took up their station at the head of the casket. "Stay," said the priest in a low voice. Matt had never seen a priest except on TV. Celia went to a small church a mile away through the poppy fields. She walked there early on Sunday mornings, along with a few other servants. She wasn't allowed to eat or even drink coffee before setting out, which was a great hardship for her. But she never missed a service. She never took Matt along, either.

"Be still," said the priest to the children's choir. They fell silent at once. He intoned a prayer and ended by sprinkling holy water over El Viejo. It didn't eat holes in El Viejo's suit, the way the Flying Priest's holy water ate through demons on TV. Matt had the vague idea it was something like acid.

"Let us remember the life of our companion," the priest said in a deep, impressive voice. He beckoned to the audience, but no one responded. Finally, Mr Alacrán said a few words, and then the priest told everyone to file past to say their final good-byes. Matt looked up at Celia, hoping they could go now. She seemed grimly determined. She pushed him ahead as they joined the long line of mourners shuffling past the casket.

What am I supposed to do now? Matt thought. He tried to see what other people were doing when they reached the casket. Most merely nodded and hurried out of the salon. When Matt and Celia arrived, Celia crossed herself and murmured, "May God be merciful to you." Matt felt a hand clamp down on his shoulder and pull him out of the line.

"What . . . is *this?*" growled the priest. He was a lot bigger close up than he was at a distance.

"El Patrón wanted him to come," Celia said.

"*This* does not belong here!" the priest thundered. "This

unbaptised limb of Satan has no right to make a mockery of this rite! Would you bring a *dog* to church?" The people in line had halted. Their eyes glittered with malice.

"Please. Ask El Patrón," begged Celia. Matt couldn't see why she wanted to argue. They weren't going to win, and he couldn't bear all those eyes watching him be humiliated. He looked around desperately, but El Patrón had already gone.

"Saint Francis would take a dog to church," María said in a clear, high voice. Where had she come from? Matt turned to find her right behind him. She was even more beautiful close up.

"Saint Francis took a wolf to church," she said. "He loved all animals."

"María," groaned Emilia, who wasn't far behind. "Dada will have a fit when he finds out what you're doing."

"Saint Francis preached to a wolf and told him not to eat lambs," María went on, ignoring Emilia.

"Miss Mendoza," said the priest, speaking much more respectfully than he had to Celia, "I'm sure your father likes you to express your opinions, but believe me, I'm an expert in these matters. Saint Francis spoke to the wolf *outside* the church."

"Then I shall too," María said haughtily. She took Matt's hand and led him back along the line of mourners.

"You're going to be in big trouble when Dada finds out," called Emilia.

"Be sure and tell him!" retorted María.

Matt was in a kind of daze. Celia hadn't come with them. He was all alone with María, being pulled through the halls to some place she'd decided was safe. He was aware only of the soft warmth of her hand and the spicy perfume she was wearing. It wasn't until they were inside with the door closed that Matt realised they were in the music room.

María pulled off her hat and ran her fingers through her hair, and suddenly she looked like a little girl again. "It's so hot!" she complained. "I don't know why El Patrón doesn't allow air-conditioning."

"He wants everything to be like his old village," Matt said. He could hardly believe his good luck. María was here! And with him!

"Then why doesn't he import rats and cockroaches too? From what I hear, his village was *covered* with them."

"He only wanted the good things from it," said Matt, trying to pull himself out of his daze.

"Oh, let's not waste our time with that!" cried María, throwing her arms around him and giving him a big kiss. "There! That shows I've forgiven you. Gosh, I've missed you!"

"You have?" Matt tried to kiss her back, but she slid out of his arms. "Then why did you avoid me after – after . . . the hospital?" Now he'd done it. He'd reminded her of MacGregor's clone.

"It was a shock," María said, growing solemn. "I knew – I didn't want to tell you – "

"Knew what?"

"Hey, is that people in the hall?"

Matt heard the noise outside as well. He pulled María to the closet, pressed the hidden switch and heard her gasp as the secret passageway opened.

"It's like a spy novel," she whispered as he drew her inside. Matt closed the door and found the flashlight he kept by the entrance. They tiptoed along the passage with Matt in the lead. Finally, he allowed her to stop and catch her breath.

16

BROTHER WOLF

I t's even hotter in here than outside," María said, wiping her
face.

"I'll find an empty room we can hide in," said Matt. He
showed her the hidden peepholes, and María was both repelled
and fascinated.

"Don't tell me you sit in here and *watch* people," she said.

"No!" Matt was offended. He wasn't above eavesdropping at
a dinner where he wasn't invited. That was simply getting back at
people who'd snubbed him. But what she'd suggested was nasty,
like peeking through a keyhole. "You must think I'm a creep!"

"Hey, I'm not the one with the secret passage. Who do you
think made it?" María's whisper sounded explosive next to
Matt's ear. It tickled and sent shivers down his neck.

"El Patrón, I guess," said Matt.

"That figures. He's so paranoid, he's always spying on
people."

"Maybe he needs to."

"He can't be using the peepholes anymore," said María. "Can you imagine trying to squeeze a wheelchair in here?"

"Don't make fun of him."

"I'm not. Really. Listen, can we find a room before I melt into a puddle?"

Matt rejected several rooms because he'd seen people in them, but at a bend in the passage he remembered a warehouse with computers and other equipment. Everything had been covered with plastic sheets. It seemed to be a place for things El Patrón needed but didn't want in full view to spoil the effect of his old-fashioned house.

Matt helped María over a tangle of wires into the darkened room. "Wow! It's cool in here," she said.

It was more than cool, Matt realised. It was icy. It smelled faintly of chemicals. A slight breeze stirred the hair on his arms, and a hum vibrated almost out of the range of his hearing. "I guess computers need air-conditioning," he said.

"Isn't that just typical," María said. "*We* can shrivel up in the heat, but the machines get a first-class hotel room."

They tiptoed around the equipment and spoke in whispers. Matt saw things glowing under the plastic covers, so the machines were on. What were they doing and what were they for?

"Let's sit somewhere and talk," whispered María. Matt found a nook between two shrouded hulks where he thought they might be warmer. The coolness, at first so welcome, was beginning to get uncomfortable.

They sat close together, as they had often done before María was sent away. "I decided to forgive you after reading *The Little Flowers of Saint Francis*," María began. "You remember the wolf

I talked about? Well, he was a monster who terrorised everybody until Saint Francis gave him a talking-to. He was sweet as a lamb and never ate anything but vegetables after that."

"I didn't know wolves could digest vegetables," said Matt, who had studied biology.

"That's not the point. Saint Francis didn't say, 'I'm going to punish you for all the wickedness you've done.' He said, 'Brother Wolf, today is a new day and you're going to turn over a new leaf.'"

Matt held his tongue. He wanted to say that he hadn't poisoned Furball and didn't need forgiveness, but he didn't want to spoil María's mood.

"So I realised I was being unfair and should forgive you. After all, wolves don't know they aren't supposed to eat peasants." María leaned against him in the blue shadows of the equipment room. Matt's heart turned over. She was so beautiful, and he had missed her so much.

"Thank you," he said.

"So you have to promise to be good."

"Okay," said Matt, who would have promised her anything at that point.

"You have to mean it, Brother Wolf. No running off to the henhouse for snacks."

"I promise. What do I call you? Saint María?"

"Oh, no!" María said. "I'm not a saint. I have all kinds of faults."

"I don't believe it," said Matt.

María told him about how she struggled not to lose her temper at Emilia, how she copied someone's paper when she forgot to do her homework, and how she ate ice cream when she was supposed to be fasting. Matt, who didn't bother about being good, thought it a waste of time to worry about faults. "Have you been baptised?" he asked.

"Yes. They did it when I was a baby."

"Is it a good thing?"

"Well, of course. Without it, you can't go to heaven."

Matt didn't know much about heaven. Hell was mentioned a lot more often in the shows he watched on TV. "What did the priest mean – that I'm an unbaptised limb of Satan?"

María leaned against him and sighed. "Oh, Matt. I'm sure Saint Francis wouldn't have agreed with him. You aren't evil, only . . . "

"Only what?"

"You don't have a soul, so you can't be baptised. All animals are like that. I think it's unfair and sometimes I don't believe it. After all, what would heaven be without birds or dogs or horses? And what about trees and flowers? They don't have souls either. Does that mean heaven looks like a cement car park? I suppose this is what the nuns call a theological problem."

"Do animals go to hell when they die?" said Matt.

"No! Of course not! You can't get *there* without a soul either. I guess – I thought about it a lot when Furball died – you simply *go out*. Like a candle. I'm sure it doesn't hurt. You're there one minute and then you're not. Oh, let's not talk about this!"

Matt was astonished to find her crying. She did cry a lot, he remembered. He hugged her and kissed her tear-streaked face. "I don't mind," he whispered. "If I had a soul, I'd probably wind up in hell anyway."

They sat together for a long time saying nothing. The room was so cold, they both were shivering. "I do like being with you," María said at last. "There's nobody at my school so easy to talk to."

"Can't you visit me again?" said Matt.

"Dada says I have to stay away. He thinks – Oh no! I hear voices again."

Matt and María jumped up and ran for the door at the same time. She tripped on the wires, and he caught her and boosted her into the passageway. He slid the door shut just as a door on the opposite side of the room opened. They stood for a moment to catch their breaths.

"Warm at last." María contentedly sighed, rubbing her arms. Matt listened attentively to the voices outside.

"That's Tom," he said quietly.

"Really? Where's the peephole? Let me see."

"I thought you didn't like spying on people."

"I only want a peek." María put her eye to the hole. "It *is* Tom. And Felicia." Matt put his ear to the wall so he could hear better.

". . . find them here . . . if they're anywhere in the . . . house," said Felicia's slow, hesitant voice. For an instant Matt thought she meant the passage, but then he heard the sound of chairs being moved and the whir of a machine.

"Hey, that's the salon," said Tom. "It's completely empty. El Viejo is all alone."

"No one cares," Felicia murmured. "He was . . . unusable."

"What do you mean?" said Tom.

Felicia laughed, a shrill, alarming sound. "His liver was . . . gone. His heart . . . dried up. You can't get transplants from a cancer patient."

"I guess he's just compost now." Tom laughed. Felicia laughed too.

Matt was deeply shocked. He couldn't produce tears for El Viejo, but he did feel sorry for him, lying there like a starved bird in his silk-lined coffin. Matt gently moved María aside. She didn't protest as he'd expected. She seemed as stunned by what she'd just heard as he was.

Matt saw that one of the large computer screens was brilliantly lit. Then he realised it wasn't a computer at all, but some kind of camera. He saw an image of El Viejo with his beaklike nose poking out of the casket. The picture blurred and shifted. Tom was working the controls.

"That's the music room," said Felicia.

Matt saw the grand piano, stacks of music, and María's black hat sitting on a table.

"They were there!" cried Tom. He moved the camera lens to show all angles of the room.

Felicia took over now, and she seemed to have a lot of experience using the viewing screen. She moved rapidly through the house, even showing the servants' quarters and storage closets. She paused over Celia's apartment. Celia had collapsed in a big easy chair with Tam Lin not far away.

"Where could they have gone?" said Tam Lin, pacing up and down with the restless energy Matt remembered so well. The bodyguard's voice was tinny and faint until Felicia increased the volume.

"Maybe they aren't even in the house," said Celia.

"He wouldn't take her there," Tam Lin said.

"How do you know? If he was desperate enough – "

"Careful," said Tam Lin, looking straight into the view screen. Celia changed the subject and began discussing the funeral.

"Blast! They know about the cameras," said Tom.

"Tam Lin knows . . . everything," said Felicia. "El Patrón dotes on him."

"Take her *where?*" shouted Tom, smashing his fist onto a table covered with shrouded machines. Something fell over and broke. Felicia grabbed his hand.

Matt knew what Celia was talking about. Tam Lin must have told her about the hidden oasis. Matt hadn't considered taking María there, and he certainly couldn't do it now with everyone hunting for him.

"They could be . . . outside," murmured Felicia. She manipulated the image to show the stables, the swimming pool, the gardens. Matt was startled to see the lotus pond and a pair of ibises lazily stretching their wings.

"Let me see," whispered María. Matt moved to one side and pressed his ear to the wall again so he wouldn't miss anything.

"Remember this?" said Felicia's slow, insinuating voice.

"That's where Furball got snuffed, isn't it?" said Tom.

María gasped. Matt realised they must be looking at the pump house.

"You know, I saw . . . the little beast that day," said Felicia.

"Furball?" Tom said.

Felicia giggled. "I meant the clone. I saw . . . wonderful, *talented* Matt . . . sneaking out of the Mendoza apartment . . . with a dog in a bag. *What's going on?* I thought, so I followed him."

There was a pause. Then Tom said, "Amazing! You can see inside!"

"The cameras are everywhere. El Patrón used to watch . . . everything. But now he's too old. He turned the job over to his security team. They don't bother . . . unless there's visitors. I spend a lot of time here."

"It's so cold!"

"The machines are more . . . efficient near freezing. I wear a coat and hardly notice," said Felicia. Matt could believe that. She was so drugged, she probably wasn't much warmer than poor El Viejo in his casket.

"Did you see Matt kill the dog?" Tom asked eagerly. Matt was startled. Why was Tom asking that question when he himself had done the crime? María's body wriggled with indignation. Matt hoped she wouldn't forget herself and yell at them.

"Matt didn't . . . do it."

María flinched as though she'd been stung.

"Oh, he had the laudanum," Felicia went on, "but he . . . didn't use it."

"Don't tell me the dog found the bottle and offed himself!"

"Oh . . . no . . . " Felicia fell silent. Sometimes it took her several minutes to marshal her thoughts and continue a conversation. Matt wished he could see what was happening, but he had no chance of prying María away from the peephole now. "I went to the lotus pond," Felicia said finally. "I was . . . so *angry* . . . at how they treated you at the birthday party. I wanted to *kill* that abomination El Patrón keeps at his heels."

Matt felt cold. He'd had no idea how much Felicia hated him.

"But I had to be satisfied with . . . that filthy, slavering rat María called a dog. I keep a small amount of laudanum for my nerves."

She keeps about enough to wipe out a city, Matt thought.

"So I poured one of . . . *my* bottles on the hamburger that idiot clone left behind. 'Come here, Furball,' I called. He didn't want to leave his bag, but I . . . dumped him out . . . on the meat. He ate the whole thing."

"How long did it take him to die?" Tom asked, but Matt didn't hear the answer. María slid to the floor, and he immediately went to her side. She didn't make a sound, but her body trembled and she turned her head from side to side in an agony of grief.

"He didn't suffer," Matt whispered as he held her. "He didn't even know what was happening." María clung to him, her face streaked by a bar of light from the flashlight Matt had propped against the wall. Finally, she calmed down enough for Matt to check up on what Tom and Felicia were doing. But they had gone, and the viewing screen was shrouded in plastic.

He led her back along the passage. María said nothing, and Matt didn't know what to do. They hadn't gone far before he saw a large shape holding a flashlight coming toward them. There was hardly room for the shape to fit between the walls.

"You utter fools," said Tam Lin in a low voice. "The whole house is buzzing like a ruddy beehive."

"How did you find us?" asked Matt.

"El Patrón told me about this passage. He guessed you'd somehow found it. Damn it, Matt, María's had enough grief out of you."

"Felicia poisoned Furball," María said.

"What are you talking about?" Tam Lin was clearly startled.

"I heard her talking to Tom. She was so — so happy about it. I didn't know people could be that evil." María looked like a wraith in her black dress. Her face was ashen.

"You need to lie down," said Tam Lin. "I'll take you out through El Patrón's study. He'll say you were there all the time. He thinks this is pretty amusing, but Senator Mendoza doesn't think it's funny at all."

"Oh. Dada," María said, as though she'd just remembered she had a father.

"Matt, you wait here a few minutes. When the coast is clear, come out wherever you went in," said the bodyguard.

"The music room," said Matt.

"I should have guessed it. María's hat was there."

"Matt," said María, pulling away from Tam Lin for a moment, "you let me forgive you for something you hadn't done."

"A little extra forgiveness never hurts," said Matt, quoting one of Celia's favourite sayings.

"You probably *liked* letting me make a perfect idiot of myself," she said with a flash of her old spirit.

"I'd never think you were an idiot," said Matt.

"Anyhow, I'm sorry I was unfair to you."

"We can't stay here," said Tam Lin.

"I expect you to keep your promise to be good," she went on, looking at Matt.

"Okay," he replied.

"And, Brother Wolf, I'll miss you." This time María let Tam Lin hurry her down the passage. Matt listened to her footsteps die away in the distance.

17

THE EEJIT PENS

The Mendozas left immediately after María, pale and miserable, emerged from El Patrón's apartment. El Patrón decamped not long afterwards with his bodyguards.

Matt was alone again. He couldn't talk to María or Tam Lin, but knowing they still liked him made all the difference. He studied things he thought they would approve of. He read survival manuals for Tam Lin and a long, confusing book about Saint Francis to please María.

Saint Francis loved everyone from murderous bandits to beggars covered with running sores (there was a picture of one of these in the book). He called a cicada to his finger and said, "Welcome, Sister Cicada. Praise God with your joyful music." Saint Francis spoke to everything – Brother Sun and Sister Moon, Brother Falcon and Sister Lark. It gave Matt the warm feeling that the world was one loving family – *very* unlike the Alacráns.

But would Saint Francis have said, *Brother Clone?*

Matt's warm feelings evaporated. He wasn't part of the natural order. He was an *abomination*.

No matter where he was, Matt couldn't rid himself of the sensation he was being watched. It was bad enough to know the security guards spied on him, but far worse to think of Felicia. She was as awful as Tom, only no one suspected it because she seemed so meek. She reminded Matt of one of those jellyfish he'd seen on TV. They floated around the ocean like fluffy pillows, trailing enough venom to paralyse a swimmer. Why hadn't he realised Felicia hated him?

Well, to be honest, because most people hated him. It was no big thing. But her malevolence was in a class by itself.

Once a week Matt went to the stables and asked for a Safe Horse. Before going out, though, he tried to have a conversation with Rosa. He didn't like her. He wasn't sure why he wanted to wake her up, only that it seemed horrible to see her so changed. If there was anything left of Rosa, it was locked in an iron box. He imagined her banging on the walls with her fists, but no one came to open the door. He'd read that coma victims hear everything people say and need voices to keep their brains alive. And so Matt talked to her about everything he'd seen and done that week. But all Rosa ever replied was, "Do you wish another horse, Master?"

After an hour or so of this, Matt rode off to the oasis. "Hello, Brother Sun," he called. "Would you mind cooling down a bit?" Brother Sun ignored him. "Good morning, Sister Poppies," Matt called to the sea of blinding white flowers. "Hello, Brother and Sister Eejits," he greeted a row of brown-clad workers bending over the fields.

One of the most amazing things about Saint Francis and his

followers was how they gave away their possessions. Saint Francis couldn't wait to strip off his shirt and sandals whenever he saw a poor person without them. Brother Juniper, one of Saint Francis's friends, even went home naked a lot of the time. Matt thought El Patrón would have a heart attack if anyone told him to give away his belongings.

Once Matt passed through the hole in the rock, it was as though he'd arrived in another world. The hawks circled lazily in a bright, blue sky, the jackrabbits crouched in the shade of the creosotes. Fish nibbled bread from Matt's fingers, and coyotes darted forward to gobble down chunks of his sandwiches. None of them cared whether he was a human or a clone.

Matt laid out a sleeping bag under the grape arbour and used a rolled-up blanket for a pillow. He placed a thermos of orange juice within reach and selected a book. This was living! The air smelled faintly of creosote and the yellow sweetness of locust flowers. A large black wasp with scarlet wings ran over the sand, searching for the spiders that were its prey.

"Hello, Brother Wasp," Matt said lazily. The insect dug furiously in the sand, found nothing, and scurried on.

Matt opened *A History of Opium,* one of the books Tam Lin had left him in the chest. He expected it to be a manual about farming, but it was something quite different and exciting. Opium, Matt read, was a whole country. It was a long, thin strip of land lying between the United States and Aztlán.

One hundred years ago there had been trouble between the United States and Aztlán, which was called Mexico in those days. Matt vaguely remembered Celia saying something about it. Many thousands of Mexicans had flooded across the border in search of work. *A drug dealer named Matteo Alacrán —*

Matt sat up straight. That was El Patrón's name! One hundred years ago he would have been a strong and active man.

This person, the book went on to say, was one of the richest and most powerful men in the world, even though his business was illegal.

Drugs illegal? thought Matt. *What a strange idea.*

Matteo Alacrán formed an alliance with the other dealers and approached the leaders of the United States and Mexico. *"You have two problems,"* he said. *"First, you cannot control your borders, and second, you cannot control us."*

He advised them to combine the problems. If both countries set aside land along their common border, the dealers would establish Farms and stop the flow of Illegals. In return, the dealers would promise not to sell drugs to the citizens of the United States and Mexico. They would peddle their wares in Europe, Asia, and Africa instead.

It was a pact made in hell, said the book.

Matt put it down. He couldn't see anything wrong with the plan. It seemed to have done everything it promised. He looked at the title page. The author was Esperanza Mendoza, and the Anti-Slavery Society of California was the publisher. Now that he looked more closely, he saw the book was printed on cheap, yellow paper. It didn't look like something you could take seriously. Matt read on.

At first, the book explained, Opium was simply a no-man's-land, but through the years it had prospered. Different areas were ruled by different families, much like the kingdoms of medieval Europe. A council of Farmers was established, which dealt with international problems and kept peace between the various Farms. Most families controlled small areas, but two were large enough to dictate policy. The MacGregors ruled the land near San Diego, and the Alacráns had a vast empire stretching from central California all across Arizona and into New Mexico.

Gradually, Opium changed from a no-man's-land to a real country. And its supreme leader, dictator, and führer was Matteo Alacrán.

Matt stopped reading so he could savour the words. His heart swelled with pride. He didn't know what a führer was, but it was obviously something very good.

A more evil, vicious, and self-serving man could hardly be imagined, wrote Esperanza on the next line.

Matt threw the book away as hard as he could. It landed in the water with its pages open. How dare she insult El Patrón! He was a genius. How many people could build a country out of nothing, especially someone as poor as El Patrón had been? Esperanza was simply jealous.

But Matt sprang up to rescue the book before it was entirely ruined. Tam Lin had given it to him, and that made it valuable. He dried it out carefully and packed it away in the metal chest.

On the way back Matt stopped at the water purification plant and talked to the foreman. Since Tam Lin's departure, Matt had thought long and hard about the excellent education he'd been given. It didn't make sense for him to spend the rest of his life as an exotic pet. El Patrón didn't waste money like that.

No, Matt realised, the old man meant him to have a higher destiny. He could never reach the status of Benito or Steven, not being human, but he could help them. And so Matt had begun to study how the enterprise of running an opium empire worked. He saw how opium was planted, processed, and marketed. He watched how the eejits were moved from field to field, how often they were watered, and how many food pellets they were allowed.

When I'm in charge — Matt quickly adjusted his thought: *When I'm* helping *the person in charge, I'll free the eejits.* Surely opium could be grown by normal people. They might not be as efficient, but anything was better than a mindless army of slaves. Now that Matt had observed Rosa, he understood that.

He asked the plant foreman about the underground river that flowed from the Gulf of California hundreds of miles away. It was used to supply water to the Alacrán estate, but it smelled — before it was purified — terrifyingly bad.

The plant foreman refused to meet Matt's eyes. Like most humans, he didn't like talking to clones, but he also didn't want to anger El Patrón. "Why does the water smell like that?" Matt asked.

"Dead fish. Chemicals," the foreman replied, not looking up.

"But you take those out."

"Yes."

"Where do you put them?"

"Wastelands," the man said, pointing north. He kept his answers as brief as possible.

Matt shaded his eyes as he looked to the north. A heat haze shimmered over the desert, and he saw a series of ridges that might be buildings. "There?" he asked doubtfully.

"Yes," the foreman replied.

Matt turned the horse and started heading northward to get a clearer view. The smell was so vile, he feared he might have an asthma attack. He felt for his inhaler.

They *were* buildings. They stretched in long rows with doors and dark little windows every so often. The roofs were so low, Matt wondered whether a person could stand up inside. The windows were covered with iron bars. Could this be where the eejits lived? The idea was appalling.

The closer Matt got, the stronger the stench became. It was a compound of rotten fish, excrement, and vomit, with a sweet chemical odour that was worse than the other smells put together.

Matt grasped the inhaler. He knew he should leave at once, but the buildings were too intriguing. He could see skeletons of fish and seashells embedded in the dirt around them. It seemed the whole place was built on waste from the Gulf of California.

Matt circled around the end of one of the buildings and rode down into a depression that must have been used for waste. The evil smell made Matt's eyes water, and he could barely focus on the dense yellow sludge on the bottom. The horse stumbled. Its legs collapsed beneath it, and Matt had to throw his arms around its neck to keep from being catapulted into the sludge.

"Get up! Get up!" he ordered, but the horse was incapable of obeying. It sat on the ground with its legs folded up under it. Then Matt felt himself getting dizzy. He threw himself off the horse and sucked desperately at the inhaler. His lungs filled with liquid. A terror of drowning swept over him, and he tried to crawl away from the trough. His fingers dug into the rotting, fish-slimed soil.

A pair of hands yanked him up. He was dragged a short way and thrown into the back of a vehicle. Matt felt the motor start. The vehicle moved away in a plume of dust that made him cough. He tried to get up and was instantly slammed down by a boot on his chest.

Shocked, Matt stared up at the coldest pair of eyes he'd ever seen. At first he thought he was looking at Tam Lin, but this person was younger and leaner. He had the same wavy, brown hair and blue eyes, the same physical alertness, but none of the good humour Matt was used to seeing in the bodyguard's face.

"Where'd you get a horse?" the man demanded. "Where'd you get the brains to make a run for it?"

"He's not an eejit, Hugh," said another voice. Matt looked up to see another man, similar to the first one.

"Then you're an Illegal," snarled Hugh. "I reckon we'll run you to the hospital and let 'em put a clamp in your brain."

"You do that," Matt said with his heart beating very fast. He was afraid, but Tam Lin had taught him it was foolhardy to show weakness. *Act like you're in control,* the bodyguard had said, *and nine times out of ten, you'll get away with it. Most people are cowards underneath.* Matt realised these men belonged to the Farm Patrol and thus, judging by Celia's stories, were very dangerous.

"You do that," Matt repeated, "and I'll tell the doctor how you treated El Patrón's clone."

"Say what?" said Hugh, lifting his boot from Matt's chest.

"I'm El Patrón's clone. I was visiting the water purification plant and got lost. Better yet, you can take me to the Big House and I'll send a message to him." Matt was very far from feeling confident, but he'd observed El Patrón give orders many times. He knew exactly how to reproduce the cold, deadly voice that got results.

"Crikey! He even sounds like the old vampire," said the second man.

"Shut your cake hole!" snarled Hugh. "Look, we weren't expecting you out there, Master, uh, Master – what do we call you?"

"Matteo Alacrán," Matt said, and was gratified to see the men flinch.

"Well, Master Alacrán, we weren't expecting you, and you were by the eejit pens, so it was a natural mistake – "

"Did it occur to you to ask what I was doing out there?" Matt said, narrowing his eyes as El Patrón did when he wanted to be particularly menacing.

"I know we should've, sir. We're really very, very sorry. We're taking you straight to the Big House, and we're most humbly begging your pardon, aren't we, Ralf?"

"Oh, yes, indeed," said the second man.

"What about my horse?"

"We'll fix that up." Ralf banged on the cab of the truck. A window opened, and he shouted instructions inside. "We'll radio for a Patrol to collect the nag. It was in a bad way from the dead air, sir. It might not survive."

"Dead air?" said Matt, startled enough to drop out of his El Patrón act.

"It sometimes happens around that trough," said Ralf. "The air doesn't move, and the carbon dioxide builds up. It's like being in a mine."

"I lost a brother like that," remarked Hugh.

"You can't tell until it's too late," said Ralf. "The nearby pens are usually okay, but on still nights we make the eejits sleep in the fields."

Matt was amazed. "Why don't you clean up the trough?"

Ralf seemed honestly puzzled by the idea. "It's how we've always done things, Master Alacrán. The eejits don't care."

Well, that's true, thought Matt. Even if the eejits knew about the danger, they couldn't flee unless they were ordered to do so.

Now that Matt appeared to accept the men's apology, they became almost friendly. They didn't act like most people did when told Matt was a clone. They were wary but not hostile. In fact, they behaved a lot like Tam Lin.

"Are you Scottish?" Matt asked.

"Oh, no," said Hugh. "Ralf here is from England, and I'm from Wales. Wee Wullie in the cab is Scottish, though. But we all like to play soccer and thump heads."

Matt remembered something El Patrón had said long ago about Tam Lin and Daft Donald: *I picked up this lot in Scotland, breaking heads outside a soccer field. Always choose your bodyguards from another country. They find it harder to make alliances and betray you.*

"Soccer sounds a lot like war," Matt said.

Both Ralf and Hugh laughed. "It is, lad. It is," said Hugh.

"The fine thing about soccer," said Ralf, with a distant look in his eyes, "is that you enjoy both the game and the trimmings."

"Trimmings?" Matt said.

"Ah, yes. That which *surrounds* the game – the buildup, the crush of fans in the trains . . . "

"The parties," said Hugh, with a dreamy look on his face.

"The parties," agreed Ralf. "You crowd into a pub with your mates and drink until the owner throws you out."

"*If* he can throw you out," Hugh amended.

"And then, either before or after, you run into the fans on the other side. So of course you have to set them straight."

"That's when the head thumping occurs," Matt guessed.

"Yes. Nothing finer, especially if you win," said Ralf.

The truck followed a zigzag course through the poppy fields. Matt saw the same eejits he'd observed that morning. They were still bending over the ripe seedpods, but he felt no impulse to call them brothers. They weren't brothers and never would be until they lost the clamps in their brains.

"If you liked it so much, why did you come here?" Matt asked Hugh and Ralf.

The men lost their dreamy expressions. Their eyes became cold and distant. "Sometimes . . . ," Hugh began, and then fell silent.

"Sometimes the head thumping goes too far," Ralf finished for him. "It's okay to kill people in a war; then you're a hero. But in soccer – which is every bit as glorious – you're supposed to shake hands with the enemy afterward."

"Kiss his ruddy backside, more like," said Hugh in disgust.

"And we didn't like that, see."

Matt thought he understood. Hugh, Ralf, and Wee Wullie in the cab were murderers. They were the ideal candidates for the Farm Patrol. They would have to be loyal to El Patrón, or he would dump them into the arms of whatever police were looking for them.

The lush gardens and red tile roofs of the Big House were visible now. Nothing could have been further from the long, low dwellings where the eejits lived – that is, when they weren't sleeping in the fields to keep from being gassed.

"Did Tam Lin kill anyone?" Matt said. He didn't much want to ask, but this might be his only opportunity to find out.

Hugh and Ralf exchanged looks. "He's in a class by himself," said Ralf. "He's a bloody *terrorist.*"

"Can't think why El Patrón trusts him so much," said Hugh.

"They're like father and son – "

"Put a cork in it! Can't you see who we're talking to?" Hugh said.

The house was near, and Matt was afraid they'd let him out before he learned what he wanted to know. "What did Tam Lin do?" he urged.

"*Only* set a bomb outside the prime minister's house in London," replied Hugh. "He was a Scottish nationalist, see.

Wanted to bring back Bonnie Prince Charlie or some other fat slug. He wasn't motivated by beer like the rest of us."

"No, he's a cut above," Ralf said, "with his fancy ethics and social conscience."

"It's a shame a school bus pulled up at the wrong moment," said Hugh. "The blast killed twenty kiddies."

"That's what social conscience gets you," Ralf said as he helped Matt climb down. The truck drove off at once – the men seemed eager to get away, or perhaps they were forbidden to show themselves around the civilised halls of El Patrón's mansion.

18

The Dragon Hoard

"Wake up!" said Celia, so close to his ear that Matt fell out of bed with his arms flailing.

"What's wrong?" he cried, trying to untangle himself from the sheets.

She yanked the sheets away and pulled him to his feet. Even though Matt was as tall as Celia now, she was stronger. It must have been all those years of lugging pots of stew around the kitchen. She pushed him into the bathroom.

"Should I get dressed?" Matt asked.

"There's no time. Just wash your face."

Matt splashed water on his face in an effort to wake up. He'd gone straight to bed after the Farm Patrol had brought him home. He'd felt sick from the bad air at the eejit pens.

He was disturbed by the conflicting images he had of the Farm Patrol. Before he had met them, Celia had filled Matt's head with enough stories to make his blood run cold. They were creatures of the night, she said, like the *chupacabras*. They infested the trails that wound out of the Ajo Mountains, and they hunted their prey with heat-sensitive goggles.

Matt remembered Hugh's cold eyes as the man slammed him onto the bed of the truck. To Hugh — at that point, at least — Matt was only a rat to be crushed underfoot.

But once he'd revealed himself as Matteo Alacrán, the Farm Patrol had transformed themselves into good-natured boys, out for a drink at the pub with a little head thumping for dessert.

Yeah, right, Matt reminded himself. *And Tom's the Angel Gabriel.*

"Hurry up! It's important!" shouted Celia from the other side of the bathroom door.

Matt dried his hands and emerged.

"Have a quesadilla before you go." Was it Matt's imagination, or was Celia's hand shaking as she handed him the plate.

"I'm not hungry," he protested.

"Eat! It's going to be a long night." Celia planted herself at the table and watched as he mechanically chewed. She made him finish every bit of it. The salsa tasted funny, or perhaps it was the aftereffects of the bad air. Matt still felt sick. He'd gone to bed with a metallic taste in his mouth.

The minute Celia and Matt emerged from the apartment, they were met by a pair of bodyguards and hustled through the halls. It must have been very late, because all the corridors were deserted.

They rushed down the front steps and along a winding path, going through darkened gardens until they reached the edge of the desert. Behind them Matt saw the great mansion with its white pillars and orange trees decorated with lights. His bare foot crunched down on a bullhead thorn.

"Ow!" Matt crouched down to remove the thorn.

The bodyguards whisked him off the ground before he could reach his foot. Then Matt realised where they were heading.

"The hospital!" he gasped.

"It's all right, *mi vida,*" said Celia, but it didn't sound all right. Her voice was choked.

"I'm not sick!" Matt cried. He hadn't been to the hospital since he'd seen the thing on the bed.

"You're not sick. El Patrón is," said one of the guards.

Matt stopped struggling then. It was perfectly natural for them to bring him to El Patrón. He loved El Patrón, and the old man would want to see him if he was very sick.

"What happened?" Matt said.

"Heart attack," grunted the guard.

"He's not . . . dead?"

"Not yet."

Matt suddenly felt faint with shock. His vision blurred and his heart pounded. He twisted his head away from the bodyguard's arm and vomited.

"What the – ?" The man gave a startled shout followed by a string of curses. "Crikey! Look at what he did to my suit!"

Matt no longer bothered about the thorn in his foot. Far worse problems overwhelmed him. His stomach felt like he'd swallowed a barrel cactus. Something was wrong with his eyes, too. The hospital walls swarmed with weird colours.

Orderlies lifted him onto a stretcher, quickly wheeled him down a hall, and transferred him to a bed. Someone shouted, "His heartbeat's all over the place!" and someone else ran a needle into his arm. Matt was no longer sure of what was real and what was a nightmare. He seemed to be in the trough at the eejit pens, floating in yellow sludge. He vomited again and again until only a thin, bile-flavoured liquid dribbled out. He saw Furball sitting at the foot of his bed, looking reproachful. Was this how Furball suffered after he'd ingested the laudanum?

Then it was Saint Francis who sat at the foot of the bed. *Brother Wolf, you have done much evil so that all folk are your enemy. Yet I would be your friend,* he said.

Sure. Okay, thought Matt.

The figure of Saint Francis shifted to that of Tam Lin. The bodyguard looked grey and haggard. He bowed his head as though in prayer, although praying was very far from the activities Matt associated with the man.

A faint, blue light illuminated the window. Dawn was approaching, and the horrors of the night were ebbing away. Matt swallowed. His throat was so raw, he wasn't sure he could speak.

"Tam Lin," he croaked. The bodyguard's head snapped up. He looked — Matt couldn't quite put a name to it — both relieved and miserable.

"Don't talk unless you have to, laddie."

"El Patrón," whispered Matt.

"He's stable," said Tam Lin. "They had to do a piggyback transplant on him." Matt raised his eyebrows. "That's where they put a donor heart next to his, to regulate the beat. The donor was — the heart was — too small to do the job by itself."

Matt understood something of the process from his science classes. When someone died in an accident, his organs were used to save the lives of sick people. If the heart El Patrón got was small, it must have come from a child. Maybe that was what had depressed Tam Lin.

"I was at . . . eejit pens," Matt said, and paused to let the pain in his throat subside. "Got sick. Farm Patrol . . . found me."

"You were in the wastelands?" Tam Lin exploded. "Good God! No wonder your heart went wonky! There's a witch's brew of chemicals in that soil. I want you to promise me never, *never* to go there again."

Matt was overwhelmed by the bodyguard's anger. How was he to know where the dangers were when no one told him? His eyes began to leak tears in spite of his efforts not to appear cowardly.

"Heck, I'm sorry," said Tam Lin. "I shouldn't yell at you when you're down. Look, you did a daft thing, nosing around the eejit pens, but maybe it wasn't such a bad mistake. They do say guardian angels guide the steps of idiots." The man looked speculatively at Matt, as though he wanted to say more.

"Sorry," whispered Matt.

"And so you should be. Celia's been wearing a groove in the floor outside for hours. Do you feel up to a little weeping and wailing?"

"If you take . . . thorn out of foot," croaked Matt.

The bodyguard yanked back the covers and found the problem at once. "Bloody idiots," he growled under his breath. "Can't find anything unless it has a bull's-eye painted around it." He pulled out the thorn and swabbed Matt's foot with rubbing alcohol.

Matt wanted badly to ask him questions. *Do you feel sorry about killing twenty children?* for instance, and *Why were you angry about Furball when you did something far worse?* But it took more confidence than Matt had to confront Tam Lin.

Weeping and wailing was exactly what Celia had in mind. She lamented over Matt until he felt hysterical. Still, it was nice to be loved. Even better, she stood up to the hospital orderlies like a tigress. "He's not needed here anymore!" she cried in both English and Spanish.

Matt was loaded onto a stretcher and carried back through the fresh, cool dawn air to Celia's apartment. She tucked him into bed and stood guard over him for the rest of the day.

El Patrón's piggyback heart performed valiantly, but it was clear the old man had passed a kind of milestone. He no longer purred around restlessly in his motor-driven wheelchair. Physical therapists worked his arms and legs to keep the muscles from wasting away, but something vital had gone.

Once El Patrón would have roared with laughter when Tam Lin described how his enemies in the U.S. and Aztlán governments had been disgraced or met with strange accidents. Now he merely nodded. Such pleasures were beyond El Patrón now, and he had few enough left at the age of 148.

Tam Lin had treasures brought from the vast hoard of gifts the old man had amassed. El Patrón ran his gnarled fingers through a box of diamonds and sighed. "In the end they're only rocks."

Matt, who spent much time by El Patrón's bed these days, said, "They're very beautiful."

"I no longer see the life in them. The fire that made men go to war for them is gone."

And Matt understood that what El Patrón missed was not the beauty of the stones, but the joy he once took in owning fine things. He felt very sorry for the old man and didn't know how to comfort him.

"Saint Francis says it's good to give stuff away to the poor," Matt suggested.

The change that came over El Patrón then was extraordinary. He drew himself up in the bed. His eyes flashed, and energy bubbled up from some unknown reservoir. *"Give . . . things . . . away?"* he cried in the voice of a man one hundred years younger. *"Give things away?* I can't believe I heard that! What have they been teaching you!"

"It was only a suggestion," Matt said, aghast at the reaction he'd provoked. "Saint Francis lived a long time ago."

"Give things away?" mused the old man. "Was that why I fought my way out of Durango? Was that why I built an empire greater than El Dorado's? El Dorado bathed in gold dust every day. Did you know that?"

Matt did. El Patrón had told him at least a dozen times.

"He stood on the porch of his golden house," said El Patrón, his black eyes shining, "and his servants dusted him with metal until he shone like the sun. His people worshipped him like a *god.*"

The old man was lost in the fantasy now, and his eyes looked far away to the jungles where the fabled king had lived.

Later Tam Lin complimented Matt on his cleverness. "Brought the roses back to his cheeks, suggesting he give away his dragon hoard. I've been too soft on him. What he really needed was a boot up the rear end."

"What's a dragon hoard?" asked Matt. He and Tam Lin were sitting in Celia's garden sharing a pitcher of lemonade. The bodyguard rarely had time to visit since El Patrón's heart operation. Now, though, because of Matt's incautious remark, the old man was roaming around the house by himself. Tam Lin said he was counting the spoons.

"Ah, now," said Tam Lin. "That's what a dragon amasses from pillaging castles. He keeps his wealth in a deep, dark cave in the mountains, and at night he sleeps on it. It's probably uncomfortable with all those jewel-encrusted daggers and so forth. But the dragon is so covered with scales, he can't feel it."

Matt loved it when Tam Lin spoke of things he must have heard as a child. A soft, musical lilt came into his voice. Matt could imagine him as a boy, long before the events that had blunted his nose and reamed him with scars from head to toe.

"Does it make the dragon happy?" Matt asked.

"Does it make the dragon happy?" echoed Tam Lin. "Why, I never thought of that. I suppose it does. What other pleasure can a creature have whose life consists of making everyone else miserable? To go on, though: The most amazing thing about dragons is that they know when anything, no matter how small, has been taken from their hoard. They can be in a deep slumber. But if some foolish lad creeps up in the middle of the night and takes *only one coin,* the dragon wakes up. You wouldn't want to be that lad then. The dragon burns him right down to a lump of coal. And tosses him onto a heap with the other lumps of coal who made the mistake of trying to steal from a dragon hoard."

Bees hovered over banks of flowers in the warm afternoon sun. Normally, Celia preferred growing vegetables, but she'd recently taken an interest in flowers. Black-eyed Susans climbed one of the walls, and a passionflower vine decorated another. Foxgloves and larkspurs formed a tidy bed framed by other plants Matt didn't recognise. Some were sensitive to sunlight, so Tam Lin had constructed a latticework arbour. Matt thought it made the garden much nicer.

"Does El Patrón know how much stuff he has in his store-room?" Matt knew, of course, who was being referred to with the dragon story.

"Probably not. But you don't want to take a chance on it," said Tam Lin.

19

COMING-OF-AGE

El Patrón's burst of energy didn't last long. Soon he was as pale and weak as ever. He rambled on about his childhood and his seven brothers and sisters who had all died young. He listened to Matt play the guitar, although the boy's fingers weren't long enough yet to play really complicated pieces.

Matt's voice was high and sweet – an angel's voice, Celia said. El Patrón went into a quiet daze when he listened to it. Matt loved to see the old man then, with his eyes half closed and his mouth curved up in a gentle smile. It was better than any compliment.

One day, as Matt was singing a Spanish ballad, his voice cracked. It dropped more than an octave to produce a sound more like a braying donkey than a boy. Embarrassed, he cleared his throat and tried again. At first the song went smoothly, but after a few moments the same thing happened again. Matt stood up in confusion.

"So it has happened," murmured El Patrón from his bed.

"I'm sorry. I'll ask Celia for cough drops," said Matt.

"You don't know what's wrong, do you? You're so cut off from the rest of the world, you don't know."

"I'll be okay tomorrow."

The old man laughed: a dry, dusty sound. "Ask Celia or Tam Lin to explain. Just play for me without singing. That's good enough."

But when Matt asked Celia later, she threw her apron over her face and burst into tears. "What is it? What's wrong?" cried Matt, thoroughly alarmed.

"You've grown up!" wailed Celia from behind the apron.

"Isn't that okay?" Matt's voice, to his horror, boomed out like a bass drum.

"Of course it is, *mi vida,*" said Celia, wiping her eyes with the cloth and putting on an unconvincing smile. "It's always a shock when a little lamb sprouts horns and turns into a big, handsome ram. But it's a good thing, darling, really it is. We must have a party to celebrate."

Matt sat in his room with the guitar as he listened to Celia bang pots in the kitchen. He didn't believe it was a good thing to grow up. He could read Celia's moods no matter how many smiles she produced. He knew that underneath she was upset, and he wanted to know why.

He'd become a man. No, that was wrong. Since he wasn't a boy to begin with, he couldn't turn into a man. He was an adult *clone.* An old memory surfaced of the doctor telling Rosa that clones went to pieces when they got older. Matt no longer feared he would actually fall apart. But what did happen?

Matt felt his face for the first hint of whiskers. There was nothing except a couple of bumps left over from his last bout of acne. *Maybe it's a mistake,* he thought. He attempted the ballad again and made it through only the first line before his throat betrayed him. It was extremely disappointing. His new voice wasn't nearly as good as the old one.

I wonder if María's voice will change too, he thought.

The party that night was subdued. Celia and Tam Lin sat in the courtyard with glasses of champagne to celebrate Matt's new status. As a special treat Matt was allowed one too, although Celia insisted on watering it down with lemonade. Fireflies Matt had ordered from a catalogue pulsed across the warm, humid garden. A heavy odour filled the walled-in space from Celia's new and somewhat creepy plants. She said she had ordered them from a *curandera* in Aztlán.

A sudden thought struck Matt. "How old am I?" he asked, holding out his glass for a refill. Celia, ignoring a frown from Tam Lin, poured him lemonade instead of champagne. "I know I don't have a birthday like humans," Matt said, "but I was born. Or something like it."

"You were harvested," said Tam Lin. His speech was slurred. He had polished off a bottle by himself, and Matt realised he'd never seen the bodyguard drink alcohol before.

"I grew inside a cow. Did she give birth to me like a calf?" Matt saw nothing wrong with being born in a stable. Jesus had found it perfectly acceptable.

"You were harvested," repeated Tam Lin.

"He doesn't need the details," Celia said.

"And I say he does!" roared the man, slamming his fist on the picnic table. Both Celia and Matt flinched. "There's been enough damn secrecy around this place! There's been enough damn lies!"

"Please," Celia said urgently, placing her hand on Tam Lin's arm. "The cameras — "

"The cameras can go to blazes for all I care! Take a look, you lying, spying wretches! Here's what I think of you!" The man made an extremely rude hand gesture at the black-eyed Susan vines covering one wall. Matt had copied that gesture once and had been yelled at by Celia.

"Please. If you won't think of yourself, think of us." Celia had gone on her knees by the bodyguard's bench. She clasped her hands the way she did in prayer.

Tam Lin shook himself like a dog. "Ach! It's the drink talking!" He grabbed the remaining champagne bottle and hurled it against the wall. Matt heard the fragments shower over the black-eyed Susans. "I'll tell you this much, lad." He hauled Matt up by the front of his shirt. Celia watched with a pale, frightened face. "You were grown in that poor cow for nine months, and then you were cut out of her. You were harvested. She was *sacrificed*. That's the term they use when they kill a poor lab animal. Your stepmother was turned into ruddy T-bone steaks."

He dropped Matt, and Matt backed away out of reach.

"It's all right, Tam Lin," Celia said gently. She eased onto the seat beside him.

"It's *not* all right." The man buried his head in his arms on the table. "We're bloody lab animals to this lot. We're only well treated until we outlive our usefulness."

"They won't get their way forever," Celia whispered, putting her arms around him.

Tam Lin twisted his head until he could peer at her from the shelter of his arms. "I know what you've got in mind, and it's too dangerous," he said.

Celia leaned against him and rubbed his back with her large, gentle hands. "This Farm has been here for a hundred years. How many eejits do you think are buried under the poppies?"

"Thousands. Hundreds of thousands." Tam Lin's voice was almost a groan.

"Don't you think that's enough?" Celia smiled at Matt as she rubbed the bodyguard's back. It was a real smile this time, and it made her beautiful in the shadowy garden light. "Go to bed, *mi vida,*" she said. "I'll look in on you later."

Matt was annoyed that the two seemed to have forgotten it was *his* party, his coming-of-age. He sulked in his bedroom. He twanged the guitar, hoping the noise would disturb the pair huddled in the garden. But after a while his anger faded away.

It was replaced by a feeling that he had overlooked something important. Hints had been as thick as fireflies in the courtyard garden. They brightened with promise. They stayed alight almost long enough to show Matt what they were. But then, like the fireflies, they vanished. Tam Lin and Celia were far too careful.

It had been like that for years. Matt knew there was vital information he was missing. It had to do with clones. He wasn't supposed to know how they were made. He wasn't supposed to know that all of them – except for him – were brain dead.

Now, for the hundredth time, Matt thought about why anyone would create a monster. It couldn't be to replace a beloved child. Children were loved and clones were hated. It couldn't be to have a pet. No pet resembled the horrible, terrified thing Matt had seen in the hospital.

Matt remembered Mr MacGregor and El Patrón sitting in adjoining wheelchairs after their operations. *Got me a new liver,* MacGregor had said, patting his stomach, *and went in for a set of kidneys while I was at it.* He'd looked at Matt with those bright blue eyes that were so much like Tom's, and Matt had been revolted.

No! It couldn't be!

Matt remembered the birthday party where El Patrón had so suddenly recovered his mental abilities. *Foetal brain implants — I must try that sometime,* MacGregor had said. *It's done wonders for you.*

Don't put it off too long, El Patrón had replied. *You have to give the doctors at least five months' lead time. Eight is better.*

It couldn't be! Matt pressed his hands against his temples to keep the idea inside. If he didn't think it, it wouldn't be real.

But it slipped through his fingers anyway. MacGregor had created a clone so he could have transplants when he needed them. The thing in the hospital had every reason to howl! And what was the source of El Patrón's foetal implants? Or the piggy-back heart that kept his old, leaky one going?

The evidence was all there. Only Matt's blindness had kept him from seeing the truth — and his unwillingness to think about it. He wasn't stupid. The clues had been there all along. The truth had been too overwhelming to bear.

El Patrón, too, had created clones to provide himself with transplants. He was exactly the same as MacGregor.

No, not the same. Because I'm different, Matt thought desperately, staring up at the ceiling of his bedroom. Celia had pasted glow-in-the-dark stars all over the surface. From the time Matt had moved into her apartment, he'd gone to sleep under a faintly shining canopy of stars. Their presence soothed and comforted him now.

I'm different. I wasn't created to provide spare parts.

El Patrón had refused to let the doctors destroy Matt's brain. He'd protected him and given him Celia and Tam Lin for company. He'd hired Mr Ortega to teach Matt music. The old man took great pride in the boy's accomplishments. That was *not* the behaviour of someone who planned to murder you later.

Matt consciously slowed his breathing. He'd been panting like a bird trapped inside a room. Matt had seen birds die of panic when they couldn't beat their way through a closed window. He had to think the situation through, reason it out. It was clear, whatever had happened to the other poor clones, that Matt wasn't meant to be one of them.

El Patrón was moved by a motive very different from Mac-Gregor's. It was, the boy realised, simple *vanity*. When the old man looked at Matt, he saw himself: young, strong, and sound of mind. It was like looking into a mirror. The effect wouldn't be the same if Matt were a drooling, blubbering thing on a hospital bed.

Matt clutched the pillow the way he'd hugged stuffed animals before he was too old for such things. He felt like he'd been yanked back from a high cliff. There was still the terrible fate of the other clones to consider.

My brothers, thought Matt.

He trembled as he tried to recall his devotion to the man who had created him. El Patrón loved him, but he was evil. *A more evil, vicious, and self-serving man could hardly be imagined,* Esperanza had written in her book on the land of Opium. Matt had hurled the book away violently when he read that. But Matt had been a boy then. He was a man now – or something like it. Men, Tam Lin often told him, had the courage to look things in the eye.

"You have a fever!" cried Celia when she and Tam Lin came to say good night. She hurried off to make herbal tea. Tam Lin stood and watched from the doorway. The silhouette of the bodyguard looked menacing, and Matt remembered he'd killed twenty children with a bomb intended for the English prime minister. The man seemed to soak up the faint starlight from the ceiling.

When Celia returned with the tea, Tam Lin shrugged and said, "In answer to your question, lad, you're fourteen years old." Then he was off to his room in El Patrón's heavily guarded wing of the house.

20

ESPERANZA

Matt woke up sick and feverish. He felt as if a boulder was resting on his chest. The only way he could roll it off would be to learn that his fears were unfounded. He could ask Celia, but she'd be afraid to answer.

Matt felt the pressure of unseen eyes on him. Someone could be watching through the cameras, or the spy room might be empty. He had no way of knowing. Felicia could be in there, wrapped in a fur coat, eagerly searching for a way to destroy him.

As for asking Tam Lin, Matt didn't know how to bring up the subject. *By the way, is anyone planning to cut me up into T-bone steaks?* Even more terrifying was the bodyguard's possible answer: *You hit the nail on the head there, laddie. I always said you were bright as a button.*

How much truth could he endure?

Matt's mood lightened, though, after getting up. A hot

shower and a breakfast of French toast helped drive away the fear. It made no sense for El Patrón to lavish education on someone who was valued only for his spare parts. Transplants didn't need straight A's. Matt went to the stables and ordered a Safe Horse.

A ground fog hung over the poppy fields as he rode through. It was common in the early morning, when the water sprinklers misted the cool air next to the soil. The sun would burn it off later, but now it formed a milky sea that reached halfway up Matt's legs as he sat astride the horse. It was a wonderful feeling to move through this fog with only the horse's back and head showing. It was like swimming through an enchanted lake.

I'm fourteen years old, Matt thought. *I'm an adult.*

It made him feel strong and adventurous. Medieval princes went to war when they were fourteen or even younger.

The oasis was shadowy and cool. Recent rains had filled the pool until it lapped at the edge of the grape arbour. Matt dragged the metal chest to higher ground. He took off his clothes and stepped into the water. Tam Lin, who let Matt do quite a few dangerous things, had discouraged swimming here because the bottom was murky with unexpected depths. To Matt, the danger was part of the attraction.

He dog-paddled across the pool. Shoals of tiny fish darted away from his hands. He reached the shore and pulled himself onto a rock by a creosote bush. He shivered slightly. The day would soon heat up, but for now the desert air was chill with night.

Matt looked up at the sky. It was such an intense blue, it almost hurt his eyes. The rain had washed out the dust, leaving the air so clean and pure that it was like breathing in light. The sense of enchantment grew stronger.

What was to keep him from climbing these mountains and going south to Aztlán? It was a poor country, according to Celia, and yet her face lit up when she spoke of it. It was full of people and life, too. It was a new world where he might escape the cameras and the malice of Felicia. He wouldn't have to meet MacGregor with his patchwork of body parts.

But would he want to live without Celia and Tam Lin? Or María?

Matt's spirits rose still higher as he thought about travelling through those grey-brown mountains. He didn't have to make the decision yet. El Patrón could live for years — *would* live for years, the boy assured himself. After all, the old man had the finest doctors in the world. Matt could plan his move carefully, perhaps even take María with him. The sick fears of the previous night had vanished, and he felt like a king: Matt the Conqueror.

He swam back across the water. The sun was beginning to flood the little valley as he unpacked Tam Lin's books and maps. Now he saw the use of them, and he intended to study them carefully for his future escape.

The history of Opium, he read in Esperanza's book, *is soaked in terror and blood.* Matt settled against a roll of blankets with a slice of cold French toast. He still found the author's preachy manner annoying, but he couldn't argue with her facts.

Matteo Alacrán, or El Patrón as he soon came to be known, planted opium from the Pecos River to the Salton Sea, Matt read. *He needed a vast workforce to tend it. This was no problem, as thousands of Mexicans flooded across the border every day. All he needed was to trap them.*

To this end, he established the first Farm Patrol. He recruited his army from the foulest criminals ever vomited up by corrupt prison systems anywhere in the world.

Matt slammed the book shut. There she went again with a tirade against El Patrón. Esperanza had to be a complete witch. He drank a bottle of juice he'd brought from the house and tried again.

Even so, El Patrón found it hard to control the Illegals. They slipped through his fingers. They helped one another escape. They flooded across Opium to the border of the United States until that government threatened to put El Patrón out of business.

It was then the Despot of Dope, fearful of losing his slave empire, came up with eejits.

On the surface, Matt read, *nothing could have seemed more humane. After all, what is suffering but an* awareness *of suffering? The eejits felt neither cold nor heat nor thirst nor loneliness. A computer chip in their brains removed those sensations. They toiled with the steady devotion of worker bees. As far as anyone could tell, they were not unhappy. So could anyone say they were being mistreated?*

I could! thundered Esperanza. *El Patrón sold those people's souls to the Devil! When they died, he ploughed their bodies into the dirt for fertilizer. The roots of Opium are watered with blood, and anyone who buys its foul weed is no better than a flesh-eating cannibal.*

That was definitely enough reading for one day. Matt rested the book on his chest and tried to picture Esperanza's face. She was probably covered with warts like an old witch. She'd have yellow fangs and cheeks that collapsed in like a rotten pumpkin. He flipped through the book, looking for her photo.

On page 247 he found it. She was dressed in a black suit with a pearl necklace. Her black hair hung in a shiny veil on either side of her pale and beautiful face.

She looked a lot like María.

Matt read the blurb under the picture: *Esperanza Mendoza, the ex-wife of Senator Mendoza, is a charter member of the*

Anti-Slavery Society of California. She has written numerous, best-selling books. She was a recipient of the Nobel Peace Prize in –

Matt dropped the book. María couldn't possibly know about this. She thought her mother was dead. Esperanza had walked out of the house when María was five years old and never returned. The little girl imagined her mother had got lost in the desert, and she woke up night after night, crying that she could hear her mother's voice. That was why María clung so desperately to keepsakes. She was terrified of losing the things she loved.

And all this time her mother had been living it up in California. Matt felt a deep, burning rage against the woman and against Senator Mendoza too. He certainly knew what had happened, but he'd preferred to let María suffer. Well, Matt wasn't going to let the situation go on any longer. The next time María visited – and she'd have to come to Steven and Emilia's wedding in two months – Matt would hit her between the eyes with this evidence.

Matt discovered the reason Tam Lin had forbidden him to swim at the oasis. That night he came down with the worst stomach flu he could ever remember. He spent hours retching into a bucket until his throat burned like fire. Celia insisted on treating him herself. She forced glass after glass of milk down him, and she didn't leave him alone for a second. In the periods between attacks, he noticed that her hands were as cold and clammy as his own.

Finally, he recovered enough to lie down. Celia pulled a chair up by his bed and sat there all night while Matt drifted in and out of sleep. At one point he woke to find Tam Lin's face only an inch from his own. The bodyguard straightened up and said, "His breath smells of garlic."

Why wouldn't it smell of garlic? Matt thought drowsily. Practically everything Celia cooked was loaded with it.

"I warned you not to try this. We have to talk," said Tam Lin to Celia.

"I'll get the dosage right next time," she said.

"Do you want to ruin everything?"

"Maybe your plan won't work out. We need a backup," Celia said.

"You'll kill him."

She looked up at the secret camera. "I'd die rather than let that happen."

The voices stopped. Matt tried to stay awake, to see whether they would reveal more, but he was too weak.

The illness left Matt nervous and headachy for days. Just when he thought he was getting better, another bout of nausea occurred. The second attack wasn't as bad as the first, so it seemed he was fighting off the disease. He did wonder why Celia didn't call for the doctor, but he was grateful at the same time. It would have meant a trip to the hospital, and Matt wanted to avoid that at all costs.

When he had recovered sufficiently, he resumed spending his days at El Patrón's side, listening to the old man ramble. It seemed that a fog was gradually enveloping El Patrón's memories. He sometimes called Matt by another name, and he was confused about other things, too. "I built this shack with my own hands," he told Matt. Matt looked around. The last thing you'd call the mansion with its gardens and fountains was a shack.

"I put in the grapevine, too," El Patrón said. "It's doing very well. It covered the arbour in only two years. I think it's the water. There's nothing finer than one of these desert pools."

He's talking about the oasis, Matt thought with a chill. El Patrón must have been the person who had lived there long ago. The shack had fallen down, but the grapevine was still doing very well. "Is that the place behind the hole in the rock?" Matt asked, to be sure he was correct.

"Of course, Felipe!" El Patrón snapped. "You climb through that hole every single day." He fell into another reverie, his eyes seeing things no one else could. "This is the most beautiful place in the world," he said with a sigh. "If there's a heaven and I'm allowed inside, I'm sure this pool and grapevine will be there."

Then he wandered off into an even older memory. El Patrón's voice filled with wonder as he described the hacienda where he had attended fiestas so long ago. "They had a fountain," El Patrón marvelled. "The water sounded like music, and there was a statue of a little angel in the middle. He looked so cool and clean. And you can't imagine the food, Felipe. Tamales — as many as you wanted — and barbecued ribs! There were chillis rellenos and moro crabs flown in from Yucatán and a whole table of caramel puddings, each with its own little dish."

Matt felt sure that if there was a heaven, it contained moro crabs flown in from Yucatán and a table covered with caramel puddings. But then El Patrón's voice became sad. "Mamá brought my little sisters to the fiesta. She carried one, and the other held on to her skirt and followed behind. My little sisters caught typhoid and died in the same hour. They were so small, they couldn't look over the windowsill — no, not even if they stood on tiptoe."

It struck Matt that El Patrón was a lot nicer when he remembered the past. He seemed kinder and more vulnerable. Matt still loved the old man, but there was no question he was evil.

"Who's Felipe?" Matt asked Celia in the large, wood-burning kitchen of the mansion.

"You mean the sauce cook or gardener?" she said.

"It must be someone else. El Patrón's always calling me that."

"Oh, no," murmured Celia, pausing from the pie dough she was rolling out. "Felipe was his son. He died almost eighty years ago."

"Then why? . . ."

"Some people are like that, *mi vida*. First they get older and older, and then they stop and get younger and younger. El Patrón believes he's about thirty-five years old now, so he thinks you're his son, Felipe. He can't possibly know who you really are."

"Because I won't exist for another hundred years."

"That's right," replied Celia.

"So what should I do?"

"Be Felipe for him," Celia said simply.

Matt went to the music room and played the piano to calm his nerves. If El Patrón's mind was slipping, it meant he was ready for another dose of foetal brain implants. That meant an embryo — *Matt's brother* — was growing inside a cow. Could embryos understand death? Could they be afraid? Matt crashed into a rendition of the "Turkish March" by Mozart, playing loud enough to make a servant drop a tray in the hallway outside. When Matt finished, he played it again. And again. The orderliness of Mozart made him feel as though he had control of his own life. It transported him beyond the stifling world of the mansion.

More and more he wanted to escape. Once the possibility had occurred to him at the oasis, the longing returned until it became a constant ache. He felt trapped like a worm in a nut.

Esperanza's book had opened his eyes to the horrors of the empire El Patrón had built, and he had seen for himself the low, dark dwellings of the eejits that were no better than coffins.

He could run away through the grey-tinged mountains that ringed the oasis. He could go to Aztlán. Tam Lin had given him a chest full of maps and food for that very reason. Matt was sure of it.

But he couldn't leave before Steven and Emilia's wedding. María would be there, and he couldn't go without seeing her.

21

BLOOD WEDDING

The mansion seethed with activity. Potted orange trees were dragged in and placed around the perimeter of the salon. The scent of their flowers filled the house. The gardens were planted with jasmine, honeysuckle, and baby's breath. So many powerful perfumes made Matt queasy. His stomach hadn't felt right since his swim at the oasis.

The freezers adjoining the kitchen filled up with ice sculptures. Mermaids, lions, castles, and palm trees swirled with mist when Matt looked inside. They would be placed in bowls of punch for the wedding reception.

The old curtains and rugs were packed away, and new ones in white, pink, and gold took their place. The walls were repainted, the red tile roofs cleaned and polished. The house began to look like a giant birthday cake covered with frosting.

Matt skirted around the edge of these festivities. He knew he'd be confined to Celia's apartment during the party. *Big deal,* thought Matt, scuffing his shoes along a newly laid stretch of white carpet. He didn't want to go to the stupid wedding anyway. Everyone had known for years that Steven and Emilia were going to get married. El Patrón had decreed it. He wanted to bind the Alacráns to the powerful political machine Senator Mendoza ruled in the United States. It was simply good luck that Steven and Emilia liked each other. If they hadn't, it wouldn't have mattered.

Benito, Steven's older brother, had married the daughter of the Nigerian president because Nigeria was one of the richest countries in the world. Benito and Fani, his bride, had loathed each other on sight; but El Patrón liked Nigerian money, so their opinions didn't count.

As the day drew near, Matt felt more and more isolated. Celia was too distracted to talk. Tam Lin was shut away with El Patrón, whose health was too poor to allow visits. Matt could have gone to the oasis, but a strange tiredness had come over him. He fell asleep early, only to find his nights disturbed by evil dreams. By day his mouth tasted of metal and his head ached. He made only one brief trip to fetch Esperanza's book on Opium.

The house filled up with guests. MacGregor arrived with a new wife – number seven, Matt thought; this one was as young as Emilia. And Felicia consumed so much alcohol that a cloud of whiskey followed her wherever she went. She drifted from one garden party to another, staring at people with bright, feverish eyes until they became uncomfortable and moved away.

As for MacGregor, he was in fine spirits. He'd had hair transplants. His scalp was a riot of springy red hair just like Tom's, and he kept patting it as though it might fall out if he didn't push the roots back in.

Matt observed everything from behind pillars or wall hangings. He didn't want anyone to point at him and say, *What's this? Who brought this creature into a place for people?*

On the day of the wedding, a Nigerian hovercraft landed, carrying Benito, Fani, and Steven. Mr Alacrán greeted them and kissed Fani, who grimaced as though she'd touched something nasty. She had a hard, bitter face, and Benito was beginning to get a potbelly. Steven, on the other hand, was as handsome as a storybook prince.

Matt disliked him less than the other Alacráns. It was Steven who had carried him away from the little house in the poppies. And if he and Emilia had ignored Matt since, neither had they been cruel.

Matt watched the milling crowd of guests and recalled their names, business connections, and scandals. He thought he understood the Alacrán empire every bit as well as Steven. For the hundredth time Matt felt the gulf that separated him from humanity. All these people were here to honour Steven. No one would ever honour Matt, nor would he ever marry.

A familiar hovercraft landed, and Matt's heart leapt to his throat. The guests turned toward the landing pad and craned their necks to see the bride. Emilia didn't disappoint them. She was dressed in a shimmering blue gown, surrounded by a cluster of little girls as attendants. Each carried a basket of rose petals, which she tossed in handfuls at the crowd. Matt thought they made a pretty picture until he realised the little girls were eejits.

Everyone applauded as the bride was led up the stairs to the salon by Senator Mendoza. But Matt had no eyes for them. The only person he cared about stepped out of the hovercraft without any fanfare at all. No one noticed María slip through the crowd, or that she wasn't going in the same direction as her sister. Matt understood, though, and he worked his stealthy way around the edge of the crowd to the music room.

Most people shunned the music room. The servants entered only when they cleaned, and Felicia had stopped playing altogether. The room was Matt's territory and thus tainted.

He closed the door behind him and went straight to the closet. María was waiting in the secret passage. "At last!" she cried, flinging her arms around him. "Have you missed me?"

"All the time," he said, hugging her back. "I thought about you every day. I wanted to write, but I didn't know how."

"I'm in an awful convent," she said, disengaging herself and flopping down on the floor. "Oh, it's not too bad. I just don't fit in. I wanted to do charity work in the town, but the Sisters wouldn't let me. Imagine! They think they follow the teachings of Saint Francis, but they'd curl up and die rather than wash a beggar's sores."

"I wouldn't like to wash a beggar's sores either," said Matt.

"That's because you're a wolf. You'd gobble him up instead."

"I'd find a healthy beggar first," Matt said.

"You're not supposed to eat *any* of them. Tell me what you've been up to. Gosh, the other girls are boring! They don't do anything but read love comics and eat chocolates." María snuggled against Matt, and he felt amazingly good. He realised he was happy and that he hadn't been for a long time.

"Love comics?" he inquired.

"Wolves wouldn't find them interesting. Tell me what you've been watching on TV. We aren't allowed TV unless a show improves our souls."

"I don't have a soul," Matt said.

"I think you do," said María. "I've been reading modern church doctrine about ecology. According to recent studies, people think Saint Francis was the first ecologist. They say he preached to animals because they had little souls that could grow into big ones. With work, even a sparrow or cicada could make it into heaven."

"Or hell," said Matt.

"Don't be negative." And then María was off with her new ideas and the arguments she'd had with the morals instructor at the convent. She moved on to how she liked gardening, but hated harvesting the poor little plants, and how she was top in maths, but had her grades lowered when she sunbathed naked on the roof.

She seemed to have stored up months of conversation and couldn't wait to let it all out. Matt didn't care. He was content to sit there in the dark with her head leaning against his chest.

"Oh! But I've done all the talking and haven't let you say a word!" María cried at last. "That's one of the things I do penance for all the time. Except that no one at the convent listens to me like you do."

"I like listening to you," Matt said.

"I'm going to shut up now, and you're going to tell me what you've been doing." She put her arms around him, and he smelled her perfume, a warm and somehow exciting scent of carnations. Matt never wanted to move again.

He told her about the eejit pens and meeting the Farm Patrol and how he had to go to the hospital. María trembled when he told her about El Patrón's heart attack. "He's so old," she murmured. "Not that there's anything wrong with that, but he's *too* old."

"I don't think his piggyback heart is going to last," Matt said.

"He shouldn't have one at all," María said.

"Do you know where he got it?"

"I – I – " María seemed confused. "I'm not supposed to talk about it, but yes, I do know where he got it! And it's evil!" She hugged Matt more tightly. He didn't know what to say. The fears he'd thrust away came back. He wanted to ask María what she meant, but he was afraid of the answer.

"I'm not like the other clones," he said, more to reassure himself than anything. "El Patrón gave me the best education anyone can have. He bought me musical instruments, computers, anything I wanted. And he's really pleased when I get an A or play a new piano piece. He says I have genius."

María said nothing. She snuggled her face into his chest, and from the dampness, Matt guessed she was crying. *Great. What is she crying about?* "He wouldn't bother" – Matt stepped very carefully over this point – "if I wasn't going to live very long."

"That's true," she said in a watery voice.

"Of *course* it's true," said Matt firmly. "I've had better schooling than Steven. Someday I can help him run the estate – from behind the scenes, of course. Opium is a big country, and it takes a lot of work to control it. Benito's too dumb, and Tom is – well, a lot of things. For starters, El Patrón can't stand the sight of him."

María stiffened. "He likes him better than you think."

"Tom doesn't even belong in the family. He's here only because El Patrón refuses to give things up once he's laid claim to them."

"That's a lie!" María said hotly. "Tom's one of the heirs, and he's not stupid!"

"I never said he was stupid. Only corrupt."

"He's considered good enough to marry me!" María said.

"What?" Matt couldn't believe what he was hearing. María was only a kid. She wouldn't get married for years and years.

"Oh, let's not fight," María said miserably. "None of us has a choice in the matter. I mean, look at Benito and Fani. Fani said she'd rather drink cyanide than marry Benito, and see how much good it did her. El Patrón gave the order, and her father drugged her until she didn't know what was happening."

Matt was incapable of speech. How could anyone want María to marry *Tom?* He was such a – such a *rotten little pustule!* It was unthinkable! He turned on the flashlight he always left in the passage and leaned it against the wall. He could see her pale face in the shadows.

"Steven and Emilia like each other, and I don't mind Tom – much. He's getting more like MacGregor, but I can change him."

"You can't change Tom," Matt said.

"Patience and love can do anything," María said. "Anyhow, the wedding won't take place for years. Maybe El Patrón will change his mind." She didn't sound hopeful.

Matt's mind was almost numb with despair. He'd refused to think about the future. He knew on some level that María would have to marry someday. Then he'd never see her again. But it had never in his darkest moments occurred to him that she'd be handed over to that monster.

"Wait," he said as an idea came to him. "I have something for you."

"A present?" María looked surprised.

Matt fished *A History of Opium* from its hiding place. He turned to page 247 and shone the flashlight directly on Esperanza Mendoza's portrait.

María gasped. "M-Mother?"

"You remember what she looked like?"

"Dada has pictures." She took the book and stared at the portrait and its accompanying biography as though she'd been turned to stone. "Mother got the Nobel Peace Prize," she whispered at last.

"And a lot more," said Matt.

"But she n-never came back." María's face looked so forlorn, Matt's heart turned over.

"She couldn't, dearest," said Matt, unconsciously using one of Celia's words. "She's utterly and completely opposed to Opium and everything your father stands for. Do you think he'd let her come home? Or that El Patrón would?" In fact, Matt silently realised, El Patrón was capable of ordering her death. It wouldn't have been the first time he'd got rid of an enemy.

"She never even wrote me a letter," murmured María.

"Don't you see? Your father would have destroyed any message she sent. But you can contact her now. Your convent – where is it?"

"In Aztlán, at the mouth of the Colorado River. It's in a town called San Luis."

"I've read your mother's book," said Matt, taking *A History of Opium* from María's cold hands and laying it on the floor. He held her hands to warm them up. "She says the Aztlános don't like Opium and would do anything to destroy it. Someone at the convent could send a message to your mother. I'm sure she wants to find you. I'm sure she'll keep you from marrying Tom."

And take you where I'll never see you again, thought Matt with a lump in his throat. But it didn't matter. He was going to lose her in any case. The important thing now was to save her.

"I have to go," María said suddenly. "Emilia will be asking for me."

"When will I see you again?"

"The wedding's tomorrow and I won't have a second to myself. I'm maid of honour. Will you be able to come?"

Matt laughed bitterly. "Maybe if I disguised myself as an eejit flower girl."

"I know. It's horrible. I asked Emilia why she couldn't have real children, and she said they couldn't be depended on to do the job right."

"You know I won't be invited," said Matt.

"Everything's so unfair." María sighed. "If I could, I'd skip the wedding and stay with you."

Matt was touched by her offer, although he knew there wasn't a chance of it happening. "I'll wait for you here," he said. "Do you want to take the book?"

"No. I can't guess what Dada would do if he found it." She gently kissed him on the cheek, and Matt kissed her back. The feel of her skin stayed on his lips for a long time after she was gone.

It wasn't a front-row seat, but it was the best he could do. Matt was positioned behind the peephole with a pocket telescope.

He had hoped to find the machine room deserted, but the place was packed. Every view screen had at least two gorilla-like bodyguards watching it. They flicked restlessly from scene to scene and spent a lot of time studying boring places, like the spaces behind pillars or curtains. Matt wondered whether they'd seen him hiding there on other occasions.

But as the wedding ceremony drew closer, the men's attention was concentrated on the salon. An altar had been erected, and the priest was prowling back and forth to one side. The eejit choir was lined up like mechanical toys, and someone was

sitting at Matt's piano. Matt adjusted the eyepiece of the telescope. It was awkward to use at a peephole, and his neck was
beginning to ache.

He saw Mr Ortega. He felt sorry for the dusty little man.
He'd gone beyond Mr Ortega's skill level long ago, but Matt
had covered for him. He feared the music teacher would suffer
the same fate as Rosa if El Patrón found out.

On another screen Matt saw El Patrón sitting in the front
row, attended by Tam Lin and Daft Donald looking bunchy in
suits.

Emilia waited in a dressing room. She wore a white gown
with a long train embroidered with pearls and carried by the
girl eejits. Celia had said the gown had been owned by a Spanish queen three hundred years before. The eejits' faces reminded
Matt of the winged babies perched on pillars throughout the
house. Their eyes were as lifeless as marbles.

María bounced around the room, talking animatedly. Matt
couldn't hear what she said, but there was no question she was
giddy with excitement. That was the difference between her
and everyone else, he thought. She was overflowing with life.
Everything delighted or devastated or fascinated her. There was
no middle ground. Next to her Emilia looked faded, and Fani,
who was drinking out of a brandy bottle in the corner, was pos-
itively drab.

The bodyguards turned up the sound. Matt heard the wedding march, and Senator Mendoza took Emilia by the arm. The
eejits lifted the train, and María and Fani took their places
behind the bride. They left the room with a stately, impressive
walk. A whisper passed over the crowd, and the priest signalled
everyone to stand.

Steven waited at the altar with Benito and Tom.

Tom. For a moment all Matt could see was his lying face. What you saw was *not* what you got with him. Underneath that angelic exterior was the boy who'd shot a helpless child with a peashooter, who had pulled chairs out from under El Viejo, who'd nailed frogs to the lawn so they could be devoured by herons. You didn't want to leave anything vulnerable around Tom.

A bodyguard blocked Matt's view for a moment. He cursed under his breath.

The next thing he saw was Emilia approaching the altar on her father's arm. María had a tight grip on Fani to keep her from swaying. Benito's wife was almost as loaded as Felicia, who was being held upright by Mr Alacrán. *What a family,* thought Matt. The women were alcoholics, Benito was as dumb as a goldfish, and Tom was a moral black hole. Steven was okay, though. Even the Alacráns couldn't strike out 100 per cent of the time.

Now Emilia was given away by her father. Steven placed a ring on her finger and lifted her veil for a kiss. They were married for better or for worse, in sickness and in health, till death should them part.

But maybe they wouldn't have to part, Matt thought. Maybe they'd all waft up to heaven together, to a special wing reserved for the Alacráns. They'd have moro crabs and caramel pudding and a vat full of whiskey for Felicia.

"Bloody hell! It's the old vampire!" swore one of the bodyguards.

Matt pressed his eye to the peephole. He was so startled, he dropped the telescope.

He saw, far away but hideously clear, El Patrón jerk upward in his wheelchair. The old man clutched his heart and tipped forward. Tam Lin scrambled to catch him. Mr Alacrán yelled for help. Willum and several other doctors who had recently taken up residence in the house shoved their way through the crowd. They knelt around El Patrón, completely hiding the old man. They reminded Matt of vultures huddling over an antelope.

Bodyguards streamed out of the machine room, and a moment later Matt saw them on the screens. They rushed into the salon and herded the wedding guests out.

Tam Lin suddenly rose from the huddle with El Patrón in his arms. Matt saw with horror how small and withered the old man was. He looked like a dry leaf clutched to the bodyguard's chest as Tam Lin hurried out with the doctors in his wake.

The salon was deserted, except for Steven and Emilia, who were standing alone and forgotten at the altar.

22

BETRAYAL

W hat should I do? What should I do?" whispered
Matt, hugging himself and rocking back and forth
in the dark passageway. He loved El Patrón. He
wanted to be with him at the hospital, to watch over him and
urge him back to health. But at the same time Matt remembered María saying that she did know the source of El Patrón's
transplants: *And it's evil!*

Celia would be looking for him. Unbidden, another memory surfaced. Celia was fussing with the suit Matt had worn to
the birthday party long ago. *If anything bad happens,* she had said,
*I want you to come straight to me. Come to the pantry behind the
kitchen.*

What do you mean, bad? Matt had asked.

I can't say. Just promise me you'll remember.

And even longer ago Matt remembered Tam Lin speaking to
him soon after his rescue from Rosa: *I'll tell you this: El Patrón has*

his good side and his bad side. Very dark indeed is his majesty when he wants to be. When he was young, he made a choice, like a tree does when it decides to grow one way or the other. He grew large and green until he shadowed over the whole forest, but most of his branches are twisted.

So many hints! So many clues! Like a pebble that starts an avalanche, Matt's fear shook loose more and more memories. Why had Tam Lin given him a chest full of supplies and maps? Why had María run from him when they found MacGregor's clone in the hospital? Because she knew! They all knew! Matt's education and accomplishments were a sham. It didn't matter how intelligent he was. In the end the only thing that mattered was how strong his *heart* was.

And yet Matt wasn't – quite – sure.

What if he was wrong? What if El Patrón really loved him? Matt thought about the old man lying on a hospital bed, waiting for the one person who could bring him a glimpse of his youth. It was too cruel! Matt curled up on the floor of the passage. He lay in a welter of fine dust that had drifted into this dark, secret space over the years. He felt like the inhabitant of an ancient tomb, an Egyptian pharaoh or Chaldean king. El Patrón loved to talk about such things.

The old man enthusiastically described the wealth that filled the pyramids, for the use of the old kings in their afterlife. He liked the tombs of the ancient Chaldeans even more. Not only did they have clothes and food, but their horses were slaughtered to provide transport in the shadowy world of the dead. In one tomb archaeologists had discovered soldiers, servants, and even dancing girls laid out as though they were sleeping. One girl had been in such a hurry, the blue ribbon she was meant to wear in her hair was still rolled up in her pocket.

What a fine thing that was, El Patrón had told Matt: that a

king got to rule in this life but also had his entire court to serve him in the next. That was even better than El Dorado powdered with gold on the balcony of his great house.

Matt choked on the dust and sat up to clear his throat. He didn't want to make any noise. He didn't want anyone to find him until he'd decided what to do. He leaned against the wall, and the darkness outside was equalled by the darkness inside his mind. What was he to do? What *could* he do?

Footsteps running up the passage made him jump to his feet. He saw a flashlight bobbing in front of a slight figure. "María," he whispered.

"Oh, thank heavens! I was afraid you'd gone somewhere else to hide," she whispered back.

"Hide?" he said.

"They're looking for you everywhere. They tore up Celia's apartment, and they've been through every room in the house. They've sent bodyguards to comb the stables and fields."

Matt held her by the shoulders and looked closely at her face. In the dim light he saw her face was wet. "Why are they looking for me?"

"You *have* to know. Tam Lin said you were too clever not to figure it out."

Matt felt turned to stone. The bodyguard evidently gave him more credit than he deserved. Matt hadn't figured it out – not really – until a few minutes ago.

"I'm supposed to be throwing a hysterical fit in my room. Emilia says I'm always getting hysterical. She says you're only the latest edition of Furball; but she's wrong! You're not a dog. You're so much, much more."

Ordinarily, Matt would have been thrilled by María's words, but the situation was too dire for happiness.

"Tam Lin says you're to stay put for now. He's going to spread a rumour that you've taken a Safe Horse north to the United States. He says that should keep the Farm Patrol busy."

Matt felt dazed by all that was happening. He couldn't seem to get his mind working. "How's El Patrón?" he asked.

"Why do you care?" María said passionately. "You should pray that he dies."

"I can't," murmured Matt. And it was true. No matter how treacherous El Patrón had been, Matt loved the old man. No one was closer to him in the whole world. No one understood him better.

"You're exactly like Tam Lin," said María. "He says El Patrón is like a force of nature – a tornado or volcano or something. He says you can't help being awestruck even when you might get killed. I think it's all rubbish!"

"What am I supposed to do?" Matt said. He felt drained of willpower.

"Stay here. I'll go throw the hysterical fit everyone's expecting. When it gets dark, I'll come back for you."

"Where can we go?" said Matt. He could think of only the oasis, but it was a long way without a Safe Horse to carry them.

"To Dada's hovercraft," said María.

Matt's eyes widened. "You know how to fly?"

"No, but the pilot was going to take me back to the convent after the wedding. I told him to expect us."

"How will you explain me?"

"You're my new pet eejit! Emilia has a dozen, and I told the pilot I was jealous and demanded one of my own." María had to cover her mouth to keep the giggles from spilling out into the dark passage. "Nobody ever asks questions about eejits. They're just part of the furniture."

• • •

Matt slept most of the time he was waiting. He was tired from the illness that had come over him recently and exhausted by all that had happened. He woke, parched and thirsty, and realised he had no water.

The passageway was dry and dusty. Matt swallowed, trying to soothe his burning throat. His throat hurt all the time these days, with or without water.

He found the machine room stuffed with bodyguards. Every view screen was being watched, and Matt realised there wasn't a single safe place in the house. He couldn't go out for water. He began to worry about María. How had she got past them before, and how would she get back in? He leaned against the wall, sunk in the deepest despair.

Time passed slowly. Matt thought about the lemonade Celia always left in the fridge. He imagined the juice sliding down his throat. Then, because the air had grown cooler, he thought about hot chocolate instead. Celia made it with cinnamon. One of his earliest memories was of her hands holding a cup to his lips and of a wonderful, spicy aroma swirling around his head.

Matt swallowed painfully. It didn't help to think about drinking when you couldn't do it. Long ago he'd seen a dead eejit in the poppy fields. Tam Lin said the man had died of thirst. Matt wondered how long it had taken.

He heard footsteps. He sprang up and was immediately swept with dizziness. He must be more dehydrated than he thought.

"I'm sorry. I forgot about water." María thrust a bottle at him, and Matt snatched it and drank ravenously.

"How's El Patrón?" he asked after he drained the bottle.

"Better, unfortunately."

"You sound like you don't want him to get well."

"Of course I don't!"

"Keep your voice down," said Matt. "If he lives, I can come out."

"No, you can't. He needs a new heart if he's going to survive, and there's only one place to get it."

Matt put his hand out, to keep from swaying. It was one thing to understand his fate and very different to hear María say it out loud. "El Patrón loves me," he said.

María made a small, impatient noise. "He loves what you can *do* for him. We don't have time to waste. Here's an eejit uniform to wear — Tam Lin got it for me. Remember, you can't say a word if we meet anyone."

Matt quickly changed clothes. The uniform reeked of sweat and a chemical odour that awoke evil memories in Matt. *The wastelands,* he thought. The person who wore this had lain in the fields on still nights, when the air near the eejit pens had gone bad.

"Here's your hat," said María.

She led him through the passage. They were moving away from the music room and past El Viejo's old apartment. Matt wondered who was living there now or if perhaps it had been sealed up. A lot of the mansion was, but you couldn't count on a place being empty.

They came to a stretch where Matt had been unable to find a peephole. María shone the flashlight along the wall.

"There's nothing here," Matt said.

"Wait." She slid a piece of red plastic over the flashlight. The walls turned the colour of dried blood. It made the place look darker and more sinister. The air suddenly seemed stale, like a tomb that hadn't been opened for a very long time.

"There!" cried María.

In the middle of the wall, where Matt could have sworn nothing had been a minute ago, was a red, glowing patch. He bent close. The patch disappeared.

"You're in the beam," said María. Matt stepped back and the patch appeared again.

It reminded him a little of the stars Celia had pasted on his bedroom ceiling. It was a different colour, though, and it wasn't a star. "It's a *scorpion*!" he cried.

"The mark of the Alacráns," said María. "Tam Lin told me about it. It shows up only in red light."

"What does it mean?"

"I think – I *hope* – it's a way out."

Matt put out his hand to touch the scorpion, and María grabbed his arm. "Wait! I have to explain something. I've been going in and out of this passage from El Patrón's bedroom. The view screens can't see in there, according to Tam Lin, but they can watch everything around it. You couldn't escape from there."

Matt was hypnotised by the red scorpion. It seemed to shimmer with a life all its own.

"This is another way out," said María. "I thought this passage was built so El Patrón could spy on people. Of course, he *did* spy on people – Tam Lin said he called it his private soap opera – but El Patrón really made the tunnel to escape from his enemies. He has a lot of enemies."

"I know," said Matt.

"The problem is, I don't know whether you want to take the chance – "

"What?" Matt said impatiently.

"It works only for El Patrón. That's to keep enemies from

sneaking in. When he presses his hand against the red scorpion, the wall opens, and he can get in and out of the house without being seen. The escape route goes to the hovercraft landing field. But, if the wrong person touches the scorpion, it sends a lethal jolt of electricity through his arm and the whole passage fills with a poisonous gas. At least that's what Tam Lin says. He hasn't tried it."

Matt stared at María. "*This* is your plan to rescue me?"

"Well, it might work," she said. "Tam Lin says the scorpion recognises the fingerprints and DNA of El Patrón. And you're his clone."

Matt suddenly felt light-headed. She was right. He *was* El Patrón's clone. His fingerprints would be the same, his DNA identical. "If you're wrong," he told María, "we'll die."

"We'll die together, dearest."

Matt's heart jolted when he heard *dearest.* "I can't let you do it. I'll go alone. I have a secret hiding place."

"The oasis?" said María. "You'll never make it there ahead of the Farm Patrol."

So she even knows about that, Matt thought. Tam Lin must have told her everything. "I can try."

"And so can I," she said, getting that mulish look in her eyes Matt knew so well. "Either you press that scorpion and we escape together, or we stay here and *starve* together. I'm not leaving you! Not now or ever!"

"I love you," Matt said.

"I love you, too," said María. "I know that's a sin, and I'll probably go to hell for it."

"If I have a soul, I'll go with you," promised Matt. He thrust his hand against the glowing scorpion before he could change his mind. He felt a strange sensation, like hundreds of tiny ants crawling up his arm. The hairs on the back of his hand stirred. "Run! It's not working!" he yelled. Instead, María grabbed him.

A door slid back before them, and a long, dark tunnel was revealed.

"If we had time to waste, I'd faint," María sighed, shining the flashlight into the new opening.

The tunnel smelled even older than the passageway, and it was clear it hadn't been used for a very long time. The floor was packed dirt with a forlorn little heap of soil here and there where some burrowing animal had got in. But there was nothing alive in the tunnel now, not a mouse or a spider or even a toadstool. It gave Matt the creeps.

Their footsteps were muffled. The sound of their breathing seemed to die in the cold, lifeless air. It struck Matt that there might not be much oxygen in the tunnel, and he hurried María along.

After a while they came to another wall blocking the way. María put the red plastic over the flashlight again and revealed another shimmering scorpion. This time Matt didn't hesitate. He pressed his hand against the wall and felt the same sensation of crawling ants. A second door slid open.

This entrance was concealed by thick bushes. Matt carefully pushed them aside for María, and they found themselves on the edge of the hovercraft landing field.

"That's our ship," whispered María, pointing out a small craft with its landing lights on. She walked ahead and Matt followed, pulling the broad-brimmed sombrero down to hide his face. They didn't hurry. They looked, Matt hoped, like they had all the time in the world. If bodyguards were watching this part of the house, all they'd see was an honoured guest attended by an eejit. Eejits didn't rate any more attention than dogs.

Matt was sweating with nerves. It was harder acting brainless than he'd imagined. He wanted to look around, but eejits didn't do such things. He tripped on a rock and caught himself before he actually fell. *Mistake,* he thought. A real eejit would land flat on his face. Would he yell if he got hurt? Matt didn't know.

"Stay," said María. Matt halted. She climbed into the hovercraft and then ordered him to come inside. He heard her talking to the pilot.

"Sit," said María, pointing at a chair. She buckled him in and continued chatting to the pilot, telling him about the convent and how glad she'd be to get back.

"I'm sorry to bother you, Miss Mendoza," the pilot said with great respect, "but do you have a permit for this eejit? They're not exactly welcome in Aztlán."

"The mother superior will have one," María said airily.

"I hope so," said the man. "Otherwise, he'll have to be put to sleep. I know a sensitive girl like you wouldn't like that."

María turned pale, and Matt realised she hadn't known about this law.

"We'll take off as soon as your sister leaves."

"My sister?" María almost shrieked.

Stay calm, stay calm, Matt thought desperately.

"You didn't think I'd let you go without saying good-bye," said Emilia, coming out of the cockpit. Steven was with her and so were a pair of bodyguards. Matt sat perfectly still, his head bowed, as the bodyguards took up positions in front of the door. He couldn't think of another thing to do.

"Emilia. How nice," said María without any enthusiasm.

"I really don't think the mother superior wants an eejit at the convent," Emilia said.

"Stay out of this."

"Why should I help you indulge in another do-good project? Honestly, you're the laughing stock of the convent – like when you wanted to care for lepers. The nuns laughed themselves silly over that. There *aren't* any lepers in Aztlán. They'd have to import them. And now you want to rescue a clone – "

"Eejit," María said quickly.

"Clone," said Steven, coming forward and pulling off Matt's hat. He dropped it as though he'd touched something foul.

Matt looked up. There was no point pretending now. "I forced María to do it," he said.

"You've been getting her into trouble for years," said Emilia. "From that first day she brought you food, you've exploited her."

"He has not!" cried María.

"You're too soft," Emilia said. "You're always getting gooey about sick animals or homeless people. If you're not careful, you'll turn out like Mother."

"Mother," gasped María. "I haven't told you – I didn't have time – she's *alive!*"

"So?" Emilia said. "I've known that for years."

María stared at her sister as though she'd just seen a tarantula. "You . . . *knew?*"

"Of course. I'm older than you, remember? I saw her go, and Dada shouted that she was dead to us now. It seemed the easiest way to explain things to you."

"You let me think she was lost in the desert."

Emilia shrugged. "What difference does it make? She didn't care about us. She thought taking care of losers was more important."

"The important thing is to get this clone to the hospital,

where it can do some good," said Steven.

"Steven," whispered Matt. In all this time he'd thought Steven and Emilia were — if not his friends — not his enemies, either. He admired Steven. In many ways they were alike.

"Take him." Steven signalled to the bodyguards.

"Wait!" shrieked María. "You can't do this! Matt's not an animal!"

"He's livestock," Steven said with a cold smile. "The law is very clear. All clones are classified as livestock because they're grown inside cows. Cows can't give birth to humans."

"I won't let you do this! I won't let you!" María threw herself at the guards, and they rather sheepishly ducked their heads to avoid her blows. The pilot grabbed her from behind and pulled her away.

"I'll call Willum," Steven said, heading for the cockpit. "I can see we'll need sedatives before we can send her back to the convent."

"Emilia! Help me! Help *him!*" screamed María, but no one paid her the slightest attention.

Matt walked between the bodyguards. He hadn't a hope of fighting them off, and he didn't want María's last image of him to be of a terrified farm animal being dragged off to slaughter. He turned to look at her, but she was too busy struggling with the pilot to notice.

The bodyguards held Matt's arms, but they didn't insist on carrying him. He smelled the night air, the scent of jasmine and gardenias that had been planted everywhere for the wedding. He smelled the distant odour of the desert, perhaps even of the mesquite surrounding the oasis. Things travelled so much further at night.

He saw the fantastic gardens of the Big House, the statues of babies with wings, the orange trees festooned with lights. This was his last night on earth, and he wanted to remember everything.

Most of all, he wanted to remember Celia and Tam Lin. And María. Would he ever see them again? Or, if he was denied heaven, would he wander through the night like La Llorona, searching for something that was forever lost?

AGE 14

23

Death

Matt was strapped to a bed in a room full of alarming machinery. Two guards sat outside the door, and another two waited by the window, which was covered by iron bars.

He was utterly terrified. This was where they had kept Mac-Gregor's clone. This was where the bad things happened.

If only I'd escaped when I had the chance, he thought. *Everything was ready for me. Tam Lin gave me maps and food and showed me how to climb mountains. I didn't understand. I didn't want to understand.*

He was sick with dread. Every noise in the hall made him try to free himself. At one point Willum and two strange doctors appeared and proceeded to poke Matt's stomach and take his blood. They untied him so he could pee into a bottle, and Matt took the opportunity to run. He got only about six feet before being tackled by one of the guards.

Fool, fool, fool, Matt told himself. *Why didn't I escape when I had the chance?*

After a while Willum and the other doctors returned to discuss Matt's health. "It has mild anaemia," said one of the doctors. "Its liver functions are a little off."

"Is it cleared for transplant?" inquired Willum.

"I see nothing against it," said the strange doctor, peering at a chart.

They left Matt alone with his fear and his imagination.

What was María doing now? They would have drugged her, as Fani had been drugged before she was forced to marry Benito. Perhaps Felicia had been given laudanum in the beginning, to keep her obedient. One day there would be another grand wedding for María and Tom. María would have to be propped up as she walked towards the altar.

I can't save her, thought Matt. But perhaps he'd done the one thing that could rescue her. María knew about her mother now. She could call for help. And Esperanza, if Matt knew anything about the woman who wrote *A History of Opium,* would descend on the convent like a fire-breathing dragon.

The door opened, and a pair of bodyguards entered and proceeded to untie Matt. *Now what?* he thought. It couldn't be a good sign. Nothing was good anymore, not for him.

The bodyguards, keeping a tight hold on Matt's arms, led him down the hall to a room unlike any he'd seen in the hospital. It was decorated with fine paintings, elegant furniture, and carpets. At the far end, next to a tall window, was a small table with a teapot, cups, and a silver plate of cookies.

And next to it lay El Patrón in a hospital bed. He looked extremely frail, but life still sparkled in his jet-black eyes. In spite of himself, Matt felt a wave of affection.

"Come closer, Mi Vida," said the whispery old voice.

Matt approached. He saw more guards standing in the shadows and Celia in a beam of light from a gap in the curtains. Matt braced himself for a stormy scene, but she was dry-eyed and grim.

"Sit down, Mi Vida," said El Patrón, indicating a chair by the table. "As I remember, you like cookies."

I did when I was six years old, thought Matt. What was going on here?

"Cat got your tongue?" the old man said. "It's like the first time we met, when Celia rescued you from the chicken litter." He smiled. Matt didn't. He had nothing to be happy about. "Ah, well," sighed El Patrón. "It always comes to this in the end. My clones forget about the wonderful years I give them, the presents, the entertainment, the good food. I don't have to do it, you know."

Matt stared ahead. He wanted to speak, but his throat had closed up.

"If I were like MacGregor — a good Farmer, but a *foul* human being — I would have had your brain destroyed at birth. Instead, it pleased me to give you the childhood I never had. I had to grovel at the feet of the ranchero who owned my parents' land for every damn sack of cornmeal."

Celia said nothing. She might have been carved out of stone.

"But once a year that changed," said El Patrón. "During Cinco de Mayo the ranchero had a celebration. I and my five brothers went to watch. Mamá brought my little sisters. She carried one, and the other held on to her skirt and followed behind."

Matt knew this story so well, he wanted to scream. El Patrón slipped into it effortlessly, like a donkey walking along a well-worn trail. Once he got going, nothing could stop him until he reached the end.

The old man spoke of the dusty cornfields and purple mountains of Durango. His bright black eyes saw beyond the hospital room to the streams that roared with water two months of the year and were dry as a bone the rest of the time.

"The mayor of our village — dressed in a fine black-and-silver suit — rode on a white horse and threw money to the crowd. How we scrambled for the coins! How we rolled in the dirt like pigs! But we needed the money. We were so poor, we didn't have two pesos to rub together. On this day the ranchero gave a great feast. We could eat all we wanted, and it was a wonderful opportunity for people who had stomachs so shrunken that chilli beans had to wait in line to get inside.

"One year, during that feast, my little sisters caught typhoid. They died in the same hour. They were so small, they couldn't look over the windowsill — no, not even if they stood on tiptoe."

The room was deathly still. Matt heard a dove calling from the roof of the hospital. *No hope,* it said. *No hope. No hope.*

"During the following years each of my five brothers died; two drowned, one had a burst appendix, and we had no money for the doctor. The last two brothers were beaten to death by the police. There were eight of us," said El Patrón, "and only I lived to grow up. *Don't you think I'm owed those lives?*" El Patrón spoke so sharply, Matt jolted up in his chair. The story wasn't ending the way he'd expected.

"There were eight of us," the old man cried. "We should all have grown up, but I was the only survivor. I am meant to have those lives! I am meant to have justice!"

Matt tried to stand. He was shoved back down by the bodyguards.

"Justice?" said Celia. It was the first word she had spoken.

"You know what it was like," El Patrón whispered, his strength deserting him now after his outburst. "You came from the same village."

"You've had many lives," Celia said. "Thousands of them are buried under the poppy fields."

"Oh, them!" El Patrón was dismissive. "They're like cattle running after greener grass. They scuttle north and south across my fields. Oh, yes," he said when Matt raised his eyebrows. "In the beginning the tide was all one way. The Aztlános ran north to find the big Hollywood lifestyle. But the United States isn't the rich paradise it once was. Now the Americanos look at movies about Aztlán and think life is pretty sweet down there. I catch about as many going one way as the other."

"El Viejo was the only good man in this family," said Celia. "He accepted what God gave him, and when God told him it was time to go, he did it." Matt was amazed by her courage. People didn't argue with El Patrón if they wanted to stay healthy.

"El Viejo was a fool," whispered El Patrón. For a few moments he stopped speaking. A doctor came in and listened to his heart. He gave him an injection.

"The operating room is ready," the doctor said in a low voice. Matt was swept by an icy wave of terror.

"Not yet," murmured the old man.

"Ten more minutes," said the doctor.

El Patrón seemed to gather his strength for a last effort. "I created you, Mi Vida, as God created Adam."

Celia sniffed indignantly.

"Without me, you would never have seen a beautiful sunset or smelled the rain approaching on the wind. You would never have tasted cool water on a hot summer day. Or heard music or known the wonderful pleasure of creating it. I gave you these things, Mi Vida. You . . . *owe* . . . me."

"He owes you nothing," Celia said.

Matt was afraid for her. El Patrón was capable of destroying a person who angered him. But the old man merely smiled. "We make a fine pair of scorpions, don't we?"

"Speak for yourself," said Celia. "Matt owes you nothing, and he's going to pay you nothing. You can't use him for transplants."

The guards stirred when they heard this. The doctor looked up from the monitor he was watching.

"When you had your first heart attack, I poisoned Matt with foxglove from my garden," said Celia. "I'm a *curandera*, you know, as well as a cook. I made Matt's heart too unstable to transplant."

El Patrón's eyes bulged. He opened his mouth, but nothing came out. The doctor rushed to his side.

"I couldn't keep on giving Matt foxglove, though. It's much too dangerous. I needed something that would make him sick, but not too sick. Then someone told me about monarch butterflies."

Matt sat up, only to have a bodyguard's hands tighten on his shoulders. He knew about the monarchs. Tam Lin had talked about them in the garden, the night of Matt's coming-of-age celebration. The air had been heavy with perfumes, some pleasant, some not, from the flowers Celia had become interested in. She'd pointed out the black-eyed Susans, larkspur, foxgloves, and milkweed, and Tam Lin was stirred when she'd mentioned milkweed. *It's fed upon by monarch butterflies,* he'd said. *They're clever little buggers. Fill themselves up with poison so nothing will eat them.*

Matt had paid no attention to this remark at the time. Tam Lin was always coming up with facts he got out of the nature books he read so slowly and carefully.

"I needed something like the poison in monarch butterflies," said Celia, breaking into Matt's thoughts. "So I began feeding him arsenic."

"*Arsenic!*" the doctor cried.

"Arsenic creeps into the whole body," Celia went on, her eyes as cold as the eyes of a snake. "It grows into the hair, it makes little white lines on the fingernails, it settles into the *heart*. I didn't give Matt enough to kill him – I wouldn't do that! – but enough to kill anyone already weak who tried to steal his heart. You've had your eight lives, El Patrón. It's time to make your peace with God."

"*¡Bruja!* Witch!" shrieked El Patrón. His eyes flamed with murderous rage. His skin flushed an angry red. He struggled to claw his way up from the bed.

"Emergency!" yelled the doctor. "Take him to the operating room! Move! Move! Move!"

The guards rolled the bed away. The doctor ran beside it, pushing on El Patrón's chest. Suddenly the whole building seethed like a wasps' nest. More guards appeared – an army of them. Two of them hurried Celia off in spite of Matt's attempts to stop them. A technician snipped off a strand of Matt's hair and retreated.

He was alone. Alone, that is, except for four burly men who sat outside the window and an unknown number lurking outside the door. It was a beautiful room, with a carpet patterned in the colours of the oasis. Matt saw the red of canyon walls, the heavy green of creosote, and a blue that was the colour of the sky trapped between high cliffs. If he half closed his eyes, he

could almost imagine himself there, in the quiet shadows of the
Ajo Mountains.

He waited. It had been morning when El Patrón was wheeled
out. Now it was afternoon. The panic had died down outside,
and the halls were nearly silent. The hospital went about its
business without involving the prisoner in the elegant drawing
room.

Matt finished the tea and ate all the cookies. He felt utterly
exhausted. Everything had been turned upside down, and he
didn't know whether El Patrón's death would mean safety or
exactly the opposite.

Matt studied his arm and wondered at the arsenic that
lurked inside. Would mosquitoes die if they bit him? Could he
kill things by spitting on them? It was an interesting thought.
Matt discovered that no matter how terrified he'd been at first,
it wasn't possible to stay terrified. It was as though his brain said,
Okay. That's enough. Let's find something else to do.

Matt thought about María instead. She was probably back at
the convent. He didn't know what she did there, aside from eating chocolates and sunbathing naked on the roof. What a crazy
thing to do. What an *interesting* thing to do. Matt's face turned
warm as he thought about it. He'd seen paintings of fat, naked
goddesses from Rome in his art classes. He thought they were
nice, but no one ran around like that in real life. Or did they?
He didn't know how people behaved in the outside world.

Anyhow, María had gotten into trouble for it. Matt felt
feverish, but it wasn't surprising, being full of arsenic as he was.
He wondered what other stuff Celia had tried on him from her
garden.

The door swung open. Mr Alacrán strode in with Tam Lin.

For an instant time froze. Matt was six years old again, lying in a pool of blood with Rosa plucking fragments of glass from his foot. A fierce man had burst into the room and shouted, *How dare you defile this house? Take the creature outside now!*

It was the first time Matt had realised he wasn't human. The fierce man had been Mr Alacrán, and he had the same expression of loathing on his face now as he looked at Matt.

"I'm here to inform you we no longer need your services," Mr Alacrán said.

Matt gasped. That meant El Patrón was dead. No matter how often he'd thought about it, the reality came as a blow.

"I – I'm sorry." Silent tears began to roll down Matt's face. He could keep himself from blubbering, but there was nothing he could do about the grief that welled up inside.

"I imagine you are," said Mr Alacrán. "It means we no longer have a use for you."

Of course you have a use for me, Matt thought. He knew as much about running Opium as Steven. He'd studied the farming techniques, the day-to-day problems of water purification and food distribution. He probably knew more than anyone about the network of spies and corrupt officials in other countries. Years of listening to El Patrón had given Matt a feel for the Alacrán empire no one else could possibly have.

"Have it put to sleep," Mr Alacrán said to Tam Lin.

"Yes, sir," said Tam Lin.

"What do you mean?" cried Matt. "El Patrón wouldn't want that! He had me educated. He wanted me to help run the country."

Tam Lin looked at him in pity. "You poor fool. El Patrón had seven other clones exactly like you, each one educated and believing he was going to run the country."

"I don't believe it!"

"I have to admit, you were the first one with musical genius. But we can always turn on the radio if we want that."

"You can't do this! We're friends! You said so! You left me a note – " Matt was knocked down by a blow that made him see stars. No one had ever struck him. No one was allowed to. He crawled to his knees, holding his jaw. He was even more shocked by the person who'd done it.

Tam Lin.

Tam Lin was an ex-terrorist. He'd been responsible for the deaths of twenty children, and maybe it didn't even bother him. Matt had never considered that possibility.

"You see, lad, I'm what you call a mercenary," said Tam Lin in the lilting voice Matt had come to love. "I worked for El Patrón for donkey's years – thought he'd go on forever. But now I'm out of a job, and Mr Alacrán has been kind enough to offer me another."

"What about Celia?" whispered Matt.

"You don't think she'd get away with the game she played? By now she'll have been turned into an eejit."

But you told her about the monarch butterflies, thought Matt. *You let her walk into the trap.*

"Can you finish up here? I've got work to do," said Mr Alacrán.

"I'll dispose of the clone, sir," said Tam Lin. "I might need Daft Donald to help me tie it up."

He called me a clone, Matt thought. *He called me an "it."*

"Remember, I want you back for the wake tonight," said Mr Alacrán.

"Wouldn't miss it for the world," said Tam Lin with a twinkle in his lying, treacherous eyes.

24

A FINAL GOOD-BYE

Daft Donald held Matt firmly, and Tam Lin wrapped him in duct tape. The bodyguard slung him over a horse as he exchanged greetings with other members of El Patrón's private army, lounging by the stables. "Where are you taking it?" a man called.

"Thought I'd dump it next to the eejit pens," Tam Lin replied. The man's laughter was lost in the drum of horse's hooves striking the earth.

This animal was different from the Safe Horses. It was faster and less predictable. It even smelled different. Matt, with his nose pressed into its hide, was in a good position to know. Safe Horses had a faint chemical odour, but this one reeked of sun and sweat.

Matt suddenly realised what Tam Lin meant by dumping him next to the eejit pens. He was going to be thrown into the yellow ooze at the bottom of a pit. The horror of it, the unfairness and treachery of almost everyone he'd ever known, made Matt's blood pound in his ears. But this time, instead of fear, he felt a surge of pure animal rage. He deserved to live! He was *owed* this life that had so casually been given him, and if he had to die, he would struggle until the very last minute.

Matt tested the tape holding his arms and legs. He couldn't move an inch. *Well then,* Matt thought, *I'll have to wriggle and squirm my way out of the sludge pit.* He saw the earth fly under the horse's hooves. His stomach bounced painfully against its body. This creature didn't run as smoothly as a Safe Horse.

Finally, it slowed and Tam Lin lifted Matt down. The boy managed to jack-knife his body and drive his head into the man's stomach. "Ach! Ye pee-brained ninny!" swore Tam Lin. "Look about you before you do a stupid trick like that!"

Matt rolled onto his back, his feet up to deliver a kick. He saw blue sky and a shoulder of rock. He smelled not slime and corruption, but good, clean air scented by creosote. They weren't by the eejit pens. They were on the path to the Ajo Mountains.

"There! I hope to have a lavish apology," grunted Tam Lin, peeling the tape, none too gently, off Matt's skin.

"Are you going to drown me in the oasis instead?" Matt snarled.

"Get a grip on yourself, lad. All right, I can see you've got grounds for suspicion, but credit me with a little decency."

"How can I trust someone who killed twenty children?" Matt said.

"So they told you that." Tam Lin looked so sad, Matt felt slightly – but only slightly – sorry for him.

"Is it true?" he demanded.

"Oh, aye. It's true." Tam Lin wadded the tape into a ball and stuffed it into one of the horse's saddlebags. He took out a backpack and heaved it over his shoulder. "Come on. I don't have much time."

He started up the trail, not looking back. Matt paused. He could steal the horse and ride north. The Farm Patrol might not know yet that he was marked for disposal. *Disposal,* Matt thought with a glow of anger. But the animal didn't look easy to ride. Unlike a Safe Horse, it had to be tied to a tree. It rolled its eyes and flared its nostrils when Matt tried to get near it.

On the other hand, he could follow Tam Lin into the mountains and hope the man's friendship held. Tam Lin had disappeared among the rocks. He wasn't even bothering to see whether Matt followed.

I'm probably the world's biggest idiot, thought Matt as he trudged along the trail.

The oasis was brimming. Autumn rains had brought life to the paloverde trees, making them bright with delicate yellow and orange flowers. The grape arbour was leafier than Matt ever remembered, and a small duck paddled away across the water as he approached.

Tam Lin was perched on a rock. "That's a cinnamon teal," he said. "They migrate from the United States to Aztlán this time of year. You wonder how they find a speck of water like this in all the dry desert."

Matt settled on another rock, not too near. The sun was sliding behind the hills and shadows crept into the little valley.

"If it hadn't been for this place, I'd have run barking mad years ago," the bodyguard said. Matt watched the little duck work its way along the far shore. "I was half mad when I went to work for El Patrón. *It's a place to hide,* I thought then. *I'll leave when the police get tired of hunting for me.* But of course things didn't work out that way. Once something belongs to El Patrón, it's his forever."

"So you did kill the children," Matt said.

"I could say it was an accident – and it was – but that doesn't take away the horror. I *was* intending to blow up the prime minister, a fat toad who deserved it. I simply never considered the other people who might get in the way. Frankly, I was such a self-important ass, I didn't care. I got most of these scars from that explosion, and Daft Donald had his throat cut. That's why he can't talk."

In all these years Matt hadn't thought about why Daft Donald never spoke. He'd assumed the large, silent man was antisocial.

"El Patrón had an instinct for people he could enslave," said Tam Lin. "He was such a powerful presence. Power's a strange thing, lad. It's a drug and people like me crave it. It wasn't till I met Celia that I saw what a monster I'd become. I was too happy swaggering around in El Patrón's shadow."

"But you let the doctors turn Celia into an eejit," said Matt.

"I did not! I marked her forehead so it appeared like she was operated on. I put her in the stables with Rosa."

Matt looked at Tam Lin directly for the first time since they arrived at the oasis. A great weight shifted off his chest.

"She'll be safe as long as she remembers to act like a zombie. So now I think I've earned that lavish apology," the bodyguard said.

And Matt gave it at great length and wholeheartedly.

"I would've brought her here, but Celia isn't much for climbing rocks." Tam Lin sighed.

They looked out over the pool with the afternoon sky silvering its surface. The cinnamon teal waddled onto the bank and preened its feathers. A swallow scooped up a dragonfly hovering over the water.

"Am I supposed to live here?" Matt asked.

Tam Lin started. "Ah! My mind was wandering. I love the way swallows turn just before they're about to crash into the ground. No, lad. You wouldn't be able to survive. It's better if you go to Aztlán."

Aztlán! Matt's heart gave a bound. "Are you coming with me?"

"I can't." Tam Lin's voice was sad. "You see, I've done terrible things in my life, and I can't escape the consequences."

"That's not true," Matt said. "The police probably stopped looking for you long ago. You could give people a false name. You could grow a beard and shave your head."

"Of course I could – and may I say, you're showing quite a lawless streak. Quite a chip off the old block you are. No, I'm talking about *moral* consequences. I've spent years benefiting from the horrors of Opium, and now I have the chance to put things right. I mustn't pass it up. Celia has made me see that. She's a very strict woman, you know. Won't put up with evil."

"I know," said Matt, thinking of how Celia had stood up to El Patrón.

"I've already packed your bag," Tam Lin said, unslinging the backpack. "There's maps in the chest. Take as many water bottles as you can manage, and when you reach the Aztlán border, say you're a refugee. Your parents have been taken by the Farm Patrol. Act stupid – that shouldn't be a problem – and don't tell anyone you're a clone."

"Won't they be able to tell?" Matt imagined the Aztlános' rage when they realised they'd been duped.

"Here's the dirty little secret." Tam Lin bent down and

whispered, as though he had to hide the information from the swallows, the duck, and the dragonflies. "No one can tell the difference between a clone and a human. That's because there *isn't* any difference. The idea of clones being inferior is a filthy lie."

Tam Lin strode off to the metal chest, leaving Matt openmouthed. He watched the man remove water bottles and maps. How could a clone be the same as a human? Everything in Matt's experience argued against it.

Tam Lin unzipped a pocket in the backpack and took out a clump of paper. "This is money, see. I should have taught you about it before. Here's a hundred-peso note and here's a fifty. Always ask the price of something first and offer half. Oh, crikey! You're not going to learn it now. Just remember to take out one piece of paper at a time and don't let anyone see how many pieces of paper you have."

The sun had set and dusk was falling rapidly. Tam Lin built a fire and stacked dry wood nearby. "You should go first thing in the morning. That gives you twelve hours to reach the border. It's the ideal time because the Farm Patrol is at the house for the wake. Another thing: El Patrón has kept Opium frozen one hundred years in the past."

"I don't understand," said Matt.

"Opium, as much as possible, is the way things were in El Patrón's youth. Celia cooks on a wood fire, the rooms aren't airconditioned, the fields are harvested by people, not machines. Even rockets aren't allowed to fly over. The only places where the rules are relaxed are the hospital and the security system. It was El Patrón's way of outwitting Death. One of his ways."

"But everything's the same on TV," Matt protested.

Tam Lin laughed. "El Patrón controlled that, too. El Látigo Negro snapped his last whip a century ago. Talk about reruns. In many ways you'll find Aztlán confusing, but they've had a movement back to simpler times recently. They're trying to turn away from a machine-based economy to the old Mexican culture. You'll find some things familiar."

"Wait!" cried Matt as the bodyguard made ready to leave. "Can't you stay?" The thought of losing his friend and perhaps never seeing him again was devastating.

"I've got to attend the wake," said Tam Lin.

"Then bring Celia here. I could help her climb the rocks."

"Wait'll you see the rocks. No, lad. Celia's too old to make the trip. I'll keep her as safe as I can. You have my word on it."

"What should I do in Aztlán? Where can I stay?" Matt was beginning to feel panicky.

"Where's my head?" Tam Lin said, stopping at the edge of the firelight. "I left the most important thing out. The first thing you do in Aztlán is catch a hovercraft to San Luis and ask directions to the Convent of Santa Clara. Unless I'm very much mistaken, María will dance rings around you when you walk in the front door."

There was no stopping him this time. Tam Lin strode ahead with Matt trotting behind. When they reached the hole in the rock, the bodyguard turned and put his hand on Matt's shoulder. "I don't believe in long good-byes," he said.

"Will I ever see you again?"

Tam Lin waited a moment before saying, "No." Matt drew in his breath sharply. "I've never lied to you, and I don't intend to start now. The important thing is, you've escaped. You're the one possession El Patrón let slip through his fingers."

"What's going to happen to me?" Matt said.

"You're going to find María and, if things work out, her mother."

"You know Esperanza?"

"Oh, aye. She used to come to the house. Did you ever see that movie about dinosaurs? The one with the velociraptor?"

Matt remembered a particularly nasty dinosaur with long claws and teeth and a willingness to burrow through rock to get at its prey.

"Well, that's Esperanza when she's got a cause. She's a good person to have on your side." Tam Lin climbed through the rock and went off into the gathering dark. He didn't look back. Matt kept himself from shining the flashlight on him.

25

THE FARM PATROL

Matt felt almost light-headed as he walked back to the oasis. So much had happened so quickly. So much had changed. The little campfire seemed unbearably lonely. He built up the fire and then worried about whether the Farm Patrol could see it. He kicked some of the branches away. Then Matt thought about the animals that might come to the water at night. Coyotes for sure, a bobcat maybe. A jaguar was a long shot, but Tam Lin had seen them. Matt built up the fire again.

He found beef jerky and dried apples in the metal chest. He was ravenous, having eaten nothing but cookies since the morning of the wedding. The food lifted his spirits, and soon he was poring over the map in the flickering light. It was like an exciting novel full of possible adventures. Tam Lin had marked the route with a red pen and added comments using his own creative spelling, such as *Ratlesnakes heer* and *Saw bare under tree*.

Matt finished dinner with a handful of peanuts and a chocolate bar.

He shut the backpack into the metal chest and unrolled the sleeping bag on an exposed slab of rock. He felt safer away from places where he might meet *bare under tree.* Then he lay down and looked at the stars.

It was oddly frightening to lie on the ground without a shelter. The sky was so black and the stars so many and brilliant. He might lose his hold on the earth. He'd float away, and if he didn't grab a tree branch, he'd go on forever into those bright, inhuman lights.

Matt ran a rope from the sleeping bag to a tree. Okay, it was a dumb thing to worry about, but it didn't hurt to be careful. Celia once told him the Indians in her village carried charms to keep from being carried off by the sky. They might know something people with houses didn't understand.

Exhausted by all that had happened, Matt fell into a deep and dreamless sleep. Just before dawn the air vibrated with something that was almost – but not quite – a sound. Matt sat up and grabbed the rope. The ground shivered briefly and was still. A pair of ravens exploded off a tree branch and flew around the oasis cawing wildly. A coyote froze with its muzzle dripping from the pool where it had been drinking.

Matt listened. The sound – if it *was* a sound – had come from all around. It wasn't like anything he'd experienced. The ravens settled, grumbling between themselves, and the coyote bolted into the rocks.

Matt started a fire with a lighter he found in the backpack. He saw that the metal chest was ringed with coyote prints and something had tried to gnaw the latch.

After a quick breakfast he filled as many water bottles as he could carry, placing an iodine tablet in each one. The last time he drank oasis water, he'd been deathly sick. But that was the arsenic, he realised. How was Celia? he wondered. Would she get enough to eat in the stables? And wasn't acting like a zombie as bad as being one if you had to do it for years?

I'll ask Esperanza to help her escape, he thought.

Now that the moment for departure had come, Matt found himself dawdling. He double-checked the supplies. He added a book, tested the weight of his pack, and took it out again. The sun was already high, although the valley was still in shadow. *I could spend another night here,* he thought. But the oasis might not be safe now that El Patrón was gone.

Matt shouldered the backpack, tied extra water bottles to his belt, and set off through the grape arbour. He would go on, as Tam Lin had, without looking back.

The first part of the trail was easy. Matt had been over it many times. Soon, however, he came to a canyon choked with bushes. He had to break his way through. The dust of the leaves covered him from head to toe and found its way into his lungs. He had to rest in a dry gully to regain his breath. Only an hour had passed. If the rest of the journey went like this, he wouldn't reach Aztlán for a month.

Matt went through the backpack. In an inside pocket he found an inhaler. The relief it brought his tortured lungs was pure heaven. He also found a wicked-looking machete in a leather sheath. *I could have saved myself a lot of trouble if I'd looked earlier,* he thought.

After a rest Matt hacked his way through the bushes. It gave him a savage pleasure to get even with the plants that had scratched his arms and face all morning.

When he reached the end of the valley, he was confronted

by a high granite cliff. Matt checked the map. There it was, with a red line going straight to the top. It was higher than anything he'd ever attempted to climb. Matt looked for another way to proceed, but the map was firm on this point: *Onlee way out. Yu can do it,* said Tam Lin's note. Matt stared up at the impossibly distant bushes peeking over the top of the cliff until he was dizzy. The only good thing was that he didn't have to boost Celia ahead of him.

Matt inched from crevice to crevice until his legs began to tremble with fatigue. Halfway up he thought he couldn't move another inch. He hugged the granite face and wondered how long he could stay there before exhaustion forced him to let go. He'd fall onto jagged rocks. He'd die there. He might as well have let his heart be harvested by doctors. A shadow passed briefly over him, and after a moment it came back.

Only one thing cast a shadow on a cliff in such a deserted place. Matt was suddenly filled with rage. It was as though it came from some deep place, like lava in a volcano. He no longer felt exhausted or discouraged or anything else except a towering fury to survive. He pulled himself up, foothold by foothold, crag by crag, until he wriggled over the top and lay panting and surprised by his feat.

Matt looked up into the blinding, blue sky and heard the leathery flap of wings as the bird turned in the air. *I win, you ugly, good-for-nothing buzzard,* thought Matt. He smiled. He sounded just like El Patrón.

Matt celebrated with a bottle of water and a packet of cookies. He threw a rock at the turkey buzzard. The map showed he'd come about five miles and there were five more to go. The sun was bending to the west, so he might not make it to the border before dark. Matt wasn't particularly worried. He had plenty of food, and he felt enormously good after his battle with the cliff.

He travelled on to the top of a ridge. The going was much easier and the view was spectacular. Tam Lin had included small binoculars among the supplies, so Matt stopped frequently to look back at Opium. The land toward Aztlán was still blocked by the mountains.

He could see the long, flat poppy fields and even a brown smudge that might have been a group of eejits. He saw the water purification plant and storehouses for food and fertiliser. The red tile roofs of the mansion spread out in a patch of intense green. Matt felt a strange sensation in the pit of his stomach. It was, he realised, sorrow.

There, on the high ridge of the Ajo Mountains, Matt gave himself over to grief. He wept for Celia trapped in the stables and for Tam Lin, who was trapped in a different way. He wasted no tears on the Alacráns or their slaves Felicia, Fani, and Emilia. But he wept for El Patrón, who deserved pity less than anyone but who was closer to Matt than anyone in the world.

In an odd way it felt as though El Patrón were still alive, and in one sense he was. For Matt still existed. As long as he survived, El Patrón had not vanished from the world.

Matt camped at the top of the ridge. The recent rains had filled hollows in the rocks, and the little folds of the mountain were green with bear grass. Desert mallow spread out peach-coloured blooms in pockets of soil, and everywhere late-blooming cliff roses swarmed with bees. Matt wasn't afraid, although he saw more animals than he had ever observed on his travels with Tam Lin.

White-tailed deer fed on bushes in the late-afternoon sun.

He saw a buck rub his antlers on a tree, perhaps to sharpen them or perhaps simply because they itched. Matt didn't know. He saw a group of coatis running with their tails in the air and their long noses pointed along the ground.

Everything seemed alive. Everything scurried, flew, dug, nibbled, or chattered. Frogs cheeped from an unseen water hole, a rock squirrel whistled when a red-tailed hawk drifted by, a mockingbird sat on the topmost branch of a mesquite and performed every song Matt had ever heard, plus a few extra the bird must have composed himself.

Most of all, it was the wild music that impressed Matt. It did the same thing that playing the piano had done when he was frightened and lonely. It took him into another world where only beauty existed and where he was safe from hatred and disappointment and death.

He stayed up a long time, watching the distant lights of Opium. There weren't many. The mansion sat by itself in a sea of dark. The factories, storehouses, and eejit pens were all hidden. The air was so still, the eejits had probably been driven into the fields to sleep. Matt heard no sound from the far plain. It might have been a painting instead of a real place. Nearby he heard the hoot of a great horned owl and the incessant chirp of crickets. The mountain was darker than the plain, but it was alive and it was real.

Matt slept well, and he felt strong and confident in the morning. Opium was covered by a ground fog, as it often was in the autumn. He couldn't see anything but a white haze stretching from horizon to horizon.

With a last look at the map, Matt started along the trail. It dipped up and down, gradually leading up to a pass between two hills. He heard a noise from one of the high meadows, like someone hitting a baseball. It happened again and again. It couldn't really be people playing baseball up there, he knew, with only the hawks and turkey buzzards to watch.

As he got closer, the sound became more like someone smacking a pair of ripe watermelons together. Matt cautiously peered around a bush and saw two bighorn sheep thunder at each other like a pair of farm trucks. They crashed head-on, reeled away, and trotted off. After a few moments they repeated the performance. A group of ewes grazed among the rocks as though they couldn't be bothered to watch. Matt was so delighted, he laughed out loud. Then, of course, the sheep skittered to safety, making huge leaps as they bounded from rock to rock.

As Matt approached the cleft at the top of the mountains, he began to hear another puzzling noise. It was like the roar of fire in Celia's stove. It got louder and louder, and now Matt could pick out individual sounds: the grinding of machinery, the blast of horns, even – incredibly – music.

He stepped through the pass into another world. The same quiet hills lay below him, with hawks patrolling wooded valleys between shoulders of rock. But beyond them lay a seething mass of factories and skyscrapers. He saw roadways not only on the ground, but also going up in wide spirals among the buildings. A sea of hovercrafts restlessly prowled the air. The buildings stretched on as far as Matt could see, which wasn't far because a smudgy brown haze covered everything. It was from here that the booming, clanking, thundering noises came, and it surprised Matt so much, he sat down on the trail to think.

The sun was directly overhead. Matt fished out the hat Tam Lin had provided. So this was Aztlán. In all Matt's imaginings it had been nothing like this. He had taken Celia's tales about the *maquiladoras* and El Patrón's stories about Durango and mixed them with episodes of El Látigo Negro. What came out was a hodgepodge of factories, primitive huts, and fabulous ranches owned by evil tycoons who had pretty daughters.

How could people live in all that noise? he thought. *How could they breathe the air?* There wasn't a fence for as far as he could see, but there was a line of poles that could have supported a fence. The land on the Opium side of the border was deserted. It was as though someone had put up a big sign saying DANGER! RADIOACTIVE!

Matt went back over the mountain pass to the meadow where the bighorn sheep had tried to brain each other. He ate a small lunch of beef jerky and dry cheese. He couldn't stay here. The rainy season in the Ajo Mountains was brief, and Matt had a very clear idea of how soon the little frog ponds and hidden grottoes would dry out.

Equally, he couldn't return to the mansion. The only way out was the border of Aztlán. *You can do it,* he imagined Tam Lin saying. *I guess I have to,* thought Matt, turning to look one last time at the quiet meadow, the white plumes of bear grass, and the black-throated sparrows flitting through the trees.

He slid down parts of the hill where the ground was steep and sandy. He arrived at the bottom, hot and dusty and itching from dozens of spines he had collected from a cholla cactus on the way down. He crouched in the shade of a rock to drink the last of his water.

Matt found the spines impossible to remove. They seemed to burrow deeper into his skin when he tried to pinch them out. And somewhere along the way he'd torn his trousers and one of the straps on the backpack.

Matt observed the border through binoculars. What he saw was every bit as ugly as it sounded. A row of factories chugged smoke into the air. Behind them, on the border itself, was a tangle of cast-off machinery and tanks that seeped a black liquid onto the ground. Pools of the stuff dotted the narrow space between the buildings and the line of poles. Then something much closer moved across Matt's field of view.

He adjusted the lenses. It was a man on a horse. *It was a member of the Farm Patrol!* Moving the glasses around, he saw more of them.

Matt shrank back into the rocks. The Farm Patrol must have gone back to work after the wake. Had they seen him come slipping and sliding down the mountain? He was afraid to move. He was afraid not to. Fortunately, the hollow where Matt was hiding was deep. After a tense half hour or so he guessed the Farm Patrol had seen nothing. Or perhaps they were merely waiting for him to get thirsty and come out. Matt did get thirsty, horribly so, as the hours went by.

He counted six men. They rode slowly back and forth. At no time was the border deserted, and at no time was it possible for Matt to run the remaining few hundred yards to freedom. The sun dipped to the west. Shadows lengthened. Matt sucked on a stone to keep from feeling thirsty.

The sun set. The shadow of night rose, dividing the eastern sky into pale blue above and grey below, with a rosy border where the sunlight still shone on a haze of dust in the air. Suddenly a commotion broke out. A group of men burst from one of the junkyards and ran across the border. The instant they passed the line of poles, sirens went off. The Farm Patrol galloped to intercept them.

At once Matt was off in the other direction. It hadn't taken him a second to react. This was his chance. He raced across the ground. To his left he heard shouts and a loud crack accompanied by a flash of light. Matt had seen this weapon at El Patrón's birthday party. It was a super stun gun that fried the hair on an Illegal's head and stopped his heart cold. Most of the time the Illegal's heart started again, so he could be turned into an eejit.

Matt heard horse's hooves pounding. He didn't try to see how many men had turned to follow him. His only chance was to reach the border, and he bounded with an agility that would have impressed a bighorn sheep. He saw the body of a horse approaching. Matt swung the binoculars at the animal's head and sent it veering to one side. The rider pulled it up and forced it to turn.

The poles were close. Matt saw the ground ahead change from dirt to cement. He put on an extra burst of speed, but the Farm Patroller grabbed Matt's backpack and reined in his horse. Matt undid the snap holding the waistband and slid out of the straps. The change in speed sent him stumbling across the border into one of the oily black pools, where he fell on his stomach and skidded out the other side in a plume of goo.

Matt sat up, frantically wiping his eyes. He saw the Farm Patroller ride away and looked down to see he would have no trouble convincing the Aztlános he was a refugee. He had no backpack, no money, and he was covered from head to toe in black slime.

LA VIDA NUEVA

26

THE LOST BOYS

"¡Qué coraje! What spirit that kid has!" a man said. Matt wiped away the goo dripping off his hair. He saw a pair of uniformed men approaching from amid ruined machinery and tanks.

"Hey, kid! ¿Como te llamas? What's your name?" asked one of them.

Matt was stumped for a moment. He certainly couldn't tell the truth. "M–Matt Ortega," he said, swiping the music teacher's name.

"You're a real fighter!" said the border guard. "I thought he had you when he grabbed the backpack. Did your family go over tonight?"

"N–No. My f-family – " Now that the excitement was over, Matt felt the reaction set in. He hugged himself and his teeth chattered.

"Hey," the guard said kindly. "You don't need to explain

now. You just had the beans scared out of you. *¡Caray!* I got scared watching you. Come inside where you can have a bath and something to eat."

Matt followed carefully so he wouldn't slip on the cement. His body was covered in sludge, and his stomach was in knots over the narrow escape.

The guards led him to a large cement bathroom with showers along the walls. They gave him a brush and a chunk of green soap. "Take one of the clean bodysuits from the bin," one of them instructed him.

This is like a dream, Matt thought as he scrubbed and rescrubbed himself in the steamy shower. He'd been afraid of his welcome in Aztlán, but these men treated him like a guest. They didn't seem a bit surprised to see him.

Matt found an olive drab jumpsuit that didn't look too bad. The cloth was as rough as a floor brush, but it would help him fit in with the others. He could pass as human.

When he emerged, he was seated at a table and given a plate of tortillas and beans by a man in a black uniform with the emblem of a beehive on one sleeve. "Thank you. This is very nice," Matt said.

"Oho! We have an aristocrat here," said one of the border guards. "When was the last time someone said thank you to a Keeper, Raúl?"

"About the time America discovered Columbus," said Raúl. He pulled up a chair. "Okay, kid. What were you doing on the *frontera?*"

Matt, between mouthfuls of beans, gave him the story Tam Lin had prepared. His parents had been taken by the Farm Patrol. He got scared and ran back across the border. He wanted to go to San Luis.

"That's really tough, losing your parents like that. Do you come from San Luis?" said Raúl.

"I have — a friend there," said Matt, stumbling over how exactly to describe María.

The man shrugged. "What kind of work can you do?"

Work? Matt was confused. He knew how to run an opium empire, but he didn't think that was what the man wanted to hear. "I can play the piano," he said at last. Raúl laughed out loud.

"Now I know he's an aristocrat," said the other border guard.

"Don't get us wrong," said Raúl, noticing Matt's unhappy expression. "We like art and music, but in the new Aztlán we don't have time for hobbies. We have to contribute to the general good of the people."

"It's hard but it's fair," the other man said.

"So if you have a special skill, like balancing magnetic coils or running a positronic purifier, please tell us."

Positronic purifier, thought Matt. *I don't even know what it is.* He racked his brain. "I studied water purification," he said at last. It wasn't quite true. Matt had *toured* the water purification plant, but he thought he remembered enough to be useful.

"Those plants are automated," said the border guard.

"Wait. I'm getting an idea," said Raúl.

"Stomp on it before it gets away," the guard said.

"No, really. The plankton factory in San Luis can always use new workers. That's something like water purification. And it's where the kid wants to go."

The men seemed to think this was a brilliant plan, and Matt, who had no idea what they were talking about, said the plankton factory sounded fine. It was in San Luis, after all. He could leave right away and find his way to the Convent of Santa Clara.

Matt spent the night in the guardhouse, and in the morning Raúl took him to a large, grey building with high windows covered with iron bars. "You're in luck, *chico*," he said. "We've got a hovercraft going to San Luis tomorrow." He unlocked a metal door that led into a dimly lit hallway. A pair of border guards lounged at a table in front of another door made of reinforced glass. They were playing a game Matt had never seen.

Tiny men seemed to hang in midair over the table, along with trees, buildings, and a pot bubbling on a fire. It was the pot and fire that enchanted Matt. They were so realistic, he could even hear water splattering onto the flames. About half of the tiny men were dressed in animal skins and carried spears. The other half were clad in monk's robes. The border guards wore silver gloves and moved the game pieces by waving their fingers.

"Another one for San Luis," said Raúl. The men grudgingly turned off the game.

"Where did the picture go?" said Matt.

"Haven't you ever seen a holo-game, kid?"

"Of course I have," Matt lied. He didn't want to arouse suspicion.

"Oh, I get it," a border guard said. "You haven't seen this game before. That's because it's so old. It's all the *crotting* government sends us."

"Don't use language like that in front of a kid," said Raúl.

"Sorry," said the guard. He turned on the game, and the tiny men appeared again. "See, those are the cannibals and these are the missionaries. The aim is for the cannibals to push the missionaries into the cooking pot."

"And the missionaries?" Matt asked.

"They have to push the cannibals into the church, but first they have to baptise them."

Matt watched, fascinated, as a tiny missionary held down a yelling cannibal and sprinkled water on his head. So that's what baptism was. "It looks like fun," he said.

"Sure, if you haven't played it a couple thousand times." The man turned the game off and unlocked the glass door for Raúl and Matt to pass through.

"Why are all the doors locked?" Matt asked.

"The orderly production of resources is vital to the general good of the people," said Raúl.

That's a very weird thing to say, Matt thought. However, his attention was riveted on a room full of boys working at tables. They all stopped what they were doing and turned to look at Matt.

He had never played with children. He'd never been to school or played sports, and he'd never had a friend his own age, except María. The reaction of most people to him had been hatred. Thus, the experience of suddenly being thrust into a crowd of boys was like being dumped into a pool of piranhas. Matt assumed they were going to hurt him. He froze into a karate stance Tam Lin had shown him.

The boys surged forward, all talking at once. "What's your name? Where are they sending you? Got any money?" Raúl, perhaps noticing Matt's odd position, crowded them back.

"*Orale, morros.* Okay, kids. His name's Matt, and he needs to be left alone for a while. He just lost his parents in Dreamland." The boys went back to the tables, but they eyed Matt curiously, and one or two of them smiled and tried to entice him over.

Matt stood next to the door while Raúl walked around the room, commenting on the boys' work. Some were fitting small bits of machinery together, others wove strips of plastic into sandals. Still others measured powder into capsules and counted the finished pills into bottles.

Raúl stopped by a large boy who was sanding a curved piece of wood. "We don't have time for hobbies, Chacho. The orderly production of resources is vital to the general good of the people."

"*Crot* the good of the people," muttered Chacho, still sanding the wood.

If Raúl was angered by this curse — and Matt had no doubt it was a curse, although he didn't know what it meant — the man didn't show it. He took the wood from Chacho's hands. "Attention to the welfare of the nation is the highest virtue to which a citizen can aspire."

"Yeah, right," said Chacho.

"Work is freedom. Freedom is work. It's hard but it's fair."

"It's *hard* but it's *fair*," chanted the rest of the boys. "It's *hard* but it's *fair*." They banged out the rhythm on the tables, getting louder and rowdier until Raúl stilled them by raising his hands.

"I'm glad to see you in high spirits," he said, smiling. "You may think I'm a boring old Keeper, but someday you'll understand the importance of these lessons." He led Matt to the middle of the room. "This boy is going to San Luis. I want you to make him welcome, but don't push him if he wants to be alone. He's just been through a terrible loss."

Raúl's exit was done smoothly, with the door closed and locked almost before Matt was aware of it. Why did they have to be locked in? And what was a Keeper? It was the second time Matt had heard the word.

He glared at the boys, whose work slowed now that they weren't being watched. El Patrón always said it was important to establish your authority before anyone had a chance to question it. Matt walked toward the tables as though he owned the place.

"Want to join us?" said a skinny little kid who was making up pills. Matt looked grandly around the room. He nodded curtly. "You can help if you want," the kid offered.

"My advice is to sit on your butt while you have the chance," said Chacho from across the room. The big boy was twisting plastic strips into sandals. Matt walked slowly to the sandal-making table. El Patrón said you should never look anxious or needy. People always took advantage of those who were anxious or needy.

"Why is that?" inquired Matt, looking down at the tangle of plastic strips.

"'Cause the Keepers are gonna work your butt off tomorrow," said Chacho. He was a large, rough-looking boy with big hands and black hair slicked back like the feathers on a duck.

"I thought I was going to San Luis."

"Oh, you are. So am I and Fidelito." Chacho pointed at the skinny kid, who looked only about eight years old. "But you can bet we're going to work *before* we get on the hovercraft, *while* we're on the hovercraft, and *after* we get off the crotting hovercraft. You'll see."

So Matt wandered around and watched the various chores the boys were doing. He settled by Fidelito, who was ecstatic to gain the approval of the newcomer. After a while Matt could see why. Fidelito was the neediest kid in the room, and so of course everyone pushed him around.

"What kind of pills are those?" Matt asked.

"Vitamin B," said Fidelito. "They're supposed to be good for you, but if you eat ten or twelve of them, you get sick."

"What a dope!" Chacho said. "Why would anybody eat a dozen vitamin pills?"

"I was hungry," Fidelito said.

Matt was startled. "You mean, they don't feed you here?"

"Sure they do, if you produce enough work. I'm just not very fast."

"You're not very big," Matt said, feeling sorry for the earnest little boy.

"That doesn't matter," Fidelito explained. "Everyone's supposed to have the same output. As long as we're here, we're equal."

"It's *hard* but it's *fair*," intoned Chacho from across the room.

The other boys picked up the chant, banging the tables until the whole room rocked. One of the border guards told them to shut up through a loudspeaker.

"Did you see your parents taken?" asked Fidelito when the hubbub died down.

"*¡Callate!* Shut up! Let him get used to it," several voices cried, but Matt raised his hand for silence, as he'd seen Raúl do. To his great pleasure, the boys obeyed. There really was something to El Patrón's methods of gaining power.

"It happened yesterday morning," he said, improvising. Matt remembered the crowd of Illegals who had distracted the Farm Patrol. "I saw a flash of light. Papá shouted for me to go back to the border. I saw Mamá fall down, and then a man grabbed my backpack. I slipped out of the straps and ran."

"I know what that flash of light was," said a sad-faced boy. "It's a kind of gun, and it kills you dead. *Mi mamá* — " His voice choked and he didn't say any more. Fidelito put his head down on the table.

"Have — have other people lost their parents?" stammered Matt. He'd been about to create a dramatic story about his escape. Now it seemed a heartless thing to do.

"We all have," said Chacho. "I guess you haven't figured it out. This is an *orfanatorio,* an orphanage. The state is our family now. That's why the border guards wait along the *frontera.* They catch the kids of rockheads who make a run for it and turn them over to the Keepers."

"*Mi abuelita* wasn't a rockhead," said Fidelito from the cradle of his arms.

"Your grandma — Oh, heck, Fidelito," said Chacho. "She was too old to run to the United States. You know that. But I'm sure she loved you," he added as the little boy sniffled. "So you see how it is," Chacho told Matt. "We're all part of the crotting production of resources for the crotting good of the people."

"Don't let Raúl hear you," someone said.

"I'd like to tattoo it on my butt for him to read," said Chacho, going back to the tangle of plastic strips on his table.

27

A FIVE-LEGGED HORSE

The rest of the day, from Matt's point of view, went very well. He drifted from group to group, listening to conversations and storing up information. In case someone were to wonder why he was so ignorant, he didn't ask many questions. He learned that the Keepers were in charge of people who couldn't take care of themselves. They took in the orphans, the homeless, the insane and moulded them into good citizens. The orphans were known as Lost Boys and Lost Girls, and they lived in different buildings. Matt couldn't figure out why everyone seemed to hate the Keepers, although no one, except Chacho, said so directly. Raúl seemed nice enough.

Matt also learned that the country of Opium was called Dreamland here. No one really knew what lay beyond its borders. There were many stories of zombie slaves and a vampire king who lived in a castle. The *chupacabras* haunted its mountains and occasionally crossed over into Aztlán to drink the blood of goats.

Boys who had not seen their parents taken believed they had made it to the United States. Several boys assured Matt they were only waiting for their parents to send for them. Then they would all be rich and happy in the golden paradise that lay beyond Dreamland.

Matt doubted it. The Farm Patrol was very efficient, and besides, El Patrón had told him just as many people ran away from the United States as towards it. If a golden paradise had ever lain to the north, it wasn't there anymore.

Matt helped Fidelito make pills. It seemed monstrously unfair that the little boy was deprived of food simply because he was slower than the larger boys. Fidelito responded with such adoration that Matt began to regret his good deed. The kid reminded him a little of Furball.

They had a half-hour break for lunch. First the guards checked everyone's work output for the morning. Then they brought in a steaming cauldron of beans and handed out tortillas. Before anyone was allowed to eat, the boys had to recite the Five Principles of Good Citizenship and the Four Attitudes Leading to Right-Mindfulness. The food was doled out according to whether a boy had reached his quota or not. Fidelito looked at Matt with shining eyes as his bowl was filled to the brim.

After lunch the work started again. Matt helped Fidelito for a while then switched to Chacho's table for variety. He very quickly figured out the pattern he was supposed to weave. "Enjoy it while you can," grunted Chacho.

"Enjoy what?" said Matt, holding up a finished sandal.

"The thrill of moving from one job to another. Once you

settle in, the Keepers will let you do only one thing. It's supposed to be efficient."

Matt considered this information as he continued to weave plastic. "Can't you ask for something else?"

Chacho laughed. "Sure, you can *ask*. You won't get it, though. Raúl says worker bees do the best they can with whatever job they're given. That's his way of saying, 'Tough toenails, sucker.'"

Matt thought a while longer. "What was that piece of wood you were working on when I arrived?"

For a moment Matt thought the boy wasn't going to answer. Chacho twisted his strip of plastic so viciously it broke. He had to start over with a new one. "It took me weeks to find that wood," he said at last. "I think it was from an old packing crate. I polished it and sanded it. I was going to find more pieces and glue them together." Chacho fell silent again.

"And make what?" Matt urged.

"Promise you won't tell?"

"Of course."

"A guitar."

That was the last answer Matt expected. Chacho had such clumsy-looking hands, he didn't seem capable of playing a musical instrument. "Do you know how to play?"

"Not as well as my father. He taught me to make guitars, though, and I'm pretty good at that."

"Was he — was he taken in Dreamland?" said Matt.

"*¡Caramba!* Do you think I belong with the rest of these losers? *Me encarcelaron por feo.* I was locked up for being ugly. I'm no orphan! My dad's living in the United States. He's got so much money, he can't even fit it into his pockets; and he's going to send for me as soon as he buys a house." Chacho looked absolutely furious, but Matt could tell from his voice that tears weren't far below the surface.

Matt worked on his sandal, not looking at Chacho. He noticed the other boys were absorbed in their work too. They knew – they had to know – that Chacho's father wasn't going to send for anyone anytime soon. But only Matt understood what had really happened to him. Chacho's father was bending and cutting, bending and cutting poppies all day in the hot sun. And on still, breathless nights he was sleeping in the fields to keep from being suffocated by the bad air from the pits.

In the evening the lunchtime ritual was repeated. The food was exactly the same. Afterward the boys washed dishes, tidied up the workroom, and moved the tables to one side. From a storage room they dragged out beds and fitted them on top of one another to form bunks three levels high. "Put Fidelito's bed on the bottom," someone told Matt.

"Which one is it?" asked Matt.

"Smell the mattress," said Chacho.

"I can't help it," the little boy protested.

They were marched into a communal shower by the border guards. Matt had never seen anyone naked outside the art classes on TV. He found it embarrassing. He kept his right foot planted on the floor so no one could see the writing that proclaimed him a clone. He was very glad to shrug on a coarse nightshirt and retreat to the workroom, now bedroom.

"Do we go to sleep now?" he asked.

"Now we get the bedtime story," said Chacho. The boys seemed energised by something. They clustered around a bunk bed under a window, and Chacho put his ear to the wall. After a moment he pointed at the window and nodded.

Fidelito climbed the bunk bed like a little monkey and lifted his nightshirt. This was his moment of glory. *"Voy a enseñarle la mapa mundi,"* he announced.

I'm going to show him the map of the world? thought Matt. Show who? And what did he mean by the map of the world? Fidelito stuck his skinny backside between the bars of the high window and waggled it. A minute later Matt heard Raúl's voice say, "One of these days I'm going to bring a slingshot."

Fidelito scrambled off the bed to the cheers of the rest of the boys. "I'm the only one small enough to fit," he said, swaggering around like a bantam rooster.

When Raúl entered, he said nothing at all about being mooned. He pulled up a chair, and the boys settled on the bunk beds to listen. The title of his talk was "Why Individualism Is Like a Five-Legged Horse." Raúl explained that things went smoothly only when people worked together. They decided on a goal and then helped one another achieve it. "What would happen," the Keeper asked all the boys, "if you were rowing a boat and half of you wanted to go one way and the other half another?"

He waited expectantly, and after a while someone put up his hand and said, "We'd go in circles."

"Very good!" said Raúl, beaming at his audience. "We all have to paddle together to reach the shore."

"What if we don't want to reach the shore?" Chacho said.

"A very good question," said the Keeper. "Can anyone tell us what would happen if we stayed out in the boat for days and days?" He waited.

"We'd starve to death," a boy said.

"There's your answer, Chacho," said Raúl. "We'd all starve to death. That brings me to the problem of the five-legged horse. A horse runs very well on four legs. It's what he's made for. But suppose he grew a fifth leg that only wanted to please itself. The other four legs would be running and running, but the fifth leg – which we'll call individualism – would want to walk slowly to enjoy a beautiful meadow, or it might want to take a nap. Then the poor animal would fall over! That's why we take that unhappy horse to a vet and have the fifth leg cut off. It may seem harsh, but we've all got to pull together in the new Aztlán, or we'll all wind up lying in the dirt. Does anyone have a question?"

Raúl waited a long time. Finally, Matt put up his hand and said, "Why don't you put a computer chip in the horse's brain? Then it wouldn't matter how many legs it had." A gasp went around the room.

"Are you saying – ?" the Keeper stopped, as though he couldn't believe what he was hearing. "Are you suggesting we turn the horse *into a zombie?*"

"I don't see much difference between that and sawing off the extra leg," said Matt. "What you're after is a horse that works hard and doesn't waste time looking at flowers."

"This is great!" Chacho said.

"But you – don't you see the difference?" Raúl was so outraged, he could hardly speak.

"We recite the Five Principles of Good Citizenship and the Four Attitudes Leading to Right-Mindfulness every time we want to eat," explained Matt. "You keep telling us the orderly production of resources is vital to the general good of the people. It's obvious we're supposed to follow the rules and not walk slowly through meadows. But horses aren't as smart as people. It makes sense to programme them with computer chips." Matt thought this was a brilliant argument, and he couldn't see why the Keeper was so upset. El Patrón would have seen the logic of it in an instant.

"I can see we have our work cut out with you," Raúl said in a tight voice. "I can see we have a nasty little aristocrat who needs to be educated about the will of the people!" Matt was amazed at the man's reaction. The Keeper had asked for questions. In fact, he'd almost demanded them.

"Well!" said Raúl, brushing off his uniform as though he'd touched something dirty. "The sooner this nasty little aristocrat goes to the plankton factory the better. That's all I can say." And he flounced out of the room.

Instantly, all the boys crowded around Matt. "Wow! You showed him!" they cried.

"You mooned him even better than I did," said Fidelito, bouncing up and down on a bed.

"He didn't even make us recite the Five Principles of Good Citizenship and the Four Attitudes Leading to Right-Mindfulness," exulted a boy.

"Heck, I had you down as a wuss," said Chacho "You've got more nerve than a herd of bulls."

"What? What did I do?" said Matt, completely bewildered.

"You only told him the Keepers were trying to turn us into a bunch of crots!"

Late that night Matt lay on a top bunk and went over the events of the day. He didn't know how much trouble he was in or what kind of revenge to expect. He didn't dislike Raúl. He only thought the man was an idiot. Matt realised he'd better walk carefully around people who took offence at mere words. What harm could words do? Tam Lin loved a good argument, the more spirited the better. He said it was like doing push-ups in your brain.

Matt felt his right foot under the scratchy wool blanket. This was his one weakness, and he despaired of keeping it hidden. Tam Lin might have said there was no difference between humans and clones, but everything in Matt's experience argued against it. Humans hated clones. It was the natural order of things, and Raúl could use it to destroy him. No one must ever see the tattoo that tied Matt to Dreamland and to the vampire who lived in its castle. *Vampire!* thought Matt. El Patrón would have enjoyed that description. He loved to inspire fear.

Matt had added a few more crumbs to the stash of information he was accumulating about this new world in which he found himself. An aristocrat was the lowest form of life, a parasite who expected honest peasants to be his slaves. A crot – the deadliest insult anyone could utter – was a simple, harmless eejit, like the thousands who had cut grass, washed floors, and tended poppies as far back as Matt could remember. The clean word for them was *zombies*. Whatever they were called, Matt thought they deserved pity, not hatred.

He couldn't bring himself to think about Celia and Tam Lin. Sorrow threatened to overwhelm him, and he didn't want to be caught sobbing like a baby. Instead, he thought about going to San Luis. He'd look for the Convent of Santa Clara right away and find María. The thought of María cheered him up immensely.

Matt basked in the approval of his newfound friends. It was the most wonderful thing that had ever happened to him. The boys accepted him as though he were a real human. He felt like he'd been walking across a desert all his life and now he'd arrived at the biggest and best oasis in the world.

28

THE PLANKTON FACTORY

Raúl gave the boys an inspirational talk in the morning. It was all about aristocrats and how attractive they might seem on the surface but how vile they really were inside. No mention was made of Matt. A few of the younger boys seemed uneasy, but Chacho and Fidelito proclaimed Matt a national hero after the Keeper left.

Matt was put to work the instant the talk was over. He was told to measure pills with the younger children, and his quota was twice theirs, "to teach him the value of labour." Matt wasn't worried. When they reached San Luis, he'd be off to the convent faster than Fidelito could say, *It's hard but it's fair.*

For breakfast he was given only half a bowl of beans and three tortillas instead of six. Chacho told each of the bigger boys to give him a spoonful of theirs, so he wound up with a full bowl anyway.

At mid-morning Raúl called out the names of the three

who were to go to San Luis and marched them to the hover-craft. "You've had it easy here," he told them. "This is a holiday camp compared to where you're going; but if you work hard and keep your record clean, you can move up to full citizenship when you reach eighteen."

"Crot that," muttered Chacho.

"That's not a good beginning. That's not a good beginning at all," said Raúl.

Matt had been inside a hovercraft only once – the disastrous night when he'd been betrayed by Steven and Emilia. This ship wasn't nearly as nice. It was full of hard plastic seats, and it smelled of sweat and mould. Raúl sat them in the middle, as far from the windows as possible. He gave them a bag of plastic strips to weave into sandals.

"Told you we'd have to work," said Chacho under his breath.

The Keeper strapped them in and left without a word. The rest of the hovercraft was filled with bales of plastic sandals piled so high, the boys couldn't see out the windows. They couldn't move around, either, because the straps were locked into place. *What is it with these people?* thought Matt. They couldn't seem to relax unless they had total control.

The hovercraft lifted, and Fidelito announced that he always got sick on airships. "You puke on me, you've had it," snarled Chacho.

Matt solved the problem by transferring the bag of plastic strips to the little boy's lap.

"You're a genius," said Chacho. "Go ahead, Fidelito. Knock yourself out."

What were Steven and Emilia doing now? Matt wondered as they flew on. Steven was the crown prince of Opium now.

He'd be celebrating. His friends from school would come over, and tables would be set in the garden where El Patrón used to have his birthday parties. Emilia would have her eejit flower girls to wait on her, or perhaps she'd sent them away to the fields. They weren't capable of much else.

Those girls must have tried to run with their parents, Matt thought with a thrill of horror. They weren't any older than Fidelito, who had lost his battle with airsickness and was coating the plastic strips in secondhand beans and tortillas.

"They should have starved you at breakfast time," said Chacho.

"I can't help it," said Fidelito in a muffled voice.

The rest of the trip – mercifully short – was spent in a cloud of sour vomit. Matt leaned one way and Chacho leaned the other in a vain attempt to escape the smell. Fortunately, the hovercraft landed soon. When the pilot saw what had happened, he unlocked the seat belts and shoved the boys out the door.

Matt tumbled to his knees on hot sand. He sucked in air and immediately regretted it. The smell outside was even worse. It was like thousands of fish rotting and oozing in the hot sun. Matt gave in to the inevitable and emptied his stomach. Not far away Chacho was doing the same. "I was in purgatory. Now I'm in hell," he groaned.

"Make it stop," sobbed Fidelito.

Matt pulled himself to his feet and dragged the little boy toward a building shimmering in the heat. All around, Matt saw blinding white hills and crusted pools stained with crimson. Chacho stumbled after them.

Matt pulled Fidelito through a doorway and slumped against a wall to recover. The air inside was cooler and slightly fresher. The room was full of bubbling tanks tended by boys who morosely fished the water with nets and who paid no attention to the newcomers.

After a few moments Matt felt strong enough to get up. His legs were rubbery and his stomach was in knots. "Who's in charge?" he asked. A boy pointed at a door.

Matt knocked and went in. He saw a group of men dressed in the same black uniform as Raúl, with the emblem of a beehive on their sleeves. "There's one of *los bichos* — the vermin — who stank up my hovercraft," said the pilot.

"What's your name?" said a Keeper.

"Matt Ortega," Matt replied.

"Ah. The aristocrat."

Uh oh, thought Matt. *Raúl must have spread the word.*

"Well, you won't get away with your swanky ways here," the man said. "We've got something called the boneyard, and any troublemaker who goes through it comes out as harmless as a little lamb."

"The first thing he's going to do is clean my ship," said the pilot. And so Matt, along with Chacho, soon found himself scrubbing the floors and walls of the aircraft. Lastly — and most horribly — they had to wash each slimy strip of plastic in a bucket of hot, soapy water.

The air didn't smell as evil as before. "It's just as bad," the pilot assured them from his seat under a plastic shade. "The longer you're here, the less you notice it. There's something in it that paralyses your sense of smell."

"We should make Fidelito drink this," said Chacho, idly sloshing the contents of the bucket.

"He can't help it," Matt said. Poor Fidelito had curled up on the ground in a fit of misery. Neither boy had the heart to make him work.

After they finished, the head Keeper, who was called Carlos, gave them a tour of the factory. "These are the brine tanks," he said. "You take the stink bugs out of the tanks with this" – he held up a net – "and when the plankton's ripe, you harvest it."

"What's plankton?" Matt ventured to ask.

"Plankton!" exclaimed Carlos, as though he'd been waiting eagerly for that question. "It's what a whale filters out of the sea to make a meal. It's the microscopic plants and animals that drift in the top layer of the water. You wouldn't think an enormous creature could live on something so tiny, but that's the astonishing truth. Plankton is the eighth wonder of the world. It's full of protein, vitamins, and roughage. It's got everything a whale needs to be happy and everything people need too. The plankton we manufacture here is made into hamburgers, hotdogs, and burritos. Ground up fine, it takes the place of mother's milk."

Carlos went on and on. It appeared his life's work was to make people love and appreciate plankton. He seemed blind to the bleak desert that surrounded them, now that they had gone outside.

Matt saw high security fences in the distance, and his heart sank. The air was foul, the temperature broiling, and the humidity so high that his jumpsuit clung to his body like a second skin. This was the place he was supposed to inhabit until he turned eighteen.

"Where's San Luis?" he asked.

"That's on a need-to-know basis," said Carlos. "When we feel you need the information, that's when you get to know it. Don't get any ideas about going over the fence, either. The top wire has enough power to spit you back like a melon seed. Here are the salt mountains." He indicated the white dunes Matt had noticed before. "After we harvest the plankton, the brine is evaporated and the salt is processed for sale. These are the highest salt mountains in the world. People come from all over to admire them."

What people? thought Matt, looking at the depressing landscape.

A siren wailed. "Time for the first lunch setting!" Carlos said. He led them up a dune. It was more solid than it looked. At the top was a picnic area with tables. Plastic flowers were planted around the edge, and a weather vane topped by a spouting whale stood in the centre. A slight breeze blew a fine dusting of salt over Matt's skin. "The lunch area was my idea," Carlos said, plopping himself onto a bench. "I think it's raised everyone's morale."

The boys, trudging up the slope with pots and dishes, didn't look especially happy. They set down their burdens and lined up between the tables like rows of soldiers. Carlos told Matt, Chacho, and Fidelito to stand at the end of a line. Everyone recited the Five Principles of Good Citizenship and the Four Attitudes Leading to Right-Mindfulness, and then a sullen, acne-scarred boy began dishing up.

"What *is* this stuff?" said Chacho, sniffing his bowl.

"Delicious, nutritious plankton," the boy growled.

"Everything a whale needs to be happy," said another, pretending to gag. They straightened up when Carlos gave them a sour look.

"I will not have you insulting food," the Keeper said. "Food is a wonderful thing. Millions of people have died because they didn't have enough, and you lucky boys get to eat your fill three times a day. In the old days aristocrats feasted on roast pheasant and suckling pig, while the peasants had to eat grass and tree bark. In the new Aztlán everything is shared equally. If only one person is deprived of roast pheasant and suckling pig, the rest of us should refuse to eat them. Plankton is the most delicious dish in the world when it is shared by all."

No one said anything after that. Matt guessed he was the only one there who'd actually feasted on roast pheasant and suckling pig. For the life of him, he couldn't see why plankton was supposed to taste better if everyone was stuck with it. It was sticky and crunchy at the same time, and it coated his mouth like rancid glue.

From the high plateau the guard fence was visible. Matt squinted his eyes into the blinding light, but he couldn't see much beyond it. He thought he saw a glint of water far to the west.

"That's the Gulf of California," said Carlos, shading his eyes as he followed Matt's gaze.

"Are there whales in it?" Matt asked.

"They'd have to bring their own bathtubs," a boy said.

Carlos looked sorrowful. "There used to be whales. Once this whole area was covered by water." He pointed at a ridge of hills to the east. "That was the coastline. Through the years the water flowing from the Colorado River got so polluted, the whales died."

"What happened to the gulf?" asked Chacho.

"That's one of the great engineering triumphs of Aztlán," Carlos said proudly. "We diverted the Colorado River to an underground canal that runs into Dreamland. Once the pollutants were removed, we started harvesting the gulf for plankton. Fresh seawater comes in from the south, but what with harvesting and the loss of river water, the gulf has shrunk to a narrow channel."

So that was where Opium's water came from, Matt realised –

a river so polluted that it could kill a whale. He wondered whether El Patrón had known about it. Yes, probably, Matt decided. The water was free, and El Patrón loved a bargain.

After lunch Matt, Chacho, and Fidelito were put to work tending the brine shrimp tanks. These stretched in a long line to the west of the central factory, with a pipeline for water running to one side. The shrimp filled up the tanks in a pulsing, squirming mass. They gobbled red algae until their bodies turned the colour of blood. It was this that had stained the pools Matt had noticed when he first arrived.

He found the job interesting. He liked the busy little creatures and thought their tiny bodies, rippling with feathery gills, were every bit as nice as flowers. He and the others sieved out insects and added water as needed. There were, unfortunately, miles of tanks and thousands of suicidal bugs. After a few hours Matt's arms ached, his back was stiff, and his eyes burned from salt. Fidelito whimpered to himself as they trudged along.

The desert stretched ahead of them without so much as a dead tree for shade. The tanks seemed to be heading for the distant channel Matt had seen during lunch. It was definitely blue now, not merely a flash of light on the horizon. The water looked cool and deep.

"Can you swim?" he asked Chacho.

"Where would I learn a swanky thing like that?" Chacho got mean when he was tired. Matt knew that *swanky* meant something only an evil, rotten, spoiled aristocrat would do.

"I know how to swim," announced Fidelito.

"Where'd a puny loser like you pick it up? In a shrimp tank?" snarled Chacho.

Instead of getting angry, Fidelito treated the suggestion seriously. Matt had noticed that the little boy was amazingly good-natured. He might wet the bed and puke at the drop of a hat, but his goodwill more than made up for it. "I am puny, aren't I? I could probably swim in these tanks."

"Yeah, and the shrimp'd eat your weenie off."

Fidelito cast a startled look at Chacho. "Ooh," he said. "I didn't think of that."

"Where did you learn to swim?" Matt asked, to change the subject.

"*Mi abuelita* taught me in Yucatán. We lived on the seashore."

"Was it nice?"

"*Was* it?" cried Fidelito. "It was heaven! We had a little white house with a grass roof. My grandma sold fish at the market, and she took me out in a canoe on holidays. That's why she taught me to swim, so I wouldn't drown if I fell overboard."

"If it was so great, why did she run for the border?" Chacho said.

"There was a storm," the little boy said. "It was a hurry – a hurry – "

"A hurricane?" Matt guessed.

"Yes! And the sea came in and took everything away. We had to live in a refugee camp."

"Oh," said Chacho as though he instantly understood.

"We had to live in a big room with a lot of other people, and we had to do everything at the same time in the same way. There weren't any trees, and it was so ugly that *mi abuelita* got sick. She wouldn't eat, so they force-fed her."

"It is the duty of every citizen to survive and contribute to the general good," said Chacho. "I've had that yelled at me a couple million times."

"Why wouldn't they let your grandma go back to the seashore?" asked Matt.

"You don't understand," Chacho said. "They kept her locked up so they could *help* her. If they turned all the poor suckers loose, there'd be no one left to help, and then there wouldn't be any point to a crotting Keeper's life."

Matt was astounded. It was the craziest thing he'd ever heard, and yet it made sense. Why else were the boys locked up? They'd run away if someone left the door open. "Is all of Aztlán like this?"

"Of course not," said Chacho. "Most of it's fine; but once you fall into the hands of the Keepers, you're lost. See, we're certified losers. We don't have houses or jobs or money, so we have to be taken care of."

"Did you grow up in a camp?" Fidelito asked Matt. It was an innocent question, but it opened the door to things Matt didn't want to talk about. Fortunately, he was saved by the arrival of Carlos in a little electric cart. It purred up so silently, the boys didn't notice it until it was almost upon them.

"I've been watching you for fifteen minutes," said Carlos. "You've been loafing."

"The heat was getting to Fidelito," Chacho said quickly. "We thought he was going to faint."

"Eat salt," Carlos told the little boy. "Salt is good for everything. You should turn back now, or you won't make it home before dark." He started to go off.

"Wait! Can you take Fidelito?" Chacho said. "He's really tired."

Carlos stopped and backed up. "Boys, boys, boys! Hasn't anyone told you labour is shared equally among equals? If one person has to walk, everyone has to."

"You're not walking," Matt pointed out.

Carlos's grin vanished instantly. "So the aristocrat presumes to lecture us about equality," he said. "The aristocrat is only a snot-faced boy who thinks he's too good for the rest of us. I am a true citizen. I've earned my privileges through hard work and obedience. No food for you tonight."

"Crot that," said Chacho.

"No food for any of you! You'll learn to obey the will of the people if it takes the next fifty years." Carlos rode off in a plume of dust and salt.

"I'm sorry, Fidelito," said Chacho. "You didn't deserve to be lumped in with the two of us."

"I'm proud to be with you," the little boy cried. "You're my *compadres!* Crot Carlos! Crot the Keepers!" Fidelito looked so fierce with his scrawny chest thrust out and revolution blazing from every pore that both Matt and Chacho broke down with hysterical laughter.

29

WASHING A DUSTY MIND

Why does everyone keep calling me "the aristocrat"?" asked Matt as they trudged back along the line of shrimp tanks.

Chacho wiped the sweat from his face with the sleeve of his jumpsuit. "I don't know. It's how you talk, partly. And you're always thinking."

Matt thought about the education he'd received. He'd read a mountain of books. He'd listened to conversations between El Patrón and the most powerful people in the world.

"You're like – I don't know how to put it . . . my grandfather. Your manners, I mean. You don't gobble your food or spit on the floor. I've never heard you swear. It's okay, but it's different."

Matt felt cold. He'd always copied El Patrón, who was, of course, one hundred years behind the times.

"*Él me cae bien*. I think he's cool," said Fidelito.

"Of course he's cool. It's only . . . " Chacho turned to Matt. "Well, you seem used to better things. The rest of us were born in the dirt, and we know we'll never get out of it."

"We're in this place together." Matt pointed at the hot desert.

"Yeah. Welcome to hell's baby brother," Chacho said, scuffing puffs of salt with his feet.

Dinner that night was plankton burgers and boiled seaweed. Matt didn't mind fasting, but he felt sorry for Fidelito. The little boy was so skinny, it didn't seem like he could survive a missed meal. Chacho solved the problem by staring at a nervous-looking kid until he managed to get half his food. Chacho could come on like a werewolf when he wanted to.

"Eat," he told Fidelito.

"I don't want food if you can't have any," the little boy protested.

"Test it for me. I want to know if it's poison."

So Fidelito choked the burger down.

As in the first camp, a Keeper arrived to give them an inspirational bedtime story. This one's name was Jorge. They all melted together in Matt's mind: Raúl, Carlos, and Jorge. They all wore black uniforms with beehives on the sleeves, and they were all idiots.

Jorge's story was called "Why Minds Gather Dust Like Old Rooms." "If we work all day in the hot sun," said Jorge, "what happens to our bodies?" He waited expectantly, just like Raúl had.

"We get dirty," a boy said.

"That's right!" the Keeper said, beaming. "Our faces get dirty, our hands get dirty, our whole bodies get dirty. Then what do we do?"

"Take a bath," the boy said. He seemed used to the drill.

"Yes! We clean off that old muck, and then we feel good again. It's *good* to be clean."

"It's *good* to be clean," said all the boys except for Matt, Chacho, and Fidelito. They'd been taken by surprise.

"Let's back up so our new brothers can learn with the rest of us," said Jorge. "It's *good* to be clean."

"It's *good* to be clean," said everyone, including Matt, Chacho, and Fidelito.

"Our minds and our work may also collect dust and need washing," the Keeper went on. "For example, a door that's always being opened and closed doesn't stick because the hinges never get rusty. Work is the same way. If you don't loaf" – and Jorge looked straight at Matt, Chacho, and Fidelito – "you form good habits. Your work never gets rusty."

Wait a minute, thought Matt. Celia's kitchen door was in constant use, but it swelled up on damp days and then you had to force it open with your shoulder. Tam Lin got so irritated by it, he put his fist right through the wood. Then it had to be replaced, and the door worked a lot better afterward. Matt thought these things, but he didn't say them. He didn't want to miss another meal.

"So if we work steadily and don't loaf," said Jorge, "our work doesn't have time to get dirty. But our minds can fill up with dust and germs too. Can anyone tell me how to keep our minds clean?"

Chacho snickered, and Matt poked him with his elbow. The last thing they needed now was a wisecrack.

Several boys raised their hands, but the Keeper ignored them. "I think one of our new brothers can answer that question. What about you, Matt?"

Instantly, everyone's eyes turned to Matt. He felt like he'd been caught in the cross beams of El Patrón's security lights. "M-Me?" he stammered. "I just got here."

"But you have so *many* ideas," Jorge purred. "Surely you wouldn't mind sharing them with us."

Matt's thoughts raced through the arguments the Keeper had already presented. "Isn't keeping your mind . . . clean . . . like keeping the rust off door hinges? If you use your brain all the time, it won't have time to collect germs." Matt thought it was a brilliant answer, considering the question had been thrown at him out of the blue.

But it was the wrong answer. He saw the other boys tense and Jorge's mouth quiver on the edge of a smile. He'd been set up.

"Diseased opinions not suited to the good of the people have to be cleaned out with self-criticism," Jorge said triumphantly. "Would anyone like to show Matt how this is done?"

"Me! Me!" shouted several boys, waving their arms in the air. The Keeper picked one with really spectacular acne covering his neck and ears. All of the boys had bad skin, but this one took the prize. He even had spots nestling in his hair.

"Okay, Ton-Ton. You go first," said Jorge.

Ton-Ton had a face that looked like it had been slammed into a wall. You could see right up his nostrils and maybe, Matt thought, get a peek at his brain.

"I, uh, I thought about stealing food this morning," said Ton-Ton eagerly. "The cook left it unguarded for a minute, and I – I, uh, wanted to take a pancake, but I, uh, didn't."

"So you harboured thoughts contradictory to the general good of the people?" said Jorge.

"I, uh, yes."

"What punishment should a person have who harbours contradictory thoughts?"

What language were they talking? wondered Matt. Each word seemed clear enough, but the meaning of the whole slipped away.

"I – I ought to, uh, have to recite the Five Principles of Good Citizenship and the Four Attitudes Leading to Right-Mindfulness twice before, uh, getting food next time," said Ton-Ton.

"Very good!" cried Jorge. The Keeper selected several more hands after that, and each boy confessed to weird things, like not folding his blanket correctly or using too much soap. The punishments all had to do with chanting the Five Principles of Good Citizenship and the Four Attitudes Leading to Right-Mindfulness, except for the case of one boy who admitted to taking a three-hour siesta.

Jorge frowned. "That's serious. No breakfast for you," he said. The boy looked crestfallen.

No more hands shot up. The Keeper turned to Matt. "Now that our new brother has been educated as to the meaning of self-criticism, perhaps he'd like to share his personal shortcomings." He waited. Ton-Ton and the other boys leaned forward. "Well?" said Jorge after a moment.

"I haven't done anything wrong," said Matt. A gasp of horror went around the room.

"Nothing wrong?" said the Keeper, his voice rising. "*Nothing wrong?* What about wanting to put computer chips into the heads of innocent horses? What about fouling the bag of plastic strips used for making sandals? What about inciting your brothers to loaf when you were supposed to be cleaning the shrimp tanks?"

"I fouled the plastic strips," squeaked Fidelito.

He looked scared out of his wits, and Matt quickly said, "It's not his fault. I gave him the bag."

"Now we're getting somewhere," Jorge said.

"But I puked!" insisted the little boy.

"It's not your fault, brother," the Keeper said. "You were led astray by this aristocrat. Be quiet!" he said with a hint of anger when Fidelito looked ready to take the blame again. "The rest of you must help this aristocrat see the error of his ways. We do this because we love him and want to welcome him into the hive."

Then they all attacked him. Every single boy in the room – except Chacho and Fidelito – hurled an accusation at Matt. He talked like an aristocrat. He folded his blanket in a swanky way. He cleaned under his fingernails. He used words people couldn't understand. Everything Chacho had mentioned – and more – was thrown at Matt like balls of sticky mud. It wasn't the unfairness of the accusations that so hurt him as much as the venom that lay behind them. Matt thought he'd been accepted. He thought he'd at last come to an oasis – ugly and uncomfortable, but still an oasis – where he could feel welcome.

But it was all a sham. They knew what he was. They might not understand how appallingly different he was, but they knew he didn't belong. They would keep hurling mud at him until he suffocated under its weight.

He heard the boys go away. He heard Chacho swear as he was forced to climb into a bunk bed. Matt was left alone, curled up in the middle of the floor, like the unnatural creature he was. And yet –

Inside, from a place Matt didn't know existed, a host of voices rose:

Here's the dirty little secret, Tam Lin whispered in his ear. *No one can tell the difference between a clone and a human. That's because there isn't any difference. The idea of clones being inferior is a filthy lie.*

Then Celia's arms were around him, and Matt could smell the cilantro leaves she chopped up when she was cooking. *I love you,* mi hijo, she said, hugging him. *Never forget that.*

Next El Patrón put his gnarled old hand on Matt's head and said, *How I scrambled for the coins the mayor threw me! How I rolled in the dirt like a pig! But I needed the money. I was so poor, I didn't have two pesos to rub together. You're just like I was at that age.*

Matt shivered. El Patrón hadn't loved him, but the emotion the old man had given him was just as strong: the will to live, to put out branches until he overshadowed the whole forest. Matt turned away from El Patrón and saw — in his mind — María.

Gosh, I've missed you! said María, giving him a kiss.

I love you, Matt said.

I love you, too, María replied. *I know that's a sin, and I'll probably go to hell for it.*

If I have a soul, I'll go with you, promised Matt.

Matt rose from the floor and saw that the room had been darkened. Chacho and Fidelito were watching him from the top bunks near the ceiling. Someone was going to be sincerely sorry he put Fidelito on a top bunk. Chacho pointed at the door and made an extremely rude hand gesture. Fidelito lifted his nightshirt and mooned the missing Jorge.

Matt had to swallow hard to keep the tears from rolling down his face. He wasn't alone after all. With friends like these, he would triumph, as El Patrón had triumphed over poverty and death so long ago.

30

WHEN THE WHALES
LOST THEIR LEGS

One thing was certainly true: Something did paralyse your sense of smell in this place, because Matt no longer noticed the foul air. The food tasted better, too. Not good, but not totally disgusting, either. Day after day he, Chacho, and Fidelito walked the long row of shrimp tanks and cleaned out bugs. Every evening they trudged back to a meal of plankton burgers or plankton pasta or plankton burritos. Carlos never seemed to run out of ideas for things to do with plankton.

When the growing cycle was over, Ton-Ton came out with a huge, slow-moving harvester. It groaned along like an arthritic dinosaur and dumped the contents of the tanks into its cavernous belly. Matt filled them again from a pipe running out of the Gulf of California.

At the far western end of the shrimp farm, the boys could look through the fence at the channel that had once been as wide as the sea. It was a deep blue, with hordes of seagulls. Chacho balanced on the rim of a tank to get a better view.

The lower part of the fence was safe to touch, although the top wire buzzed and popped with electricity. Fidelito stretched his arms through the mesh, as though he could touch the enticing blue if only he tried a little harder. Matt searched for weak places in the mesh. Escape was never far from his mind.

"What's that?" asked Chacho, pointing north.

Matt shaded his eyes. He saw something white peeping over a fold in the ground.

"Doesn't look like trees," said Chacho. "Want to take a look?" The sun was beginning to lower in the west, but the lure of something new was too great to resist.

"This is going to take a while. You wait here," Matt told Fidelito. He knew the little boy didn't have the strength for an extra walk.

"You can't leave me. We're *compadres,*" said Fidelito.

"We need you to guard our stuff," said Chacho. "If anyone tries to steal it, kick them where I showed you."

Fidelito grinned and saluted like a midget commando.

Matt and Chacho walked over a landscape even more desolate than the area near the saltworks. There, if it rained, a few stunted weeds struggled to the surface. Here there was nothing except white patches of salt. Seashells dotted the surface, evidence of the living sea that had once stretched from horizon to horizon.

"Maybe it's only a salt bed," said Chacho.

As they got closer, Matt saw odd shapes thrusting up. Some were paddlelike, others were thin and curved. It was the strangest thing he'd ever seen. They came up a slight rise and looked out over a deep chasm. It was filled from side to side with *bones.*

For a few moments Chacho and Matt stood on the edge of the chasm and said nothing. Finally, Chacho murmured, "Somebody lost a heck of a lot of cattle down there."

"Those aren't cattle," Matt said. The skulls were huge, the jaws shaped like monster bird beaks. One rib alone was longer than a cow. Mixed in with them were the paddlelike bones, massive enough to make tables or even beds. So many skeletons were jumbled together, Matt couldn't begin to count them. He guessed there were hundreds. Thousands.

"Isn't that a human skull?" said Chacho.

Matt squinted at the shadows partway down and saw what Chacho was pointing at.

"Think about it," the big boy said. "If someone fell in there, he'd never get out."

Matt thought about it. He'd been about to explore the pit, stepping from bone to bone like climbing down a large tree. Now he saw that the whole pit was delicately balanced. Put one foot in the wrong place, and the whole structure would collapse. He clenched his teeth, sickened by what he'd almost done.

"We'd better go back," said Chacho. "We don't want Fidelito poking around here."

Fidelito had been entertaining himself by splashing his feet in a shrimp tank. He'd draped a net over his head for a sunshade. "What was it?" he called to Matt and Chacho.

Matt described the bones, and to his surprise, the little boy recognised them. "They're whales," said Fidelito. "Eight of them beached themselves where I lived in Yucatán. They swam right up on shore and then couldn't get back. *Mi abuelita* said that was because they used to walk on land and had forgotten they didn't have legs anymore. ¡*Fuchi!* Yuck! They smelled like Jorge's sneakers! The villagers had to bury them in sand."

Fidelito chirped and warbled about rotting whales all the way back to the factory. Anything to do with his grandmother got him going.

What could have lured all those whales to their death? thought Matt as they trudged along the line of shrimp tanks. Maybe the chasm was still full of water when the Gulf of California dried up. Maybe the whales decided to wait there until the rains came and the gulf filled up again. Only it didn't fill up and the whales had lost their legs, so they couldn't walk home anymore.

Every night Jorge told a bedtime story and afterwards invited the boys to confess sins. And every night the boys, led by Ton-Ton, hurled accusations at Matt. It was meant to humiliate him, but the odd thing was that the attacks hurt less the longer they went on. Matt thought it was like listening to a barnyard full of turkeys. El Patrón sometimes ordered dozens of the ridiculous birds when he was planning a party, and Matt liked to lean over the fence to watch them. Tam Lin said turkeys were the stupidest birds in the world. If they were looking up when it was raining, they'd drown.

At any rate, turkeys went into a wild-eyed, head-banging panic when a red-tailed hawk went over. *Gobble-obble-obble-obble,* they shrieked, even though they weighed five times as much as a hawk and could have stomped it into the ground. That was what Matt heard when the boys trotted out his crimes: *Gobble-obble-obble-obble.*

Jorge's eyes narrowed and his mouth tightened into a thin line when Matt refused to confess, but he said nothing. Chacho and Fidelito quickly learned that the easiest way to avoid trouble was to give the Keeper what he wanted. They confessed to all sorts of creative sins, and Jorge was so pleased that he hardly ever punished them.

Matt was especially tired this night after the walk to the whale pit. He mumbled his way through the Five Principles of Good Citizenship and the Four Attitudes Leading to Right-Mindfulness. He barely heard Jorge's story. It was something about how you needed all ten fingers to play a piano. The fingers had to support one another and not try to show off by being individualists.

Fidelito admitted to gagging over plankton milk shakes, and Chacho said he used bad words when the wake-up bell went off. The Keeper smiled and turned to Matt. But Matt remained silent. He knew he was being stupid. All he had to do was confess to something small, but he couldn't force himself to grovel in front of Jorge.

"I see our aristocrat needs further education," said the Keeper. His gaze passed over the assembled boys, and all at once the atmosphere changed in the room. Everyone stared down at the floor, and no one put up his hand. Matt roused himself out of his stupor long enough to notice. "You!" barked Jorge so suddenly that several boys flinched. He pointed at Ton-Ton.

"M-Me?" squeaked Ton-Ton as though he couldn't believe it.

"You stole a holo-game from the Keepers' rooms! We found it under a pile of rags in the kitchen."

"I, uh, I, uh – "

"Cleaning the Keepers' rooms is a privilege!" yelled Jorge. "It is earned through obedience and good behaviour, but you've failed in your duties. What should be done with a boy who sneaks around and takes things the others don't have?"

The Keepers have things the others don't have, thought Matt. He didn't say it aloud.

"He should work extra hard," a boy guessed.

"No!" shouted Jorge.

"Maybe he can – he can apologise," someone else faltered.

"Haven't you learned anything?" the Keeper bellowed. "Worker bees must think of the whole hive. If they gather nectar for themselves and don't bring anything home, the hive will starve when the cold weather comes. That's not what workers do. It's how *drones* behave. They steal from others. But when winter comes, what happens to the drones?"

"The good bees kill them," said a boy almost as small as Fidelito.

Wait a minute, thought Matt.

"That's right! The good bees sting the evil drones to death. But we don't want to go quite that far," said Jorge.

Matt let out the breath he'd been holding. In Opium murder was a casual thing. He didn't know what the rules were here.

By now Ton-Ton was reduced to absolute terror. Tears and snot ran down the boy's unlovely face. Matt was surprised to feel sorry for him. Ton-Ton was a slimy crawler who deserved whatever was coming.

"Assume the position," said Jorge.

Ton-Ton stumbled to a wall. He leaned against it with his arms stretched out before him and his hands flat against the wall. He spread his legs.

"Remember, if you move it will be worse for you."

Ton-Ton nodded.

The Keeper unlocked a small storage closet and selected a cane. Matt could see they were of all sizes. Jorge took his time making the decision. Ton-Ton whimpered softly.

Finally, the Keeper brought out a cane about the thickness of his thumb. He thwacked it against a bed to test its strength. Otherwise, the room was perfectly silent, except for Ton-Ton's snuffles.

Jorge paced back and forth. He seemed to be deciding what part of Ton-Ton to hit. The boy's arms and legs were trembling so hard, it seemed likely he'd fall over before Jorge laid a hand on him. Matt could hardly believe what was happening. It was so cruel, so *pointless*. Ton-Ton had shown himself eager to obey. He humbled himself whenever the Keepers asked. But maybe that was the point. El Patrón said easy targets were opportunities to frighten enemies you weren't ready to tackle just yet.

That's me, thought Matt. *I'm the enemy Jorge wants to frighten.*

The Keeper suddenly broke off his pacing and hurled himself across the room. At the very last instant Ton-Ton panicked and ran. Jorge was on him at once, flailing away, hitting anything he could reach. He struck again and again until blood flew off the cane. Fidelito scrambled over to bury his face in Matt's chest.

Finally, the Keeper stepped back, panting, and pointed at the boys cowering near the door. "Take him to the infirmary," he ordered. The boys scurried to obey. They dragged Ton-Ton, limp as a rag, from the room.

Jorge propped the cane against a bed and wiped his face with a towel. No one moved or spoke. Everyone looked too terrified to even breathe. After a moment Jorge looked up with the kindly expression of a beloved teacher. The fury had drained from his face as completely as it had once drained from Tom's face, and the change was even more frightening than rage. "I think our young aristocrat has understood the lesson," he said gently. "Well, Matt. Do you have any personal shortcomings you'd like to share?"

"No," said Matt, pushing Fidelito out of harm's way. Everyone gasped.

"I beg your pardon?"

"I haven't done anything wrong." Matt understood the lesson all right. It was this: Even slavish obedience didn't protect you from punishment.

"I see," sighed the Keeper. "Then there's no help for it. Assume the position."

"I don't see how it makes any difference," Matt said. "You beat up Ton-Ton when he was lying on the floor."

"Do it. It makes things easier," someone dared to whisper. Jorge whirled around but didn't catch who spoke.

Matt stood with his arms crossed. Inside he was quaking with fear, but outside he gave the Keeper as cold and imperious a look as El Patrón had ever mustered to terrify an underling.

"Some boys," Jorge said in a thin, almost wheedling voice that sent chills down Matt's back, "some boys have to learn the *hard* way. They have to be broken and mended and broken again until they learn to do what they're told. It may be simple, like sweeping a floor, but they do it eagerly to keep from being broken again. And they do it forever, for as long as they live."

"In other words, you want to turn me into a zombie," said Matt.

"No!" several voices cried out.

"How *dare* you accuse me of that!" Jorge reached for the cane.

"I'll confess for him! I'll do it!" shrieked Fidelito, running to the centre of the room. "He dropped the soap in the shower and didn't pick it up again. He threw away porridge 'cause there was a stinkbug in it."

"Fidelito, you idiot!" groaned Chacho.

"He did those things. Honest!" cried the little boy.

Jorge looked from Fidelito to Matt with an interested look in his eyes.

"Go sit down," Matt said in a low voice.

"Stop!" shouted the Keeper. "I see we have social contamination of the worst order here. The aristocrat has turned this boy into his lackey. And thus, it is the lackey who should be punished."

"A beating would kill him," said Matt.

"No one is too little to learn the value of education," Jorge said. "Why, even child kings used to be thrashed until they learned not to cry at public meetings – as young as six months of age."

He's got me, thought Matt. No matter how much he wanted to resist Jorge's authority, he couldn't do it at the little boy's expense. "Very well, I confess," said Matt. "I dropped the soap in the shower and didn't pick it up again. I threw away the porridge because there was a stinkbug in it."

"And?" the Keeper said pleasantly.

"I peed in a shrimp tank – don't ask me which one. I don't remember. And I left water running in the kitchen sink."

"Assume the position."

Matt did so, hating himself, but hating the Keeper even more. He kept a stony silence as Jorge pranced around, trying to work on Matt's nerves. And he didn't scream, although he wanted to very much when the man hurled himself across the room and struck him with a force that made him almost pass out with pain.

He straightened up and endured another blow, and another. After six blows Jorge decided he'd done enough. Or – more likely – the Keeper had exhausted his strength beating up Ton-Ton. Matt figured he'd been lucky, but he didn't doubt that more agony was down the road. Jorge wasn't going to give up that easily.

Matt staggered to a bunk and collapsed. He was barely aware of Jorge's departure, but the instant the door closed the boys scrambled off their beds and clustered around Matt. "You were great!" they cried.

"Jorge's such a loser," said a tall, skinny boy named Flaco.

"Loser?" said Matt weakly. "I'm the one who gave up."

"*¡Chale!* No way!" said Flaco. "Jorge crossed the line tonight. If news of this gets back to the Keepers' Headquarters, he's history."

"No one's going to tell them," Chacho said scornfully. "This place might as well be on the moon."

"Soon I'll be old enough to leave," said Flaco. "I'll go to Headquarters then and tell them."

"I'm not holding my breath waiting," Chacho said.

"Anyhow, you were *muy bravo* to take the beating for Fidelito," Flaco told Matt. "We thought you were a wussy aristocrat, but you're really one of us."

"I kept telling you that," Fidelito piped up.

Then everyone started arguing about when they discovered Matt wasn't a wussy aristocrat and when they knew he was *muy gente,* a great guy. Matt let the warm tide of their approval flow around him. He was dizzy with pain, but it was worth it if the others liked him.

"Hey, we've got to get him fixed up," Flaco said. The boys checked the hallway to be sure it was clear. Then they carried Matt to the infirmary, where Ton-Ton was already sound asleep. A pockmarked boy in a green uniform dressed Matt's wounds and measured three drops of liquid into a spoon.

That's laudanum, Matt realised as his eyes caught the label on the bottle. He fought against taking the medicine. He didn't want to turn into a zombie like Felicia or die like poor Furball, but he was too exhausted to resist for long. If he died, Matt wondered as he drifted off into a drug-induced haze, would he meet Furball in whatever afterlife non-humans inhabited? And would the dog sink his teeth into Matt's ankle, for taking him away from María?

31

TON-TON

I feel awful," groaned Ton-Ton, reaching blindly for the glass of water by his bed.

"You look awful," observed the pockmarked boy.

"You, uh, you take that back, Luna. I can still beat the stuffing out of you."

"Not now that I'm a Keeper," Luna said, smugly.

"You're only a trainee." Ton-Ton managed to reach the water, but he spilled half of it on his chest when he tried to drink.

"Wait a minute," Matt said. He was unwilling to reach for his own glass, even though he was extremely thirsty. He suspected that serious pain was waiting for him if he moved. "You're training to be a Keeper?"

"Well, duh," said Luna. "Everyone does, eventually."

Matt watched the light dancing on the glass of water just out of his reach. "But there's only 20 Keepers here and — how many boys?"

"210 at the moment," said Luna.

"They can't all become Keepers. There aren't enough places," Matt said.

Ton-Ton and Luna looked at each other. "Carlos says every boy who keeps the Five Principles of Good Citizenship and, uh, the Four Attitudes Leading to Right-Mindfulness until he reaches 18 becomes a Keeper," said Ton-Ton.

No matter how carefully Matt explained to them the difference between 210 job seekers and only 20 jobs, it didn't penetrate.

"You're, uh, you're just jealous," Ton-Ton said.

But in one area Ton-Ton was knowledgeable. He knew what went on inside the Keepers' compound, which was surrounded by a high wall. The Keepers had holo-games and a television and a swimming pool. They had all-night parties with delicious food. And Ton-Ton knew all this, Matt now discovered, because he cleaned the Keepers' rooms and washed their dishes. Matt figured they allowed Ton-Ton inside because they thought he was too slow-witted to understand what he saw.

But as Celia often said, some people may think slowly, but they're very *thorough* about it. As Matt listened to Ton-Ton, he realised the boy wasn't stupid. His observations of the Keepers' activities and his understanding of the factory's machinery showed an intelligent mind. Ton-Ton was simply careful about his opinions.

Matt could see the boy was deeply disturbed about the punishment he'd received the night before. He kept going back to it, picking at it like a scab.

"I don't get it," Ton-Ton said, shaking his head. "I, uh, didn't do anything wrong."

"You must've done something. He sure whacked the heck out of you," said Luna.

"No, uh, I *didn't*."

Matt could see the gears churning slowly in the boy's brain: Whatever Jorge said was good. Ton-Ton did what Jorge said. Therefore, Ton-Ton was good. So why did Ton-Ton get the heck whacked out of him?

"Jorge is *un loco de remate,* a complete weirdo," said Luna.

"No," Ton-Ton insisted. "He's something else."

Matt couldn't guess what conclusion the boy was working toward. "What's it like inside the compound?"

Ton-Ton's eyes lit up. "You, uh, you can't believe it! They've got roast beef and pork chops and pie à la mode."

"What's pie à la mode?" Luna asked.

"It's got *ice cream* on it! Not melted or anything."

"I had ice cream once," Luna said in a dreamy voice. "My mother gave it to me."

"The Keepers drink real milk, too, not ground-up plankton, and they eat chocolates wrapped in gold paper." Ton-Ton had stolen a chocolate once. The memory hovered in his mind the way the Virgin of Guadalupe had hovered over Matt's bed when he was little.

"Doesn't it bother you that the Keepers have these things and we don't?" said Matt.

Both Ton-Ton and Luna drew themselves up like offended rattlesnakes. "They earned it!" Luna said. "They put in their time; and when we put in our time, we'll have those things too!"

"Yeah," said Ton-Ton, but something seemed to be working at the back of his mind.

"Okay, okay. I was just curious," Matt said. He braced himself and reached for the glass of water. The pain was worse than he expected. He gasped and fell back.

"Pretty bad, huh?" Luna folded Matt's fingers around the glass. "Want some laudanum?"

"No!" Matt had spent years watching Felicia turn into a zombie. He didn't want to follow her example.

"Your choice. Personally, I love the stuff."

"Why do you need it? Are you in pain?" asked Matt.

Luna sniggered as though Matt had said something completely stupid. "It's a trip, see. It's a ticket out of this place."

"You're only a trainee," Ton-Ton said scornfully. "You're not supposed to, uh, trip out until you move into the compound."

"Says who?" Luna picked up the laudanum bottle and sloshed it around. "How're they going to count all the drops in here? It's my reward for running the infirmary."

"Wait a minute," said Matt. "You mean the Keepers take this stuff?"

"Sure," Ton-Ton said. "They *earned* it."

Matt's mind was working very fast. "How many of them? How often?"

"All of them and, uh, every night."

Matt felt light-headed. This meant that every single night the Keepers turned into zombies. This meant the factory was left unguarded. The power plant that electrified the fence was left unguarded. A big sign flashing FREEDOM lit up in Matt's mind. "Do either of you know where San Luis is?" he asked.

It turned out both boys did. Ton-Ton had grown up there. He described, in his halting way, a city of whitewashed houses and tile roofs, of vines spilling over walls, of busy marketplaces and beautiful gardens. It sounded so pleasant, Matt wondered why Ton-Ton didn't want to return. Why was he looking forward to life inside a compound with a bottle of laudanum for company? It was totally insane.

"San Luis sure sounds great," Matt said.

"Uh, yes," said Ton-Ton as though the thought had just occurred to him.

Matt was bursting to tell him to dump the Five Principles of Good Citizenship and the Four Attitudes Leading to Right-Mindfulness and head over the fence to San Luis. But that would have been foolish. Ton-Ton worked toward a conclusion with the same, slow deliberation as the shrimp harvester he drove along the tanks. Nothing could hurry him. And nothing, Matt hoped, would turn him aside, either.

When Matt hobbled to the bathroom and looked into the mirror, he got a shock. All the boys had zits. Matt knew he had them too, but this was the first time he'd had a good look at the damage. There was no mirror in the dormitory. He looked like a loaded pizza! He scrubbed and scrubbed with the grey, seaweed soap, but it only made his skin turn a violent red.

Ton-Ton and Luna guffawed when Matt returned. "They don't wash off, you know," said Luna.

"I look like a planktonburger," mourned Matt.

"Hunh! You, uh, look like a planktonburger that's been, uh, puked up by a seagull and, uh, left out in the sun," said Ton-Ton in an unusual flight of poetry.

"I get the picture!" Matt painfully crawled into bed. He lay on his side to spare the welts on his back.

"We all have zits," said Luna. "It's the mark of people who work with plankton."

Great, thought Matt. Now that he thought about it, he realised the Keepers were only mildly scarred but not covered in the same active little pus volcanoes that dotted the boys' faces. Maybe it had something to do with their food. A diet of pork chops, pie à la mode, and chocolate was obviously better for your skin than healthy, nutritious plankton.

Jorge forced Matt and Ton-Ton back to work the next day. Ton-Ton really needed another day in the infirmary, but he obeyed without a murmur. Matt was eager to get back. He couldn't wait to get going on an escape plan. Before, it had seemed pointless. Now he knew San Luis lay a few miles to the north, beyond a low range of hills.

As Tam Lin once said, a jailer has a hundred things on his mind, but a prisoner has only one: escape. All that concentrated attention was like a laser cannon melting through a steel wall. Given his background, Matt figured Tam Lin knew a lot about escaping from jails.

All Matt had to do was shut down the electricity to the fence and climb over. It sounded simple, but it wasn't. The powerhouse was locked after dark. The Keepers counted the boys every night at ten o'clock and every morning at five. That left seven hours in which to walk the five miles to the fence (while hoping the power hadn't been turned on again) and then twenty more miles to San Luis in the dark. If the ground was covered with cacti, the trip might take a lot longer.

What would the Keepers do when they discovered three boys missing, because Matt intended to take Chacho and Fide- ito with him? Could Jorge use a hovercraft to hunt them down? Fidelito should probably be left behind. He couldn't walk twenty-five miles. And yet how could Matt abandon him?

Friendship was a pain, Matt thought. All these years he'd wanted friends, and now he discovered they came with strings attached. Very well, he'd *take* Fidelito, but he'd need more time. If he overloaded the boiler next to the Keepers' compound, it would explode and –

Was it wrong to blow twenty men to smithereens? El Patrón wouldn't have worried one second over it. Tam Lin had tried to blow up the English prime minister, but he'd killed twenty children instead.

Murder is wrong, Brother Wolf, said a voice in Matt's mind. He sighed. This was probably what María called having a conscience. It was even more of a pain than friendship.

"*Why* do we have to wait for him?" asked Chacho as they watched the shrimp harvester chug and wheeze its slow way towards their tank.

"Because he knows things we need to find out," Matt explained patiently. They were sitting by the farthest tank. The fence loomed up behind them, its top wire humming and crackling in the dry air.

"He's a crawler, He has a go at us every night."

"Not since the beating," Matt pointed out.

"Well, that's because he's taking a vacation." Chacho was unwilling to believe Ton-Ton had any good qualities.

"Be nice to him, okay?"

"*Mi abuelita* says people's souls are like gardens," Fidelito said brightly. "She says you can't turn your back on someone because his garden's full of weeds. You have to give him water and lots of sunlight."

"Oh brother," said Chacho, but he didn't argue with the little boy.

A plume of dust rose from the back of Ton-Ton's harvester. It settled slowly across the barren ground. The air was so still, the plume barely drifted away from the road. "You, uh, you should be working," Ton-Ton called as his machine jerked to a halt.

"And you should be head down in a shrimp tank," muttered Chacho. Matt kicked him.

"If you're, uh, waiting to beat me up, don't bother," said Ton-Ton. "I can, uh, beat the stuffing out of you."

"Why would you assume that three people innocently sitting by the road are planning to attack you?" said Chacho. "Although it could be true."

"We only want to be friendly," Matt said, frowning at Chacho.

"Why?" Ton-Ton's eyes narrowed with suspicion.

"Because *mi abuelita* says people have to be tended like gardens," Fidelito chirped. "They need sunlight and water, and their souls need to – need to – "

"Be weeded," finished Chacho.

Ton-Ton's eyes rounded as he processed this curious statement.

"We just want to make friends, okay?" Matt said.

Ton-Ton took another minute to consider that, and then he stepped off the harvester.

"When was the last time you went to San Luis?" asked Matt.

If Ton-Ton was surprised by the question, he didn't show it. "About, uh, about a year ago. I went with Jorge."

"Do you have family there?"

"My m–mother went across the, uh, border years ago. My f–father tried, uh, tried, uh, to find her. He didn't come back."

Matt noticed that Ton-Ton's speech problem got worse when he talked about his parents.

"No *abuelita*?" Fidelito asked.

"I, uh, I did. M–Maybe she's still there." Ton–Ton's mouth turned down at the sides.

"Well, why don't you go look for her!" said Chacho. "¡Hombre! If I had a grandma only twenty miles to the north, I'd rip up this fence to find her! What's wrong with you, man?"

"Chacho, no," said Matt, putting his hand on the boy's shoulder.

"You, uh, don't understand," Ton–Ton said. "Jorge saw me on the wrong side of the border. There were Farm Patrols and, uh, dogs, big mud–coloured dogs with big teeth. They did everything the Farm Patrol said, and, uh, the Farm Patrol told them to *eat* me." Ton–Ton shuddered at the memory. "Jorge came over the border and shot them. He got into a lot of trouble for it, too. He, uh, he saved my life, and I owe him everything."

"Did Jorge tell you not to look for your grandmother?" Matt said.

"He said I was born to be a Keeper. He said that Keepers don't have families, only one another, but that it's, uh, better because families only run off and abandon you."

"But your *abuelita* must have cried when you didn't come home," Fidelito said.

"I wouldn't have come home, you idiot!" shouted Ton–Ton. "I would've been inside a dog's belly!"

"It's okay, Fidelito," Matt told the little boy. "That's enough weed pulling for one day." He asked Ton–Ton about San Luis, and Ton–Ton was eager to talk about that. The longer he spoke, the less he stumbled over his words. The scowl on his face smoothed out. He looked a lot younger and happier.

Ton–Ton described the city so thoroughly, he seemed to have a map spread out in his mind. He recalled every detail – an oleander bush with peach-coloured flowers, an adobe wall with paloverde trees draped over it, a fountain tinkling into a copper basin. It was like following a camera down a street. And gradually, he lowered his guard enough to talk about his *mamá* and *papá*. He had lived in a crowded house with aunts and uncles and brothers and cousins and a tiny *abuelita* who ruled the whole establishment. But it hadn't been an unhappy place, even though they'd been poor.

At last Ton-Ton stretched and smiled as though he'd had a fine meal. "I, uh, I won't tell anyone why we're late," he said. "I'll say the harvester broke down." He let Fidelito ride most of the way back with him, putting the little boy down only when they came within sight of the Keepers' compound.

"I don't get it," whispered Chacho as the harvester shuddered its way back. He and Matt walked to one side, away from the plume of dust. "It's like you turned a light on inside his head. I didn't know Ton-Ton was that bright."

Matt smiled, pleased to be proven right about the big boy. "Celia used to say slow people are just paying close attention."

"Who's Celia?"

Matt almost dropped in his tracks. He'd carefully hidden any reference to his life before he'd arrived in Aztlán. Listening to Ton-Ton's memories had made him careless. "Why, Celia . . . she's my . . . my m-mother." And he knew that it was true. All those years she'd told him not to think of her as his mother fell away. No one else cared for him the way she did. No one protected him or loved him so much, except, perhaps, Tam Lin. And Tam Lin was like his father.

Suddenly all the memories, so carefully suppressed in his new life, came flooding back. Matt had trained himself to stop thinking about Celia and Tam Lin. It was too painful. Now he found himself helpless. He crouched on the ground, tears pouring down his face. He held himself tight to keep from crying out loud and totally ruining his image in front of Chacho.

But Chacho understood. "I should've kept my fat mouth closed," he said, kneeling in the dust next to Matt. "It's the one thing none of us are supposed to bring up until someone's ready. Heck, I bawled my eyes out the first few weeks."

"Are you sick?" called Fidelito's voice from a distance as he rode on the harvester.

"He sure is," said Chacho. "You would be too if you ate a handful of raw shrimp." And he shielded Matt from view until he was able to gain control of himself and go on.

32

FOUND OUT

That night Jorge, with his instinct for weakness, pounced on Matt again. He insisted that more and more crimes be confessed, and Matt soon found himself repeating the same sins. He hardly cared what he said.

Matt felt bruised inside. In a strange way he wasn't even in the same room with Jorge, because his mind was back in El Patrón's mansion. He was in Celia's apartment. At any moment she'd call him to dinner and they'd sit down with Tam Lin. The illusion was painful, but it was so much better than anything in Matt's current life.

"If the aristocrat won't listen," came Jorge's smooth voice, "I'll have to talk to his lackey."

Matt woke from his reverie to see Fidelito being pulled to the centre of the room. The little boy's face was pale with fear.

"You've been bad, haven't you?" purred Jorge.

"Not *very* bad," said Fidelito, glancing at the cane closet.

"That's for me to say, isn't it?" the Keeper said.

"Okay," said Fidelito.

Matt knew the scene before him was important. He tried to keep his mind on it, but he kept slipping back to Celia's apartment.

"I think the aristocrat needs to understand why his behaviour must be controlled," Jorge said. "Worker bees know that everything they do affects the whole hive. If a lazy worker sleeps all day and isn't punished, he teaches others to follow his example. If enough workers follow his example, the hive will die."

Fidelito's face showed the argument had gone over his head.

"So we have to correct the weak little lackeys who think it's fun to follow a bad example. Isn't that so?"

"I — I don't know."

Matt forced himself to concentrate on the present. "If you want to punish me, why don't you just do it?" he said.

"Because that doesn't work," Jorge replied. His face glowed with joy, as though he'd discovered a wonderful truth he couldn't wait to share with everyone. Once more Matt was reminded of Tom.

"I confess. I obey. I take my punishment," Matt said.

"Yes, but you don't mean it," said the Keeper. "You go through the motions, but in your heart you're still an aristocrat. I puzzled over it a long time. Then I realised the thing that *makes* an aristocrat is the presence of a lackey. If I remove the lackey, poof!" He snapped his fingers. "No more aristocrat. Assume the position, Fidelito."

Matt was frozen with shock. This time it was clear his confessions weren't going to save the little boy. He glanced at the others. They looked stunned. The last time Jorge had threatened Fidelito, Matt had come to his rescue. But this time was different. It seemed the Keeper had crossed an invisible line and the boys were appalled by what they were about to witness. It had been okay to beat Ton-Ton for no reason. He was big and able to take it. Fidelito was skinny and frail in spite of his tough spirit. And he was only eight years old.

Fidelito did what he'd seen the others do: Lean his hands against the wall and spread his legs. The other boys murmured. Matt couldn't hear what they were saying.

Jorge went to the closet. Matt felt as though he were floating over the scene. Like other times in his life when things had gone wrong, he wanted to retreat into his own private kingdom. If he imagined being in Celia's apartment hard enough, it might actually happen.

Jorge paced back and forth, whisking the cane. Any second now he'd break into a run. He stopped. He gathered his strength for the initial blow. He lunged forward –

Matt hurled himself at the Keeper. He drove his head into Jorge's stomach and tore the cane from the man's hands. Jorge reeled back, gasping for breath. Matt brought the cane down hard on his shoulder and then used it to force the Keeper to the floor. Chacho came out of nowhere and threw himself into the battle, pummelling Jorge with his fists.

"You – hit – little – kids!" Chacho shouted between blows. "You – deserve – to – be – hit – back!" The other boys were shouting and cheering. They surged forward, forming a ring around the Keeper and his two attackers. Flaco dragged Fidelito away from the fight.

Matt's head spun. Jorge was curled into a ball. Maybe he was seriously hurt. The boys were dancing around excitedly, and Matt guessed they were about to join in. "Stop!" Matt cried, dropping the cane. He grabbed Chacho and pulled him back.

"We mustn't kill him!"

"Why not?" demanded the boy. But the interruption was enough to bring him to his senses. He sat down hard on the floor and clenched his fists. The other boys groaned with disappointment, but they moved aside when Jorge rolled onto his hands and knees and scuttled to the door.

No one said a word. Chacho sat on the floor, breathing heavily. Fidelito whimpered in a corner, where he was being held firmly in place by Flaco. Matt shivered as though he had a high fever. He couldn't imagine what was going to happen next.

But he didn't have long to wait. Footsteps thundered down the hall, and the door was slammed open by an army of Keepers. All twenty of them stormed into the room. They were armed with stun guns, and the boys retreated against the walls. First Matt, then Chacho was seized. Their hands were bound behind their backs and their mouths were sealed with tape.

"You're going to be locked up," Carlos roared at the remaining boys. "We'll decide what to do with you tomorrow. But understand we won't – repeat, *won't* – tolerate this kind of mob behaviour."

"Don't you want to know what Jorge did?" said Flaco.

"What you did was far worse!" shouted Carlos.

"He was going to kill Fidelito."

That did seem to startle Carlos. He stopped and looked at the little boy hiding behind Flaco.

"He's lying," said Jorge, who was holding his injured shoulder with one hand.

"There are 200 of us," said Flaco. "We all witnessed it."

And in that statement, Matt realised, was an implied threat. There were two hundred boys in the dormitory. No matter how well armed the Keepers were, they couldn't hope to control a crowd that size.

The thought seemed to have occurred to Carlos as well. He backed towards the door and signalled the other men to follow. But like a swirl of dust on the dry salt flats outside, a stream of boys moved to cut off the exit. Now the Keepers were surrounded on all sides.

"I think you should listen to us," said Flaco.

"We can talk about it tomorrow," Carlos said.

No, thought Matt. *Don't let them put it off. The minute the men are outside the room, they'll bolt the door. They'll never listen to the facts.* He could say nothing because his mouth was covered with tape.

"I think now is better," said Flaco.

Carlos swallowed. He fingered the stun gun.

"They've been corrupted by the aristocrat," said Jorge. "Things have gone wrong ever since that arrogant swine arrived. He's the one who led the attack, and the rest followed. He's the leader. The rest are his filth-eating lackeys."

"Don't make things worse," Carlos said.

"Luna in the infirmary has an interesting tale," Jorge went on. "When the aristocrat was brought in, Luna helped load him into bed. He saw writing on the boy's right foot."

Oh no, oh no, thought Matt.

"There was an old scar across it, but he managed to make out the writing: 'Property of the Alacrán Estate.'"

"Alacrán?" said Carlos. "That's the name of the old vampire who runs Dreamland."

"I know," Jorge said pleasantly. "I wondered how a person could belong to an estate, unless he worked there. *Or unless he was an escaped crot!*"

A gasp ran through the room.

"Don't use that filthy word," Carlos said.

"I'm sorry." Jorge smiled. "I was only using language I thought the boys would understand. I was still thinking about what to do with the information when tonight's problem cropped up. It *is* funny, you have to admit, that all these lackeys have sworn their loyalty to a stinking *crot* – excuse me, zombie – instead of a real aristocrat."

No, no, no, thought Matt. His weakness had been found out. Even though the Keeper had drawn the wrong conclusion about the tattoo, it was just as devastating.

"I don't believe it," said Flaco.

"Why don't we look?" invited Jorge. Flaco came forward and knelt on the floor next to where Matt was standing. He looked up, apologising with his eyes. Matt didn't resist. It wouldn't have done any good. He allowed the boy to turn his foot toward the light and waited for the inevitable reaction.

"Jorge is right. It does say 'Property of the Alacrán Estate,'" said Flaco.

The rebellion went out of the boys then. They were so used to obeying, Matt realised, that very little was needed to make them surrender. They moved away from the door and slowly drifted toward the bunks.

"W-Wait," said a voice Matt never expected to hear. "Any, uh, anyone can get trapped in Dreamland. It, uh, doesn't make him a bad person."

"Be quiet, Ton-Ton," said Jorge. "Thinking isn't your strong point."

"I have, uh, I *have* been thinking," said the big boy. "Our parents ran away to, uh, Dreamland, and they w-were turned into z-zombies." It was clearly difficult for him to say this.

"My father wasn't," protested Flaco. "He's living it up in the United States. He's running a movie studio, and when he gets enough money, he'll send for me."

"We, uh, tell ourselves stuff like th-that," stammered Ton-Ton, "but it isn't t-true. All our parents are crots." A flurry of voices rose telling Ton-Ton to shut up. "Our *mamás* and *papás* aren't b-bad, just unlucky," the boy went on in his relentless way, "and M-Matt isn't bad either!"

"Oh, go to bed," said Jorge. "Do you think anyone wants to listen to your ravings? You've always been stupid and you'll always be stupid. You're lucky I pulled you out of Dreamland before I found out what an idiot you are."

"I'm n-not stupid!" cried Ton-Ton, but no one listened to him. The boys drew away from Matt as though he were something unclean. The Keepers hurried him and Chacho out, and Carlos bolted the door behind them.

They were taken to a small closet without enough space to lie down. It was dark and airless. The floor was cold. All night the boys huddled against the wall, and Matt was glad it was dark and that they had their mouths covered with tape. He couldn't have borne hearing Chacho call him a crot or seeing him shrink away from the presence of such a monster.

33

THE BONEYARD

A faint light shone under the door when two of the younger Keepers arrived to fetch Matt and Chacho. Matt was so stiff, he fell over when they pulled him to his feet. "Mph!" came from behind the tape covering Chacho's mouth.

They were urged outside to one of the carts the Keepers used to move equipment around the factory. Jorge was in the driver's seat, smoking a cigarette. More tape was wound around the boys' ankles.

The cart rolled slowly at first because it was solar powered, but as the sun rose higher and flooded the salt flats, it picked up speed. Matt saw the shrimp tanks move past. He realised they were heading toward the western fence. The cart's wheels crunched along the gritty path, and sand hissed across the ground in an early-morning breeze.

Matt was thirsty. He was hungry too. He saw, with a kind of

bitter pleasure, that Jorge's shoulder was encased in a plaster cast. Matt hoped he was in a lot of pain.

After a while the cart turned and bumped along rougher ground. Matt saw they were driving parallel to the fence. He saw a white swirl of seagulls as they rose and sank along the Gulf of California. Their cries floated to him on the dusty wind.

On and on the cart struggled. When it floundered in sand, the men had to jump out and put creosote branches under the wheels to urge it on. At last it jerked to a stop, and Matt was carried off by the two young Keepers.

They came over a rise. Before thcm stretched the wide basin that had once been full of living water and was now filled with dead whales. The bones stuck up like a gigantic bowl of thorns.

"This is what we call the boneyard," Jorge said pleasantly.

Matt remembered someone saying, when he first arrived, *You won't get away with your swanky ways here. We've got something called the boneyard, and any troublemaker who goes through it comes out as harmless as a little lamb.*

"Shall I take the tape off now?" one of the Keepers inquired.

"Only from his mouth," said Jorge.

"But that means he won't be able to climb out."

"He tried to kill me!" Jorge shouted. "Do you want a murderer crawling back to stir up revolution?"

"Carlos won't like it."

"You leave Carlos to me," said Jorge. Matt felt the tape rip off. He flexed his mouth, ran his tongue over his bruised lips. "You think you're thirsty now," Jorge said, smiling. "Wait till tomorrow."

"*He's* the murderer," cried Matt, but he had no time to say anything else. The men swung him up and out. He came down with a crash, and the bones shifted and let him fall through. Down he tumbled, rolling this way and that until he arrived at a plateau of skulls. He hung in the midst of a sea of bones, with the blue sky visible through a fretwork of ribs and vertebrae. He turned his head cautiously. Below was a pit whose dark depths he could only guess at.

A few minutes later he heard Chacho land not far away. The mass shifted again, and Matt slipped down a few more feet. He felt a rib poke into his back. A fine dust of salt and sand pattered over his face. He heard Chacho cough. He heard the men's feet crunch away and then the purr of the cart growing fainter and fainter until it was gone.

"Are you okay?" called Chacho.

"Depends on what you mean by okay." Matt was amazed he could still laugh, although he did it weakly. "Are you hurt?"

"Not much. Got any good escape plans?"

"I'm working on it," said Matt. The salt powdered his face and got into his mouth. "I wouldn't mind a drink."

"Don't talk about it!" said Chacho. "I think I could cut this tape if I could find a sharp bone."

"There's one sticking into my back," said Matt. He spoke cheerfully, as though they were working on a way to snatch an extra ten minutes of sleep, not trying to escape a long, painful death.

"Some people have all the luck." Chacho spoke lightly too, but Matt suspected he was just as frightened.

Matt wriggled until his wrists touched the jagged bone. He sawed back and forth, but before he could make any progress, the bones shifted and he slid down into deeper darkness.

"Matt!" cried Chacho with an edge of panic.

"I'm here. Well, that didn't work. Why don't you give it a

try?" In fact, Matt's heart was pounding and he was afraid to move. The whole basin quivered, and he didn't know what would happen if he fell all the way to the bottom.

"Heck! Oh, heck!" shouted Chacho. Matt heard him slither through the fretwork of bones.

"We've got all day. You don't have to hurry," said Matt.

"Shut up! I think there's something else in this pit."

Matt thought he heard a high-pitched noise. Was it possible something lived in the darkness below? And what kind of creature would choose such a home?

"They're *bats!* Horrible, slimy bats!" yelled Chacho.

"Bats aren't slimy," Matt said, relieved. A real creature was much better than the monsters he'd imagined.

"Stop making jokes! They'll suck our blood!"

"No, they won't," said Matt. "Tam Lin and I watched them dozens of times."

"They'll wait for dark. I saw it in a movie. They'll wait for dark and then they'll come up and suck our blood." Chacho's panic was shrill and infectious. Matt began to get scared too.

"Tam Lin says they're just mice with wings. They're as afraid of us as we are of — "

"One's coming at me!" screamed Chacho.

"Keep still! Don't move!" yelled Matt. A horrible idea had just occurred to him, and he had to warn Chacho before anything else happened.

Chacho kept screaming, but he must have heard Matt's advice because he didn't struggle. After a moment his cries stopped and were replaced by sobbing.

"Chacho!" called Matt. The boy didn't answer. He wept on and on, hiccupping to catch his breath. Matt turned carefully, searching for another sharp bone. Below, in the ghostly near blackness, tiny bats fluttered and squeaked. They must have found the pit almost as comfortable as a cave. They flitted here and there, navigating between the bones like fish in a sea. A sour smell, disturbed by their wings, filtered up.

"Chacho?" Matt called. "I'm here. The bats are settling down. I'm going to try to cut the tape again."

"We'll never get out," groaned Chacho.

"Sure we will," Matt said. "But we have to be very, very careful. We mustn't fall down any farther."

"We're going to die," said Chacho. "If we try to climb out, the bones will shift. There's tons of them here. We'll fall to the bottom, and they'll come down on top of us."

Matt said nothing. That was exactly the thought he'd had. For a few moments he was swept with despair, unable to think clearly. Was this the end to the chance at life he'd been given by Tam Lin and Celia? They'd never know what had happened to him. They'd think he had deserted them.

"Tam Lin says rabbits give up when they're caught by coyotes," Matt said after he'd calmed enough to trust his voice. "He says they consent to die because they're animals and can't understand hope. But humans are different. They fight against death no matter how bad things seem, and sometimes, even when everything's against them, they win."

"Yeah. About once in a million years," said Chacho.

"*Twice* in a million," said Matt. "There's two of us."

"You are one dumb bunny," said Chacho, but he stopped crying.

As the sun slowly worked its way across the sky, Matt became more and more thirsty. He tried not to think about it, but he couldn't help it. His tongue was glued to his mouth. His throat was gritty with sand.

"I've found a sharp bone," said Chacho. "I think it's a tooth."

"Great," said Matt, who was working his bonds against a rib. The tape had an amazing ability to stretch. He sawed and sawed, and the tape merely lengthened and didn't break. But after a while it became loose enough for Matt to slip his hands free. "I did it!" he called.

"Me too," said Chacho. "I'm working on my feet."

For the first time Matt felt real hope. He drew his legs up carefully and picked at the bonds with a fragment of bone. It was horribly exhausting. He had to move extremely slowly to keep from sliding deeper, and he had to stop and rest every other minute. He realised he was growing weak.

Chacho seemed to rest for longer periods too. "Who's Tam Lin?" he asked during one of these breaks.

"My father," said Matt. This time he didn't stumble over the words.

"That's funny, calling your parents by name."

"It's what they wanted."

There was a long pause. Chacho said, "Are you really a zombie?"

"No!" said Matt. "Do you think I could talk like this if I were?"

"But you've seen them."

"Yes," said Matt.

The wind had died down, and the air felt heavy and still. The silence was eerie, because it felt like the desert was waiting for something to happen. Even the bats had stopped chittering.

"Tell me about zombies," said Chacho.

So Matt described the brown-clad men and women who toiled endlessly over the fields and the gardeners who clipped the vast lawns of El Patrón's estate with scissors. "We called them eejits," he said.

"It sounds like you were there a long time," said Chacho.

"All my life," said Matt, deciding, for once, to be honest.

"Were your parents . . . eejits?"

"I guess you could call them slaves. A lot of work has to be done by people with normal intelligence."

Chacho sighed. "So my father could be okay. He was a musician. Did you have musicians there?"

"Yes," said Matt, thinking of Mr Ortega. But Mr Ortega couldn't have been Chacho's father. He'd been around too long.

The sun was low in the west now. It was darker than Matt expected for this time of day, even with the light cut down by the pit. The breeze picked up again. It moaned like a lost spirit in the bones and turned surprisingly cold.

"It sounds like La Llorona," said Chacho.

"That's just a story," said Matt.

"My mother used to tell me about her, and my mother didn't lie." Chacho reacted instantly to any real or imagined insult to his mother. Matt knew she'd died when Chacho was six.

"Okay. I'll believe in La Llorona if you'll believe the bats aren't dangerous."

"I wish you hadn't brought them up," said Chacho. The wind blew even harder, sending a swirl of dust over the basin. The topmost bones rattled, and all at once Matt saw a blinding flash of light followed by a crack of thunder.

"It's a *storm*," he said in wonder. The chill wind pushed the smell of rain at him, making his thirst even more unbearable. Desert storms were rare, except in August and September, but they weren't unheard of. They blew up suddenly, wreaked havoc, and vanished almost as quickly as they'd come. This one promised to be spectacular. The sky turned white and then peach-coloured in the sunset light as a giant cloud loomed overhead. Lightning forked. Matt counted from flash to thunder, to gauge how far away it was: a mile, a half mile, a quarter, and then right on top of them. The bottom of the cloud opened, pouring out hailstones as big as cherries.

"Catch them!" shouted Matt, but the roar of the storm was so loud, Chacho probably couldn't hear. Matt caught them as they skittered down through the bones and crammed them into his mouth. They were followed by rain, buckets and buckets of rain. Matt opened his mouth and let it pour in. In the flashes of light he saw bats clinging to the bones. He heard water rushing over the side of the basin.

And then it was gone. The thunder retreated across the desert. The lightning grew fainter, but water still poured into the pit. Matt bunched up his shirt and sucked out as much moisture as he could. The rain had revived him, but he hadn't got nearly as much water as he wanted.

The sky was almost dark now. "Aim yourself at the nearest edge while you can still see," Matt called to Chacho. "My legs are free. Are yours?"

The boy didn't answer.

"Are you okay?" Matt had the awful thought that Chacho had slipped to the bottom during the violent storm. "Chacho! Answer me!"

"The bats," said the boy in a hollow voice. He was still nearby. Matt felt a rush of relief.

"They won't hurt you," he said.

"They're all over me," said Chacho in that odd voice.

"Me too." Matt suddenly became aware of the little creatures creeping onto his body. "They – they're trying to get away from the water," he stammered, hoping it was true. "Their nesting place is flooded. And I guess they want to get warm."

"They're waiting for it to be dark," Chacho said, "and then they'll drink our blood."

"Don't be a complete idiot!" shouted Matt. "They're frightened and they're cold!" All the same, he felt an instinctive horror at their stealthy movements. A distant flash of lightning showed him a tiny creature huddled against his chest. It had a flat nose and leaflike ears, and its mouth disclosed delicate, needle-sharp teeth. But it also had a baby tucked under one leathery wing. It was a mother trying to rescue her young from the flood.

"You wouldn't bite me, would you?" he whispered to the mother bat. He turned slowly, freezing in place when the bones threatened to shift, then moving again, aiming toward where he thought the nearest edge lay. The bat clung briefly to his shirt before sliding off into the darkness.

It was like being a swimmer in a strange and terrible sea. Every time Matt moved forward, he sank down a little. At one point the bones weighed upon his back and he feared they had trapped him. But they shifted slightly and allowed him to move on. Yet every stroke toward shore increased their weight. Soon he would be unable to move, and then he would have to wait, like an insect imprisoned in amber, for death to find him.

The pit was completely black when his hands struck against rock instead of bone. Matt grasped the wall and inched himself upward until he was able to plant his feet against the stone. Now the bones seemed even heavier, but that was because he was trying to force his way up through them. He leaned against the rock, panting with exhaustion. He found a trickle of storm water still flowing and lapped it like a dog. It was cold and mineral. It tasted wonderful.

"Chacho?" he called. "If you come toward my voice, you'll reach the edge. There's water." But the boy didn't answer. "I'll keep talking, so you'll know where to go," said Matt. He talked about his childhood, leaving out things that would be hard to explain. He described Celia's apartment and his trips into the mountains with Tam Lin. He described the eejit pens and the opium fields that surrounded them. Matt didn't know whether Chacho could hear him. The boy might have fainted. Or the bats really might have drunk his blood.

It was the middle of the night when Matt pulled himself over the edge and collapsed onto wet earth. He was unable to move. All the willpower he'd used to work his way free deserted him. He lay on his side with his face half in mud. He couldn't have moved if Jorge had shown up with an army of Keepers.

As he drifted in and out of consciousness, he heard a strange sound coming from the pit. Matt listened, trying to decide what animal made such a noise, and then it came to him: Chacho was snoring. The boy had fallen asleep from sheer exhaustion. He might still be trapped in the pit, but he was alive. And the bats hadn't drunk his blood after all.

34

THE SHRIMP HARVESTER

The sky was dark blue and the mud bore a powdering of frost when Matt pulled himself from the ground. He crouched to protect what little warmth his body produced. A wind ruffled the little pools of water that dotted the desert. The east was a blaze of pink and yellow.

Matt had never been so cold in his life. His teeth chattered; his body felt like one giant goose bump. In the growing light he saw that his clothes had been torn in a dozen places during his journey through the pit. His arms and legs were covered with scratches. He hadn't noticed the injuries during the desperate fight to survive, but now he hurt all over.

"Chacho?" he called to the sea of bones turning grey in the predawn light. "Chacho!" Matt's voice was carried off by the breeze. "I'm outside. I'm safe. You can be too. Just come toward my voice."

No answer.

"You'll go down a little, but after a while you'll come to the edge of the pit. I can help you then," called Matt.

No answer.

Matt paced back and forth along the edge of the basin. He had a fair idea where Chacho was, but he couldn't see him. "There's water out here from the storm. I can't get it to you, but you can come to it. It'll make you feel a lot better. *Please*, Chacho! Don't give up!"

But the boy made no reply. Matt found a rain-filled hollow in a rock and drank until his head stabbed with pain. The water was freezingly cold. He went back to the edge of the basin, calling, begging, and even insulting Chacho to get a response. There was nothing.

As the sun came over the rim of the desert and light flooded the little hillocks and bushes all around, Matt curled up in the shelter of a rock and cried. He couldn't think of a thing to do. Chacho was out there, but he couldn't find him. Even if he did find him, Matt couldn't go to him. And there weren't any plants in the desert that would make a decent rope.

Matt wept until he was exhausted, which didn't take long because he was tired already. The sunlight brought a slight warmth to the air, although the wind whipped it away the minute Matt stood up.

What could he do? Where could he go? He couldn't stay here until Jorge came back to check up on things. But he couldn't leave Chacho behind, either. He limped back to the basin and sat on the edge. He talked and talked, sometimes exhorting Chacho to come towards his voice, sometimes only rambling on about his childhood.

He talked about El Patrón and the fantastic birthday parties. He talked about María and Furball. He talked until his throat was raw, but he didn't stop because he felt this was the only rope he could throw Chacho. If Chacho could hear him, he wouldn't feel completely alone and he might try to stay alive.

The sun rose high enough to shine into the pit. Matt saw, not far down, a patch of brown. It was the uniform all the boys wore in the factory. "I can see you, Chacho," said Matt. "You aren't far from the edge. You can make it if you try."

In the distance he heard a clanking, mechanical noise. It wasn't Jorge's cart, but perhaps the Keeper had borrowed something sturdier. Matt shaded his eyes. He wanted to hide, but he saw with dismay that he'd left muddy footprints all over the ground. He couldn't possibly wipe them out before someone arrived.

He waited hopelessly for the Keeper to find him, but instead, to his amazement, he saw Ton-Ton's shrimp harvester shuddering and groaning over the desert. Fidelito sat on the hood. As soon as he saw Matt, he jumped off and started running.

"Matt! Matt!" shrieked the little boy. "You got out! Where's Chacho?" He flung himself at Matt and almost knocked him over. "I'm so happy! You're alive! I was so worried!" Matt held on to him, to keep him from dancing over the edge of the basin.

The shrimp harvester jerked to a stop. "I, uh, I thought you might need help," said Ton-Ton.

Matt began to laugh. Only it wasn't a laugh, more like hysteria. "Need help?" he wheezed out. "I guess you could say that."

"I did say it," said Ton-Ton, looking puzzled.

Matt began to shiver. His laughter turned into stormy weeping. "Don't do that!" wailed Fidelito.

"It's Chacho," sobbed Matt. "He's in the bones. He won't talk. I think he's dead."

"Where?" said Ton-Ton. Matt pointed out the brown uniform, all the while clutching Fidelito's arm. He was terrified the little boy would fall into the pit.

Ton-Ton positioned the harvester at the edge. He reached into the bones with the mechanical arm he used to tip shrimp tanks into his collecting bin. At the end was a large claw. Slowly, methodically, Ton-Ton cleared away the top layer until they could see Chacho's face. The boy's eyes were closed. Ton-Ton moved away more bones until Chacho's chest appeared. The cloth was torn and his uniform was streaked with blood, but he was breathing.

"It'd work better if he could, uh, help," said Ton-Ton. He manoeuvered the machine as delicately as a surgeon performing an operation.

"Could I climb out on the arm and tie a rope around him?" Matt had stopped crying, but he couldn't seem to stop shivering.

"Humph," grunted Ton-Ton. "You'd be, uh, as much help as a drunk buzzard trying to, uh, carry off a dead cow." He continued working so slowly and carefully that Matt wanted to scream. Yet it made sense. Any wrong move could send the bones slithering back down to cover Chacho.

Finally, Ton-Ton closed the jaws of the shrimp harvester around Chacho's body. The jaws were strong enough to crush rock, but Ton-Ton lifted the boy as gently as if he were an egg. He backed up the machine. The arm swung around until it cleared the basin and deposited Chacho on the ground. Ton-Ton pulled the arm up and over the top of the shrimp harvester, folding it into the storage position. Careful in everything, he wasn't about to leave this job half done.

Matt knelt by Chacho and felt his pulse. It was slow but strong. Fidelito patted his face. "Why won't he wake up?"

"He's, uh, in shock," said Ton-Ton, alighting from the machine. "I've seen it before. People can take only so much fear, and then they go into a kind of, uh, sleep. Hold him up. I've got to get fluids into him."

Matt propped Chacho up while Ton-Ton dribbled red liquid from a plastic bottle into the boy's mouth. "It's cherryade," explained Ton-Ton. "The Keepers drink it all the time. It's got electrolytes in it. Good for dehydration."

Matt was surprised by Ton-Ton's medical knowledge. But of course he stored away everything he heard. Luna at the infirmary must have talked about dehydration.

Chacho coughed, licked his lips, and swallowed. His eyes flew open. He grabbed the bottle and began gulping for all he was worth. "Slow down!" said Ton-Ton, wrenching the bottle away. "If you drink too fast, you'll, uh, puke."

"More! More!" croaked Chacho, but Ton-Ton forced him to take sips. Chacho said some bad words, but the older boy shrugged them off. He continued to dole out the cherryade until he was satisfied Chacho had had enough.

He unpacked another bottle and gave it to Matt. *Heaven can't possibly be better than this,* thought Matt, swirling the sweet, cool liquid around his mouth. The taste of cherryade had to be right up there with El Patrón's moro crabs flown in from Yucatán.

"We'd better get going," said Ton-Ton, firing up the shrimp harvester.

Matt's euphoria came down with a thump. "Go back? Jorge wants to kill us. I heard him say so."

"Keep your hair on," said Ton-Ton. "We're going to San Luis to find my *abuelita*."

"It was my idea," said Fidelito.

"It was *my* idea," Ton-Ton said firmly. Matt held his hand over Fidelito's mouth to shush him. It didn't matter who thought of it as long as Ton-Ton didn't get sidetracked.

"I don't know how far I can walk," murmured Chacho. He looked dazed.

"That's why I brought the, uh, shrimp harvester," said Ton-Ton. "You and Matt can ride in the tank. Fidelito can, uh, sit up front with me."

That, as far as Ton-Ton was concerned, was the end of the discussion. Matt didn't argue. By some slow, careful process Ton-Ton had decided to make a break for it. And if he wanted to make a break at five miles an hour, nothing Matt said was going to talk him out of it. Matt wondered how he hoped to evade the Keepers.

Matt helped Chacho climb down a metal ladder into the tank. Even with the old water flushed out, it reeked of rotten shrimp. Matt thought he'd throw up, except he didn't have anything to throw up. At least he wouldn't get hungry on the way.

Chacho fell asleep on the damp floor, but Matt climbed up the ladder and faced into the breeze.

Five miles an hour! Matt saw he'd been wildly optimistic. Fidelito could have skipped faster than the shrimp harvester moved. Ton-Ton had to manoeuver around rocks and away from holes. Several times the machine threatened to tip over, but it ground on relentlessly and righted itself.

They went north around the vast basin of bones, and then west. The soil was littered with boulders, the spaces between with deep sand, where the harvester wallowed and complained before struggling on. Finally, they arrived at the fence and Ton-Ton halted. "Everyone out," he announced.

He had to help Matt pull Chacho from the tank. Chacho was too weak to stand. With Fidelito dancing attendance, they carried him to a soft patch of sand. "Stay here," Ton-Ton told Fidelito. "I mean it. If I, uh, catch you near the harvester, I'll, uh, beat the stuffing out of you."

"He wouldn't really," whispered Fidelito as the older boy strode away.

"What about the Keepers?" Matt said. "Isn't he afraid they'll catch us?"

"Not a chance!" Fidelito wriggled with excitement. "They're locked up in their compound. The doors and windows are covered with bags of salt — mountains and mountains of salt! All the boys helped."

"Didn't the Keepers try to stop them?"

"They were asleep," Fidelito said. "Ton-Ton said they wouldn't wake up no matter how much noise we made."

Matt had a bad feeling about this, but he was too startled by what Ton-Ton was doing now to ask more questions. The boy had clamped the jaws of the shrimp harvester on to a single wire in the fence. He backed up slowly, pulling the wire with a horrible, grinding, screeching noise until *snap!* The wire parted. Ton-Ton attacked another wire, and another. The more he broke, the easier it was to unthread the fence, and soon he'd created a hole big enough to drive through.

Matt watched the top of the fence anxiously. The one wire they had to worry about was still up there, snapping and humming in the breeze. As long as Ton-Ton didn't disturb its insulation, they would be safe.

"How do you feel?" Matt asked Chacho.

"I don't know," said the boy in a faint voice. "I'm not sure what's wrong. I tried to reach you last night, but the bones came down so hard, I could hardly breathe. It was like being squeezed under a rock." He paused, seeming too weak to go on.

"Does your chest hurt?" said Matt. Now he understood why Chacho had never answered him.

"A bit. But I don't think I broke anything. It's just . . . I can't seem to get enough air."

"Don't talk," Matt said. "We'll take you to a doctor as soon as we get to San Luis." He was deeply worried, but he didn't understand what was wrong either.

Ton-Ton drove through the opening he'd created and helped Matt carry Chacho to the tank. The next part of the trip was much better. A road paralleled the fence, and the shrimp harvester was able to move much faster. Now and then Ton-Ton stopped to stretch his legs and to let Fidelito run off some of his energy. "If you, uh, jump up and down on my seat *one more time,* I'm going to, uh, beat the stuffing out of you," he growled. The little boy quieted down for a minute or two.

All of them drank cherryades. Ton-Ton had a crate of them in the cab. He took a break for lunch, producing wonderful food the likes of which Chacho and Fidelito had never seen. They ate pepperoni sausages and cheese, bottled olives, and cream crackers. And if the food made them thirsty, it didn't matter because they had more cherryade than they could drink. They finished with chocolates wrapped in gold paper.

"I'm so happy, I could fly," Fidelito said with a contented sigh.

Matt worried about the slow, leisurely trip they were taking. "Aren't you afraid the Keepers will dig their way out?" he asked Ton-Ton.

"I told him about the salt bags," said Fidelito.

"They, uh, they're asleep," said the older boy.

"Not after all this time," Matt said. "Unless — Oh, Ton-Ton! You didn't give them laudanum?"

"They earned it," he said, in the same dogged way he'd defended them in the infirmary.

"How much?"

"Enough," said Ton-Ton. Matt could see he wasn't going to supply any more information.

"It was wonderful!" Fidelito piped up. "Ton-Ton told us we were going to rescue you, only we had to wait for sunrise."

"The harvester works on, uh, solar energy," said Ton-Ton.

"So Flaco checked to be sure the Keepers were really asleep. He and the others carried off their food, and then they piled as many bags of salt around the building as they could find. Flaco said he'd wait for the supply hovercraft to fly him to the Keepers' Head — Head — "

"Headquarters," said Ton-Ton.

"Yes! And tell them what Jorge did."

"Flaco trusts Headquarters. I don't," said Ton-Ton.

"Me neither," murmured Chacho. He was propped against the side of the harvester with a bottle of drink. He seemed barely awake.

"Maybe we should hurry," Matt said, looking at Chacho.

"Yes," Ton-Ton agreed.

And so the shrimp harvester ground on until it reached the corner where the fence turned right. The road continued north toward a low range of hills. To the left lay the remnants of the Gulf of California, but presently it vanished and was replaced with drifting sand. Whiffs of foul-smelling air drifted over the harvester. It was the same smell Matt had met in the wastelands near the eejit pens, only here it was sharper and more alarming.

The sun was low in the west. Shadows began to lengthen

across the desert. The shrimp harvester slowly climbed the road through the hills, but when it came to a pass, where the road was entirely in shadow, it stopped. "That's it," said Ton-Ton, jumping from the cab. "That's as far as it will go until dawn."

Matt helped him lift Chacho from the tank. They laid him next to the road, wrapped in blankets Ton-Ton had brought. He and Matt walked to the end of the pass and hunkered down, watching the sun slide into a violet haze. "How much farther is San Luis?" asked Matt.

"Three miles. Maybe four," said Ton-Ton. "We have to cross the Colorado River."

"I don't think Chacho can wait until morning."

Ton-Ton continued to gaze at the disappearing sun. It was hard to tell what was going through his mind. "I, uh, I followed my parents into Dreamland over there." He pointed at the haze. "Jorge saved me from the dogs. I thought he was – he was . . . wonderful. But he only thought I was stupid." Ton-Ton put his head down.

Matt guessed he was crying, and he didn't want to embarrass him by noticing. "Something like that happened to me," Matt said at last.

"It did?" said Ton-Ton.

"Someone I cared about more than anyone in the world tried to kill me."

"Wow!" said Ton-Ton. "That's really bad."

They said nothing for a while. Matt could hear Fidelito telling Chacho how much fun it was to camp out under the stars and how he used to do it with his *abuelita* after the hurricane blew away their house.

"I guess you and, uh, Fidelito had better walk to San Luis," said Ton-Ton. "If you can find a doctor, bring him here. If you haven't, uh, returned by dawn, I'll go on."

Ton-Ton gave Matt and Fidelito flashlights. He supplied them with blankets to ward off the cold and lemons to survive the smell. "The Colorado River's b-bad," he said. "It goes into, uh, a pipe before it gets to the road, but it's still dangerous. Stay away from it, Fidelito," he warned. "Pay attention, or I'll, uh – "

"Beat the stuffing out of me," the little boy said cheerfully.

"I mean it this time," said Ton-Ton.

35

EL DÍA DE LOS MUERTOS

The walk downhill was easy, but Matt found he had to stop and rest frequently. He ached all over from his ordeal the night before, and some of his scratches were infected. He looked back to see Ton-Ton watching gravely from shadows at the top of the pass. The snout of the shrimp harvester was just visible.

Fidelito bounced up and down, waving the flashlight. "Do you think he can see me?"

"I'm sure he can," said Matt. Sometimes Fidelito's energy made him feel tired.

They went on, with Fidelito asking questions about who they were going to see. Matt told him about María and the Convent of Santa Clara. He didn't know what the convent looked like, but he made up a description to entertain the little boy. "It's a castle on a hill," he said. "It has a tower with a red roof on each corner. Every morning the girls raise a flag in the garden."

"Like the Keepers," said Fidelito.

"Yes," said Matt. Every morning the Keepers lined up the boys and raised a flag with the emblem of a beehive over the factory. The boys recited the Five Principles of Good Citizenship and the Four Attitudes Leading to Right Mindfulness before trooping into the cafeteria for plankton porridge. "This flag has a picture of the Virgin of Guadalupe. The girls sing 'Buenos Días, Paloma Blanca,' her favourite song, and then they have toast and honey for breakfast."

Fidelito sighed.

Matt wondered whether the Keepers had managed to wake up from their drugged sleep. Were they all lying dead like poor Furball? And would Ton-Ton be arrested for murder? "Can the Keepers get water in their compound?" he asked.

"Flaco said they could drink out of the toilet," said Fidelito.

It's hard but it's fair, Matt thought with a grim smile.

"That smell is making me sick," said Fidelito.

Matt lifted his head. The stench had been growing so gradually, he hadn't registered it. "We must be close to the river," he said. He scratched the skin of a lemon and held it to Fidelito's nose. "This won't kill the smell, but it should keep you from throwing up."

Matt heard a gurgling, thrashing noise somewhere to the left and shone the flashlight at it. A wide, black ribbon of water disappeared into a giant drain. It glistened with oil, and here and there shapes struggled to the surface and were pulled down again.

"Is that a fish?" whispered Fidelito.

"I don't think so," Matt said, shining the light on a long, greasy-looking tentacle that whipped out of the flood and struggled wildly to hang on to the shore. "I think that's the reason Ton-Ton told you to stay away from the river." The tentacle lost the battle and disappeared down the drain with a horrible sucking sound.

"Let's run," begged the little boy.

The ground trembled as the vast river plunged underneath the road. The smell almost made Matt faint. *Bad air. Bad air,* he thought wildly. If they passed out here, no one would rescue them. "Faster!" Matt gasped, but in fact it was he who was slow. Fidelito bounded ahead like a monkey.

They went up a rise. A slight breeze blew the nauseous stench of the river away, and Matt collapsed with his chest heaving. He began to cough. He felt like he was being strangled. *Oh, no,* he thought. *I can't have an asthma attack now.* He'd been free of the illness since he'd left Opium, but the smell of the river had brought it back. He bent over, trying to fill his lungs.

Fidelito frantically scratched his lemon and held it to Matt's nose. "Smell! Smell!" he cried. But it didn't help. Matt was drenched in sweat from his efforts to get air. "I'll go for help," shouted Fidelito into his ear, as though Matt were deaf as well. *Stop, it's dangerous,* Matt wanted to say. But maybe it was just as well the little boy went on. There was nothing Matt could do to protect him.

How much time passed, Matt couldn't say. The world had shrunk to a tiny patch of road, where he struggled to stay alive. But all at once he felt hands lift him and an inhaler – *an inhaler!* – held to his face. Matt grabbed it and breathed for all he was worth. The attack faded. The world began to expand again.

He saw a brown, weathered face etched by deep wrinkles. "Look what the river coughed up, Guapo," said the woman.

Guapo – a name meaning "handsome" – hunkered by the

side of the road and gave Matt a big, almost toothless grin. He was at least eighty years old. "The kid picked a lousy place to swim," he said.

"I was joking," said the woman. "Nobody swims in that river and survives. Can you walk?" she asked Matt.

Matt got to his feet. He took a few unsteady steps and nodded.

"Stay with us," the woman said. "I don't suppose your mother's expecting you home tonight."

"He's a runaway orphan. Look at his uniform," said Guapo.

"You call those rags a uniform?" The woman laughed. "Don't worry, niño. We won't tell anyone. We hate the Keepers as much as you do."

"Chacho," Matt gasped out.

"The little one told us about him," said Guapo. "Look. The ambulance is already on its way." He pointed up, and Matt saw a hovercraft pass overhead. The anti-gravity stirred the hair on his arms.

With Guapo on one side and the woman, who identified herself as his sister Consuela, on the other, Matt made his way along the road. He felt light-headed. Everything seemed unreal: the dark road, the starry sky, and the old man and woman who guided his steps.

Presently they came to a high wall. Consuela pressed a button, and a door slid open to show a scene so unexpected, Matt wondered whether he was dreaming after all.

Inside, flanked by graceful paloverde trees, were graves as far as Matt could see. Each one was decorated with palm fronds, flowers, photographs, statues, and hundreds of glittering candles. The candles sat in red, blue, green, yellow, and purple glasses and looked like fragments of rainbow dancing over the ground.

Some of the graves had offerings of food as well: tortillas, bowls of chilli, bottles of drink, fruit, and whole herds of tiny donkeys, horses, and pigs made out of pastry or sugar. On one grave was a beautiful little cat with a pink sugar nose and a tail curled around its feet.

Matt saw people sitting in the shadows and speaking to one another in quiet voices. "Where are we?" he murmured.

"A cemetery, *chico*," said Consuela. "Don't tell me you've never seen one?"

Not like this, Matt thought. The Alacráns were buried in a marble mausoleum not far from the hospital. It was the size of a house and decorated with so many angels, it looked like a convention of them. You could see through the front door to what appeared to be chests of drawers on either side. The name of a departed Alacrán was inscribed on each long drawer. Matt guessed you could slide them out like the ones in his room, where Celia packed his shirts and socks.

The eejits, of course, were buried in mass graves out in the desert. Tam Lin said their resting places were impossible to distinguish from landfill.

"This looks like a – a party," Matt faltered.

"It *is*," cried Fidelito, suddenly appearing from amid a group of women who were unpacking picnic baskets. "We're so lucky! Of all the days we could've come, we picked *El Día de los Muertos*, the Day of the Dead. It's my favourite holiday in the whole year!" He munched on a sandwich.

Matt couldn't understand it. Celia had celebrated every holiday on the calendar, but never had she mentioned this one. She put out shoes for the Wise Men to leave gifts at Christmas. She coloured eggs for Easter. She served roast turkey on Thanksgiving and heart-shaped cakes on Saint Valentine's Day.

She had special ceremonies for San Mateo, Matt's patron saint, and for her own Santa Cecilia. And of course there was El Patrón's birthday party. But never, never, never had anyone dreamed of throwing a party for Death!

Yet here Matt saw, on grave after grave, statues of skeletons playing guitars or dancing or driving around in little plastic hovercars. Skeleton mothers took skeleton children for walks. Skeleton brides married skeleton grooms. Skeletons dogs sniffed lampposts, and skeleton horses galloped with Death riding on their backs.

And now Matt became aware of an odour. The foul stench of the river was kept away by the wall, but the air was full of another scent that made every nerve in Matt's body tighten with alarm. It smelled like Felicia! It was as though her ghost hovered before him, breathing the heavy fumes of whiskey into his face. He sat down, suddenly dizzy.

"Are you sick?" asked Fidelito.

"Guapo, find another inhaler in my bag," said Consuela.

"No . . . no . . . I'm all right," said Matt. "The smell here reminded me of something."

"It's only the copal incense we burn for the dead," Consuela said. "Maybe it reminds you of your *mamá* or *papá,* but you mustn't be unhappy. Tonight is when we welcome them back, to let them see how we're doing and to offer them their favourite foods."

"They . . . eat?" Matt looked at the tamales, bowls of chili, and loaves of bread decorated with pink sugar.

"Not as we do, darling. They like to smell things," said Consuela. "That's why we serve so many foods with a good odour."

"*Mi abuelita* said they come back as doves or mice. She said I mustn't chase anything away if it wants to eat," said Fidelito.

"That's also true," said Consuela, putting her arm around the little boy.

Matt thought about the Alacráns in their marble mausoleum. Perhaps El Patrón was there – in the top drawer, of course. Then Matt remembered Celia saying El Patrón wanted to be buried in an underground storeroom with all his birthday presents. Was anyone putting out food for him tonight? Had Celia prepared tamales and bowls of *menudo*? But Celia was hiding in the stables. And Mr Alacrán wouldn't put out so much as a single chilli bean because he hated El Patrón.

Matt blinked away tears. "How can anyone celebrate death?"

"Because it's part of us," Consuela said softly.

"*Mi abuelita* said I mustn't be afraid of skeletons because I carry my own around inside," said Fidelito. "She told me to feel my ribs and make friends with them."

"Your grandmother was very wise," said Consuela.

"I'm off to town now for the fiesta," said Guapo, who had put on a handsome black sombrero and slung a guitar over his shoulder. "Do you kids want me to drop you off anywhere?"

Consuela laughed. "You old rogue! You only want to chase women."

"I don't have to *chase* anyone," the old man replied haughtily.

"Come home in one piece, Guapito. I worry about you." She kissed him and straightened the sombrero on his head.

"What about it, kids? Shall I take you to see Chacho? He's in the hospital at the Convent of Santa Clara."

"That's where we were going!" Fidelito cried.

"What about the Keepers?" Matt said.

"They stay off the streets when there's a party. Too much fun," said Consuela. "But just in case . . . " She fished around in her large bag and brought out a pair of masks. "I was saving

these for my grandchildren, but I'll get them something else."
She fitted a mask over Fidelito's face.

Matt felt a strange tightening in his chest when he saw the
skull staring back at him from Fidelito's skinny body. "Put yours
on too," urged the little boy. Matt couldn't move. He couldn't
take his eyes off Fidelito's face.

"I've got one of my own," said Guapo, slipping on his mask.

"That's an improvement, believe me," said Consuela. Guapo
capered around, his black sombrero bobbing over his skullface.
Matt knew they were trying to cheer him up, but he felt only
horror.

"Listen, *mi vida,*" said Consuela. Matt flinched at the sound
of his old name. "I don't know what bad things happened to
you, but it's a matter of safety to wear the mask now. The Keepers won't bother you if you're wearing a costume."

Matt saw the wisdom of her suggestion. Very reluctantly, he
pulled the mask over his head. It fitted him like a second skin,
with holes for his eyes, nose, and mouth. It felt like being buried
alive, and he had to struggle against panic. He took a deep
breath and willed the horror away.

"Muchas gracias," he said.

"De nada," Consuela replied.

36

THE CASTLE ON THE HILL

As he followed Guapo, Matt noticed that all the graves were dotted with golden flowers. When they reached the road, he saw a trail of their bright petals leading from the cemetery.

"What's that?" he whispered to Fidelito.

"*Cempasúchil* flowers. For the dead to find their way back home."

Matt couldn't help feeling a chill as they trod the delicate petals into the dust.

The old man had a small, personal hovercar, and it took a while for him to coax it into the air. Even then, it hovered only a few feet off the ground. "Cheap anti-grav," muttered Guapo, fussing with dials and buttons. "I got it at a discount. I'm sure it's mixed with electrons."

The car left the graveyard behind and came to the first houses. All had paths of flowers to their doors. What struck Matt was how beautiful the houses were. They didn't look at all like the hovels he'd seen on TV. They were made of a shining material moulded into fantastic shapes. Some were like small castles, while others looked like ships or space stations, and still others grew like trees, with fanciful balconies and rooftop gardens.

As Guapo's hovercar went by, holographic displays were triggered in the yards. Skeletons zoomed around on rockets. A skeleton wedding, complete with priest and flower girls, marched across a lawn. Fidelito leaned out the window and tried to touch them.

In the distance Matt heard music and the sputter of fireworks. Fidelito pointed at a shower of red and green sparks in the sky. Soon the road became crowded with bands of partygoers until Guapo could hardly move at all. In a good hovercar he could have soared over people's heads. The best he could manage was to blare his horn and push his way through the mob. There was so much music and shouting, no one paid attention to the horn.

Matt watched the stream of people in wonder. In all his life he'd never seen so many. They sang and danced. They hoisted children onto their shoulders to see the fireworks painting the skies. They playfully rocked the hovercar until Guapo yelled at them. And the costumes! Gorillas, cowboys, and astronauts mobbed the food stalls. Zorro cracked his whip at a trio of space aliens ahead of him in line. La Llorona and the *chupacabras* waltzed by with bottles of beer. But most of the people were dressed like skeletons.

Matt grabbed Guapo's shoulder and cried, "Who's that?"

The old man glanced at the figure in a black-and-silver suit. "Him? That's only the Vampire of Dreamland." And Matt saw a line of brown-clad, skull-faced eejits shuffling after a terrifyingly real El Patrón. Matt shrank into his seat. He had to breathe deeply to overcome his shock. He felt a wrenching sense of loss, which didn't make any sense at all. If El Patrón had lived, he – Matt – would be dead.

"Keepers," whispered Fidelito. Matt saw the group of men standing by the side of the road. They scowled at the revellers as if to say, *All of you are drones, and when winter comes, the worker bees will throw you into the snow to die.* "I'm going to show them the map of the world," announced Fidelito, but Matt grabbed him and held him down.

"You kids stop wrestling back there," said Guapo. "You're making the magnetic coils overheat."

At last they passed through the seething fiesta. The carnival booths fell behind, the smell of fried meat and beer died away, and they came to the base of a hill. Above them wound a lovely and peaceful lane lined with pomegranate trees. At intervals globes of burning gas cast a white-hot light over the ground.

"The hovercar can't make it up there," said Guapo, "but it isn't far to the top. Give my best to the Sisters at the hospital. They stitched me up after the last fiesta and threw in a free lecture to boot." The old man gave Matt a wolfish grin.

Matt was sorry to see him go. He hadn't known Guapo and Consuela long, but he liked them very much. He removed his mask and helped Fidelito do the same.

"Is that where María lives?" asked the little boy, craning his neck to see the top of the hill.

Matt's heart sank. He desperately wanted to find María. He'd been thinking of little else for weeks. But would she want to see him? Hadn't she merely befriended him out of pity? Matt knew he'd been, quite literally, an underdog, and María couldn't resist a crusade.

At least he'd been an appealing underdog then. Now his face was covered with acne. His body was scarred with welts from Jorge's cane, as well as sores from the scratches he'd got in the boneyard. His clothes were filthy. He reeked of rotten shrimp. Would María be so embarrassed by his appearance that she'd slam the door in his face?

"That's where she lives," he told Fidelito.

"I wonder if they're having a party," said Fidelito.

Me too, thought Matt as they started up the steep hill. He imagined the convent girls dressed in fine clothes, like the bridesmaids at Emilia's wedding. He combed his hair with his fingers and felt the heavy coating of sand and salt. If Fidelito was anything to go by – and the little boy was at least cute in a basic sort of way – the two of them were as attractive as a pair of mangy coyotes.

"It *is* a castle," said Fidelito in awe. The white walls and towers of the Convent of Santa Clara rose out of bougainvillea hedges dense with violet and crimson flowers. The same bright lights that bordered the winding path hung in the air over the walls. The building was made of the same shining substance as the houses in San Luis. Matt didn't know what it was, but it shimmered like silk.

"They have toast and honey for breakfast," murmured Fidelito. "I wonder if they'll give us some."

"First we have to find the door," said Matt. They followed a flagstone path around the building. It showed them windows high in the walls, but no doors. "This has to go *somewhere,*" Matt said. At that instant lights came on and the wall opened, as though someone had drawn aside a curtain. They saw an archway leading to a lighted courtyard. Matt took a deep breath and put his hand on Fidelito's shoulder.

The little boy was trembling. "Is it magic?" he whispered.

"A hologram," said Matt. "It's part of the security system. It makes the wall look solid from a distance, but once you get beyond the projectors" – he pointed at the cameras in the trees – "the hologram goes away."

"Is it okay? I mean, if it turns on again, will we be trapped inside?"

Matt smiled. "It's perfectly safe. I've seen this before where I – where I used to live."

Fidelito looked up at him. "Was that when you were a zombie?"

"Oh brother!" Matt said. "Don't tell me you believed Jorge's lies?"

"Of course not," said the little boy, but Matt noticed he seemed relieved.

Matt led Fidelito through the archway and past a white marble statue of Saint Francis feeding the doves. On the far side they came to a hallway. Nurses and orderlies ran here and there with bandages and medicines. The beds lining the hallway were full of injured people, and because most of the people were in costume, it looked like the beds were occupied by skeletons.

"What are you doing here?" cried a flustered nurse, bumping into the two boys.

"Please. We came to see Chacho," said Matt.

"And María," added Fidelito.

"There's a hundred Marías in here tonight," said the nurse. "It happens every year with that cursed fiesta. All those people drinking and picking fights. They should outlaw it . . . But Chacho – " He stopped and looked at the boys closely. "I know of only one Chacho, and he's in intensive care. You wouldn't be boys from the same orphanage?"

"We might be," Matt said cautiously.

The nurse lowered his voice. "You'd better be careful. Keepers are nosing around. It seems there was a mutiny at the salt-works."

"How's Chacho?" asked Fidelito.

"Not so good. Listen, I'll take you there a private way." The nurse opened a door to a dimly lit passage that seemed to be used for storage. Matt saw piles of bedding and boxes of equipment as they made their way through. "I used to be an orphan myself," the nurse said. "Even now, I wake up in a cold sweat reciting the Five Principles of Good Citizenship and the Four Attitudes Leading to Right-Mindfulness."

They came out to another, deserted hallway. "This is the recovery wing," explained the nurse. "Here's where the Sisters watch over the long-term patients. Chacho is in the last room on the right. If he's sleeping, don't wake him." The nurse left them and went back to his duties.

Matt heard voices coming from the end of the hall. Fidelito ran ahead. "Chacho!" he yelled.

"Don't wake him!" said Matt. But it hardly mattered how much noise the little boy made because the people in the room were shouting even louder. Matt saw a pair of Sisters guarding a bed. Facing them were two Keepers, and next to them, trussed up like a lumpy package on the floor, was Ton-Ton. Ton-Ton mouthed the word *run*.

"If you move him, he'll die," cried one of the Sisters.

"We'll do what we like, Sister Inéz," a Keeper snarled. Matt instantly recognised the voice. It was Carlos, and the other man, to go by the cast on his arm, was Jorge. "These boys have tried to commit murder – do you understand?" said Carlos.

"I understand that some of your men suffered an injury to

their pride," Sister Inéz said. "Last I heard, no one ever died of humiliation. But if Chacho's moved, it *will* be murder. I can't allow it."

"Then we'll take him without your permission," said Carlos. Matt saw Sister Inéz go pale, but she didn't back down.

"You'll have to go through us," she said.

"And us," said Matt. The Keepers whirled around.

"It's that damned aristocrat!" shouted Jorge. He made a grab for Matt, but having only one good arm, he stumbled and fell on top of Ton-Ton. Ton-Ton immediately butted his head into Jorge's side.

"Stop! Stop!" cried Sister Inéz. "This is a convent. You aren't allowed to use violence."

"Tell *them* that!" shouted Matt, who was trying to kick Carlos's feet out from under him. The Keeper had hurled himself into the fight when Jorge went down. Matt hadn't a hope of winning. He was badly weakened by his ordeal, and besides, the man outweighed him by at least three stone. But Matt had had enough of running and hiding. He wasn't going to let the Keepers win easily. They were fat toads that Tam Lin wouldn't have thought twice about blowing up. The blood sang in Matt's ears.

"Stop this at once!" came a sharp voice that cut through the red fog that had enveloped Matt's mind. He felt Carlos's hands let go. He felt himself falling to his knees. He heard Fidelito sobbing.

"This is a *disgrace!*" said the sharp voice.

Matt looked up. It would have been funny if the situation hadn't been so dire. Sister Inéz was frozen with her hands grasping Carlos's hair. The other Sister had the neck of Jorge's shirt bunched up in her fists, and Jorge was in mid-kick towards Ton-

Ton's stomach. Fidelito had thrown himself across Chacho, as though his skinny body could provide protection. And poor Chacho merely stared, as though he'd seen a dragon appear in the doorway.

Matt saw a small, but extremely fierce-looking woman with her hands on her hips. She wore a black dress, and her black hair was braided and pinned on top of her head in a kind of crown. She was little, but everything about her proclaimed that she was used to being obeyed and anyone who didn't was going to regret it.

"D-Doña Esperanza," stammered Sister Inéz. Matt's mouth dropped open. It was María's mother! He recognised her from the portrait, although she was older than he'd expected.

"Stand up, all of you," ordered Doña Esperanza. Carlos, Jorge, the two Sisters, Fidelito, and Matt all struggled to their feet. Even Ton-Ton tried to sit up straight. "I want an explanation for this," said Esperanza.

Then everyone tried to talk at once, and she crisply told them to shut up until she called on them. She looked at each person in the room, her eyes softening only when she saw Chacho. "You!" she said, pointing at Ton-Ton. "You tell me the reason for this *disgusting, unbelievable* display of brutishness."

And Ton-Ton, without a single misspoken word, told the whole story – from the time Fidelito was condemned to caning, to when Matt and Chacho were thrown into the boneyard, to when the orphans rose as an avenging army, to when Ton-Ton drove the shrimp harvester, to when he and Chacho were finally airlifted to the hospital. Esperanza had scared the stuttering right out of him.

When Ton-Ton was finished, no one said a word. The silence stretched on and on. Matt wanted to back up Ton-Ton's story, but one look at those fierce black eyes told him it was better to stay quiet.

"Please forgive me for putting forth my opinion, Doña Esperanza," Jorge said at last. "I must explain that this boy is mentally retarded. I rescued him from the Farm Patrol years ago, but he's never shown any intelligence."

"He sounds intelligent to me," said Esperanza.

"He parrots anything anyone tells him. Most of the time he can hardly string a sentence together."

"I c-can s-so," muttered Ton-Ton.

Esperanza silenced him with a frown. She turned again to Jorge. "Are you saying the canings never happened?"

"Of course they didn't," said the Keeper. "We may keep a boy on short rations for a day if he misbehaves, but we never use physical punishment. It's against everything the Keepers believe in."

"I see," said Esperanza. "And the boneyard is a myth, too."

"You know how it is," Jorge said smoothly. "Boys like to scare one another with stories after dark. They talk about vampires and the *chupacabras*. It's natural, but sometimes it gets out of hand."

Matt's heart sank. Esperanza nodded her head as if she agreed with Jorge: Boys did tell one another scary stories. They did make things up. But then she said, "The warehouse full of laudanum is also a myth, I suppose?"

Jorge flinched. "Laudanum?"

"The Aztlán police have wondered for a long time how drugs were being distributed in this country. They were extremely interested in what they found at the saltworks."

"That's a vicious lie! Someone's trying to undermine the reputation of the Keepers!" cried Carlos. "Rumours like that are spread by idiots who want orphans to lie around like pampered house cats. *We* know they're squalid little parasites until they're re-educated into good citizens. If any laudanum was found, it was planted there by the police!"

"Fine. Then you won't mind taking a drug test," said Esperanza. She stepped aside, and suddenly the doorway swarmed with men in blue uniforms. They must have been waiting just out of sight. Jorge and Carlos looked stunned as they were led away.

"I've been waiting for this a long time," said Esperanza, dusting off her hands as though she'd just finished a chore. "We knew the Keepers were trafficking drugs, but we had no legal way to get a search warrant until Ton-Ton told us what he saw at the Keepers' compound." She borrowed scissors from Sister Inéz and began snipping off the duct tape binding the boy.

"Nobody, uh, ever listened to me before," said Ton-Ton.

"You had no one you could tell about the dreadful way you were treated," said Sister Inéz. "Imagine living on plankton all those years! We use it only for animal feed."

Matt was dazed by the rapid change in his fortunes. Things had been going wrong for so long, it was hard to believe they might go right at last.

"Can we stay with Chacho?" Fidelito asked shyly.

"We'll work something out," said Sister Inéz. "To begin with, I'm *sure* you'd like a bath." The women laughed, and Esperanza looked almost friendly.

They were interrupted by a shriek. A girl in a white party dress streaked through the door and threw herself into Matt's arms. "Oh, Mother! Oh, Mother! It's Matt! He's alive! He's here!"

"Good heavens, María," said Esperanza. "We'll never get the smell of shrimp out of that dress if you don't show a little restraint."

37

HOMECOMING

Matt revelled in the clean white sheets, the soft pillows, the flower-scented air drifting in from the garden. Sister Inéz had ordered him to bed after looking at the sores on his body. Fidelito and Ton-Ton were housed at a boarding school run by the convent, but they visited Matt and Chacho every day.

Poor Chacho, thought Matt. He barely noticed when anyone visited him. He drifted in and out of dreams, sometimes calling for his father and sometimes raving about bats. Sister Inéz said his mind needed time to recover from his terrible ordeal. He had breathed far less than was good for him under the heavy whale bones. His body had been starved of oxygen, and the pressure had cracked several of his ribs.

The best part of the day for Matt was when María visited. He was content to listen, while she never ran out of things to say. She talked about stray cats she had rescued or how she had made a mistake and put salt into a cake batter instead of sugar. María's life was full of drama. A flower opening in the garden and a butterfly lighting on a window were causes for excitement. Through her eyes, Matt saw the world as an infinitely hopeful place.

Now Matt watched the door eagerly because he heard María's voice in the hall, but he was disappointed to see both her and her mother. Esperanza was dressed in steel grey. She reminded Matt of one of the guided missiles El Patrón used to get for his birthday.

"I brought you some guavas," said María, placing a basket on the bedside table. "Sister Inéz says they're full of vitamin C. She says you need them to clear up your skin condition."

Matt winced. He knew his acne was horrible. Sister Inéz said it was caused by pollution in the water the Keepers used to grow plankton.

"You look healthy," said Esperanza.

"Thank you," Matt said. He didn't trust her.

"Healthy enough to get up."

"Oh, Mother! He needs at least another week in bed," said María.

"You will *not* turn this young man into one of your invalids," Esperanza told her daughter. "I've had quite enough of three-legged cats and fish that float upside down. Matt is young and resilient. And he has a very important job to do."

Uh oh, Matt thought. What was Esperanza up to now?

"We *are* terribly worried," María admitted.

"We're more than worried," Esperanza said in her relentless way. "Something has gone wrong in Opium — not that anything was ever right in that godforsaken wasteland. But El Patrón at least had ties with the outside world. No one has heard a word from there since the day he died."

"Emilia is still in Opium," María explained, "and so is Dada. I'm still angry at them for how they treated you, but I don't want anything – anything bad to happen to them." Her eyes filled with tears.

Esperanza made an exasperated sound. "It wouldn't bother me a bit if something happened to your dada. Oh, do stop brimming over like a fountain, María. It's a silly habit and it clouds your wits. Your father is an evil man."

"I can't help it." María sniffled. Matt handed her one of his tissues. He privately agreed with Esperanza, but his heart was on María's side.

"Opium is in a state of lockdown," said Esperanza. "I can think of only three times that's happened in the past one hundred years. It means that nothing is allowed to enter or leave the country."

"Can't we just wait until they decide to contact us?" said Matt.

"The other lockdowns lasted a few hours. This one's gone on for three months."

Matt realised what this meant. Shipments of opium had to go out every day to keep money moving around the empire. Dealers in Africa, Asia, and Europe must be clamouring for their supplies. MacGregor and the other Farmers couldn't cover the shortfall. They had put most of their land to crops that produced cocaine and hashish.

"What am I supposed to do about it?" Matt said. Esperanza smiled and he knew he'd walked into a trap.

"All incoming hovercrafts have to be cleared by the security system," she said. "The pilot places his hand on an identity plate in the cockpit. His fingerprints and DNA signature are beamed to the ground. If these are cleared, the ship is allowed to land. If not – "

"It's blown out of the sky," said María. "Mother, this plan is *awful.*"

"During a lockdown," Esperanza went on, ignoring her daughter, "no ships are cleared – with one exception: El Patrón's signature overrides everything."

Matt understood at once: His fingerprints and DNA were the same as El Patrón's. "How do you know the system hasn't been changed?"

"I don't," said Esperanza. "I'm counting on the Alacráns to have forgotten about the override. They must be in some kind of trouble, or they wouldn't have sealed themselves off."

What kind of trouble? Matt thought. Could the eejits have revolted, or could the Farm Patrol have taken over? Perhaps Mr Alacrán was locked in a power struggle with Steven and Benito. "The way I see it," he said, "I'll get blown out of the sky. If I do manage to survive, the Alacráns will have me put to sleep like an old dog. I'm a clone, in case you've forgotten. I'm livestock."

María flinched. Matt didn't care. Let her understand what they were asking of him. He didn't care whether Emilia and her dada were safe. But then he heard María choke back a sob.

"Oh, very well!" he said angrily. "I'm no good for spare parts anymore. You might as well throw me away on this."

"I don't want to throw you away," María said, weeping.

"Let's all take a deep breath and start over," said Esperanza. "First of all, Matt, you aren't a clone."

Matt was so startled, he sat straight up in bed.

"Oh, you *were* a clone. There's no mistake about that. But we're talking about international law now." Esperanza started pacing around the room as though she were lecturing a class. "International law is my speciality. In the first place, clones shouldn't exist."

"Fat lot of good that does me," said Matt.

"But if they do exist, they're livestock, as you say. That makes it possible for them to be slaughtered like chickens or cattle."

María moaned and put her head down on the bed.

"You can't have two versions of the same person at the same time," Esperanza went on. "One of them – the copy – has to be declared an *unperson*. But when the original dies, the copy takes his place."

"What . . . does that mean?" Matt said.

"It means you really are El Patrón. You have his body and his identity. You own everything he owned and rule everything he ruled. It means you're the new Master of Opium."

María raised her head. "Matt's human?"

"He always was," her mother replied. "The law is a wicked fiction to make it possible to use clones for transplants. But bad law or not, we're going to use it now. If you survive the landing, Matt, I'll do everything in my power to make you the new reigning drug lord. I have the backing of the Aztlán and U.S. governments on this. Only you must promise me that once you're in control, you'll destroy the opium empire and tear down the barrier that has kept Aztlán and the United States apart for so long."

Matt stared at the small, fierce woman as he tried to understand the sudden shift in his fortunes. He guessed that Esperanza cared less about her daughters than her desire to destroy Opium. She'd gone off without a backward glance when María was only five. In all the years since, she'd never contacted her. It was only when María made the first move that Esperanza returned and proceeded to order everyone around.

Matt thought she would easily sacrifice him to realise her goal. But how could he refuse after the terrible suffering El

Patrón had caused? He understood the full extent of it now. It wasn't only the drug addicts throughout the world or the Illegals doomed to slavery. It was their orphaned children as well. You could even say the old man was responsible for the Keepers. If Matt had become El Patrón, then he'd got the whole package: wealth, power . . . and the evil that created it.

"I promise," he said.

The hovercraft trembled as it was scanned by beacons from the ground. Matt glanced at the pilot. The man's face was grim. "When the red light goes on, press your right hand on the identity plate," he said. WARNING! GROUND ARTILLERY DEPLOYED, flashed a panel over the controls.

They'll shoot first and ask questions later, thought Matt. He carried messages from the Aztlán and U.S. presidents, but they wouldn't do much good if he got blown out of the sky.

"There's the signal!" cried the pilot.

The identity plate lit up. Matt slammed his hand down. He felt the tingling he'd noticed when he'd pressed the glowing scorpion outside the secret passage in the mansion. The red light faded, and the panel turned a welcoming green.

"You did it, sir! Well done!" The pilot began to bleed off anti-gravity in preparation for landing. Matt felt a glow of happiness. The man had called him "sir"!

Matt watched anxiously through the window. He saw the *estancia* as he'd never seen it before. The water purification plant lay far to the east, and the little church Celia visited – could she still visit as an eejit? – was to the west. In between were storehouses, drug purification labs, and a factory where food pellets for the eejits were made. Slightly to the north was the grey, featureless hospital. Even from here, it looked sinister. Next to it was the mausoleum where the Alacráns slept in their marble drawers.

The swimming pool flashed with sunlight as they passed over. Matt searched the grounds for people. He saw eejits crouching by a lawn. He saw maids hanging out washing, and someone seemed to be repairing a roof. No one looked up. No one showed the slightest interest in the hovercraft that was now descending to the ground.

"Where's the welcoming committee?" he murmured. A platoon of bodyguards always ran out to greet visitors.

The ship bumped gently to a landing. "Do you need a weapon, sir?" asked the pilot, handing him a gun. Matt looked at it with dismay. Such guns had been used by the Farm Patrol to stun – and kill – the parents of Chacho, Flaco, Ton-Ton, and the other orphans.

"It's probably better to appear friendly," he said, handing the weapon back.

"I'll remain here in lift-off mode, in case you want to leave quickly," the pilot said.

Matt opened the door and climbed down. The landing field was empty. The only sounds were of birds, fountains, and – briefly – the hammer of the man fixing the roof.

Matt followed a winding path through the gardens. His job was to confront the Alacráns and end the lockdown. He could disable the lockdown system himself – when he found it. Tam Lin or Daft Donald would know its location. Then Esperanza and top officials from both countries on the border would descend on Opium and try to install Matt as leader.

I had better odds for survival in the boneyard, he thought. He saw a peacock strut across a lawn. A mob of red-winged blackbirds shrieked at one another from a crowded tree. A winged baby watched him from atop a fountain.

Matt's nerves were raw. Any minute now Mr Alacrán would stride out of the house and shout, *Take this creature away! Dispose of it at once!* Memories threatened to overwhelm him. He didn't know what he'd do if he saw Celia.

Matt went up the broad steps leading to the salon. It was there that El Patrón had introduced him to the family so long ago. It was there that El Viejo had lain like a starved bird in his coffin and Emilia, surrounded by eejit flower girls, had married Steven. It was as though the great hall thronged with ghosts. They hovered behind the white, marble pillars. They breathed over the dark pond covered with water lilies. Matt saw an ancient fish rise from the depths to look at him with a round, yellow eye.

Matt froze. Someone was playing a piano. The person was certainly skilled, but he – or she – was attacking the music with such ferocity that it bordered on madness. Matt raced towards the sound. The noise rolled like a tidal wave out of the music room, and he had to cover his ears.

"Stop!" he yelled. But the person didn't react. Matt crossed the room and grabbed the man's arm.

Mr Ortega spun around. He took one look and fled. Matt heard his footsteps disappear down the hall. "I wasn't *that* bad a student," Matt murmured. But of course Mr Ortega had thought he was dead. He was probably crying alarm from one end of the house to the other. Now it was only a matter of time before someone showed up.

Matt sat down. His hands were callused from the work he'd done at the salt factory, and he was afraid the hard labour had made his fingers clumsy. But as he began the Adagio from Beethoven's Piano Concerto No. 5, the awkwardness fell away. The music swelled through his body, transporting him from the horrors of the past few months. He felt as light as a hawk coasting the upper air over the oasis. He played until he felt a hand on his shoulder.

Matt turned, still in a daze of music, and saw Celia dressed in the flowered dress he remembered so well. "*Mi hijo!*" she cried, gathering him into a ferocious bear hug. "Oh, my darling, you're so thin! What happened to you in all this time? How did you get back? What's wrong with your face? It's so thin and — and — "

"Covered with spots," said Matt, struggling to catch his breath.

"Ah, well, it's part of growing up," declared Celia. "They'll go away with the right food." She held him at arm's length to look at him. "I'm sure you're taller."

"Are you okay?" said Matt. Her sudden appearance shocked him. He was afraid of bursting into tears.

"Of course. But you took about five years off Mr Ortega's life."

"How did you — I mean, Tam Lin said you had to hide . . . "

Matt couldn't trust his voice enough to say any more.

"Tam Lin. Oh, my." Celia suddenly looked very tired. "We've been in lockdown for months and couldn't send out a message."

"Why didn't Mr Alacrán or Steven do something?" said Matt.

"You'd better come with me." Celia led Matt through the halls, and once again he was struck by how silent everything was.

They came to the kitchen, and at last Matt saw something reassuringly normal. Two undercooks were kneading bread, and a maid was slicing vegetables. Strings of garlic and chillies hung from the ceiling. The odour of roast chicken wafted over him from the big, wood-fired oven.

Mr Ortega and Daft Donald were sitting at a table with cups of coffee and two laptop computers. "See? I wasn't making it up," said Mr Ortega. Daft Donald typed something onto his computer. "I was *not* running around like Chicken Little," said Mr Ortega, reading his screen. "You'd be upset too if a ghost grabbed your shoulder."

Daft Donald smiled.

Matt stared at them. He'd never thought of the two men outside their duties as music teacher and bodyguard. He'd never tried to communicate with them, and besides, he'd always assumed Daft Donald wasn't bright.

"I'd better begin," sighed Celia. She settled Matt between the two men and fetched him a mug of hot cocoa. The odour brought back memories so profound, the room wavered before his eyes. For an instant Matt was in the little house in the poppy fields. A storm raged outside, but in the house it was warm and safe. Then the scene faded, and he was back in the kitchen.

"You remember what I said about El Patrón never letting anything go?" Celia began. Matt nodded. "Tam Lin used to say that things – and people – became part of El Patrón's dragon hoard."

Used to say, Matt thought with a chill. What did that mean?

"That's why he wouldn't let Felicia run away and why he kept Tom close to him, although he hated the boy. We all belonged to him – the Alacráns, the bodyguards, the doctors, me, Tam Lin, and you. Most of all, you."

38

THE HOUSE OF ETERNITY

Matt saw that last evening in his mind's eye as Celia and the others told the story. When she faltered, Daft Donald would take up the narrative on his computer. Sometimes Mr Ortega would burst in with an opinion.

While he, Matt, was lying under the stars at the oasis, Tam Lin and everyone else had been called to the wake. Celia was missing because she was supposed to be an eejit. Mr Ortega was missing because he hadn't heard about it. Besides, he'd lived such a quiet existence for so many years that everyone had forgotten about him.

The Farm Patrol stood at attention in the gathering dusk. Six bodyguards, including Tam Lin and Daft Donald, carried the coffin from the hospital to the desert beyond the mausoleum. One man alone could have carried El Patrón, but the coffin was so encrusted with gold that six could barely lift it.

They walked slowly as a choir of eejit children sang the "Humming Chorus" from the opera *Madama Butterfly*. It was one of El Patrón's favourite pieces, and the eejits' voices were high and sweet.

"I heard it from the stables," said Celia, wiping her eyes. "He was an evil man, but the music would have broken your heart."

A door had been opened in the ground. A ramp led deep down into a vast underground chamber lit by candles. It was only the first of many chambers leading off under the earth. Daft Donald said he didn't know how many there were.

The coffin was a wonder, Daft Donald wrote on his computer. It had an image of El Patrón on the lid, like the portrait of an Egyptian pharaoh. El Patrón looked about twenty-five. You couldn't recognise him, except – and here Daft Donald glanced up – that he looked a great deal like Matt.

Matt felt cold.

Everyone went down into the chamber, the bodyguard continued typing, *which was filled with drifts of gold coins. You had to wade through them like sand on a beach.* Daft Donald saw some of the bodyguards scoop some up and hide them in their pockets. The priest performed the funeral rites. Then the eejits and Farm Patrol were sent away. It was time for the wake.

"Which is just another name for a party," interrupted Mr Ortega. "You celebrate the dead man's life – or in this case, his eight lives. You were supposed to be the ninth, Matt."

Matt felt even colder.

Everyone was in a fine mood, what with the food and wine, wrote Daft Donald. *Everyone talked about what an old beast El Patrón was and how they were glad he was dead.*

It had gone on for hours when Tam Lin brought out a special wine that had been bottled the year El Patrón was born. It was in a musty crate covered with cobwebs and sealed with the Alacrán scorpion mark. "This is what El Patrón was saving for his 150th birthday," announced Mr Alacrán. "If he didn't make it, it was supposed to be served at his funeral. I propose we drink it to celebrate the old buzzard's death!"

"Hear! Hear!" everyone cried.

Steven opened the first bottle and sniffed it. "It smells like someone opened a window in heaven," he said.

"Then it doesn't belong with this crowd!" Tom yelled. Everyone roared with laughter. They passed around fine crystal glasses. Mr Alacrán said they were all supposed to toast El Patrón at the same time and then smash their glasses on his coffin.

I had a glass, wrote Daft Donald, *but Tam Lin came up to me and said, "Don't drink it, laddie. I've got a strange feeling about this wine." And so I didn't.*

We raised our glasses for the toast. Mr Alacrán said, "Tomorrow we'll send a truck down here and haul this stuff away! Here's to greed!" Everyone cheered and then they drank – except for me. Before the next minute had passed, they had all fallen to the ground. Just like that. As though someone had reached inside and turned off a switch.

"What happened?" Matt asked, gasping.

I went from one person to the next, trying to wake them up, but they were all dead, wrote Daft Donald.

"Dead?" cried Matt.

"I'm so terribly, terribly sorry," said Celia.

"Not Tam Lin!"

"The poison was very quick. I don't think he felt it."

"But he knew something was wrong with the wine," shouted Matt. "Why did he drink it?"

"Listen to me," said Celia. "El Patrón had ruled his empire for one hundred years. All that time he was adding to his dragon hoard, and he wanted to be buried with it. Unfortunately" – Celia stopped and wiped her eyes – "Unfortunately, the dragon hoard included people."

Matt remembered with a chill how often the old man had spoken of the Chaldean kings. Not only were they buried with clothes and food, but their horses were slaughtered to provide transport in the shadowy world of the dead. In one tomb archaeologists had discovered soldiers, servants, and even dancing girls laid out as though they were sleeping. One girl had been in such a hurry, the blue ribbon she was meant to wear in her hair was still rolled up in her pocket.

The plan must have been in El Patrón's mind all along. He'd never intended to let Mr Alacrán or Steven inherit his kingdom. Their education was as hollow as Matt's. None of them was meant to survive.

"Tam Lin knew what was going to happen," said Celia. "El Patrón told him everything. He was closer to the old man than anyone, except, perhaps, you."

I laid out the bodies, wrote Daft Donald, *as many as I could manage. I was crying. I don't mind admitting it. It happened so fast. It was so awful. I went outside and got dynamite from a storage shed. I wired it to the entrance passage and set it off.*

"I didn't hear the explosion, but I felt it," said Mr Ortega.

"Everyone ran out to see what had happened," said Celia. "We found the passageway buried and Donald lying stunned on the ground."

"I felt the explosion too," Matt murmured. "Just before dawn the ground trembled, and it woke me up."

"Tam Lin saw it as his chance to free the eejits," said Celia. "That's why he didn't warn anyone except Donald about the wine. I know it sounds terrible, but how else was he to break the power of the Alacráns? El Patrón had ruled this country for one hundred years. His children might rule for another hundred."

Matt could see the buried tomb in his mind's eye – the broken wineglasses, El Patrón's portrait staring up from the coffin, the bodyguards laid out in their dark suits. Only instead of ribbons, they had gold coins in their pockets.

Tom was there too, his lying, oh-so-believable voice stilled forever. How many times had Matt entertained himself with thoughts of Tom's downfall? Now that it had happened, Matt felt numb. Tom had been no more in charge of his fate than the dullest eejit.

"Tam Lin did what he wanted to do," Celia said. "He was guilty of a terrible crime when he was young, and he could never forgive himself for it. He believed this last act would make up for everything."

"Well, it didn't!" shouted Matt. "He was an idiot! A stupid, *crotting* idiot!" He jumped up. Mr Ortega tried to stop him, but Celia shook her head.

Matt ran through the gardens until he came to the stables. "Get me a horse!" he yelled.

After a moment Rosa shuffled out. "A Safe Horse, Master?" she said. For a moment Matt was tempted to ask for Tam Lin's steed, but he wasn't skilled enough to ride it.

"A Safe Horse," he said.

Soon he was moving through the fields as he had done so many times before. Some were misted with the bitter green of opium seedlings. Some dazzled his eyes with the glory of full-grown poppies. A faint, corrupt perfume hung in the air.

Matt saw the first labourers. They walked slowly, bending

down with tiny knives to slash the seedpods. What was he going to do about them? He was their lord now. He was the master of this vast army.

Matt felt utterly drained. Somehow, he'd expected everything to work out. He'd expected himself, María, Tam Lin, and Celia to someday be happy together. Now it was all ruined.

"You fool!" he shouted at the vanished Tam Lin.

Could the eejit operation be reversed? Even with a restaffed hospital, it might take years – that is, if Matt could lure doctors to Opium after they found out what had happened to the last batch. He'd have to get rid of the Farm Patrol. They were felons wanted in countries all over the world. He could tell their police forces to come and get them. He would have to hire other, less violent men to replace them because the eejits couldn't exist without orders.

It was an overwhelming problem. He'd need to hire another army of bodyguards. Wealth such as Opium possessed lured criminals. *Always choose your bodyguards from another country,* whispered El Patrón. *They find it harder to make alliances and betray you.*

Okay, thought Matt. He would ask Daft Donald about it tomorrow. A pack of Scottish soccer louts sounded about right.

He gave the horse a drink and made his way into the mountains. A clear blue sky cast its light over the oasis. The sand next to the water was marked with animal prints, and the metal chest was still hidden under the grape arbour. Matt rummaged through it until he found Tam Lin's old note.

Deer Matt, he read. *Im a lousy writer so this wont be long. El Patron says I have to go with him. I cant do anything about it. I put supplise in this chest plus books. Yu never know when yu mite need things. Yor frend Tam Lin.*

Matt folded it and put it into his pocket, along with a flash-light for when it got dark. He made a fire and warmed his hands as he listened to the sounds of the oasis. It was too cold to swim.

He would dig up the poppy fields and put in normal crops. Once the eejits were cured, Matt would give them the choice of returning home or of working for him. He would help them find their children.

Matt sat up straight. Of course! Chacho, Fidelito, and Ton-Ton! He could invite them to live with him. He could imagine Fidelito's wide-eyed astonishment. *This is really yours?* the little boy would cry. *You're not making it up?*

It's all right, Chacho would say, refusing to be impressed. Matt could give him his old guitar. Mr Ortega could teach him music. Ton-Ton could have his own machine shop. He could maintain the equipment Matt needed to create his new farms.

He could invite María to stay – and hope that Esperanza was busy somewhere else. María would love reuniting the eejits with their children. And they could have picnics and ride horses, and she could keep as many three-legged cats as she liked.

Matt looked up at the sky. Sunset wasn't far off. The light was turning gold, and sunlight shone through a gap in the mountains and made a bar of radiance on a wall of rock just beyond the oasis. Matt saw something dazzle.

He jumped up and ran to the spot before the radiance slipped behind the mountains. When he arrived, shadow had almost hidden the mark, but he saw, in the red light of the setting sun, a shining scorpion. He pressed his hand against it.

Slowly, silently, a door opened in the cliff. Matt felt the rock. It wasn't stone after all, but a clever imitation. The door revealed a dark passage going down into the earth. Matt shone the flash-light inside.

The floor glittered with gold coins. Farther on were weird statues that might have been Egyptian gods. Matt lay back against the cliff, breathing hard. It was part of El Patrón's dragon hoard. It was the first of the underground chambers that stretched all the way to El Patrón's coffin and his attendants.

Around the old man were bodyguards to protect him in the shadowy world of the dead. There were doctors to attend to his health. Mr Alacrán could entertain him with matters of business, and Steven could offer opinions about the farming of poppies. There would certainly be an opium farm in El Patrón's version of heaven. Felicia, Fani, and Emilia could admire him from tables covered with moro crabs and caramel puddings.

And Tam Lin? Matt took out the note again: *El Patron says I have to go with him. I cant do anything about it.*

"You could have done something about it," Matt whispered. "You could have said no." He stepped away, and the door slid shut again. He ran his fingers over the surface. He couldn't tell where the opening had been, but he could find it again with red light.

Late that night Matt sat by the fire and smelled the good mesquite smoke as it spiralled up into the starry sky. Tomorrow he would begin the task of breaking down the empire of Opium. It was a huge and terrifying job, but he wasn't alone. He had Chacho, Fidelito, and Ton-Ton to cheer him on. He had Celia and Daft Donald to advise him and María to be everyone's conscience. He also had Esperanza, but he couldn't see a way out of that.

With everyone's help, it would get done.

You can do it, said Tam Lin from the darkness on the other side of the fire.

"I know I can," said Matt, smiling back.

ABOUT THE AUTHOR

Nancy Farmer grew up on the border between Arizona and Mexico in the landscape that she evokes so strongly in her disturbing futuristic adventure. She has won both the National Book Award and the prestigious Newbery Honour for *The House of the Scorpion*. Nancy Farmer lives with her family in Menlo Park, California.